COVEN OF ANDROMEDA

Copyright   2025 RONALD BLACKSMITH

All rights reserved.

No part of the publication may be reproduced, distributed, or transmitted in any form or by any means, including photocopying, recording, or other electronic or mechanical methods, without the prior written permission of the publisher, except as permitted by U.S. copyright law.

For permission requests, contact:

RON BLACKSMITH, 441 W BAGLEY RD, PMB 108
BEREA, OH 44017
ATTN: FIRST-WORLD BOOKS
OR GO TO: RONBLACKSMITH.COM

The story, all names, characters, and incidents portrayed in this production are fictitious. No identification with actual persons (living or deceased), places, buildings and products is intended or should be inferred.

1st Printing 2025
Hardcover ISBN-13: 979-8-9919479-5-4
Paperback ISBN-13: 979-8-9919479-6-1
Kindle   ISBN-13: 979-8-9919479-7-8
Library of Congress Control Number: 2025908778
Printed in the United States of America
Coven of Andromeda

COVEN OF ANDROMEDA

RON BLACKSMITH

FIRST-WORLD BOOKS

TABLE OF CONTENTS

1. Eldoria — 1
2. Homecoming — 9
3. The Necropolis — 19
4. The Funeral — 29
5. The Gardens of Necropolis — 51
6. Secrets Between Bookstacks — 63
7. The Drakorian Attack — 85
8. A Brief History — 95
9. The Voodoo Queen — 107
10. The King's Farewell — 119
11. The Path of Magic — 129
12. The Fall of the Palace — 147
13. Shadows — 157
14. The Conqueror — 177
15. Lights of the Fair — 187
16. The Necromancer's Last Stand — 205

17.	Street Fight	217
18.	The Apprentice's Choice	233
19.	Aunt Carol	237
20.	The Portal to Earth	257
21.	Secrets Behind Closed Doors	261
22.	The Oath of Vengeance	281
23.	Morning Revelations	287
24.	New World Dawn	299
25.	Beyond the Door	309
26.	What Was Lost	317
27.	The Winter Court	333
28.	Revelations	347
29.	The Necromancers Return	359
30.	An Unexpected Confession	365
31.	Preparations	377
32.	Bayou Betrayal	393
33.	The Crossroads Guardian	405
34.	The Coven Gathers	419
35.	Dark Crossing	433
36.	Through the Veil	445
37.	Souls in Combat	463
38.	Second Homecoming	491

Chapter 1
ELDORIA

On the planet Eldoria, the lavender sky blazed with the rising sun, casting long shadows across the spires of Lumina. The city's arcane symbols pulsed along ancient walls, their rhythmic glow matching the heartbeat of magic that flowed through every stone and citizen.

Sameril slipped through the morning crowd, his dark blue apprentice robes marking him as a student of the Arcane Academy. The sweet scent of spellberry tarts from a nearby stall made his empty stomach growl.

"Late again, Sam?" called Merith, an elderly potion merchant with laugh lines etched deep into her face. She tossed him a small, wrapped package. "Can't conjure knowledge on an empty stomach."

He caught it deftly, grinning. "You're a lifesaver, Merith. Master Thorne would have my head if I missed another lesson."

"Your coin purse next time, young man!" she called after him as he darted through the plaza.

The grand plaza teemed with activity, but the center had been cleared for the morning's lesson. Master Thorne, silver-bearded and straight-backed despite his advanced years, stood waiting as students gathered in a loose circle around him.

"Magic," Master Thorne's voice carried across the plaza, silencing the chattering students, "is not a tool to be wielded carelessly. It is a living force that demands respect."

Sameril slid into place just as the Master's piercing gaze swept over the assembly. He unwrapped Merith's gift—a spellberry tart still warm from the oven—and took a quick bite before tucking the rest away.

"Today," Master Thorne continued, "we practice elemental attunement. Find your partner and begin."

Students shuffled into pairs, but Sameril remained still, his eyes drawn across the circle to where Briella of House Tanner stood alone. Her copper hair caught the morning light, seeming to ignite like living flame around her shoulders. She wore the emerald-trimmed robes of an advanced student, her witch's hat—a family heirloom—perched atop her head at a precise angle.

"Waiting for an engraved invitation, Sameril?" Master Thorne's voice broke through his thoughts.

Sameril felt heat rise to his cheeks. "No, Master. I just—"

"Was hoping someone would ask you to partner with?" The old mage's eyes twinkled with amusement. "Sometimes fate requires a gentle push. In your case, that will come later. Not now."

Master Thorne gestured across the circle. "Talien needs a partner. Your theoretical knowledge balances his practical strength."

Sameril nodded, trying to mask his disappointment as he moved to join the lanky student on the far side of the circle. Talien greeted him with a friendly clap on the shoulder that nearly sent Sameril stumbling.

"Thought you'd be paired with Briella today," Talien whispered as Master Thorne began explaining the exercise. "The way you two locked eyes across the plaza was rather obvious."

"I have no idea what you're talking about," Sameril muttered, though his flushed cheeks betrayed him.

"Focus, students!" Master Thorne called out. "Elemental attunement requires perfect concentration. One partner will create an elemental sphere, the other will transform it. Begin!"

The plaza filled with the shimmer of magic as students summoned their elemental energies. Floating orbs of fire, water, earth, and air formed between partners, each pulsing with raw power.

Talien extended his hands, brow furrowed in concentration. Between his palms, a sphere of flickering flame materialized. "Your turn to transform it," he said, sweat beading on his forehead from the effort of maintaining the unstable element.

Sameril raised his hands, drawing on the arcane knowledge that had always come so naturally to him. He visualized the transformation, feeling the magical currents shift around him. The fire sphere trembled, then slowly morphed into a swirling orb of water, its surface rippling with perfect control.

"Excellent form, Sameril," Master Thorne commented as he passed. "Though perhaps too methodical. Magic requires not just knowledge, but intuition."

Across the plaza, Sameril caught sight of Briella working with Vessa, a sharp-featured student with silver-white hair. Unlike the controlled transformations happening elsewhere, Briella wasn't simply changing one element to another—she was creating something entirely new. Her water sphere pulsed with an inner light, luminescent plants growing and twisting within it.

"Show-off," Talien muttered, following Sameril's gaze. "Though I must admit, her grasp of creative transformation is impressive."

The lesson continued through the morning; each exercise more complex than the last. As the sun climbed higher, Master Thorne finally called for them to conclude.

"Remember, tomorrow we begin specialized training," he announced. "You've all received your assignments. Some will continue with traditional elemental magic; others will explore alternative disciplines."

Sameril's heart quickened. He had waited months for this moment—the day when students would be divided into their specialized fields of study. While most would continue along the path of witchcraft at Lumina, a select few would be chosen for other disciplines.

As the students dispersed, Master Thorne beckoned Sameril to follow him away from the plaza. They walked in silence until they reached a quiet courtyard where a stone bench sat beneath a twisted silverleaf tree.

"You've sensed it, haven't you?" Master Thorne asked, settling onto the bench. "The way your magic differs from the others."

Sameril nodded slowly. "I've always felt... drawn to different aspects of magic than my peers. When they focus on creation and growth, I find myself thinking about the cycles of energy, the transformation between states of being."

"Including the transformation between life and death," Master Thorne stated, his voice matter of fact.

Sameril tensed. "I've never practiced—"

"Of course not," the old mage interrupted gently. "But you've thought about it. Wondered about it. That's not wrong, Sameril. It's simply who you are."

From his robes, Master Thorne produced a sealed letter bearing the emblem of a skull entwined with thorny vines. "This arrived for you this morning. From the Necropolis."

Sameril's fingers trembled slightly as he accepted the letter. "The Academy of Necromancy? But I didn't apply—"

"They've been watching you," Master Thorne explained. "As have I. Your talents lie in a different direction than what Lumina can offer. Necromancy is not the dark art many believe it to be—it's about understanding the balance between life and death, the transfer of energy through all states of existence."

"But what about my training here? My friends?" Sameril's thoughts flashed to Briella, to their brief exchanges that had always felt charged with possibility.

Master Thorne's eyes softened. "Different paths sometimes lead to the same destination, my boy. Open the letter."

Sameril broke the seal and unfolded the heavy parchment. The elegant script inside invited him to present himself at the Necropolis the following morning to begin his studies under Master Xaloth, the ancient necromancer whose reputation reached even to Lumina.

"This is... a great honor," Sameril said, his voice barely above a whisper.

"Indeed, it is," Master Thorne agreed. "Master Xaloth rarely takes personal students. He must see exceptional potential in you."

Sameril carefully folded the letter, his mind racing. "I need to prepare, to gather my things—"

"All arrangements have been made," Master Thorne assured him. "Tonight, will be your last in Lumina's dormitories. Tomorrow, you begin a new chapter."

As the sun began its descent toward the horizon, casting a golden glow across Lumina's spires, Sameril found himself wandering the familiar paths of the academy gardens. The moonflowers were beginning to open, their pale petals unfurling to catch the last light of day.

"I heard the news," a voice said from behind him. "The Necropolis beckons its newest student."

Sameril turned to find Briella standing there, her copper hair now loosely braided, her witch's hat absent. Without its shadow, her emerald eyes seemed even brighter.

"Word travels fast," he observed, trying to keep his voice steady.

"In academic circles, always." She stepped closer, studying his face. "You don't seem entirely pleased."

"It's a great opportunity," Sameril said carefully. "Master Xaloth is legendary."

"But?" Briella prompted.

Sameril sighed. "But I've spent my whole life in Lumina. And necromancy... it's not exactly well-regarded by most witches."

"By most, perhaps," Briella conceded. "But I've always believed that arbitrary divisions between magical disciplines limit our understanding. Witchcraft, necromancy—they're different approaches to the same fundamental energies."

She reached out, surprising him by taking his hand. "The gardens between our academies are neutral ground. Perhaps, one day, we could meet there—to discuss theories, share discoveries."

Sameril felt warmth spread from where her fingers touched his. "I'd like that," he said softly.

As twilight descended over Eldoria, Sameril returned to his dormitory to pack his few belongings. Tomorrow, he would stand before Master Xaloth in the heart of the Necropolis, beginning a journey into the mysteries of life and death. And perhaps, in the moonflower grove at sunset, he would discover connections between magical disciplines that few had ever explored.

His final night in Lumina was spent in quiet contemplation, watching the twin moons rise over the city he had called home. Tomorrow would bring new challenges, new knowledge—and the first steps along a path that would forever change his understanding of magic.

Chapter 2

Homecoming

Golden hour light spilled across the dashboard as Bree Tanner stared out the passenger window. The familiar streets of Ballad rolled by, smaller somehow than in her memories. Ten years away had changed her perspective, but the town itself seemed frozen in time—the same storefronts, the same manicured lawns, the same feeling of secrets hiding behind picket fences.

"Look," Molly nudged her, pointing at the town square. "They still have that ridiculous statue of the founder."

Bree smiled despite herself. "Complete with that historically inaccurate witch's hat."

"If they only knew," Molly muttered, twisting a strand of dark hair around her finger.

From the driver's seat, Mary Ann Tanner let out a sharp breath. "Girls, please. Today is difficult enough without your commentary."

Bree caught her mother's eyes in the rearview mirror. The dark circles underneath spoke of sleepless nights since the call about Grandma Nancy's passing. Mary Ann had been dreading this homecoming for years, though she'd never admitted as much aloud.

"Sorry, Mom," Bree said softly. She placed a hand on her mother's shoulder. "How are you holding up?"

Mary Ann's knuckles whitened against the steering wheel. "I'll be fine once we get settled. It's just... being back here..."

"Brings up everything we left behind," Molly finished.

The unspoken hung between them: their father's sudden death, the whispers that followed, the midnight departure from Ballad. Bree had been twelve then, Molly fourteen. Old enough to feel the loss, young enough to be sheltered from the worst of it.

As they turned onto Willow Street, Bree felt a familiar tingle at the base of her skull—a sensation she'd experienced since childhood but had learned to suppress in the outside world.

"The wards are still up," she whispered.

Molly nodded, her eyes going distant. "Strong as ever. Grandma Nancy didn't let anything slip, even at the end."

"What do you mean, 'even at the end'?" Mary Ann asked sharply.

"Just that maintaining protective wards takes energy," Molly explained. "Most witches let them fade when they're... when they know their time is coming."

"Your grandmother wasn't 'most witches,'" Mary Ann said, a hint of pride cutting through her grief.

They fell silent as the car rounded the final corner, revealing the grand Victorian mansion that had been in the Tanner family for generations. Three stories of weathered elegance, with gingerbread trim and a widow's walk that Bree had always imagined was made for moon-gazing and spell-casting. The massive oak in the front yard had grown, if possible, even larger in their absence.

"Home sweet home," Molly murmured.

Bree swallowed hard. "It feels like it's watching us."

"All houses built by witches watch their inhabitants," Mary Ann said matter-of-factly as she pulled into the circular driveway. "It's part of their protection."

As the engine died, none of them made a move to exit. The weight of their return hung heavy in the car.

"Girls," Mary Ann finally broke the silence, turning to face her daughters. "I know this isn't easy. Coming back to Ballad, joining the coven officially... it's not what I had planned for you."

"It's what we are, Mom," Molly said gently. "You can't outrun blood."

Mary Ann's eyes glistened. "I wasn't running from our heritage. I was trying to give you normal lives, time to grow up without all the... complications."

"The complications found us anyway," Bree said, thinking of the unexplainable incidents that had followed them through the years—lights flickering during arguments, dreams that came true, the way plants seemed to reach for them. "At least here we'll learn how to control it."

Before Mary Ann could respond, movement on the porch caught their attention. The front door swung open, and a crowd of women spilled out, their faces bright with welcome despite the somber occasion of their return.

"They're all here," Mary Ann whispered, a mix of dread and longing in her voice.

"The whole coven?" Molly asked, peering through the windshield.

"Looks like it," Bree replied, recognizing faces from her childhood—Susan Fond with her short blonde hair, Elaine Warren and her daughter Lucy both wearing round glasses, Trudie Catshill still wearing her signature purple.

Mary Ann squared her shoulders. "It's not the entire coven... but it's enough. Well, we can't sit in the car forever. Remember what I told you—the coven will expect you to step into your places now. You're both of age, and with Nancy gone..."

"Her hat passes to one of us," Molly finished.

Bree felt her stomach twist. The witch's hat—a physical repository of power, knowledge, and memory, passed down through generations. She'd grown up hearing stories about them but had never expected to inherit one so soon.

"I'm not ready," she whispered.

Mary Ann reached back and squeezed her hand. "None of us ever are, sweetheart. But Nancy believed in you both. So do I."

With that, she opened her door, and the spell of hesitation broke. As they stepped out into the golden afternoon light, a chorus of warm greetings enveloped them.

Susan Fond reached them first, pulling Mary Ann into a fierce embrace. "It's been too long," she murmured, her voice thick with emotion. "Nancy watched for you every day."

Mary Ann stiffened momentarily before returning the hug. "I'm sorry we didn't come back sooner."

"You're here now," Susan replied simply. She turned to the girls, her wise eyes assessing them. "My goodness, look at you both. All grown up and practically vibrating with untrained power."

Bree, now a young adult woman, shifted uncomfortably under her scrutiny. "Is it that obvious?"

"Only to those who know what to look for," Susan winked. "Don't worry, we'll help you harness it. That's what the coven is for, after all."

The Warren women, Elaine and her daughter Lucy, moved with synchronized grace that had always fascinated Bree as a child. Their deep brown skin seemed to glow in the afternoon light, Lucy's braids adorned with small silver charms that clinked softly as she moved.

"Such a joy to see you girls," Elaine said warmly, her rich voice carrying the same musical cadence Bree remembered from childhood lessons on herb lore.

"Though we wish it were under happier circumstances," Lucy added, adjusting her glasses.

"Grandma Nancy wouldn't want us to be sad," Molly said, her voice stronger than Bree expected. "She always said death was just another transition."

"Wise beyond your years, just like your grandmother," Trudie Catshill remarked, joining their circle. Her eyes, a startling amber, seemed to see straight through Bree. "She spoke of you both constantly."

"She did?" Bree couldn't hide her surprise. After their abrupt departure from Ballad, she'd sometimes wondered if her grandmother had forgotten them.

"Oh yes," Trudie nodded emphatically. "She was so proud of you, kept track of everything. Your academic achievements, your hobbies, even that poetry contest you won last year."

Bree's mouth fell open. "But how? We barely spoke..."

"Nancy had her ways," Susan said cryptically. "Come inside, all of you. We've prepared a little welcome home gathering."

As they made their way up the porch steps, Bree couldn't shake the feeling of being watched. She glanced over her shoulder at the neighboring house—a smaller Victorian that had always stood empty in her childhood memories.

A man sat on the porch next door, partially obscured by climbing roses. Even at a distance, something about him struck Bree as familiar, though she was certain they'd never met. He raised a hand in acknowledgment, and she found herself returning the gesture before Molly tugged her through the front door.

Inside, the Tanner house was exactly as Bree remembered—the grand staircase sweeping up from the foyer, the stained-glass windows casting jewel-toned light across the hardwood floors, the scent of rosemary and sage permeating everything.

"We've kept it just as Nancy left it," Susan explained, seeing their expressions. "The coven has been taking turns tending to the house, keeping the energy flowing."

Mary Ann ran her fingers along the mahogany banister. "It feels like she might walk through the door any minute."

"In many ways, she's still here," Elaine Warren said softly. "The most powerful witches never truly leave their homes."

The gathering in the parlor was intimate but lively, with coven members sharing stories of Nancy that had Bree and Molly alternating between laughter and tears. The evening stretched on, food appearing and disappearing, glasses of wine being refilled, and gradually, the formality gave way to genuine connection.

As the night deepened, Bree slipped away from the group, needing a moment of quiet. She found herself in her grandmother's study, a room lined with bookshelves and dominated by a massive oak desk. On a stand beside it sat Nancy's formal witch's hat—not the pointed caricature of fairy tales, but an elegant, wide-brimmed creation of midnight blue velvet, adorned with silver stars that seemed to twinkle even in the dim light.

"I wondered when you'd find your way in here."

Bree startled, turning to find Susan Fond in the doorway.

"Sorry," Bree said automatically. "I just needed some space."

Susan waved away her apology. "This was always your favorite room as a child. You used to sit at Nancy's feet while she worked her spells, asking a thousand questions."

Bree smiled at the memory. "She never minded. Not once."

"Because she saw the potential in you," Susan said, crossing to stand beside her. "The same potential I see now."

Bree's gaze returned to the hat. "I don't know if I can do this," Bree admitted. "Take her place in the coven, possibly inherit her hat, carry on her work. It's too much."

"You don't have to take her place," Susan said gently. "You only need to find your own. And you and Molly still have time to decide between yourselves who will take the hat."

"That's what scares me," Bree admitted. "What if I'm the one who ends up with it? What if I see things through her eyes that I'm not ready for? What if I learn truths about our family that Mom has been protecting us from?" Bree was visibly concerned, and not just for herself, but for Molly as well.

Susan's expression grew serious. "There are always truths we must face, Bree. That's part of being a witch—seeing reality without flinching from it."

Before Bree could respond, a movement outside the window caught her attention. The man from next door was visible again, this time standing in his own garden, looking directly at the Tanner house.

"Who is that?" she asked, nodding toward the window.

Susan followed her gaze, her lips curving into a knowing smile. "That's Sam Sorken. He moved in about 3 years ago. Quiet type, keeps to himself mostly."

"Was he friends with Grandma Nancy?"

"In a manner of speaking," Susan replied cryptically. "She took quite an interest in him when he arrived. Used to bake for him every Sunday."

Bree frowned. "That doesn't sound like Grandma. She wasn't exactly the neighborly type."

"Perhaps she saw something in him worth nurturing," Susan suggested. "Nancy always did have an eye for potential."

As they watched, Sam turned away, disappearing into his own house.

"You'll meet him soon enough, I imagine," Susan continued. "Ballad is a small town, after all. Hard to avoid anyone for long."

Bree nodded absently, her attention returning to the hat. In the moonlight streaming through the window, it seemed almost alive, waiting.

"Tomorrow will be difficult," Susan said, changing the subject. "The funeral will bring out everyone in town, not just the coven. Then in about ten or twelve days, we'll have the Passing of the Hat ceremony, once you and Molly have made your decision."

"I'm not sure I'm ready," Bree murmured.

"None of us ever are," Susan's laugh was gentle. "Not really. Some things happen whether we're ready or not." She squeezed Bree's shoulder. "Come back to the gathering when you're ready. Your mother could use your support."

Left alone in the study, Bree approached the hat cautiously. She didn't touch it—that would come during the ceremony in ten days, if she and Molly decided she would be the one to receive it—but she felt its energy reaching for her, recognizing her bloodline.

"I hope whoever wears you does Nancy proud," she whispered.

From outside came the soft hoot of an owl, a sound Bree had always associated with her grandmother's magic. A coincidence, perhaps, or perhaps something more—a sign, a greeting, a promise.

Either way, Bree knew there was no turning back. She was home, back where she belonged, standing on the threshold of a power and responsibility larger than herself. Whatever secrets lay buried in Ballad, whatever connection existed between her family and the mysterious neighbor, whatever destiny awaited her and Molly as they stepped into their roles within the coven—it would all unfold in its own time.

For now, she had a funeral to prepare for, a hat to possibly inherit, and a legacy to understand.

Bree cast one last glance out the window at Sam Sorken's darkened house before rejoining her family. Something told her their paths would cross soon enough, and when they did, nothing would ever be the same again.

Chapter 3
The Necropolis

Shadow and light danced across ancient stone as Sameril stood before Master Xaloth in the heart of the Necropolis. Unlike the bright, open spaces of Lumina's arcane academy where witches trained, the great hall of necromancy embraced darkness. Giant obsidian pillars rose to vaulted ceilings where phantom lights slowly drifted in lazy spirals, high above, casting an ethereal glow over the proceedings below.

Master Xaloth's weathered face seemed to be carved from the same stone as the chamber walls. His eyes, however, burned with an inner power; two points of violet flame within deeply recessed sockets. The centuries had bent the mans once-imposing frame to make him appear as something less, but those who knew him would never mistake this fragility for weakness.

"You seem nervous, Sameril," Xaloth observed, his voice carrying the weight of centuries. "There's no need for such anxiety. This is a moment of triumph."

Sameril straightened his shoulders, forcing his hands to remain steady at his sides. "Forgive me, Master. I just... I didn't expect to be summoned from Lumina so suddenly."

"The timing of destiny is rarely convenient," Xaloth replied with a dry chuckle. He gestured to the circular platform they stood upon, where ancient runes pulsed with a subtle green luminescence. "Do you know why you're here?"

"I believe my final examination—"

"That was merely a formality." Xaloth waved dismissively. "You surpassed my expectations long ago. No, you stand here today because you have accomplished something far more significant."

The ancient necromancer turned toward a stone alcove behind him, passing his hand over its surface. The solid stone rippled like water, and from within emerged a large tome bound in rich brown leather. Its cover bore the embossed emblem of a skull entwined with thorny vines—the symbol of advanced necromancy.

"The Codex Mortis," Sameril breathed, his academic composure momentarily abandoned.

Xaloth's lips curved into a rare smile. "You recognize it. Good. This grimoire contains knowledge accumulated over fifteen generations of master necromancers. Each adding their discoveries, their breakthroughs—the culmination of our discipline's highest achievements."

He held the book with reverence between his ancient hands, the leather seeming to absorb the chamber's phantom light. "Sameril, you have proven yourself to be my most promising pupil. Your understanding of the delicate balance between life and death surpasses students twice your age."

Sameril's heart hammered against his ribs. "Master Xaloth, I-I'm deeply honored, but surely there are others more deserving—"

"False modesty doesn't become you," Xaloth interrupted sharply. "I have watched you master techniques in weeks that took me years to comprehend. Your intuitive grasp of necromantic principles is unmatched in my three centuries of teaching."

The old necromancer extended the tome. "Today, I bestow upon you a gift given only to the most dedicated and skilled of our order. The Codex Mortis is now yours to study and, eventually, to add your own discoveries."

Sameril accepted the book with trembling hands, feeling its substantial weight—both physical and metaphorical. His fingers traced the embossed skull and vines, feeling the subtle energy that thrummed beneath the cover.

"I... thank you, Master Xaloth," he managed, his voice thick with emotion. "I will honor this gift with every fiber of my being."

"See that you do," Xaloth replied, his momentary warmth receding behind his customary severity. "Remember, Sameril—necromancy is not about conquering death, but understanding it. Not about defying the natural order but perceiving the hidden patterns within it."

"I understand, Master. Life and death in balance, as has always been our way."

Xaloth nodded approvingly. "Now, go join your peers. Knowledge hoarded is knowledge wasted. Practice what you've learned and share it with those worthy of receiving it."

Sameril bowed deeply, clutching the codex to his chest. "I won't disappoint you."

"I know you won't, my boy." Something almost paternal flickered in Xaloth's ancient eyes. "Now go before you're late for Magister Vreen's practical demonstration. I hear she's quite irritable when students disrupt her rhythm."

With another quick bow, Sameril turned and strode across the grand chamber, his footsteps echoing against the stone. The massive doors swung open of their own accord as he approached, spilling daylight into the dim hall.

Outside, the Necropolis grounds spread before him—a stark contrast to the somber interior. The academy's gardens bloomed with exotic flora specifically cultivated to harness necromantic energies. Black roses with yellow-edged petals grew alongside luminescent fungi that pulsed with an inner light. Pale, ghost-like butterflies flitted between skeletal trees whose bare branches were perpetually covered in frost despite the warm Eldorian sun.

Sameril breathed deeply, relishing the complex aroma of herbs and incense that permeated the air. In the distance, he could see a gathering of students in the central courtyard. His fellow necromancers were easily recognizable by their slate-gray robes trimmed with silver sigils—a stark contrast to the colorful attire favored by the witches of Lumina.

"Sameril!" A familiar voice called out. Talien waved enthusiastically from the edge of the group, his lanky frame towering over most of the other students. "Over here! You've missed half the discussion already!"

Sameril quickened his pace, weaving through the garden paths until he reached his friend. Talien's eyes immediately dropped to the book clutched against Sameril's chest.

"By the Void," Talien whispered, recognition dawning on his face. "Is that—?"

"The Codex Mortis," Sameril confirmed, unable to suppress his pride. "Master Xaloth just presented it to me."

Talien's eyes widened. "Sam, that's... that's unprecedented. Students don't receive the Codex until after formal graduation, and even then, only the exceptional few."

"I'm still in shock myself," Sameril admitted.

Another student, Vessa, overheard their exchange and abandoned her position in the circle to join them. Her silver-white hair was pulled back in a severe braid that accentuated her sharp features and calculating eyes.

"So, the rumors were true," she said, eyeing the codex with barely concealed envy. "Xaloth's favorite has received special treatment again."

"It's not like that, Vessa," Sameril protested.

"Isn't it?" She raised an eyebrow. "The rest of us spend hours in the crypts practicing elementary reanimation while you're granted private lessons in the restricted archives."

Talien stepped subtly between them. "Perhaps Sameril receives additional instruction because he completes the standard curriculum in half the time the rest of us require."

Vessa's lips thinned, but before she could respond, a hush fell over the gathering. The circle of students parted, and Sameril turned to see a figure approaching from the direction of Lumina's academy.

The late afternoon sun set Briella's copper hair ablaze, the illusion of a living flame cascading down her back. Unlike the muted grays and silvers of the necromancy students, she wore the emerald-trimmed robes of a senior witch apprentice. Her witch's hat—that marked her as a daughter of House Tanner—cast a shadow across her face, but Sameril could still discern her bright emerald eyes assessing the gathering.

The necromancy students shifted uncomfortably. While not forbidden, interactions between the two magical disciplines were uncommon. Witchcraft drew power from life and growth; necromancy explored the boundaries of death and transformation. Both were respected, but their practitioners rarely mingled.

Briella seemed either unaware of or unconcerned by the stir her presence caused. She walked directly toward Sameril, her gaze fixed on the book in his arms.

"Is that the tome everyone's been whispering about?" she asked without preamble, stopping before him. "The one containing the highest necromantic secrets?"

Sameril blinked, momentarily thrown by her directness. "The Codex Mortis, yes. Though I wouldn't say it contains 'secrets' so much as advanced theoretical frameworks and practical applications of—"

"May I see it?" Briella interrupted, extending her hand.

Talien made a strangled noise beside him. "That's not—one doesn't simply—"

"Why?" Sameril asked, genuinely curious rather than defensive.

Briella's lips curved into a smile that transformed her face from merely beautiful to radiant. "Because knowledge shouldn't be confined to arbitrary boundaries. Witchcraft and necromancy are not opposing forces but complementary aspects of the same universal energy."

Vessa scoffed audibly. "That's not what your Archmagi Elindra teaches. Didn't she call necromancy 'a perversion of natural order' in her last public address?"

"I form my own opinions," Briella replied coolly, her eyes never leaving Sameril's. "Just as I imagine you all do. Or do you blindly accept everything Master Xaloth teaches without question?"

A tense silence followed her words. Questioning one's master wasn't openly encouraged in either discipline.

"I respect my master's wisdom," Sameril said carefully, "but true understanding comes from exploration and questioning." He hesitated only briefly before opening the codex to its first page, angling it so Briella could glimpse its contents. "I cannot let you handle it—there are binding spells that would... react poorly to someone untrained in our arts. But you may look."

The page revealed elegantly inscribed text surrounding intricate diagrams of energy flows between life and death. Briella leaned closer, her scent—like fresh herbs and something distinctly floral—momentarily distracting Sameril.

"Fascinating," she murmured. "The underlying principles aren't so different from our advanced transmutation theory. The application and focus differ, but the fundamental understanding of energy conversion is remarkably similar."

"That's exactly what I've been researching," Sameril said, excitement overcoming his usual reserve. "The theoretical intersection of witchcraft and necromancy could potentially yield entirely new magical disciplines."

Briella's eyes lit up. "You're researching magical convergence? I've been exploring similar concepts from the witchcraft perspective. The elders think it's a waste of time, but I'm convinced there's merit to it."

"I would be very interested in hearing your approach," Sameril said, closing the book carefully. "Perhaps we could meet specifically to discuss it?"

"The gardens at sunset?" Briella suggested. "Near the moonflower grove? It's a neutral ground between our academies."

"I believe that someone mentioned that to me once before. I'll be there," Sameril agreed, acutely aware of his classmates' stares burning into his back.

Briella nodded, her eyes lingering on his for a moment longer than necessary before she stepped back. "Until then, Sameril."

As she turned to leave, her hand brushed against his arm—the contact brief but electric. Sameril watched her depart, her confident stride carrying her back toward Lumina's spires in the distance.

The moment she was out of earshot, the quiet erupted into a cacophony of voices.

"Have you lost your mind?" Vessa hissed. "Sharing the codex with a witch?"

"I didn't share it," Sameril defended. "I showed her a single page of introductory theory."

"And arranged a private meeting," Talien added, a hint of teasing in his voice despite his obvious concern. "With Briella Tanner, no less. Half the apprentices in Lumina would trade their hats for such an opportunity."

"It's purely academic," Sameril insisted, though the flush creeping up his neck suggested otherwise.

"Academic," Vessa repeated skeptically. "Well, when your 'academic' meeting gets you expelled for sharing necromantic knowledge with outsiders, don't expect sympathy."

"The prohibition is against sharing practical applications," Sameril corrected, "not theoretical discussion."

"A convenient interpretation," Vessa sniffed, turning away. "Come, Talien. Magister Vreen will begin the demonstration soon."

Talien hesitated, looking between Vessa's retreating form and Sameril. "She's not entirely wrong to be concerned, Sam. The divisions between our disciplines exist for historical reasons. But," he added with a small smile, "I've never known you to follow a path simply because it was traditional."

He clapped Sameril on the shoulder. "I'll save you a place at the demonstration. Try not to get so lost in thoughts of Briella Tanner that you forget to attend."

As Talien jogged to catch up with the other students, Sameril carefully secured the codex in his satchel. His fingers lingered on the embossed cover, tracing the skull and vines emblem thoughtfully.

Convergence between witchcraft and necromancy. The idea had occupied his research for months, but he'd never dared share it openly. Yet Briella had arrived at the same conclusion independently.

The sunlight caught the distant spires of Lumina, making them gleam like beacons against the lavender sky. In a few hours, he would meet Briella in the gardens to exchange ideas and theories.

Purely academic, he told himself again, even as his heart quickened at the thought of her emerald eyes and the brief touch of her hand against his arm.

With a deep breath, Sameril turned toward the demonstration grounds. First, his responsibilities as a student of the Necropolis. Then, at sunset, a conversation that might change everything.

Chapter 4
The Funeral

Morning light streamed through the curtains as Bree awoke in her childhood bedroom. For a disorienting moment, she felt twelve again, until the weight of why they'd returned crashed over her. Grandma Nancy was gone, and today they would lay her to rest.

She pulled herself from bed and crossed to the window, drawn by voices from outside. In the garden next door, Sam Sorken sat on a wrought-iron chair, laptop open before him, coffee mug in hand. Even from a distance, there was something compelling about him—a quiet intensity that made it difficult to look away.

A knock at her door broke the spell.

"Bree?" Molly's voice called. "Mom's made breakfast. We need to leave for the church in an hour."

"Coming," she replied, reluctantly stepping away from the window.

Downstairs, Mary Ann stood at the stove, flipping bacon with practiced precision. The normality of the scene—her mother cooking breakfast on the morning of a funeral—struck Bree as both bizarre and comforting.

"Morning," she mumbled, sliding onto a stool at the kitchen island.

Mary Ann turned, offering a strained smile. "Sleep well?"

"As well as could be expected," Bree answered honestly. "The house still... feels things."

Mary Ann nodded in understanding. "Witch houses always do. They absorb emotions, hold memories."

Molly entered, hair damp from the shower. "Speaking of memories," she began, accepting a plate of eggs and bacon from their mother, "I had the strangest dream last night. About Grandma Nancy and... someone else. A man I didn't recognize."

Mary Ann froze momentarily before resuming her cooking. "Dreams in this house often carry messages," she said carefully. "Especially on significant days."

Bree glanced out the kitchen window toward Sam's house. "Who's that?" she asked, nodding in his direction. "The neighbor."

Mary Ann followed her gaze. "Sam Sorken. Writer, I believe. Science fiction or something."

"Did Grandma know him well?"

"According to Susan, they were friendly," Mary Ann replied, her tone deliberately casual. "She mentioned Nancy used to bake for him."

"That's odd," Molly interjected. "Grandma wasn't exactly the cookie-baking type."

Mary Ann shrugged. "People change. Nancy was getting older, maybe she was feeling nostalgic for simpler connections."

Molly leaned forward, eyes narrowing with interest. "He's kind of cute, in a brooding, mysterious writer way."

Bree rolled her eyes. "We're here for a funeral, Mol, not to check out the neighbors."

"Who says we can't do both?" Molly grinned, some of her usual spark returning.

Mary Ann placed her hands on the counter, expression serious. "Girls, I need you to focus today. The funeral will be difficult enough without distractions. And afterward... afterward comes the ceremony."

The levity drained from the room. The ceremony—the formal passing of Nancy's witch hat to one of her granddaughters, the transfer of power and knowledge that would irrevocably change their lives.

"Have you two thought about which of you will receive Grandma's hat?" Mary Ann asked quietly.

Bree and Molly exchanged uncomfortable glances before Molly spoke. "We haven't really discussed it yet."

"You still have ten days or so," Mary Ann said gently. "But you'll need to decide before that ceremony. As the direct descendants, it's your choice to make between yourselves."

"Couldn't you take it?" Bree asked. "You're her daughter."

Mary Ann shook her head firmly. "No. That part of my life is behind me. The hat needs to go to one of you girls—whoever feels ready to carry Nancy's knowledge forward."

She glanced at the kitchen clock. "We should finish eating. The Fonds will be here soon to drive us."

As if summoned by her words, a gentle knock sounded at the front door. Molly went to answer it, returning moments later with Sarah and her mother, Susan Fond.

"Good morning, dears," Susan greeted them warmly, though her eyes held the appropriate solemnity for the day. "Are you ready?"

Mary Ann nodded, gathering her purse. "As ready as we'll ever be."

Bree noticed that Susan carried a small wicker basket covered with a checkered cloth. Catching her curious gaze, Susan smiled sadly.

"Lavender scones," she explained. "Nancy's recipe. I thought... for after."

"She'd like that," Mary Ann said softly.

The drive to the church passed in contemplative silence, broken only when Sarah began sharing memories of Nancy's infamous summer solstice celebrations.

"Remember how she used to string fairy lights through every tree in the garden?" Sarah smiled; her eyes distant with memory.

Molly laughed softly. "And make us dance barefoot in the grass until sunrise."

"The lavender lemonade," Mary Ann added with a wistful smile. "I swear it had actual magic in it."

Susan chuckled from behind the wheel. "Oh, there was definitely something in it! Left everyone feeling lighter for days afterward."

"Happiness potion," Sarah confirmed with a wink directed at Bree and Molly. "One of Nancy's specialties. She always said joy was the most powerful magic."

As they approached the church, Bree was struck by the number of cars already lining the street. It seemed half the town had turned out to pay respects to her grandmother.

"I didn't realize so many people would come," she murmured.

"Your grandmother touched many lives," Susan said gently. "Whether they knew she was a witch or not, she was beloved in Ballad."

The church itself was a small white building with stained glass windows depicting scenes of local history. As they entered, Bree felt a wave of emotion seeing the oak casket at the front, covered in wildflowers and lavender sprigs—Nancy's favorite.

People filled the pews, some Bree recognized, others strangers. The coven members were easy to spot, clustered near the front, their energy distinct even without any outward magical display.

"Breathe," Molly whispered, squeezing her hand as they made their way down the aisle.

The service itself was beautiful in its simplicity—hymns Nancy had loved, readings that spoke of cycles and rebirth rather than endings, stories that brought both laughter and tears. The pastor, a kind-faced woman who Bree vaguely remembered from childhood, spoke of Nancy's generosity, wisdom, and fierce independence.

The hardwood floor of the church creaked as Mary Ann rose from the pew. Each click of her heels echoed through the hushed room as she approached the podium, her fingers trembling slightly as they clutched the folded paper containing her eulogy. The sea of faces before her—some familiar, others nearly forgotten over the years—blurred together as tears threatened to spill from her eyes. She blinked them back, determined to maintain her composure for her daughters' sake.

The closed casket sat at the front of the room, adorned with a spray of white lilies—Nancy's favorite. Mary Ann had chosen the arrangement herself, remembering how her mother would point them out in gardens during their evening walks around Ballad. "There's magic in those petals," Nancy used to say with a knowing smile. Now, their sweet fragrance filled the church, a gentle reminder of the woman they had all come to honor.

"When I went over this in my head, it sounded better than I think it does now," Mary Ann began, her voice wavering slightly as she smoothed the crinkled paper. She glanced at the casket, shaking her head with a wistful smile. "Even though Mom isn't with us, I can't help wondering how she feels about all of this."

She paused, taking a moment to look around the room. The Warren family sat in the second row, Elaine dabbing at her eyes with a lace handkerchief while her daughter Lucy squeezed her shoulder. Sarah and Susan Fond were directly behind Bree and Molly, their faces solemn but supportive. Trudie Catshill, with her striking silver hair piled high in an elegant bun, nodded encouragingly from her seat near the aisle.

"She was never really a funeral person," Mary Ann continued, a hint of fondness creeping into her voice. "But, as she said more than once, they're for the living. It crossed her mind a couple of times not to bother with all the rigmarole, and she finally made the decision that it was more about us than it was about her."

Mary Ann's eyes drifted to the back of the church, where she spotted a familiar figure standing partially obscured by a column—Sam Sorken. His presence surprised her; she hadn't expected him to attend. Their eyes met briefly, and he gave a respectful nod before lowering his gaze.

"Had she been able to see you all here now, wanting to say goodbye, I think she'd be grateful she made the decision that she had, for everyone who's here. Thank you, all of you, for coming. We really do appreciate it."

In the front pew, Bree reached for Molly's hand. Her sister's fingers were ice-cold despite the warmth of the church. The sisters exchanged a glance, a silent communication passing between them as they listened to their mother speak of the woman who had shaped so much of their lives, even from a distance.

"The memories I know will never fade of the woman my mother was," Mary Ann continued, her voice growing stronger with each word. "I'm sure all of you have your own stories about her, something I hope you'll share with us, in the same way we'll share our stories with you."

Mary Ann's gaze lingered on the members of the Andromeda Coven scattered throughout the congregation. To anyone else, they appeared to be ordinary townspeople, but she could sense the subtle current of energy connecting them, the silent acknowledgment of what Nancy had meant to their circle.

"Nancy Tanner was a special woman, in many different ways. She raised me as a single mom after Dad died, making sure to keep his memory alive as best she could, but it did mean she was there for so many special moments he'd never be able to see."

Mary Ann's voice caught, and she took a moment to compose herself, reaching for the glass of water that had been placed on the podium. After taking a sip, she continued, "I remember her holding me at his funeral, the only real memory I have of it, helping me through the pain, in the same way she was there for every other emotion following."

In the pew, Molly felt a tear slide down her cheek as she watched her mother speak. She could almost picture the scene—a young Mary Ann, devastated by the loss of her father, finding comfort in Nancy's embrace. It was a cycle that seemed to repeat itself through generations: loss, grief, and the strength of the women in their family who carried on despite it all.

"When I was a teenager, I was furious at her for no reason," Mary Ann said with a small, rueful laugh that brought knowing smiles to several faces in the audience. "She put up with a lot from me then, because I wasn't easy, and yet she still made certain there were nights we'd spend together the same way we did when I was little—with a hot chocolate, staring out at the stars."

Bree smiled at this, remembering her own nights spent stargazing with Nancy. Her grandmother had a way of making the constellations come alive with stories of ancient goddesses and powerful witches who had left their mark on the heavens. Only now was Bree beginning to understand that those tales weren't entirely folklore.

"Even now when I look at them, I'm reminded of her," Mary Ann continued, "some of the stories she told me about the constellations coming back, the memory of them a comfort."

A murmur of agreement rippled through the coven members. Nancy's knowledge of the stars had been legendary among them, her ability to read the patterns in the night sky unmatched.

"Eventually, the time came when she told my own daughters those stories, her two precious granddaughters, who she loved almost more than life itself." Mary Ann's gaze softened as she looked at Bree and Molly. "I remember the day they were born; how proud she was both times. Holding them like they might break if she wasn't careful enough with them."

Molly and Bree moved simultaneously, tightening their grip on each other's hands as tears began to trickle down both their cheeks. The memory of their grandmother's gentle touch, her warm smile, and the wisdom in her eyes was almost tangible in that moment.

"At times, my own relationship with Mom was complicated," Mary Ann admitted, her voice dropping slightly. This was something they rarely spoke about—the tension that had existed between mother and daughter for years. "She never once let that stop her spending time with Molly and Bree. I'd get a call, and she'd be asking to see them, so they'd make the journey out here for another week with their Gram."

Mary Ann smiled, genuine affection warming her features. "It was one of the things I loved most about her. Now she's gone, I know she'd be proud of who I am, and who I raised my daughters to be. We're going to miss her every day, the memories slowly becoming a blessing as the pain begins to fade, all of us remembering her with a deep love."

With a final, tremulous smile, Mary Ann stepped away from the podium. As she made her way back to her seat, she noticed Sarah Fond wiping away tears, and Trudie Catshill gazing thoughtfully at Bree and Molly, as if assessing them. Mary Ann knew what they were all thinking—which of the Tanner women would take up Nancy's mantle now? Which of them would wear the hat?

She reached her daughters and sat between them, placing her hand over their clasped ones. Her fingers were shaking slightly, the emotional toll of the day catching up to her. Bree leaned her head against her mother's shoulder, offering what comfort she could, while Molly squeezed Mary Ann's hand tightly.

After the service concluded with a haunting rendition of "Amazing Grace," the attendees filed out of the church in a solemn procession. Nancy's simple oak casket remained behind, waiting to be transported to the crematorium as per her wishes. "Don't leave me in the ground," she had told Mary Ann during one of their last conversations. "Set me free to the wind and stars, where I've always belonged."

Outside the church, mourners gathered in small clusters, exchanging hushed condolences and memories of Nancy. The day was surprisingly fair for early spring, with sunlight dappling through the budding trees that lined the church grounds. It was as if nature itself was paying tribute to a woman who had always been deeply connected to its rhythms.

"Are you alright?" Bree asked her mother as they stood on the church steps, accepting hugs and handshakes from the departing crowd.

Mary Ann nodded, though the pallor of her face belied her words. "I will be. It's just... final now, isn't it?"

"She's not really gone, Mom," Molly said softly, her hand on Mary Ann's arm. "Not completely. Grandma Nancy always said that energy never truly disappears—it just changes form."

Mary Ann's lips quirked in a sad smile. "She would say that, wouldn't she? Always the witch philosopher."

"Mary Ann." A gentle voice interrupted their conversation. They turned to find Susan Fond approaching, her daughter Sarah at her side. "The eulogy was beautiful, dear. Nancy would have loved it."

"Thank you, Susan," Mary Ann replied, accepting the older woman's embrace. "Will you and Sarah be joining us at the house? I know it's early, but people will be arriving soon, and I could use the help setting up."

"Of course we will," Susan assured her. "Sarah's already got a pot of her famous stew in the car, and I've baked three batches of Nancy's favorite lemon squares."

Sarah nodded, her kind eyes meeting Bree's. "We're here for whatever you need. The whole coven is."

As if on cue, Elaine Warren appeared beside them, her short, plump frame commanding attention even in her subdued funeral attire. "Mary Ann, the girls and I will be over shortly. Lucy's just gone to pick up the food we prepared, and I've asked Trudie to bring some of her herbal tea—the calming blend. I think we could all use some today."

Mary Ann nodded gratefully. "Thank you all. I don't know what we'd do without you."

"You never have to find out," Elaine said firmly, embracing each of the Tanner women in turn. "That's what the coven is for—we're family, in every way that matters."

As they prepared to leave, Bree noticed Sam Sorken standing at the edge of the churchyard, hands in his pockets, observing the scene from a respectful distance. When he saw her looking, he inclined his head slightly in acknowledgment before turning to walk away.

"He's an interesting one, isn't he?" Sarah murmured, following Bree's gaze.

"Did you know he was friends with Grandma?" Bree asked, curious about the connection between Nancy and their reclusive neighbor.

Sarah's expression turned thoughtful. "Friends... yes, I suppose you could call it that. Nancy took him under her wing when he first moved to Ballad. Said he had 'potential,' whatever that meant." She shrugged lightly. "Your grandmother always did have an eye for seeing things in people that others missed."

Before Bree could press for more details, Mary Ann called them over, and the moment of discovery was lost in the flurry of departure arrangements.

By the time they arrived back at the Tanner house, several cars were already parked along Willow Street. The front door stood open, and the sounds of quiet conversation and movement drifted out to greet them as they walked up the path.

Inside, the house had been transformed. The Warrens, the Fonds, and several other coven members had arrived early to prepare for the reception. The dining table was laden with food—casseroles, salads, breads, and desserts of all kinds—while the living room furniture had been rearranged to create conversational nooks. Vases of fresh flowers adorned every available surface, their vibrant colors a stark contrast to the somber attire of the guests.

"Oh my," Mary Ann breathed, taking in the scene. "You've done so much already."

"Least we could do," Trudie Catshill replied, appearing from the kitchen with a tray of delicate teacups. Her salt and peppered hair caught the light as she moved, creating an almost ethereal halo effect. "Nancy would have done the same for any of us."

As more guests arrived, the house filled with the murmur of conversation and the occasional burst of laughter as someone shared a particularly fond memory of Nancy.

The coven members stood creating a circle. As Bree, Molly, and Mary Ann appeared within it, they began to hum—a single note that seemed to vibrate through the very foundations of the house.

Finally, Susan stepped forward, her usually warm features solemn. "We gather to honor Nancy Tanner, daughter of Cecilia, granddaughter of Eleanor, witch of the Coven of Andromeda. We gather to witness the passing of her power, her knowledge, her legacy."

The humming grew louder as Susan gestured for the Tanner women to enter the circle.

"Mary Ann Tanner, daughter of Nancy, mother of Bree and Molly, step forward and speak your farewell."

Mary Ann moved to stand beside the table, her hands hovering over the hat. "Mother," she began, her voice thick with emotion, "you taught me strength when I was weak, courage when I was afraid, and wisdom when I was foolish. Your magic flows through me, through my daughters, through all who loved you. Go peacefully into the great beyond, knowing your legacy continues. Blessed be."

"Blessed be," the coven echoed.

Susan turned to Molly. "Molly Tanner, granddaughter of Nancy, daughter of Mary Ann, step forward and speak your farewell."

Molly approached the table, her usual confidence tempered by the solemnity of the moment. "Grandma Nancy," she said, her voice clear despite the tears in her eyes, "you showed me that power comes with responsibility, that magic is both a gift and a burden. I promise to honor your teachings, to protect our family's legacy, to use what you've left me for good. Blessed be."

"Blessed be," came the response.

Susan turned to Bree; her gaze gentle but expectant. "Bree Tanner, granddaughter of Nancy, daughter of Mary Ann, step forward and speak your farewell."

Bree took a deep breath and approached the table. The hat seemed to pulse with an energy she could almost see—threads of light and memory woven into its fabric. She placed her trembling fingers near it, not quite touching but feeling the warmth radiating from its surface.

"Grandma Nancy," she began, her voice soft but steady, "you planted seeds of magic in me that I'm only now beginning to understand. You saw something in me that I couldn't see in myself. I promise to nurture that gift, to seek the knowledge you valued so highly, and to honor the connection between past and future that you always cherished." Her voice caught slightly before she continued, "Thank you for the stories, the wisdom, and the love that will guide me even in your absence. Blessed be."

"Blessed be," the coven members intoned, their voices blending in perfect harmony.

The short farewell ceremony complete, the coven converged on the three women with hugs and smiles. Bree then found herself moving from group to group, accepting condolences and listening to stories about her grandmother that she had never heard before.

"Did you know your grandmother once hexed old Mayor Hensley's toupee right off his head during a town council meeting?" Trudie whispered to her with a mischievous glint in her eye. "The man had tried to push through a development project that would have destroyed the ancient oak grove at the edge of town. Nancy wasn't having any of it."

Bree's eyes widened. "She did what?"

Trudie chuckled, the sound low and throaty. "Oh yes. A sudden gust of wind, they all said—came right through the closed windows and snatched that ridiculous hairpiece clean off his head. Flew it right into the punch bowl. The proposal was tabled indefinitely after that 'omen.'"

Across the room, Molly was deep in conversation with Lucy Warren, the heavy-set woman was gesticulating animatedly as she spoke.

"Your grandmother's spellcraft was something else," Lucy was saying, her voice pitched low enough that only Molly could hear. "She could infuse her cooking with intent like nobody I've ever seen. One bite of her apple pie, and feuding neighbors would be shaking hands by dessert's end. One sip of her mulled cider, and winter colds vanished overnight."

Molly smiled, remembering the special treats Nancy would prepare during their visits. "She never told us about any of that. We just thought she was an amazing cook."

"Oh, she was," Lucy assured her. "But she was so much more, too. The magic enhanced what was already there—it didn't create it." She leaned closer, her eyes serious despite her lighthearted tone. "That's something you and your sister will learn, when one of you takes up her hat."

Before Molly could respond, the front door burst open, and in walked Lucy's mother, Elaine Warren, her arms laden with even more food and drinks. Lucy jumped up to meet her, a look of mild exasperation crossing her face.

"Mama, I told you we didn't need to bring all this," Lucy chided, her voice carrying across the room as she took some of the containers from her mother's arms. "The Tanners have plenty of food already."

Elaine's eyebrows rose imperiously. "Lucy Warren, when have I ever listened to you about how much food is appropriate for an occasion?"

Lucy, undeterred, made her way to the kitchen, calling over her shoulder, "Never, Mama, but there's always hope that one day you might start!"

Elaine shook her head, a smile playing on her lips as she followed Lucy into the kitchen. Their good-natured bickering brought a welcome lightness to the somber atmosphere.

Moments later, with her mother in tow, Lucy emerged from the kitchen, balancing a plate piled high with slices of her sweet potato pie. She made a beeline for Bree and Molly, who had gravitated back toward each other as they often did in social situations.

"Girls, you have got to try this pie," Lucy declared, thrusting the plate toward them. Her warm brown eyes sparkled with pride as she announced, "I used Grandma Nancy's secret recipe, and let me tell you, it's even better than hers!"

Bree and Molly exchanged an amused glance, well aware of Lucy's culinary ambitions. For years, she had been trying to replicate—and improve upon—Nancy's legendary recipes, with varying degrees of success.

"Lucy Warren, you bite your tongue!" Elaine called from across the room, her voice stern but her eyes twinkling with mirth. "Nancy's sweet potato pie was the best in the county, and you know it!"

Lucy rolled her eyes dramatically, mouthing her mother's words mockingly before turning back to Bree and Molly with a conspiratorial wink. "Don't listen to her, girls. I've been working on this recipe for months, and I've finally perfected it."

As Bree took a bite of the pie, her eyes widened in genuine surprise. The flavors were complex and harmonious—sweet but not cloying, spiced with what she recognized as cinnamon, nutmeg, and something else she couldn't quite place. "Lucy, this is incredible!" she exclaimed, savoring the perfect texture and balance of flavors.

Molly, too, let out an appreciative sound as she tasted the dessert. "I hate to say it, but I think you might have actually outdone Grandma Nancy this time."

Lucy beamed with pride, casting a triumphant glance toward her mother. "See, Mama? I told you!"

Elaine, unable to hide her smile, shook her head in mock despair. "Lord help us all, the child's going to be insufferable now."

The room erupted in laughter, the tension and sorrow of the day momentarily forgotten as everyone reveled in Lucy's infectious joy. It was a moment of respite, a reminder that life and joy continued even in the face of loss—something Nancy herself had always emphasized.

As the laughter died down, Lucy's expression grew more serious, a rare vulnerability showing in her usually confident demeanor. "In all honesty, though, Nancy was an incredible woman. She taught me so much about baking, about life, about being a part of this coven. I'm going to miss her more than words can say."

Her voice caught on the last words, and for a moment, she looked much younger than her twenty-eight years—like the little girl who had followed Nancy around the kitchen, absorbing every lesson with wide-eyed wonder.

Bree and Molly, touched by Lucy's heartfelt words, pulled her into a tight hug. "We all will," Bree murmured, feeling the warmth and love of the coven surrounding them like a protective circle.

As Lucy moved away to offer pie to the other guests, the conversation shifted naturally to the topic that had been simmering beneath the surface all day: Nancy's role within the Andromeda Coven and what her passing meant for its future.

"Nancy was more than just a member of the coven," Elaine said softly, her voice carrying an authority that commanded attention. As she spoke, the other coven members drew closer, forming a loose circle around the

Tanner women. "She was our High Priestess, the guiding light that led us through times of darkness and uncertainty."

Trudie Catshill nodded solemnly, her gaze moving between Mary Ann, Bree, and Molly. "And now, with her passing, it falls to one of you Tanner women to take up her mantle."

A hushed silence fell over the group as the weight of Trudie's words settled on the three women. Bree felt a flutter of both excitement and apprehension in her chest. The idea of stepping into Nancy's role—of wearing her hat and carrying all the knowledge and power it contained—was both exhilarating and daunting.

Mary Ann's expression remained carefully neutral, though Bree noticed her mother's hands had clenched into tight fists at her sides. There was a history there, something unspoken between Mary Ann and the coven that Bree had yet to fully understand.

Molly broke the silence, her voice barely above a whisper. "But how will we decide which one of us should take it?"

Sarah Fond stepped forward, her gentle presence a calming influence in the charged atmosphere. "That's a decision you and your sister will need to make together," she said kindly. "The Passing of the Hat ceremony can only happen once you've both come to an agreement."

"And what if neither of them feels ready?" Mary Ann asked suddenly, her voice carrying an edge that surprised Bree. It was the first time she had spoken since the conversation had turned to coven matters.

Trudie leaned forward, her silver bracelets jingling softly. "The coven needs its High Priestess, Mary Ann. We cannot remain without leadership for long."

"How long do they have to decide?" Mary Ann pressed; tension evident in her posture.

Elaine's eyebrows rose sharply. "The traditional period is ten days of reflection. After that..." She let the sentence hang meaningfully in the air before continuing, "Mary Ann Tanner, your bloodline has produced some of the most powerful witches the Andromeda Coven has ever known. One of your daughters will rise to this occasion—of that, I have no doubt."

Before the conversation could continue, an unexpected knock at the door drew everyone's attention. The circle broke apart naturally, the coven members drifting back to their previous positions as if nothing unusual had been discussed. It was a practiced movement, Bree realized—the instinctive discretion of those who were accustomed to keeping their true nature hidden from the world.

Molly, seizing the opportunity to escape the intense conversation, hurried to answer the door. Standing on the porch was Sam Sorken, looking somewhat out of place in his simple black suit. In his hands, he held a covered dish, the scent of something savory wafting from beneath the foil.

"I'm so sorry for your loss," he said, his voice low and sincere. His eyes, a striking shade of gray that reminded Bree of storm clouds, held genuine sympathy. "I didn't want to intrude, but I did want to drop off some food and let you know that if there's anything I can do, please don't hesitate to ask."

Molly, who was utterly surprised and touched by the gesture, accepted the dish with a grateful smile. "Thank you, Sam. That's very kind of you."

Sam nodded, his gaze moving past Molly to where Bree stood in the living room. For a brief moment, their eyes met, and Bree felt an inexplicable pull, as if some invisible thread connected them across the space. It was gone as quickly as it had come, leaving her to wonder if she had imagined it.

"I won't stay," Sam said, stepping back from the door. "I know you have a lot of people here, and I don't want to impose. But please, if you need anything at all, I'm just next door."

With a final, sympathetic smile, he turned and made his way back down the path, his tall figure silhouetted against the late afternoon sun.

As Molly carried the dish into the kitchen, Bree found herself watching Sam through the window. There was something about him—something beyond his striking looks and the mystery surrounding his friendship with her grandmother—that intrigued her deeply. She made a mental note to ask Nancy's friends more about him, to try and unravel the enigma that surrounded her neighbor.

But for now, there were more pressing matters at hand. The question of who would take up Nancy's hat and become the new High Priestess of the Andromeda Coven loomed large, casting a shadow over the day's events. It was a decision that would not be made lightly, Bree knew, and one that would irrevocably change the course of their lives.

As the afternoon wore on and the house gradually emptied of guests, Bree found herself drawn to the window overlooking the street. The sun was beginning to set, casting long shadows across Willow Street and bathing the Victorian houses in a warm, golden light. It was the kind of evening Nancy had loved—perfect for stargazing, she would have said.

The Fonds were the last to leave, but living next door made for a quick trip for them both. Bree stepped outside to say goodbye to Susan and Sarah, watching as they made their way down the path with promises to check in on the Tanners the following day.

As she turned to step back inside the house, she noticed Sam sitting on his porch, slowly moving in his glider swing. A steaming mug of what she assumed was coffee cradled in his hands, his expression pensive as he gazed out at the street. When he saw her looking, he raised his mug in a silent toast, acknowledgment passing between them across the space that separated their homes.

Bree waved back, a small smile curving her lips. There was something comforting about his presence, a sense of continuity in a day filled with endings and beginnings. As she lowered her head in thought and stepped back inside, she couldn't shake the feeling that Sam Sorken would play a more significant role in their lives than any of them yet realized.

Behind her, through the closing door, the last light of day caught the edge of a hat box sitting on the mantelpiece—a box that hadn't been there that morning. Inside, Nancy Tanner's witch hat waited patiently for its new owner, its centuries of accumulated knowledge ready to be passed on to the next generation of the Tanner line.

Chapter 5
The Gardens of Necropolis

The twin suns of Eldoria cast long shadows across the ancient stones of the Necropolis as Sameril made his way toward the gardens. He had changed from his formal academy robes into a simpler tunic of midnight blue, embroidered with subtle silver runes along the hem—casual by necromancer standards, yet still presentable for an evening in the city.

The Codex Mortis remained safely locked in his quarters. While he yearned to show Briella more of its contents, Vessa's warning had planted seeds of caution. Instead, he carried a smaller journal filled with his own research notes—less controversial to share, yet still substantive enough for meaningful discussion.

As he approached the garden entrance, the stark architecture of the Necropolis gave way to living beauty. Here, the boundaries between the disciplines blurred. Necromancers and witches had jointly created this space centuries ago as neutral ground—a physical manifestation of magical cooperation that had since become more symbol than reality.

The tinkling of water drew Sameril forward. At the heart of the garden stood an elaborate fountain where carved serpents and birds twisted around each other in eternal dance, water cascading from their open mouths. Nearby sat Briella, her copper hair now loosely braided and draped over one shoulder. She had exchanged her formal witch's attire for a flowing dress of emerald silk that caught the dying sunlight with each subtle movement.

She looked up at his approach, a smile transforming her face. "You came."

"Did you doubt I would?" Sameril asked, suddenly conscious of his quickened pulse.

"Not doubt, exactly." Briella rose gracefully. "But I heard whispers that showing the codex to a witch might have earned you some disapproval."

Sameril's eyebrows rose. "News travels fast between the academies."

"Faster than you might think." Her eyes sparkled with amusement. "Especially news involving Xaloth's star pupil and a Tanner witch."

"I hope I haven't caused you any trouble," he said, genuinely concerned.

Briella waved this away. "My family has a reputation for... unconventional interests. One more won't raise many eyebrows." She gestured to the bench beside her. "Please, sit. Tell me more about your research into magical convergence."

Sameril settled beside her, carefully maintaining a respectful distance despite his desire to be closer. "I've been exploring the theoretical foundations of our disciplines. At their core, both manipulate the same fundamental energies, just from different perspectives."

"Life and death as complementary forces rather than opposites," Briella nodded. "I've reached similar conclusions through my studies of transformative magic."

Sameril leaned forward eagerly. "Exactly! Consider reanimation—necromancers view it as infusing lifeless matter with directed energy. But isn't that fundamentally similar to a witch's transmutation of one living form into another?"

"The difference being our source of power and intended outcome," Briella said, her expression thoughtful. "Witchcraft channels life energy toward growth and change, while necromancy..."

"Redirects residual energy from what has ended toward new purpose," Sameril finished. "Neither creates nor destroys—both transform."

Their conversation flowed effortlessly, two minds finding unexpected harmony in topics that would scandalize their respective mentors. As they spoke, the last rays of the twin suns painted the sky in brushstrokes of amber and deep violet.

A distant bell tolled, marking the evening hour. Around them, garden lamps flickered to life—not with common flame but with captured wisps of magical luminescence that cast a soft, pearlescent glow over the flowering paths.

"I hadn't realized how late it's grown," Briella said, looking at the darkening sky with surprise. "We've been talking for hours."

Sameril hadn't noticed either, so engrossed was he in their exchange of ideas. His stomach chose that moment to rumble audibly, prompting a small laugh from Briella.

"It seems your body is more aware of the time than your mind," she said. "I'm feeling rather hungry myself."

"I should probably return to—" Sameril began, but Briella interjected.

"Nonsense. The night is young, and Lumina's markets are at their most vibrant after sunset." Her eyes held a challenging gleam. "Unless you're uncomfortable venturing beyond the Necropolis walls with a witch?"

"Not at all," Sameril replied quickly, though in truth, he rarely visited the city proper. Most of his time was spent within the academy grounds, buried in studies or practice. "I would be honored to accompany you."

"Excellent!" Briella stood in a fluid motion. "I know a marvelous place near the southern quarter. The owner, Madame Erissa, serves kalak roasted with eleven different spices that will make you forget every other meal you've ever tasted."

Sameril rose to join her, his academic reserve melting under her enthusiasm. "Lead the way. Though I should warn you, my knowledge of Lumina's geography is somewhat limited."

"All the more reason to explore it," Briella said, offering her arm in a gesture that inverted traditional Eldorian etiquette where men typically extended such courtesy to women. "Consider this your guided tour of the witch's city."

Sameril hesitated only briefly before linking his arm with hers, hyperaware of the warmth where their bodies connected. "My education would be incomplete without it."

They walked together through the gardens and out into the streets of Lumina. The transition was immediate and striking—from the serene quiet of the garden to the vibrant energy of the evening market district. Lanterns in every color imaginable hung from buildings and floated midair, enchanted to drift lazily above the crowds.

Vendors called out their wares from stalls overflowing with exotic goods. The aromas of cooking food mingled with the scent of incense and herbs, creating an intoxicating perfume that pulled them deeper into the labyrinth of commerce.

"Is it always this lively?" Sameril asked, fascinated by the organized chaos surrounding them.

"This is actually rather subdued," Briella replied as they navigated through a cluster of laughing children chasing enchanted paper birds. "You should see it during the Lunar Alignment Festival. The entire city stays awake for three days straight."

They passed a stall where an elderly woman with indigo-stained fingers sold crystallized flowers preserved in perpetual bloom. Recognizing Briella, she beckoned them closer.

"Young Tanner! It's been too long since you've visited old Mestra," the woman called. Her sharp eyes shifted to Sameril, narrowing slightly at his distinctly necromantic attire. "And with interesting company, I see."

"Mestra creates the most exquisite preserved botanicals in all of Eldoria," Briella explained to Sameril before addressing the vendor. "My friend is a scholar from the Necropolis. He's interested in the intersection of our magical traditions."

The old woman's expression softened marginally. "Is he now? Well, that's something you don't hear every day." She selected a delicate blue blossom suspended in clear crystal and pressed it into Sameril's hand. "Frost orchid. It grows only in the shadow of death but produces the most vibrant life. Rather fitting, wouldn't you say?"

"It's beautiful," Sameril said honestly, examining the perfect preservation of each petal. "Your work shows remarkable precision."

"Take it," Mestra insisted when he tried to return it. "A gift for a young man brave enough to cross boundaries."

Before he could properly thank her, Briella was tugging him onward. "If we stop at every stall, we'll never reach Erissa's before midnight," she laughed.

They continued their walk through the market, still wanting roasted kalak, stopping occasionally when something caught their interest. At one stall, Sameril found himself fascinated by an assortment of mechanical curiosities—tiny clockwork creatures that moved with uncanny realism.

"These remind me of animated constructs," he observed, watching a metallic hummingbird hover above his palm. "But they contain no necromantic energy."

"Enchantment rather than animation," Briella explained. "Infusing nonliving matter with purpose without the need for life energy as a bridge."

"Fascinating," Sameril murmured. "I've never considered that approach."

The vendor, a bespectacled man with oil-stained hands, perked up at their conversation. "The young man has a good eye! These operate on pure magical mechanics—no life force involved. Perfect for those who find necromancy a bit... unsettling." He winked at Briella.

"Not all of us fear what we don't understand, Tinker Melv," she replied with good humor. "Some of us seek to learn from it."

They left the tinker's stall with the clockwork hummingbird tucked safely in Sameril's pocket—a gift from Briella despite his protests.

"To remind you that there are many paths to similar outcomes," she said, touching his hand briefly. "Just as there are many ways to approach magic."

The gesture left Sameril momentarily speechless, warmth spreading from her touch up his arm and into his chest.

Finally, they arrived at a modest building with rounded windows that glowed amber from within. Delicious aromas wafted from its open door, accompanied by the sounds of lively conversation and distant music.

"Madame Erissa's," Briella announced. "The best-kept secret in Lumina. Witches, merchants, artists, scholars—everyone is welcome here, regardless of their magical affiliation or social standing."

As they entered, Sameril realized why Briella had chosen this place. Unlike the stratified dining halls of the Necropolis, where rigid hierarchies determined everything from seating to food quality, Erissa's was a democratic chaos of mingled company.

A robust woman with elaborate braids piled atop her head spotted Briella and bellowed a greeting over the din. "Tanner! About time you showed your face here again!" Her gaze shifted to Sameril, and her eyebrows rose dramatically. "And with necromantic company! My, my, you do like to stir the cauldron, don't you?"

"Madame Erissa," Briella greeted her with obvious affection. "This is Sameril, a brilliant scholar who appreciates good food and open minds."

"Then he's come to the right place," Erissa declared, ushering them to a small table near a window overlooking a courtyard filled with bioluminescent flowers. "Sit, sit! I'll bring you my best—no arguments!"

Before they could respond, she had disappeared into the bustling kitchen, shouting orders in a language Sameril didn't recognize.

"She seems... formidable," he commented, adjusting to the unfamiliar environment.

Briella laughed. "Erissa was my mother's closest friend at the academy before she left to pursue culinary magic instead. She treats half of Lumina like her personal children."

"Culinary magic?" Sameril asked, intrigued.

"You'll understand when you taste the food," Briella promised, her eyes twinkling. "Some say she infuses emotions directly into her dishes. Happiness in the sweet courses, courage in the spicy ones."

Their conversation paused as servers arrived bearing plates of steaming food and decanters of amber liquid that sparkled when poured. The promised roasted kalak—a game bird native to Eldoria's southern plains—was indeed seasoned with a complex blend of spices that danced across Sameril's palate.

"This is incredible," he admitted after his first bite. "We have nothing like this at the Necropolis."

"What do necromancers eat?" Briella asked, genuinely curious. "I've always wondered about daily life in your academy."

"Nothing nearly as exciting," Sameril chuckled. "Mostly simple, nourishing foods. There's a belief that excessive pleasure dulls magical precision."

Briella rolled her eyes. "How utterly dreary. Witches believe the opposite—that joy and pleasure heighten magical connection."

"Perhaps that explains your greater success with weather manipulation," Sameril mused, giving a quick thought to both approaches of their crafts. "It's known to be notoriously difficult for necromancers."

"While you excel at transmutation beyond what most witches can achieve," Briella countered. "Each approach has its strengths."

As they ate, their discussion ranged from magical theory to childhood memories, from favorite books to dreams for the future. Sameril found himself sharing thoughts he'd never voiced aloud—his occasional frustration with necromancy's rigid traditions, his desire to expand the discipline beyond its current boundaries.

"I sometimes wonder," he admitted after their plates had been cleared and replaced with delicate pastries filled with honeyed neffra cream, "if our separate academies do more harm than good. How much knowledge is lost because we refuse to learn from each other?"

Briella's expression grew serious. "My mother says it wasn't always this way. The separation grew more pronounced over centuries. What began as specialization became isolation."

"And yet here we are," Sameril said softly, "a witch and a necromancer, finding more common ground than difference."

"Here we are," Briella agreed, her eyes meeting his with an intensity that made his heart skip.

The moment stretched between them, charged with unspoken possibility. Around them, the restaurant's other patrons continued their meals and conversations, unaware of the small revolution occurring at the corner table—two young people from opposed magical traditions discovering connection where there should be division.

Finally, Briella broke the silence. "It's growing late. I should return to the academy before curfew."

Sameril nodded, suddenly aware of how much time had passed. "As should I. Master Xaloth expects me for early practice tomorrow."

They settled their bill—Briella insisting on paying despite Sameril's protests—and stepped back into the night. The streets had quieted somewhat, though plenty of people still wandered between the now-shuttered market stalls.

"May I escort you back to your academy?" Sameril offered.

"I would like that," Briella replied, once again taking his arm.

They walked slowly, neither eager for the evening to end. The moons of Eldoria had risen—one bright grey, one with a distinct blue tinge—casting dual shadows behind them on the cobblestone path.

"I've enjoyed this evening more than I can express," Sameril said as they approached the halfway point between their academies.

"As have I," Briella replied. She stopped walking and turned to face him. "Sameril... would you be willing to meet again? To continue our discussions?"

"Nothing would please me more," he answered without hesitation.

"Good." Her smile was radiant in the moonlight. "Because I believe what we're exploring—this convergence of magical understanding—could be important. Not just for us, but perhaps for all of Eldoria."

"I feel the same," Sameril said, though magical theory wasn't foremost in his mind as he looked at her.

They stood there, momentarily suspended between their separate worlds, until Briella rose on her toes and placed a gentle kiss on his cheek.

"Until next time, Necromancer," she whispered.

Before he could respond, she had turned and continued toward the academy of witchcraft, her figure gradually blending with the shadows until only the subtle glow of her enchanted hairpins remained visible in the distance.

Sameril stood rooted to the spot, his hand unconsciously rising to touch the place where her lips had brushed his skin. In his pocket, the clockwork hummingbird hummed gently, as if responding to the quickened pace of his heart.

The night air felt charged with possibility as he finally turned toward the Necropolis. Something had changed this evening—something beyond magical theory or culinary discoveries. A connection had formed, delicate yet undeniable.

And as the ancient walls of the necromancers' academy came into view, Sameril knew with absolute certainty that his life would never be quite the same again.

CHAPTER 6

SECRETS BETWEEN BOOKSTACKS

Golden light spilled across Willow Street as Bree pulled her cardigan closer against the morning chill. Beside her, Molly yawned, still not fully awake despite the mug of coffee she'd drained before they left the house. The funeral had exhausted them both, but when Sarah had called with an invitation to visit the bookstore, neither sister could resist.

"Do you think Mom will be okay alone today?" Molly asked as they approached the Fonds' cheerful yellow Victorian with its white gingerbread trim and wrap-around porch. "It bothers me leaving her alone so soon."

Bree glanced back toward their own house. "I think she needs the space. She was already in the backyard working in the garden when I woke up—said something about Nancy's herbs needing attention."

As they climbed the porch steps, the screen door swung open before they could knock. Susan Fond stood framed in the doorway, her elfin face brightening at the sight of them. Her short, blonde hair caught the morning light, giving her an almost ethereal appearance.

Unlike yesterday's funeral attire, she wore a flowing floral sundress that celebrated life rather than mourning death.

"Molly, Bree, come on in," she said, her voice warm as honey. "Sarah will be down in just a moment." She ushered them inside with a gentle hand on each of their backs.

The Fond house smelled of cinnamon and something deeper, more herbal—perhaps rosemary or sage. Bree inhaled deeply, finding comfort in the familiar scent that reminded her of summers spent with her grandmother. The living room was a cozy space filled with well-worn furniture and bookshelves that climbed from floor to ceiling. Potted plants occupied every available surface, their leaves reaching toward the sunlight streaming through lace-curtained windows.

"How are you girls holding up?" Susan asked as she gestured for them to sit on the floral-patterned sofa. "Yesterday was quite a day."

"We're managing," Bree answered, settling onto the cushions. "It still doesn't feel real that she's gone."

"And now there's this whole thing with the hat," Molly added, dropping her voice slightly even though they were among friends.

Susan nodded, her expression softening with understanding. "Nancy's hat carries a tremendous legacy. But remember, your grandmother believed in both of you so deeply. She knew this day would come."

The creak of steps from the staircase drew their attention. Sarah appeared, dressed in jeans and a flowing blouse the color of autumn leaves, her blonde hair pulled back in a loose braid. Her face broke into a wide smile at the sight of them.

"I'm so glad you two could come over," she said, crossing the room to pull each sister into a quick, firm hug. Unlike her mother's delicate frame, Sarah was tall and solidly built, with a presence that filled the room. "I thought we could walk together to the bookstore, if you're up for it."

"That sounds perfect," Bree said. "I could use some fresh air and..." she hesitated, "normal life, I guess."

Sarah squeezed her shoulder. "I understand completely. Sometimes the best cure for grief is routine—finding your way back to the everyday magic of living."

After saying goodbye to Susan, who promised to have tea waiting when they returned, the three women stepped out into the morning sunshine. Ballad was coming alive around them—shopkeepers opening their doors, neighbors walking dogs, the distant sound of children's laughter from the playground at the end of the street, reminding the girls of when they were children.

"It's strange," Molly observed as they walked, tucking a strand of auburn hair behind her ear. "Everything looks exactly the same as I remember, but somehow it all feels different."

"That's because you're different," Sarah replied. "You're seeing the town through the eyes of who you are now, not who you were when you left."

They turned onto Main Street, where the heart of Ballad's small business district began. The buildings here were older, mostly brick and stone structures from the early 1900s that had been lovingly preserved and updated. Window boxes overflowed with spring flowers, and hand-painted signs swung gently in the breeze.

"There's Tina's Café," Sarah pointed out as they passed a cheerful storefront with red-and-white striped awnings. "Still makes the best cinnamon rolls in three counties, and has the ribbons to prove it. And over there is Hartwell's Hardware—old man Hartwell passed a few years back, but his son Ray runs it now."

As they walked, Sarah provided a running commentary on the businesses and people they passed, filling in the decade of town history the sisters had missed. Bree found herself mentally mapping the changes, connecting her childhood memories with the present-day reality of Ballad.

"I can't believe we're finally going to be joining the coven," Molly said when there was a lull in the conversation, her voice a mix of excitement and nervousness. "I feel like we've been waiting for this moment our whole lives."

Sarah nodded, her expression thoughtful as they waited for a car to pass before crossing the street. "It's a big step," she agreed, "but one I know you both are ready for. Your grandmother always said that you two had a special destiny within the coven."

Bree felt a flutter of anticipation in her chest at Sarah's words. "What do you think she meant by that?"

Sarah glanced around subtly before answering, lowering her voice. "The Tanner bloodline has always been powerful—particularly strong in certain areas of magic. Nancy could commune with spirits in ways that most witches can only dream of." She gave Bree a meaningful look. "She believed those gifts would manifest in you girls as well."

They walked in contemplative silence for a block, each lost in their own thoughts. The street widened as they approached the town square, a charming park with a central gazebo and ancient oak trees that had witnessed generations of Ballad's history. On the far side of the square stood Infinitely Books, its deep blue facade and gold-lettered sign a beacon for literary souls.

"So, Bree," Sarah said casually as they crossed the square, "have you given any more thought to what we discussed the other day? About working at the bookstore?"

Bree stopped mid-stride, turning to face Sarah with wide eyes. "You were serious about that?" she asked, hardly daring to believe it. When Sarah had mentioned it in passing at the funeral reception, Bree had assumed it was just a kind gesture, not a genuine offer.

Sarah laughed, the sound bright and clear in the morning air. "Of course I was serious! I could really use the help, and I know how much you love books. It seems like the perfect fit."

A genuine smile spread across Bree's face, the first she'd felt since before her grandmother's passing. "I would love to work at Infinitely Books," she said, her voice filled with gratitude. "Thank you, Sarah."

"What about me?" Molly teased, nudging her sister with her elbow. "Am I not literary enough for employment?"

Sarah's eyes twinkled with mischief. "I seem to recall you saying, and I quote, 'If I have to organize one more shelf of books, I'll hex myself into next Tuesday.' That was during your last summer visit, I believe."

Molly laughed, a slight blush coloring her cheeks. "Fair point. Though I'd spend all day organizing shelves if it meant being around Lucy's baking again. Is she still dropping off treats at the store?"

"Every Monday and Thursday like clockwork," Sarah confirmed. "Her cinnamon-cardamom cookies have developed quite a following. We actually have customers who schedule their visits around Lucy's delivery days."

As they approached the bookstore, Bree felt a magnetic pull toward the building. The large display windows showcased artfully arranged stacks of books, interspersed with antique reading lamps and comfortable-looking chairs that invited browsing. A hand-lettered sign announced "Book Club Meeting: Thursday 7 PM – Discussing 'The Midnight Library'" next to a pyramid of the featured novel.

Sarah produced a set of keys from her pocket and unlocked the door, the gentle tinkling of bells announcing their arrival as they stepped inside. The scent enveloped Bree immediately—paper and ink, leather bindings, the faint hint of coffee from the small café area in the corner, and something else—something indefinable that smelled like possibilities.

"Welcome to Infinitely Books," Sarah said with a proud sweep of her arm. "Home away from home for the literary-minded citizens of Ballad—and a few other special folks as well."

Bree moved deeper into the store, trailing her fingers along the spines of books as she passed. The interior was larger than it appeared from outside, with row upon row of bookshelves creating a labyrinth of literary treasures. Comfortable reading nooks were scattered throughout, featuring overstuffed chairs and small tables. Soft classical music played from hidden speakers, adding to the peaceful atmosphere.

"This place is incredible," Bree breathed, turning in a slow circle to take it all in. "It's exactly how I remember it, but somehow even better."

Sarah smiled, clearly pleased by Bree's reaction. "Nancy helped me design it when I took it over from my mother. She said a bookstore should feel like stepping into another world—a place where magic seems possible."

"Speaking of which," Molly said in a hushed tone, glancing around to ensure they were alone, "are there any... special sections here? Books that aren't for regular customers?"

Before Sarah could answer, a voice called out from the back of the store. "Sarah? Is that you?"

"Back here, Kristy!" Sarah called in response. "I've brought visitors!"

A petite woman with a cloud of blonde curls emerged from between the bookshelves, a stack of paperbacks balanced precariously in her arms. Her bright blue eyes widened in recognition, and a warm smile spread across her face as she carefully set the books down on a nearby table.

"You must be Molly and Bree," she said, extending a hand in greeting. Her voice was melodic, with a slight Southern drawl that suggested she wasn't a Ballad native. "Sarah has told me so much about you both. I'm so sorry for your loss."

"This is Kristy Baker," Sarah explained. "She's been working at Infinitely Books for about three years now, and I honestly don't know how I managed before she came along."

Kristy waved away the praise with a laugh. "She's only saying that because I can reach the top shelves without a ladder." The woman was nearly a head taller than Sarah's height.

As they shook hands and exchanged pleasantries, Bree felt an immediate connection with Kristy. There was a quiet intelligence in her eyes and a gentle, calming energy about her that put Bree at ease.

"Sarah mentioned you might be joining our little team," Kristy said to Bree with an encouraging smile. "Fair warning—once you start working in a bookstore, you'll never look at your paycheck the same way again. Most of mine goes right back into the register."

They all laughed, and Bree felt some of the tension she'd been carrying since the funeral begin to melt away. This was what she needed—normal conversation, friendly faces, the promise of purpose.

"Let me show you around," Sarah said, leading them deeper into the store. "If you're going to work here, you'll need to know the lay of the land."

For the next hour, Sarah guided them through the bookstore, explaining the organization system, pointing out specific sections, and sharing stories about regular customers and their reading preferences. Kristy occasionally chimed in with anecdotes or clarifications, her easy laughter a counterpoint to Sarah's more methodical approach.

Bree absorbed it all, already imagining herself behind the counter, helping customers find their next favorite book. It felt right, somehow—as if a piece of her that had been adrift was finally settling into place.

While Sarah explained the inventory tracking system to Bree, Molly wandered off, drawn to a section of historical fiction. She was soon lost in the pages of a novel about ancient Egypt, curled up in a window seat with sunlight streaming over her shoulder.

"Your sister looks right at home," Kristy observed, coming to stand beside Bree. "Do you both share the same taste in books?"

Bree shook her head with a fond smile. "Not at all. Molly loves historical fiction and biographies—real stories about real people. I've always been more drawn to fantasy and the supernatural."

"Interesting," Kristy said, a knowing glint in her eye. "Fiction that contains deeper truths than reality sometimes."

Before Bree could respond to the curious comment, Sarah returned from helping a customer who had entered the store while they were talking.

"So, how about we all take a break and catch up properly?" Sarah suggested, glancing at her watch. "It's nearly lunchtime, and we haven't had a chance to really talk about everything that's happened."

Together, they collected Molly from her reading nook and made their way to the small café area in the corner of the store. Kristy excused herself to attend to a customer who had approached the register, leaving the three friends to settle around a small circular table to speak in private.

"So," Sarah said, leaning forward with her elbows on the table, "tonight's meeting is going to be important for both of you. It's not just about welcoming you back to Ballad—it's about formally introducing you to the coven as potential leaders."

Bree and Molly exchanged a nervous glance. "What exactly should we expect?" Bree asked.

Sarah's expression turned thoughtful. "The Passing of the Hat ceremony is an ancient tradition, dating back to the founding of the coven. Normally, it would be a joyous occasion—a celebration of the transfer of knowledge and power from one generation to the next."

"But these aren't normal circumstances," Molly added softly.

Sarah shook her head. "No, they're not. Nancy's passing was unexpected, and there hasn't been time for the usual preparations that the coven would normally do." She hesitated, seeming to choose her words carefully. "And then there's the matter of your mother's reluctance."

"Do you know why?" Bree asked, the question that had been nagging at her since the funeral finally escaping. "Why doesn't Mom want to take the hat herself? Why pass it to one of us?"

Sarah sighed, her expression a mix of understanding and sympathy. "Your mother has always been a complex woman," she said gently. "I think, in many ways, she's always felt a bit overshadowed by Nancy's legacy. She loves magic, and she loves the coven, but the idea of stepping into the role of High Priestess is daunting for her."

Sarah paused, looking thoughtfully out the window before continuing. "There was also... tension between Nancy and Mary Ann when you girls were younger. I don't know all the details—it was something they kept private—but I believe it stemmed from disagreements about how you should be raised, how much you should know about your heritage."

Bree nodded slowly, absorbing Sarah's words. She remembered the strained phone calls, the terse conversations when they would visit Ballad. There had always been an undercurrent of something unresolved between her mother and grandmother.

"I think Mary Ann wanted to protect you from some of the challenges that come with being Tanner witches," Sarah continued. "Nancy believed you should embrace your heritage fully, from a young age. Neither was entirely wrong, but they couldn't find a middle ground."

As the conversation lulled, each of them lost in their own thoughts, Bree's gaze wandered around the bookstore. The shelves seemed to stretch endlessly, each book containing worlds and knowledge waiting to be discovered. A thought occurred to her suddenly.

"Sarah," she said softly, "do you think there might be books here that could tell us more about the coven's history? About the magic and traditions that have been passed down through the generations?"

Sarah's eyes lit up, a mischievous grin playing at the corners of her mouth. "I thought you'd never ask," she said, rising from her chair and beckoning for the sisters to follow. "Come with me. I have a feeling there's a whole world of discovery waiting for us in these stacks."

Sarah led them through the main floor of the bookstore, past shelves of contemporary fiction and reference books, toward a door marked "Employees Only" at the back of the building. She produced a small key from her pocket, glancing around to ensure no customers were watching before unlocking the door and ushering them inside.

They found themselves in a storage room filled with boxes of books, office supplies, and a small desk where invoices and order forms were stacked neatly. But Sarah didn't stop there. She moved confidently toward the back wall, where a narrow wooden staircase led upward.

"Watch your step," she warned as they began to climb. "These stairs are as old as the building."

The wooden steps creaked ominously under their weight, the sound echoing in the close confines of the stairwell. The air grew warmer as they ascended, and Bree caught the faint scent of herbs and beeswax candles.

At the top of the stairs, they emerged into a small, dimly lit loft space with sloped ceilings that required Bree to duck her head at the edges. The atmosphere shifted immediately—there was a stillness here, a sense of time operating differently than in the bustling bookstore below.

"Welcome to the heart of Infinitely Books," Sarah said, her voice hushed with reverence. "This is where we keep the true treasures."

As Bree's eyes adjusted to the dimness, she gasped softly. The entire loft was lined with bookshelves, but these were no ordinary books. Ancient tomes bound in leather, scrolls tied with faded ribbons, and manuscripts whose pages had yellowed with age filled every available space.

Molly moved forward as if in a trance, her fingers hovering just above the spine of a particularly old volume. "These aren't just regular books, are they?" she whispered.

Sarah shook her head, her expression solemn. "This collection represents centuries of magical knowledge, gathered and preserved by the Andromeda Coven. Spell books, grimoires, journals of prominent witches—all the wisdom and power of our ancestors, kept safe for future generations."

Bree felt goosebumps rise on her arms as she walked slowly along the shelves, reading titles embossed in gold or silver on leather spines: "Lunar Enchantments," "Herbal Remedies for Magical Ailments," "The Art of Scrying," "Communing with the Other Side."

"This is incredible," she breathed, hardly daring to touch the books despite her longing to open them and absorb everything they contained. "I had no idea all of this existed."

"The bookstore has always been more than just a business," Sarah explained, running her hand lovingly along a shelf. "For generations, the Fond women have been the keepers of the coven's knowledge. My great-grandmother Eleanora started the tradition, converting the attic of her home into a magical library. When she opened the bookstore in 1923, she created this secret space to house the most valuable texts."

Molly had stopped in front of a glass-fronted cabinet containing what appeared to be the oldest books in the collection. "What are these?" she asked, pointing to a set of thirteen identical volumes bound in deep purple leather with silver clasps.

"Ah," Sarah said, moving to stand beside her. "Those are the journals of the founding witches of the Andromeda Coven. Each of the original thirteen kept detailed records of their magical practices, their visions for the coven, and their personal journeys."

With reverent hands, Sarah unlocked the cabinet and carefully extracted one of the volumes. The silver clasp bore an intricate design—a pentagram surrounded by what appeared to be stars in the constellation of Andromeda.

"This one," she said, holding it out to Bree, "belonged to Wilhelmina Tanner."

Bree took the book with trembling hands, feeling the weight of her ancestor's legacy physically manifested in the tome she now held. The leather was soft and supple despite its age, warm to the touch as if it contained some living essence of the woman who had written in it.

"May I?" she asked, her finger hovering over the clasp.

Sarah nodded. "It belongs to your bloodline. You have every right."

With careful movements, Bree undid the clasp and opened the journal to its first page. The handwriting that greeted her was elegant and precise, the ink faded to a warm sepia but still perfectly legible:

"I, Wilhelmina Rose Tanner, begin this record on the twenty-first day of March, in the year of our Lord eighteen hundred and twenty-three, as the spring equinox brings balance to our world and marks the founding of our

sacred circle. May these pages serve as testament to our covenant with the natural world and the powers that flow through us, and may they guide those who follow in our footsteps along the path of light and wisdom."

Bree read the words aloud, feeling a connection across time with this woman whose blood ran in her veins. "It's like she's speaking directly to us," she murmured, turning the page carefully to reveal more of Wilhelmina's elegant script.

"In many ways, she is," Sarah replied. "These journals were written not just as personal records, but as guidebooks for future generations. The founding witches knew they were creating something that would outlive them, a sisterhood that would preserve and protect magical knowledge through the ages."

Molly had moved to another shelf and was examining a large, leather-bound book whose cover was embossed with silver stars. "And what's this one?" she asked, her fingers tracing the constellations depicted on its surface.

"That," Sarah said with a smile, "is the 'Compendium of Arcane Incantations.' It's one of the oldest and most comprehensive collections of spells known to our coven. Nancy contributed quite a bit to that volume over the years—her additions are marked with her personal sigil."

Molly's eyes widened as she gently opened the book. The pages crackled softly, releasing the faint scent of sage and rosemary. Unlike the journal, this book contained not just handwritten notes but intricate diagrams, symbols, and illustrations that seemed to shimmer with an inner light.

"These spells," she murmured, her finger hovering just above the elegant script, "they're incredible. Look at this one for protection, and this one for healing..."

"The magic contained within these pages is powerful," Sarah warned gently. "It must be approached with respect and caution. But in the right hands, with the right intentions, it can be a force for incredible good."

Bree looked up from Wilhelmina's journal, meeting Sarah's gaze with newfound determination. "I want to learn," she said firmly. "I want to understand this magic, to use it to help others, just like Grandma Nancy did."

Sarah's smile widened, her eyes glistening with emotion. "I had a feeling you might say that," she said softly. "And I think, with time and training, you'll make an exceptional witch. Both of you will," she added, including Molly in her gaze.

As the three women settled into the loft, surrounded by the whispered secrets of their ancestors writings, Bree felt a sense of purpose take root deep within her. The sisters took turns reading passages aloud from various books, asking questions that Sarah answered with patience and wisdom, occasionally adding her own stories of spells she had cast or rituals she had participated in, as well as the lessons learned..

Time seemed to lose meaning in the magical space, and they might have remained there all day had the sudden creak of the staircase not jolted them from their scholarly reverie. Molly and Bree's eyes widened in alarm as Kristy's friendly face appeared in the doorway, a look of surprise mirrored on her own features.

Bree shot a panicked glance at Sarah, her heart racing at the thought of their secret being discovered. But Sarah, ever the picture of calm reassurance, simply smiled and beckoned Kristy into the room.

"It's alright, girls," she said softly, her voice warm with affection. "Kristy is one of us, in her own way. She may not have powers, but she's an honorary witch, and a true friend to the coven."

Kristy, her expression softening with understanding, stepped fully into the loft and closed the door gently behind her. "I hope I didn't startle you," she said apologetically. "I just wanted to let Sarah know that it's lunchtime, and I'm stepping out of the store for a bit."

The tension released from Bree's shoulders as she realized their secret was safe. "So you know about the coven?" she asked Kristy directly.

Kristy nodded, a warm smile lighting her features. "My grandmother was a hedge witch—not part of any organized coven, but she practiced in her own way. When I moved to Ballad after college, I felt drawn to the magical energy here. Sarah recognized a kindred spirit in me, even though I don't have the gift myself."

"Kristy helps us maintain our cover," Sarah explained. "She manages the store when we have coven meetings, helps source rare ingredients by passing them off as specialty teas, and generally acts as our eyes and ears in the non-magical community."

Sarah rose gracefully to her feet, carefully replacing the books they had been examining. "Speaking of the store, I should head down and cover the register while you're at lunch, Kristy." She turned to Bree and Molly, her eyes sparkling with mirth. "Duty calls, I'm afraid. But we'll continue this conversation tonight, at the meeting."

Molly and Bree, their initial surprise giving way to a sense of relief and camaraderie, smiled gratefully at Kristy. "It's nice to know we have another friend in Ballad," Bree said warmly. "Even if you don't have powers, your support clearly means the world to the coven."

Kristy grinned, her cheeks flushing with pleasure. "I may not be able to cast spells or brew potions," she said with a wink, "but I like to think I bring a certain practical magic to the group. Plus, someone has to keep track of the accounting and taxes—unless there's a spell for that I haven't heard about."

Laughter filled the small loft, the tension of the moment dissolving into a sense of easy companionship. As Sarah and Kristy made their way back downstairs, Bree and Molly took one last, lingering look at the shelves of ancient tomes and magical secrets.

"We should probably head home too," Molly said reluctantly, her fingers brushing against the spine of the Compendium of Arcane Incantations. "Mom will be wondering where we've been all morning."

Bree nodded, a wistful sigh escaping her lips. "You're right. But I can't wait to come back and explore more of these books. There's so much we still have to learn."

They made their way carefully down the narrow staircase and through the storage room, emerging back into the main area of the bookstore where several customers now browsed the shelves. The shift from the mystical atmosphere of the loft to the ordinary world of commerce was jarring, a reminder of the double life that witches in Ballad led.

"See you tonight," Bree called out to Sarah as they prepared to leave, a smile of anticipation on her lips.

Sarah waved from behind the counter where she was ringing up a customer's purchases. "I'll be over at seven o'clock. There's much to prepare before the others arrive."

As Bree and Molly stepped outside, the warm spring sun and the bustle of Ballad's town square seemed to bring them back to the present moment. They walked home in comfortable silence, each lost in their own thoughts of the coven, the magic that flowed through their veins, and the incredible journey that lay ahead.

The streets of Ballad felt different now, transformed by the knowledge they had gained. Every house they passed might contain hidden secrets, every person they nodded to on the sidewalk might be more than they appeared. The sisters found themselves searching faces for signs of recognition, for the subtle acknowledgment that would identify another member of the magical community.

As they approached Willow Street, Bree caught sight of a familiar figure sitting on his porch next door. Sam Sorken looked up from his laptop as they passed, raising a hand in greeting.

"Good afternoon, ladies," he called, his deep voice carrying easily across the yard. "Beautiful day, isn't it?"

Bree and Molly paused at the edge of their driveway, exchanging a quick glance before Bree responded. "It really is. Are you enjoying it?"

Sam closed his laptop and stood, stretching his tall frame. "Very much so. There's something special about spring in Ballad—the town seems to come alive in a way you don't see in larger cities."

There was something in his tone, a hint of meaning beyond his words, that made Bree wonder once again about his connection to their grandmother. Had Nancy shared the secret of the coven with him? Was he aware of the magical undercurrents that ran through the town?

Before she could find a subtle way to probe further, the front door of their house opened, and Mary Ann appeared on the porch. "There you are," she called, waving them over. "I was beginning to worry. Lunch is almost ready."

"We were at the bookstore with Sarah," Molly explained as they started up the path. "We lost track of time."

Sam nodded politely to Mary Ann. "Your daughters are in good hands with Sarah Fond. She's a remarkable woman."

Mary Ann's expression was difficult to read as she nodded in acknowledgment. "Indeed, she is. A good friend to our family for many years."

As they said their goodbyes to Sam and headed inside, Bree couldn't shake the feeling that there was an entire conversation happening beneath the surface of the exchange—meanings and history that she wasn't yet privy to.

The scent of vegetable soup and freshly baked bread greeted them as they entered the kitchen, where Mary Ann was already ladling the steaming liquid into bowls.

"So," she said, her tone deliberately casual as they settled around the table, "what did Sarah have to say about tonight's meeting?"

Bree and Molly exchanged a look, silently debating how much to share about their morning discoveries.

"She showed us around the bookstore," Bree began carefully. "And told us a bit about the coven's history."

Mary Ann nodded, breaking off a piece of bread. "Sarah's family has always been the keepers of our records. Did she show you the loft?"

The directness of the question surprised Bree. "Yes," she admitted. "We saw Wilhelmina Tanner's journal."

A small smile played at the corners of Mary Ann's lips. "I remember the first time Nancy showed it to me. I was about your age, maybe a little younger. I stayed up there for hours, reading through the founding witches' accounts of their first rituals, their hopes for what the coven would become."

"Mom," Molly asked hesitantly, "why didn't you tell us more about all of this when we were growing up? Why keep it from us for so long?"

Mary Ann's expression grew serious. "The world isn't always kind to those who are different, Molly. I wanted you both to have normal childhoods, to form your own identities before you had to take on the responsibility of the coven. Nancy..." she hesitated, "your grandmother didn't agree with my approach. She thought you should be immersed in the craft from an early age, as she had been with me."

"Is that why you don't want to take the hat?" Bree asked quietly. "Because of your disagreements with Grandma?"

Mary Ann was silent for a long moment, her gaze fixed on the steam rising from her soup bowl. "My reasons are complicated," she finally said. "But know this—I believe in the coven, in our heritage, and in both of you. Whichever of you takes up Nancy's hat will have my full support."

The conversation shifted then to practical matters—preparation for the evening's gathering, what the sisters should wear, which rooms of the house would be used for the meeting. But beneath the mundane details, Bree could sense the weight of the decision that loomed before them.

As she helped clear the lunch dishes, Bree found herself thinking about Wilhelmina Tanner's journal, about the heritage of strong women that had led to this moment. One of them—either she or Molly—would soon take their place in that lineage, assuming a mantle of leadership that stretched back two centuries.

The thought was terrifying and exhilarating in equal measure. As the afternoon sunlight streamed through the kitchen windows, casting long shadows across the floor, Bree knew that by the time night fell, their lives would be irrevocably changed.

And as she glanced out the window toward Sam Sorken's house, she couldn't shake the feeling that he, too, would play a role in the unfolding drama of their magical inheritance.

Chapter 7
The Drakorian Attack

"You must try the honeyed neffra cakes," Briella insisted as Madame Erissa led them to their table. "They're absolutely—"

The rest of her words vanished beneath a deafening roar that shook the very foundations of the building. Diners froze; conversations halted mid-sentence as the rumbling intensified. From outside came screams, first isolated, then multiplying into a chorus of terror.

Sameril reached the window first, Briella just behind him. The peaceful evening sky had transformed. Massive black ships, their hulls gleaming with an unnatural sheen, descended through the clouds. Each vessel bore the unmistakable blood-red sigil of the Drakorian Empire—a serpent devouring its own tail while clutching a shattered planet.

"Impossible," Briella whispered, her face draining of color. "The defense wards should have—"

The first volley of plasma fire cut through her words. Green-tinged energy lanced from the ships, striking the tallest spires of Lumina. Ancient stone that had stood for millennia vaporized instantly. The concussive blast shattered every window in Erissa's, showering the patrons with glass.

Sameril instinctively pulled Briella away from the window, shielding her with his body as the building trembled.

"Everyone out!" Madame Erissa bellowed, already herding stunned customers toward the rear exit. "Move to the underground shelters!"

Outside, chaos had consumed the once-vibrant market district. Buildings collapsed under direct hits, sending plumes of dust and debris skyward. The enchanted lanterns that had floated so serenely now flickered and died, plunging sections of the street into darkness broken only by the hellish glow of fires erupting throughout the city.

"This can't be happening," a man sobbed nearby, clutching a bleeding arm. "The wards were impenetrable. They were supposed to be impenetrable!"

Sameril's mind raced through possibilities. The Drakorian Empire had long been Eldoria's enemy, but open warfare had been avoided for generations. Their sudden appearance—and more concerning, their ability to bypass Eldoria's famed defensive wards—suggested treachery from within.

"We need to get to the academies," he said to Briella, gripping her shoulders. "Both of us. Our mentors will know what to do."

Briella nodded, her initial shock hardening into resolve. "The quickest route will be through the Central Plaza and then—"

Another explosion, closer this time, drowned her words. A Drakorian ship had descended almost to rooftop level, its cannons systematically targeting what appeared to be random buildings. But Sameril recognized the pattern.

"They're hitting the power nodes," he realized aloud. "The focal points where magical energy is stored and distributed throughout the city."

"How would they know where those are?" Briella asked, her voice tight with fear and growing anger. "That information is restricted to council members and senior mages."

Before Sameril could respond, the building across from them erupted in blue flame. From the wreckage emerged figures—humanoid in form but wrong somehow. They moved with mechanical precision, their armor a gleaming obsidian that seemed to absorb light rather than reflect it. Each soldier's helmet featured a featureless faceplate with a single vertical slit from which emanated the same eerie purple glow that lit the ships above.

"Drakorian shock troops," Sameril breathed, pulling Briella into the shadow of a collapsed market stall. "Elite warriors enhanced with forbidden magic."

"Enhanced how?" Briella whispered, watching as one soldier lifted a massive chunk of masonry that would require three men to move.

"Necromancy," Sameril admitted grimly. "But corrupted, twisted. They bind life energy directly to dead flesh, creating soldiers that feel no pain, need no rest, and follow orders without question."

Disgust flashed across Briella's face. "Your order would never—"

"No Eldorian necromancer would practice such abominations," Sameril assured her. "It violates every principle of the balance we maintain. This is why the Drakorians are enemies to both our disciplines."

They fell silent as a patrol passed their hiding place. The soldiers moved in perfect synchronization, their weapons—long staffs crackling with malevolent energy—sweeping methodically across the ruins, searching for survivors.

"We can't stay here," Briella murmured when the patrol had passed. "The longer we wait, the harder it will be to reach the academies."

Sameril nodded, surveying their surroundings. "If we follow the canal path, we might avoid the main contingent of troops. It's longer, but—"

"Look!" Briella interrupted, pointing skyward.

Above the chaos, a brilliant white light had erupted from the tallest tower of the Royal Palace. It expanded outward in a dome of pure energy, pushing back the Drakorian ships where it touched them. The counterattack had begun.

"The Archmage," Briella said, hope kindling in her voice. "She's activating the secondary defenses."

The dome continued to expand, forcing the closest Drakorian vessels to retreat to higher altitudes. For a moment, it seemed the tide might turn—until three of the largest ships redirected their fire, concentrating all their weapons on the source of the white energy. The dome flickered once, twice, then collapsed entirely as the tower from which it emanated crumbled.

"No," Briella gasped, her hand flying to her mouth. "If the Archmage has fallen..."

Sameril squeezed her hand. "We don't know that. But we need to move—now."

They darted from their hiding place, keeping to the shadows as they navigated the devastated streets. Everywhere, the evidence of Drakorian brutality confronted them. Citizens who had been enjoying a peaceful evening now lay broken among the rubble or fled in terror from the advancing forces. A mother cradled a small child, shielding him with her body as she ran. An elderly man stood frozen in shock, staring at the ruins of what had likely been his home and livelihood.

"We can't help them all," Sameril said softly when he saw Briella hesitate near a group of injured civilians. "The best thing we can do is reach those who can organize an effective resistance."

"I know," she replied, though the pain in her eyes showed how deeply it cost her to keep moving.

They had nearly reached the canal when a squadron of Drakorian soldiers emerged from a side street directly ahead. At their center walked a figure different from the others—taller, adorned with ornate armor that pulsed with sickly purple light. Where the soldiers' helmets were featureless, this one's was sculpted into the visage of a snarling beast, its eyes glowing with the same unnatural luminescence.

"Battlemage," Sameril hissed, pulling Briella behind a toppled statue before they could be spotted. "One of their war-casters."

"What do we do?" Briella whispered, peering around the stone. "We can't get past them, and they're headed straight for the central district."

Sameril assessed their options quickly. "We need a diversion."

Without waiting for her response, he placed his palms against the ground and closed his eyes. Necromantic energy flowed from his hands into the earth, seeking, connecting to the remnants of life that had once flourished in the soil beneath Lumina's streets. Most necromancers required extensive preparation for this kind of working, but Sameril had always possessed a natural gift for the art.

The ground trembled slightly, and from beneath the rubble emerged dozens of small creatures—rats, birds, and insects that had perished in the initial attack. Their little bodies moved with jerky animation, no longer truly alive but temporarily reanimated by Sameril's power.

"What are you doing?" Briella asked, her voice a mixture of awe and unease.

"Creating confusion," Sameril replied, sweat beading on his forehead from the effort. "I've directed them to swarm the troops and then head east—away from our path."

Sure enough, Sam's necromantic magic worked, causing the small army of reanimated creatures to surge toward the Drakorian patrol. While they posed no real threat to the armored soldiers, their sudden appearance and unnatural movement created precisely the distraction Sameril had hoped for. The troops turned to face the swarm, weapons raised.

"Now," Sameril grabbed Briella's hand. "Run!"

They sprinted across the exposed street and down a narrow alley that led toward the canal. Behind them, bursts of energy lit the darkness as the Drakorians obliterated Sameril's diversion, but by then, they had gained enough distance to slip away.

The canal path was mercifully clear, though the water itself carried floating debris and worse—evidence of the devastation upstream. They ran in silence for several minutes, the sounds of battle growing somewhat more distant, until they reached a junction where their paths would necessarily diverge.

"The Necropolis lies that way," Sameril said, pointing north. "The Witches' Academy is to the east. We should separate here."

Briella nodded, though reluctance showed clearly in her eyes. "Find Master Xaloth. Gather whoever you can. The Drakorians must be stopped before they can access either academy's repositories of knowledge."

"If they gain control of both necromantic and witch magic..." Sameril left the thought unfinished, the implications too terrible to voice.

"They won't," Briella said firmly. "We won't let them."

For a moment, they stood facing each other, the chaos of invasion raging around them, yet somehow distant from the connection that had formed between them. Then Briella stepped forward and, with surprising fierceness, pressed her lips to Sameril's.

The kiss lasted only seconds, but in it was a lifetime of possibility—the promise of what might have been in a world not suddenly engulfed in flames. When they parted, her eyes shone with emotion.

"Find me when this is over," she said, her voice barely above a whisper. "Promise me."

"I promise," Sameril replied without hesitation. "Nothing in this world or beyond will keep me from finding you again."

With visible effort, Briella turned and began running toward her academy, her copper hair catching the firelight like a beacon of defiance against the darkness.

Sameril allowed himself one moment—one precious moment—to watch her go, to burn the image of her into his memory. Then he turned north, toward the Necropolis and whatever fate awaited him there.

The path to the Necropolis led through increasingly devastated sections of the city. Drakorian forces seemed to be concentrating their heaviest attacks on the areas surrounding the academies, suggesting they understood all too well the true sources of Eldoria's power.

As Sameril navigated the ruins, he encountered pockets of resistance—witches and necromancers who had set aside their traditional rivalries to face a common enemy. He joined briefly with one such group, combining his necromantic abilities with a witch's elemental magic to collapse a building on an advancing patrol of shock troops.

"Head for the Necropolis," he told the exhausted witch after they had confirmed all enemies were neutralized. "Master Xaloth will be organizing our defense there."

"And you?" she asked, binding a wound on her arm with torn fabric.

"I need to find him first," Sameril replied, already moving onward.

As he approached the outer boundaries of the Necropolis grounds, Sameril was horrified to see the ancient walls—which had stood for thousands of years—reduced to rubble in several places. The gardens where he had met Briella just days ago now burned, the rare and magical plants releasing multicolored smoke as they were consumed by unnatural fire.

A figure staggered through the destruction—an older student Sameril recognized from advanced classes. The young man's robes were torn and stained with blood, his face a mask of shock.

"Talien!" Sameril called, rushing to support his friend before he collapsed. "What happened? Where is Master Xaloth?"

Talien's eyes focused slowly on Sameril's face. "Sam... they came from nowhere. The wards... they just failed. One moment we were safe, the next..." He gestured weakly at the devastation.

"Xaloth," Sameril repeated urgently. "Where is he?"

"The vault," Talien managed, coughing violently. "He took the senior masters to protect the most dangerous texts. Told the rest of us to scatter, to save what knowledge we could."

Sameril helped Talien to a relatively sheltered alcove. "Can you make it to the emergency rendezvous point? The caverns beneath the eastern hills?"

Talien nodded weakly. "I think so. But Sam, you can't go to the vault. The Drakorians have concentrated their forces there. It's suicide."

"I have to try," Sameril said, checking that his codex was still secure in his inner pocket. "Xaloth gave me knowledge that can't fall into enemy hands."

Before Talien could argue further, a series of explosions rocked the ground beneath them. In the distance, toward the heart of the Necropolis, a column of sickly purple energy erupted skyward.

"They've breached the inner sanctum," Talien whispered in horror.

Sameril felt a cold certainty settle in his chest. He was too late to help Xaloth—but perhaps not too late to save something even more precious.

"Get to the caverns," he told Talien firmly. "Gather whoever you can. If I don't return by dawn, assume I've fallen and proceed with the contingency plan."

Without waiting for a response, Sameril turned and ran—not toward the vault and certain death, but eastward, toward the Witches' Academy and Briella. If the Necropolis had fallen so quickly, the witches might be next. And while he had failed his mentor, he would not fail the woman who had, in the space of a few short days, come to mean more to him than he had thought possible.

As he ran through the burning city, Sameril clutched the Codex Mortis close to his heart. Whatever happened in the hours to come, whatever price he might pay in this night of devastation, he would ensure that the knowledge entrusted to him—and the woman he had come to love—would survive.

Even if he did not.

Chapter 8
A Brief History

"Tell us more about the joining ceremony tonight," Bree said, settling into her chair at the kitchen table. The afternoon sun cast long shadows across the polished oak surface, illuminating the three Tanner women as they gathered for conversation after lunch had been cleared away.

Mary Ann's fingers curled around her teacup, the silver ring on her right hand—a gift from Nancy years ago—catching the light as she considered her daughters' eager expressions. Having just finished discussing their morning at the bookstore, the conversation had naturally turned to the evening ahead.

"I know this is a big step for both of you," she began, her voice gentle but firm. "Joining the Andromeda Coven is not a decision to be made lightly. It's a commitment, a sacred bond that will tie you to the sisterhood for life."

Bree leaned forward, her eyes intent on her mother's face. "We understand that, Mom. And we're ready." She hesitated, torn between excitement and anxiety. "But we were hoping you could tell us more about the ritual itself. What should we expect?"

Mary Ann nodded, her hands folding together on the tabletop. "The joining ritual is a powerful and ancient rite," she explained, her voice taking on a reverent tone. "It's a way of formally welcoming new members into the coven, and of binding their magic and their souls to the collective."

She paused, her gaze drifting to the window where the garden—Nancy's garden, now Mary Ann's responsibility—stretched in carefully tended beds of herbs and flowers. Many of them, Bree knew now, were chosen not just for their beauty but for their magical properties.

"The ritual will take place under the light of the full moon," Mary Ann continued, returning her attention to her daughters, "in a sacred space prepared by the coven. You'll each be presented with a ceremonial robe, a symbol of your dedication and your willingness to submit to the coven's teachings."

Molly's eyebrows shot up, a flicker of apprehension crossing her face. "Submit? That sounds a bit... intense."

Mary Ann smiled reassuringly, reaching across the table to squeeze her older daughter's hand. Her fingers were warm and steady in their grip. "It's not about giving up your free will, love. It's about opening yourself to the wisdom and the guidance of those who have come before. The coven is a family, a support system. We lift each other up, and we help each other grow."

The tension in Molly's shoulders visibly eased, and she nodded, relaxing into her mother's explanation.

Bree, her own hand finding her mother's, asked softly, "What happens next? In the ritual, I mean."

The afternoon light caught the dust motes dancing in the air as Mary Ann continued her explanation, her voice painting pictures that Bree could almost see.

"Once you're robed," she said, "you'll be brought before the High Priestess. In this case, it will be Sarah, as the acting leader of the coven. She'll anoint your forehead with sacred oil, a blend of herbs and essences that have been used in our rituals for generations."

Mary Ann's free hand lifted, her index finger tracing a crescent shape on the wooden tabletop. The motion was fluid, practiced—the muscle memory of countless rituals performed over the years. "As she does this, she'll invoke the blessings of the Goddess, asking her to guide and protect you on your path. You'll then be given a candle, lit from the central flame of the altar, and asked to recite the coven's oath."

Molly sat up straighter, her full attention on her mother. "What does the oath say?" she asked, her voice hushed with anticipation.

A transformation came over Mary Ann's face—a softening, an opening, as if she were connecting to something beyond the kitchen, beyond the moment. Her eyes drifted closed for a moment, and when she spoke, her voice carried a resonance that seemed to fill the room, vibrating with the power of generations who had spoken these words before her:

"I, [your name], do solemnly swear
To honor the Goddess, with reverence and care
To walk the path of magic, with wisdom and grace
To support my sisters, in this sacred space
I pledge my heart, my mind, my soul

*To the Andromeda Coven, I give my whole
From this day forward, by moon and by sun
In perfect love and perfect trust, I am one."*

A shiver ran down Bree's spine as the words hung in the air, almost tangible in their power. She could feel them resonating deep within her, calling to something that had always been there, waiting to be awakened. Beside her, Molly had gone very still, her eyes wide and luminous in the afternoon light.

Mary Ann opened her eyes, a soft smile playing at the corners of her lips as she observed her daughters' reactions. "After you've recited the oath, you'll be welcomed into the circle of sisters. There will be a celebration, a feast in your honor, and a chance for you to get to know your new family."

Molly, still caught in the spell of the oath, asked quietly, "And then? What happens after the ritual?"

"Then," Mary Ann said, her voice warm with promise and a touch of wistfulness, "your true journey begins. You'll start your training, learning the ways of magic and the secrets of the coven. It won't always be easy, but you'll have the support and the love of your sisters to guide you."

Bree felt her throat tighten with emotion. For all the complications in their relationship, all the years spent away from Ballad and the magic that was their birthright, her mother had clearly never stopped caring about the coven and its traditions. The realization made her wonder, not for the first time, why Mary Ann had chosen to leave it all behind.

"Mom," she began hesitantly, "why did you—"

But her question was interrupted as Molly leaned forward, her brow furrowed in concentration. "Mom, could you list out the original thirteen members of the coven? I want to make sure I have them all straight in my head before the ritual."

Mary Ann seemed relieved by the change in topic. She leaned back in her chair, the wooden legs scraping slightly against the tile floor. "Let's see," she began, her eyes lifting to the ceiling as she recalled the names that had been part of coven lore for generations. "There were the Anders', the Warrens, the Bells, the Catshills, the Whites, the Kings, the Roberts', the Smiths, the Davis', the Wilsons, and the Moores. And then, of course, our family and the Fonds."

She paused, a nostalgic smile softening her features. "Most of those families you're likely to remember from when you were children. It wasn't unusual for coven members to be in and out of Gram's house all the time."

Bree sat up straighter, a memory clicking into place. "Wait... Anders. You mean Aunt Carol?"

Mary Ann nodded, amusement playing at the corners of her mouth. "That's right, love. Carol Anders. Although, as you know, she's not actually your aunt by blood."

"But she's always been there, for as long as we can remember," Molly chimed in, her expression fond but tinged with exasperation. "She's family, even if it's not by birth."

Bree remembered Carol Anders vividly—a vivacious woman with flame-red hair who always arrived at family gatherings in a whirlwind of scarves, jangling bracelets, and exotic perfume. She had been a constant presence in their childhood, bringing gifts from her frequent travels and regaling them with stories that, in retrospect, were probably heavily edited for young ears.

Mary Ann reached across the table, giving Molly's hand a gentle squeeze. "And that, my darlings, is what the coven is all about. Family, in all its forms."

Then she paused, her expression shifting to something more cautionary. "Now, I want you both to understand something about your aunt Carol. She's a good person, inside-and-out, with a kind heart and fierce loyalty to all those she loves. But she can be a bit... embarrassing at times."

Bree raised her eyebrows, intrigued by this new perspective on the woman she had always known as simply "Aunt Carol." "Embarrassing? How so?"

Mary Ann sighed, a rueful smile tugging at her lips. "Let's just say that Carol is not shy about hunting for a man. She's been known to be a bit... forward in her approach."

Molly burst into giggles. "You mean like the time she practically threw herself at the butcher during the Midsummer Festival?" she managed after a moment.

"I'd forgotten about that!" Bree exclaimed, the memory suddenly vivid in her mind—Carol Anders in a flowing emerald dress, cornering the bewildered butcher by the punch bowl, her laughter carrying across the town square.

Mary Ann joined in their laughter, her eyes crinkling at the corners. "Exactly. Carol is a free spirit, and she's not afraid to go after what she wants. But sometimes, her methods can be a bit... unorthodox."

A thought occurred to Bree, sobering her amusement. "But her magic? Is it... I mean, does she ever...?" She trailed off, unsure how to phrase the delicate question.

Mary Ann, understanding immediately, shook her head firmly. "No, love. Carol may be unconventional in her personal life, but she would never use her magic to influence or manipulate someone. That goes against everything the coven stands for."

Her expression grew more serious as she leaned forward, her gaze intent on both her daughters. "Magic is a gift, a responsibility. It's not to be used for personal gain or to control others. That's the first and most important lesson you'll learn as part of the Andromeda Coven."

Bree and Molly nodded solemnly, absorbing the gravity of their mother's words. The power they were about to formally embrace came with clear boundaries and ethics—something Bree found reassuring rather than restrictive.

The conversation paused as Mary Ann rose to refresh their tea. Through the kitchen window, Bree could see shadows lengthening across the garden as afternoon began its gradual transition into evening.

Soon, the house would fill with coven members. The ritual would begin, and she and Molly would take their first official steps into a world of magic and sisterhood. The thought sent a thrill of anticipation through her, mingled with a touch of apprehension.

As she watched her mother move around the kitchen with practiced ease, a question formed in Bree's mind—one that had been hovering at the edges of her consciousness since they'd first learned about the coven's structure and traditions.

"Mom," she began, setting down her teacup, "everyone keeps saying how great the coven is and how it supports everyone. But has there ever been someone who was disavowed or thrown out?"

The kitchen seemed to grow quieter, as if the very walls were listening for Mary Ann's answer. Her smile faded, a shadow passing over her features like a cloud across the sun. She sighed, her shoulders tensing slightly as she returned to the table.

"It's rare," she said finally, her voice measured and careful, as if weighing each word. "The coven is built on a foundation of trust, respect, and mutual support. But there have been instances, in the past, where someone has violated those principles."

Molly leaned forward, her voice dropping to barely above a whisper. "What happened?"

Mary Ann clasped her hands together on the tabletop, her knuckles whitening slightly with the pressure. Her gaze became distant, focused on a point beyond the kitchen walls, beyond the present moment.

"There was one incident, years ago, when your grandmother was still the High Priestess," she began, her voice taking on a storyteller's cadence. "A young woman who had just joined the coven, full of ambition and hunger for power."

Outside, a cloud passed over the sun, briefly dimming the kitchen. The parallel was not lost on Bree, who felt goosebumps rising on her arms despite the warmth of the room.

"She wanted to know too much, too soon," Mary Ann continued, her expression troubled. "She was always pushing, always questioning, always seeking more than she was ready for. It was as if she saw the coven as a means to an end, a way to rise to a position of authority that she hadn't earned."

The quiet in the kitchen deepened, the only sound the distant ticking of the grandfather clock in the hallway, marking the passage of time as Mary Ann's story unfolded.

"What did Gram do?" Bree asked, her voice barely audible.

Mary Ann's gaze sharpened, returning to the present. "She did what she had to," she said firmly, though there was a shadow of regret beneath her certainty. "As High Priestess, it was her responsibility to protect the coven, to ensure that its integrity and its secrets remained intact. She confronted the young woman, gave her a chance to change her ways and her attitude."

"And did she? Change, I mean?" Molly asked, her expression solemn.

Mary Ann shook her head slowly, a heavy sigh escaping her lips. "No, she didn't. If anything, the confrontation only made her more determined, more reckless. She started to lash out, to challenge your grandmother's authority at every turn."

She looked up, meeting her daughters' gazes with unexpected intensity. "In the end, Nancy had no choice. She invoked the ancient rite of banishment, casting the young woman out of the coven and stripping her of her powers."

A chill ran through Bree at the thought. To be cut off from magic, from the sisterhood that had been described as so fundamental—it seemed a punishment worse than any conventional justice could devise.

"What happened to her?" she asked hesitantly, almost afraid to hear the answer. "The woman who was banished?"

Mary Ann shifted in her chair, uncharacteristic unease flickering across her features. "No one knows for certain. She left Ballad, disappeared without a trace. Some say she sought out other covens, other sources of power. Others believe she turned her back on magic altogether, consumed by bitterness and resentment."

She didn't meet their eyes as she added, almost as an afterthought, "There are even those who whisper that she found darker paths to pursue—forms of magic that the Andromeda Coven would never condone."

The implications hung heavy in the air between them. Bree had read enough books, seen enough movies, to understand what her mother was suggesting—black magic, forbidden arts, powers that came at a terrible price.

Mary Ann straightened, her expression clearing as she seemed to make a conscious effort to shift the mood. "The point is, my loves," she said, her voice warming again, "that while the coven is a source of great strength and support, it is not to be taken lightly. The power we wield, the secrets we keep, they come with a heavy responsibility."

"We understand, Mom," Molly said quietly, her usual exuberance tempered by the gravity of the conversation. "We won't let you down."

Mary Ann smiled, reaching out to touch each of their faces in turn, a tender gesture that reminded Bree of childhood bedtimes and whispered reassurances after nightmares. "I know you won't," she said softly. "But I want you to remember, always, to be vigilant. To trust your instincts and to rely on each other. The bond between sisters, both by blood and by magic, is a powerful thing."

As she spoke, the sunlight returned, streaming through the windows and casting a golden glow across the kitchen table. It illuminated the three women, highlighting the family resemblance that connected them across generations—the curve of a cheek, the set of the jaw, the particular way their eyes crinkled when they smiled.

The story of the banished witch lingered in the air, a cautionary tale and a reminder of the complexities of the world they were about to fully enter. But as Bree looked at her mother and sister, she felt a renewed sense of purpose and unity that outweighed any lingering unease.

They were Tanners, daughters of the Andromeda Coven, and they would face whatever challenges lay ahead with courage, wisdom, and the unbreakable bond of sisterhood.

"Now," Mary Ann said, her tone deliberately lighter as she rose, "we should start preparing for tonight. The coven will begin arriving around seven, and there's much to do before then."

As Bree stood to help, she caught a glimpse of movement through the kitchen window—a tall figure passing by on the sidewalk, his face turned toward the Tanner house with what seemed like particular interest.

Sam Sorken, their mysterious neighbor, paused for just a moment, his gaze meeting Bree's through the glass. Something passed between them—not quite recognition, not quite understanding, but a connection nonetheless. He nodded once, a gesture that could have been merely neighborly but somehow felt more significant, before continuing on his way.

Bree turned back to her mother and sister, the brief encounter already fading from her conscious mind. But somewhere deeper, in the part of her that was beginning to awaken to her magical heritage, a question formed:

What role would Sam Sorken play in the unfolding story of the Tanner women and the Andromeda Coven?

Only time—and perhaps the ancient wisdom contained in Nancy Tanner's witch hat—would tell.

CHAPTER 9

THE VOODOO QUEEN

Deep in the heart of Louisiana, where the air hung heavy with humidity and the whispers of forgotten gods, stood a weathered shotgun house on the outskirts of New Orleans. From the outside, it appeared abandoned—peeling paint, sagging porch, windows perpetually shuttered against prying eyes. But appearances, as with most things in Kestrel Drach's world, were deliberately deceiving.

Inside, a labyrinth of rooms extended far beyond what the house's exterior dimensions should allow—a spatial impossibility that was just one of many rules Kestrel had broken in her pursuit of power. The air was thick with the mingled scents of dozens of burning herbs, some sweet, others acrid and nauseating. Incense smoke coiled in serpentine patterns, defying the natural movement of air as it twisted into shapes that resembled faces in agony.

In the innermost chamber, Kestrel Drach sat cross-legged on a floor of bare earth, her midnight-black skirts pooled around her like spilled ink. A dozen candles encircled her, their flames unnaturally still despite the drafts that whispered through the house. The flickering light played across her deep brown skin, accentuating her high cheekbones and the almost predatory intensity of her expression. Though approaching fifty, Kestrel maintained a terrible beauty—the kind that drew the eye but sent a primal warning through the observer's spine. Her ebony complexion seemed to absorb the candlelight, giving her an otherworldly presence in the dim room.

Just outside the doorway, twenty-three-year-old Nissa Drach watched her mother with the wariness of a small animal in the presence of a venomous snake. Her slender frame was tense, poised for flight even as she forced herself to remain and observe. Like her mother, Nissa's skin was a rich brown, though several shades lighter—the color of burnished copper. Unlike her mother's dramatic features—raven hair with a single streak of silver, eyes so dark they appeared black in certain lights—Nissa wore her tightly coiled hair in a crown of intricate braids framing a heart-shaped face dominated by eyes the color of amber in sunlight.

Kestrel's lips moved silently, forming words in a language that had never been meant for human tongues. Her entire body swayed slightly, as if moved by an unseen current. The air around her seemed to vibrate, creating a visible distortion that made Nissa's teeth ache and her skin prickle with gooseflesh.

Nissa knew better than to interrupt. The last servant who had disturbed one of Kestrel's trances had been found the next morning, his mind shattered beyond repair, his eyes frozen wide in an expression of such profound terror that even Kestrel's most hardened followers had been shaken. The man still lived—if such an existence could be called living—locked away in the attic room where he did nothing but rock back and forth, occasionally breaking into screams that sounded less than human.

So Nissa waited, her fingernails digging half-moons into her palms as the minutes stretched into an hour, then longer. The candle flames began to gutter as wax pooled on the floor, and still Kestrel maintained her trance, her consciousness traversing realms that few living souls had ever glimpsed.

Beyond the veil of ordinary reality, Kestrel's spirit moved through a landscape of perpetual twilight, where shapes formed and dissolved like smoke, and distant voices called out in languages that had been long extinct from the mortal world. She had been making this journey for over twenty years, each time pushing a little further, demanding more, her hunger for forbidden knowledge and power insatiable.

Today, her purpose was clear. For weeks, she had sensed a disturbance in the magical currents that flowed through the world—a ripple that signaled a significant shift in power. Something had happened, something that might provide an opening for her to claim what she had been denied all those years ago.

As she moved deeper into the spirit realm, the mists parted before her, revealing a crossroads illuminated by an eerie phosphorescence that seemed to emanate from the very soil. And there, standing at the center where the four paths met, was a figure both ancient and ageless, his skin as dark and gleaming as obsidian, his eyes holding the light of distant stars.

Papa Legba, the loa of the crossroads, guardian of the gateway between the living world and the realm of spirits, watched her approach with an expression that mingled amusement and contempt.

"Kestrel Drach," he said, his voice resonating not through the air but through the very fabric of the place, vibrating in Kestrel's bones. "Why do you keep coming here, child? What is it that you seek?"

Kestrel's spirit form drew closer, unafraid where most mortals would have cowered. "Power," she whispered, the word a caress and a demand all at once. "The power to bend the world to my will, to shape the fates of those who would stand in my way."

Papa Legba regarded her with ancient eyes that had witnessed the rise and fall of civilizations, the birth and death of gods. "And you believe that power is yours to take?" he asked, a hint of amusement coloring his tone. "You, who twist the ancient arts to serve your own selfish ends?"

Kestrel's face contorted in a snarl, her spirit form rippling with the force of her rage. "I alone am worthy of the true secrets of magic," she hissed, her voice dripping with venom. "The others, with their talk of balance and harmony, they are weak. They do not understand the true nature of power."

Papa Legba threw back his head and laughed, the sound echoing through the mists like thunder, shaking the very foundations of the crossroads. "Oh, child," he said, his voice softening with something that might have been pity. "You understand nothing. But perhaps it is time for you to learn."

He waved a hand, and the shadows around them shifted, coalescing into a scene as vivid as life. Kestrel saw a funeral, a gathering of mourners dressed in black, and at the center of it all, a closed casket draped in white lilies. Though the faces were indistinct at this distance, she recognized the setting immediately—the small church in Ballad, the town she had fled more than two decades ago.

"Your old friend, Nancy Tanner, has passed from the world of the living," Papa Legba said, his voice a whisper that somehow carried perfect clarity. "Her power, the secrets she guarded so carefully, they are now in play."

The scene shifted, showing a Victorian house that Kestrel remembered all too well. Two young women stood on the porch—sisters by their resemblance, both with something of Nancy Tanner in the set of their jaws, the arch of their brows.

"Her granddaughters," Papa Legba continued, "now stand at the threshold of their power. One will take the hat, become the new High Priestess of the Andromeda Coven. The balance shifts, the wheel turns."

Kestrel's eyes flew open in the spirit realm, her breath coming in sharp, ragged gasps. "When?" she demanded, her voice rising to a shrill, desperate pitch. "When did this happen? Why was I not told?"

Papa Legba's expression hardened, his eyes flashing with a dangerous light. "You dare to make demands of me?" he asked, his voice a low, menacing growl. "You, who have no place here, no right to the knowledge you seek?"

He raised a hand, and Kestrel felt a force like a physical blow strike her chest, sending her reeling back through the veils that separated the worlds, hurtling toward her physical form with bruising velocity.

"Be gone," Papa Legba commanded, his voice fading into the mists. "And trouble me no more with your petty desires and your grasping ambition."

In the physical world, Kestrel's eyes snapped open, her body jerking violently as her consciousness slammed back into her flesh. A trickle of blood ran from her nose, and her chest heaved as she struggled to catch her breath. Her mouth tasted of copper and something else—something acrid and bitter that made her want to retch.

Nissa, still watching from the doorway, felt a chill run down her spine at the look of pure, unadulterated rage that twisted her mother's features. It was an expression she had seen before, one that invariably preceded someone's suffering.

"Nissa!" Kestrel snapped, her voice cold and cutting as a blade of ice. "Prepare yourself. We have work to do."

Without waiting for a response, Kestrel rose to her feet in one fluid motion, extinguishing the candles with a dismissive wave of her hand. The darkness that followed was brief but absolute, a glimpse of a void that seemed to hunger. Then, with another gesture, Kestrel ignited the oil lamps hanging from the ceiling, filling the room with a sickly yellow light.

Eyes blazing with a feverish intensity, she crossed the room with purposeful strides, the hem of her skirts whispering across the dirt floor. She reached a bookshelf carved with symbols that seemed to shift and writhe when viewed from the corner of the eye, and pressed her palm against a particular configuration. A hidden compartment slid open with a sound like a distant scream.

From the secret space, Kestrel withdrew a book bound in leather so dark it seemed to absorb the lamplight. It was a diary of sorts, a repository of secrets and knowledge gathered over a lifetime of dark pursuits.

With trembling hands—not from fear but from barely contained excitement—she flipped through the yellowed pages, her gaze scanning the cramped, spidery handwriting until she found what she was looking for. There, in faded ink, was a detailed entry about the Tanners, their history, their location, and the power that flowed through their bloodline.

"Nissa," Kestrel called, her voice sharp and commanding. "Come here, child."

Nissa obeyed immediately, her movements graceful but careful, like someone approaching a wounded but dangerous animal. She entered the room with her eyes appropriately downcast, her shoulders hunched slightly in a posture of submission that had been ingrained since childhood.

Kestrel thrust the open book into her daughter's hands, her fingers digging into the young woman's shoulder with a painful intensity, nails like talons piercing through the thin fabric of Nissa's blouse to break the skin beneath. "Read this," she hissed, her breath hot against Nissa's ear. "Memorize every word, every detail. This is your mission, your sole purpose for existence."

Nissa, her hands shaking as she clutched the diary, began to read, her eyes widening with each revelatory sentence. The Tanners, the Andromeda Coven, the secrets of their magic—it was all laid out before her, a tantalizing glimpse into a world she had never dared to imagine.

The diary contained intimate details—the families of the coven, their relationships to one another, their particular magical affinities. Most compelling were the passages about Nancy Tanner and her unique ability to commune with spirits, a power that Kestrel had coveted above all others. And there, in the margins, annotated in red ink that Nissa suspected might be blood, were Kestrel's notes from her time in Ballad, her observations and plots.

"You have one task, and one task only," Kestrel continued, her voice low and menacing. "You will go to Ballad, to the Tanner house. You will find Nancy Tanner's hat, the repository of her power, and you will bring it back to me. At any cost, do you understand?"

Nissa, her throat tight with unshed tears, nodded mutely. She knew, with a certainty that chilled her to the bone, that failure was not an option. Her mother's wrath, her cruelty and her cunning were legendary. To disappoint her was to court a fate worse than death.

At twenty-three years old, Nissa should have been a young woman on the cusp of independence, ready to forge her own path in the world. But under Kestrel's iron rule, she was little more than a puppet, a pawn in her mother's twisted games of power and control.

Though Nissa had her own considerable magical abilities—inherited from Kestrel but tempered with an innate sensitivity that her mother lacked—she had been taught to use them only in service to Kestrel's ambitions. Any hint of independence, any suggestion that she might develop her gifts in her own way, was swiftly and brutally punished.

Kestrel, her eyes glittering with malevolent satisfaction, smiled coldly. She could see the fear in her daughter's eyes, the trembling of her limbs, and it filled her with a perverse sense of pleasure. Nissa was hers, body and soul, a tool to be wielded in the service of her dark ambitions.

"Go now," Kestrel commanded, her voice a sibilant whisper. "Pack only what you need. You leave tonight."

Nissa blinked in surprise. "Tonight? But—"

Kestrel's hand lashed out, striking Nissa across the face with enough force to snap her head to the side. "Do not question me," she hissed, her face inches from Nissa's. "Every moment we delay is a moment for them to secure the hat, to transfer its powers. Time is against us, girl."

Nissa tasted blood where her teeth had cut into the inside of her cheek. She nodded, fighting to keep her expression neutral despite the burning humiliation and fear churning inside her. "Yes, Mother. I'll prepare immediately."

As she turned to leave, clutching the diary to her chest, Kestrel's voice stopped her in her tracks.

"Remember, Nissa," she said, her tone deceptively soft. "You are nothing without me. Your life, your very existence, is a gift that I can take away as easily as I granted it. Never forget that."

Nissa, her eyes stinging with unshed tears, nodded once more. She knew, with a sinking certainty, that her mother's words were no idle threat. She had seen what happened to those who failed Kestrel Drach, and the memory of their fates was enough to make her stomach twist with dread.

"And do not fail me, child," Kestrel added, almost as an afterthought. "The consequences would be... unpleasant."

With those ominous words hanging in the air between them, Nissa fled to her small room at the back of the house. It was sparse—a narrow bed, a dresser, a small desk where she studied the magical texts Kestrel deemed appropriate. Nothing personal adorned the walls or surfaces; Kestrel's controlling grip did not permit such attachments, and having something found could prove deadly.

Quickly, methodically, Nissa packed a small suitcase with the essentials—clothes, toiletries, the few magical implements she would need to maintain contact with her mother. Last, she carefully wrapped the diary in a silk scarf and tucked it into a hidden compartment in the suitcase.

As she worked, her mind raced with conflicting emotions. Fear, of course—fear of failure, fear of her mother's wrath. But beneath that, a tiny, treacherous spark of something else. Excitement. Curiosity. Hope.

This would be her first time away from her mother's direct supervision since childhood. Her first opportunity to see the world beyond the confines of the house in New Orleans and the few carefully controlled excursions Kestrel permitted. And though her mission was clear—steal Nancy Tanner's witch hat and return it to Kestrel—the prospect of even a brief taste of freedom made her heart beat faster.

Would the Andromeda Coven be as Kestrel had described them? Weak, sentimental fools who squandered their gifts on helping others rather than pursuing true power? Or was there something her mother wasn't telling her, some reason beyond the obvious that Kestrel had been cast out all those years ago?

Despite her loyalty and fear, Nissa couldn't help but wonder. And wonder, her mother had always warned her, was the first step toward disobedience, toward destruction.

She closed the suitcase with trembling hands, smoothing her palm over the worn leather. Whatever lay ahead in Ballad, whatever secrets and dangers awaited her there, she knew one thing with absolute certainty: she could not fail. Her life depended on it.

Kestrel watched her daughter leave, her lips curled in a cruel, satisfied smile. The power of the Tanner bloodline, the secrets of the Andromeda Coven, were almost within her grasp. After more than twenty years of exile, of building her power in secret, of biding her time, the moment for revenge had finally arrived.

Nancy Tanner was dead, and soon, her legacy would belong to Kestrel Drach. The thought sent a thrill of anticipation through her, a hunger so profound it was almost sexual in its intensity.

And if Nissa proved to be a useful tool in that pursuit, then so be it. But if she failed, if she showed even a hint of weakness or hesitation, then Kestrel would dispose of her as easily as she would any other obstacle in her path.

For in the end, power was all that mattered. And Kestrel Drach, the voodoo queen of Louisiana, would let nothing and no one stand in her way.

Not even her own daughter.

Chapter 10
THE KING'S FAREWELL

What remained of the council chamber's vaulted ceiling had partially collapsed, allowing the smoke-filled sky to peer through like a malevolent eye. The once-immaculate mosaic floor—depicting the founding of Eldoria in brilliant tiles of lapis and gold—lay shattered beneath fallen columns and the bodies strewn about of royal guards who had given their lives to protect their monarchs.

King Aldric Valarion stood amidst this devastation, his grey hair matted with dust and blood, his ceremonial armor dented and scorched. The crown of Eldoria—worn by his lineage for fifteen generations—was conspicuously absent, deliberately removed when the first Drakorian ships appeared in the sky. A king in name and bearing only now, as befitted these final hours.

"Isadora," he whispered, kneeling beside his queen.

Queen Isadora lay on an improvised pallet, her elegant features marred by a deep wound across her forehead where a chunk of ornamental masonry had struck her during the last bombardment. Despite the pain evident in her tightly drawn lips, her eyes remained alert and focused—the same sharp intelligence that had made her the true political force behind the throne for three decades.

"I'm fine, Aldric," she insisted, though the pallor of her skin betrayed the lie. She attempted to rise but winced as the movement sent fresh blood trickling down her temple.

"Stay still, my love," Aldric urged, pressing a gentle hand to her shoulder. "The healers are coming."

A young witch hurried forward from the group of survivors huddled in the relative safety of the chamber's eastern alcove. Her green robes—marking her as a junior member of the healing coven—were torn and soot-stained, but her hands were steady as she knelt beside the queen.

"Your Majesty," she murmured, her palms already glowing with soft amber light. "This may feel warm."

As the healing magic flowed into the queen's wound, King Aldric turned to face the two generals who had managed to fight their way to the royal couple's position. General Thorne and General Varis stood at rigid attention despite their haggard appearance, ready to receive their king's commands even as the world crumbled around them.

General Thorne—a mountain of a man whose scarred face had become legendary across Eldoria's military—stepped forward first. "Your Majesty, the eastern and southern quadrants have fallen. The Drakorians have established fortified positions and are moving methodically toward the palace."

"And the evacuation?" Aldric asked, his voice betraying none of the despair that threatened to overwhelm him.

General Varis, her dark hair pulled back in a tight military braid, consulted a data tablet that flickered with intermittent static.

"Approximately sixty percent of the civilian population has been moved to the emergency shelters in the western highlands. The rest..." She paused, visibly struggling to maintain her professional demeanor while addressing those assembled. "The rest are either trapped by Drakorian blockades or..."

She needn't finish. The unspoken truth hung heavily in the air—many of Lumina's citizens were already beyond salvation.

"What of our orbital defenses?" the king pressed.

"Eliminated, Your Majesty," Thorne reported grimly. "The Drakorians targeted our defense platforms first. Methodical. Precise. They knew exactly where to strike."

A pained expression crossed the king's face. The implication was clear—such precision indicated betrayal from within. Someone with intimate knowledge of Eldoria's defenses had provided the Drakorians with critical intelligence.

"How much time do we have?" Aldric asked, turning back to his queen. The healing spell had stopped the bleeding, but Isadora's complexion remained alarmingly pale.

"At current advance rates, two hours before they breach the palace proper," Varis answered. "Perhaps three if the remaining defensive wards hold."

King Aldric nodded, his mind racing through possibilities that diminished with each passing moment. He gazed across the chamber at the frightened faces of those who had sought refuge within the palace walls—scholars, artisans, families with young children, the elderly. Those who could not fight but who represented the heart and soul of Eldorian culture.

"We cannot abandon them," he said softly, more to himself than his generals.

Queen Isadora reached up to grasp her husband's hand. "Nor can we save everyone, my love," she replied, her voice weak but resolute. "We must make the hardest choice of our reign."

The king closed his eyes briefly, the weight of the decision pressing down upon him like a physical force. When he opened them again, they held the clarity of purpose that comes only in moments of absolute crisis.

"General Varis," he commanded, "organize our remaining forces into two groups. The first will continue the evacuation efforts, focusing on getting as many civilians as possible to the western highlands. The second will establish a defensive perimeter around the palace complex to buy time."

General Varis nodded crisply. "A sound strategy, Your Majesty, but dividing our forces will significantly weaken our ability to hold any position for long."

"I'm aware," Aldric replied, the lines in his face deepening. "But I will not sacrifice the innocent while we make our last stand."

"As you command, Your Majesty," Varis said, bowing deeply before turning to coordinate with her officers.

General Thorne stepped forward, his massive hand resting on the hilt of his ceremonial sword. "Your Majesty, I request permission to lead the defensive force personally. My men will hold the line to their last breath."

Before the king could respond, the chamber doors opened to admit High Priestess Zara and Grand Necromancer Xaloth. Both magical leaders appeared exhausted, their normally immaculate ceremonial robes disheveled and battle-worn. Yet they carried themselves with the dignity of those who had accepted their fate but refused to be broken by it.

"Your Majesties," Zara said, offering a formal bow despite the circumstances. Her silver-and-white hair caught what little light remained in the ruined chamber, creating the illusion of a halo. "We've received reports that the Drakorians are specifically targeting practitioners of both our disciplines. They seek not just conquest but our knowledge."

"Malakai's true objective becomes clear," Xaloth added, his gravelly voice carrying across the chamber. "He wants the Nexus."

A chill settled over the gathering. The Nexus—the focal point of all magical energy on Eldoria—was the most closely guarded secret of their world. If corrupted by Drakorian hands, the consequences would be catastrophic beyond imagination.

Queen Isadora struggled to sit upright, ignoring the young healer's protests. "You've activated the Sanctuary Protocol?"

"The preparations are complete," Zara confirmed. "Selected practitioners from both orders stand ready. The knowledge vessels have been prepared."

"But we need time," Xaloth stated bluntly. "The ritual cannot be rushed without risking complete failure."

King Aldric looked between his generals and the magical leaders, understanding crystallizing in his mind. "Then we shall give you that time," he declared. "At whatever cost."

He turned back to General Thorne. "You have your permission, General. Assemble your best warriors and hold the Drakorians at bay for as long as possible."

Thorne saluted, his eyes burning with fierce determination. "We will not fail you, my King."

"And I," General Varis interjected, "will personally oversee the civilian evacuation. My forces will create a corridor to the western highlands and hold it open until the last possible moment."

High Priestess Zara stepped forward, her silver eyes reflecting the gravity of the moment they all faced. "Your Majesty, with your permission, I would lead a contingent of my witches to assist General Varis. Using our healing and protection spells could mean the difference between life and death for many civilians attempting to escape."

"I grant it gladly," the king replied, genuine gratitude in his voice.

"Then I shall remain with General Thorne," Xaloth declared, drawing himself up to his full height. "My necromancers will reinforce the palace defenses. We have... particular methods that may give the Drakorians pause."

The implication hung in the air—Xaloth intended to employ the darker aspects of his art, those normally regulated by strict ethical codes. In these final hours, such constraints had become luxuries they could no longer afford.

"Do what you must," King Aldric said solemnly. "All that matters now is the survival of our people and our knowledge."

A distant explosion shook the chamber, sending fresh debris cascading from the damaged ceiling. A reminder that time was the one resource they were rapidly exhausting.

"Go," the king commanded. "May the ancient spirits guide your paths."

As the generals departed to organize their respective forces, Zara and Xaloth lingered, exchanging a look laden with unspoken meaning. For centuries, the leaders of Eldoria's two magical disciplines had maintained a professional distance, their philosophical differences creating a gulf rarely bridged. Now, in the face of annihilation, such divisions seemed trivial.

"Zara," Xaloth said, his normally severe expression softening. "I had hoped we would face this final challenge together."

The High Priestess smiled sadly, reaching out to grasp the necromancer's weathered hand. "Our paths diverge, old friend, but our purpose remains the same—to ensure that something of Eldoria survives this darkness."

"Your students," Xaloth began, his voice dropping so that only Zara could hear. "Have you selected those who will carry the legacy of witchcraft to the stars?"

"I have," she confirmed. "Thirteen of our most promising. Including young Briella of House Tanner—her connection to the life energies is extraordinary."

Xaloth nodded thoughtfully. "I have chosen seven, including my apprentice Sameril. His understanding of the balance transcends his years."

"Perhaps not a coincidence," Zara mused. "Seven and seven. Balance even in our final act."

"Indeed." A rare smile crossed Xaloth's austere features. "After all these years of philosophical debates, we find harmony at the end."

The chamber shook again, more violently this time. The distant sounds of battle grew perceptibly closer.

"We must go," Zara said, reluctance evident in her voice. "The civilians cannot wait, and your defenses must be prepared."

Xaloth straightened, his face once more assuming its customary gravity. "Yes. There is much to do and precious little time."

Yet neither moved immediately, each seeming to search for words equal to what might be their final parting.

"Xaloth," Zara said finally, her voice barely above a whisper. "In another life, perhaps—"

"Yes," he interrupted gently. "In another life."

No further words were needed. Their hands clasped once more, a gesture that conveyed centuries of respect, rivalry, and unacknowledged affection.

"May your path be guided by light," Xaloth offered, the traditional blessing of the witches' coven.

"And may shadows grant you clarity," Zara returned, using the necromancers' benediction.

Then they parted, each moving toward their separate destinies with the dignified resolve of those who had accepted the necessary sacrifice that duty demanded.

King Aldric watched them go, a deep sadness mingling with pride in his heart. Around him, the remaining palace staff hurried to prepare the royal couple for evacuation—a journey Aldric had already privately decided they would not take. A king and queen did not abandon their world in its darkest hour.

"They will succeed," Queen Isadora said softly, reading her husband's thoughts as she had for thirty years of marriage. "Something of Eldoria will survive."

"At such cost," Aldric replied, his voice heavy with the weight of all that would be lost.

Isadora took his hand, her grip surprisingly strong despite her injury. "All great legacies are built on sacrifice, my love. We have always known this day might come."

The king nodded, drawing strength from his queen's unwavering courage. Together they had guided Eldoria through decades of peace and prosperity. Together they would face its fall.

"Come," he said, helping Isadora to her feet. "If these are to be our final hours, let us spend them not in hiding, but standing proud before our people."

Hand in hand, the royal couple made their way toward the palace's grand balcony—the traditional place from which monarchs had addressed the citizens of Lumina for countless generations. One last time, they would stand before their people, offering what comfort and courage they could in the face of approaching darkness.

Behind them, the chamber where so many crucial decisions had been made throughout Eldoria's history stood empty save for the ghosts of what had been and what might have been—silent witnesses to the end of an era.

Chapter 11
THE PATH OF MAGIC

The sky faded from periwinkle to lavender as evening descended on Willow Street. Bree stood before the hall mirror, examining her reflection with critical eyes. She'd changed outfits three times already; unsure what one should wear to a witchcraft initiation ceremony. She'd finally settled on a simple navy dress—neither too casual nor too formal—paired with a silver pendant that had been a gift from Nancy years ago.

"Stop fussing," Molly called from the top of the stairs. "You look fine."

Bree turned to see her sister descending, wearing a flowing emerald skirt and cream-colored blouse that complemented her auburn hair. Despite her reassuring words to Bree, Molly had clearly taken equal care with her appearance.

"Girls," Mary Ann called from the kitchen, "the Fonds are here!"

The headlights of Susan Fond's vintage Volvo station wagon swept across the living room walls as it pulled into the driveway. Bree grabbed the small bag she'd packed with the items Sarah had suggested—a personal token, a notebook, and comfortable shoes for afterward—and joined her mother and sister at the door.

"Ready?" Mary Ann asked, her eyes searching their faces for any sign of hesitation.

Bree exchanged a glance with Molly before nodding. "Ready."

The cool evening air greeted them as they stepped outside. The first stars had begun to appear, pinpricks of white against the deepening indigo sky. Susan Fond sat behind the wheel of the station wagon, while her daughter Sarah waited beside the passenger door, waving cheerfully.

"There they are," Sarah called, "our women of the hour!"

Her enthusiasm was infectious, and Bree felt the nervous knot in her stomach loosen slightly. Sarah was dressed more formally than Bree had ever seen her, in a flowing dress of midnight blue with silver embroidery around the neckline and sleeves.

"You both look lovely," Susan said as they approached. She wore a more subdued outfit—charcoal gray pants and a silk blouse in a soft lavender shade—but there was a festive glimmer in her eyes. "Climb in! We don't want to be late."

The interior of the station wagon smelled of lavender sachets and aged leather. Bree, Molly, and Mary Ann settled into the back seat while Sarah took her place beside her mother.

"Where exactly are we going?" Bree asked as Susan backed out of the driveway. "I thought the ceremony would be at someone's home."

Sarah turned in her seat, her expression bright with excitement. "We have a special place for important rituals—an old barn on the outskirts of town that belongs to the Warrens. Elaine's family has owned the property for generations. It's isolated, private, and perfectly suited for our needs."

"It's beautiful," Susan added, navigating through the quiet streets of Ballad. "Wait until you see what we've done with it."

As they drove, Sarah detailed what Bree and Molly could expect during the ceremony. "The initiation is sacred, but not somber," she explained. "We celebrate new members with joy. You'll be welcomed, anointed, and asked to recite the oath. Then afterward, there's food, drink, and much merriment."

"And of course, Lucy's bringing her famous Witches' Brew," Susan added with a knowing smile. "Just pace yourselves with that one, girls."

The houses of Ballad thinned as they reached the outskirts of town. Susan turned onto a narrow country road bordered by towering oak trees whose branches formed a cathedral-like canopy overhead. The headlights illuminated a worn wooden sign that read "Warren Orchard" before curving to follow a winding dirt path.

"Almost there," Sarah said, her voice dropping to an excited whisper as the car crested a small hill.

The barn came into view, silhouetted against the twilight sky. But this was no ordinary agricultural building. The massive structure had been transformed, its exterior illuminated by dozens of lanterns that cast a warm, golden glow across the weathered wood. Garlands of herbs and flowers hung from the eaves, and the double doors stood open, spilling light onto the packed earth of the yard.

Vehicles of various makes and models were already parked in neat rows beside the barn—the coven members had arrived ahead of them. As Susan brought the station wagon to a stop, Bree felt a flutter of anticipation mixed with a touch of anxiety.

"Don't be nervous," Mary Ann said, reaching over to squeeze her daughters' hands. "Everyone here loves you already."

They exited the car, the evening air alive with the sounds of crickets and distant laughter emanating from within the barn. Bree inhaled deeply, catching the mingled scents of burning sage, fresh herbs, and something sweet and spicy that hinted at the festivities to come.

"Follow me," Sarah said, leading them toward the open doors. "Your new family awaits."

As they stepped across the threshold, Bree felt it immediately—a subtle vibration that hummed through the soles of her feet and resonated in her bones. The air itself seemed charged with energy, with possibility.

Inside, the transformation was even more dramatic than the exterior had suggested. The cavernous space of the barn had been draped in fabrics of deep purple and midnight blue, creating a tent-like effect that softened the rough-hewn beams. Hundreds of candles flickered from every surface, their golden light casting dancing shadows on the faces of the gathered witches. The air was thick with the scent of incense and herbs, a heady blend that made Bree feel slightly lightheaded.

In the center of the space, an altar had been erected—a beautifully carved table draped in a cloth of pure, snowy white. Upon it rested a variety of sacred objects: a silver chalice filled with water that caught and reflected the candlelight; an ornate knife with a handle of polished antler; a pentacle fashioned from what appeared to be solid silver; and a bundle of dried herbs tied with a cord of braided silk. The altar was flanked by two tall, slender candles, their flames burning bright and steady in the still air of the barn.

Around the altar, arranged in a loose circle, stood the members of the Andromeda Coven. Bree and Molly, their eyes wide with wonder, took in the gathering. There were at least thirty people present, a diverse assembly of faces both familiar and new. The majority were women, ranging in age from early twenties to late sixties, each one radiating a unique energy and presence. But there were also men present—fewer in number but equal in their bearing and the power they emanated.

The moment the Tanners stepped fully into the space, a hush fell over the gathering. Then, as if on cue, the coven members broke into welcoming smiles, several moving forward to embrace them.

Elaine Warren approached first, resplendent in a gown of deep forest green that complemented her dark hair. "Welcome, my dears," she said, her voice warm with genuine affection. "We've been waiting for this day for a very long time."

Lucy followed close behind, wearing a dress of bright turquoise that matched her vibrant personality. "Finally!" she exclaimed, pulling Bree and Molly into a joint hug. "I've been planning the post-ceremony feast for weeks!"

One by one, the coven members came forward to greet them—Trudie Catshill with her collection of silver bracelets that jingled musically as she moved; Carol Anders, her flame-red hair piled high and her makeup perfectly applied despite the occasion; the King sisters, Alicia and Miranda, who moved with the synchronicity of twins though they were born three years apart.

And then a tall, slender man with striking blue eyes and a shock of silver hair stepped forward. His presence was commanding yet gentle, an aura of quiet strength surrounding him like a cloak.

"Blessed be, Bree and Molly," he said, his voice a rich, melodious baritone that seemed to resonate in the very air around them. "We are honored to welcome you into our circle tonight."

Mary Ann, her eyes shining with pride, placed a hand on each of her daughters' shoulders. "Marcus, these are my daughters, Bree and Molly," she said, her voice trembling slightly with emotion. "Girls, this is Marcus Thornwood, one of the elders of the coven."

Bree and Molly, their hearts racing with excitement, murmured their greetings. There was something about Marcus that inspired both respect and ease—a rare combination that marked true leadership.

"I knew your grandmother well," Marcus said, his blue eyes twinkling with fond memory. "Nancy had a way of seeing right through pretense to the heart of a matter. A quality I see reflected in both of you."

Before they could respond, Sarah stepped forward, gently taking control of the moment. "The hour approaches," she announced, her voice carrying easily through the barn. "Let us prepare for the ceremony."

The coven members moved with practiced efficiency, taking positions around the circle. Mary Ann squeezed her daughters' hands once more before joining the others, leaving Bree and Molly standing slightly apart, witnesses to the ancient ritual about to unfold.

Sarah approached them, now holding two folded garments of pure white. "These are your ceremonial robes," she explained softly. "They symbolize the purity of your intentions and your readiness to embark on this journey. There's a small anteroom where you can change."

She directed them to a curtained alcove at the side of the barn. Inside, a mirror hanging on the rough wooden wall reflected their nervous, excited faces as they helped each other don the soft, flowing robes.

"How do I look?" Molly asked, smoothing the fabric over her hips.

Bree smiled, adjusting the drape of the robe across her sister's shoulders. "Like a proper witch."

When they emerged, the coven had fully assembled in a perfect circle around the altar. The idle chatter had ceased, replaced by an expectant silence that seemed to pulse with potential. The air had grown somehow thicker, heavier with significance.

Sarah, resplendent in her gown of midnight blue, now wore a silver circlet upon her brow, marking her role as acting High Priestess. She stood at the altar, her hands resting lightly on its surface, her expression one of serene authority.

As Bree and Molly approached, the circle parted to admit them, then closed again once they stood before Sarah.

"Sisters and brothers of the Andromeda Coven," Sarah began, her voice ringing out clear and strong in the hushed barn. "We gather here tonight to welcome two new members into our circle, to initiate them into the ancient mysteries of our craft, and to bind them to us in love, loyalty, and magic."

She turned to face Bree and Molly directly, her expression softening with warmth and affection. "Bree and Molly Tanner, daughters of Mary Ann, granddaughters of Nancy, do you come here freely and of your own will, ready to embrace the path of the witch and the way of the coven?"

Bree and Molly, their hands clasped tightly together, stepped forward. Bree felt a momentary flutter of panic—what if her voice failed her? What if she stumbled over the words? But when she spoke, her voice emerged clear and steady, joining with Molly's in perfect harmony: "We do."

Sarah smiled, the candlelight catching the silver of her circlet. "Then let the ceremony begin."

With reverent hands, she guided them to stand directly before the altar. From the silver chalice, she dipped her fingers into water that smelled faintly of roses and traced a cool, damp line across each of their foreheads.

"With this sacred water, I cleanse you," she intoned, her voice rich with power. "May it wash away all doubt and hesitation, leaving only clarity of purpose and purity of intent."

Next, she carefully took a small, silver bowl filled with fragrant oil from the altar. The scent was complex—something herbal and earthy at its base, but sweet, with notes of citrus and what might have been frankincense rising above it. Holding it in one hand, she dipped her finger into the oil and traced a crescent moon on each of their foreheads, the cool, slick sensation sending a shiver down Bree's spine.

"With this sacred oil, I anoint you," Sarah continued, her voice deepening with each ritual action. "May the Goddess guide and protect you on your path, and may her wisdom flow through you like a river of light."

From the altar, she next took two slender white candles, handing one to each sister. Unlike the larger candles flanking the altar, these were unlit, their wicks pristine and waiting.

"These candles represent your individual lights," Sarah explained, "the unique gifts and talents you bring to our circle. When lit from our central flame, they symbolize how your personal power joins with and enhances the collective strength of the coven."

She gestured to a large, ornate candle at the center of the altar—the source flame that would light their individual candles. It burned with an unusually steady flame, neither flickering nor wavering despite the subtle movements of air in the barn.

"Approach the flame," Sarah instructed, "and light your candles, adding your light to ours."

Bree stepped forward first, her hand steady as she tilted her candle toward the central flame. The wick caught immediately, flaring to life with a brightness that seemed disproportionate to its size. Molly followed, her candle igniting with equal vigor.

With their candles lit, they turned back to face the circle, the flames illuminating their features from below. Bree could feel the weight of the moment, the significance of what they were about to do.

"And now," Sarah said, her voice hushed but carrying clearly through the perfect acoustics of the draped barn, "you will speak the oath that binds you to us and to the ancient traditions we uphold. Repeat after me: I, Bree Tanner, and I, Molly Tanner, do solemnly swear..."

The sisters, their voices trembling slightly with emotion but growing stronger with each word, began to recite the coven's oath, the ancient promise flowing from their lips with a power that seemed to resonate through the very air around them:

"I, [your name], do solemnly swear
To honor the Goddess, with reverence and care
To walk the path of magic, with wisdom and grace
To support my sisters, in this sacred space
I pledge my heart, my mind, my soul

To the Andromeda Coven, I give my whole
From this day forward, by moon and by sun
In perfect love and perfect trust, I am one."

As the final words of the oath faded into silence, something extraordinary happened. A burst of energy swept through the barn, a rush of wind and light that seemed to emanate from the very heart of the altar. The candles flared, their flames leaping higher for a brief, breathtaking moment before settling back to their steady burn.

Bree and Molly gasped in unison, their eyes wide as they felt the magic of the coven surround them, embrace them, welcome them home. It was a sensation unlike anything Bree had ever experienced—a feeling of connection so profound it brought tears to her eyes. She could feel the presence of every person in the circle, sense the unique signature of their magical energy.

And beyond that, something else—a deeper current, an ancient power that flowed through the coven and now through her. Was this what Nancy had experienced? This sense of being both distinctly herself and part of something vaster, older, more powerful than any individual could be alone?

Sarah, her face radiant with joy, stepped forward and took their hands in hers. "Sisters and brothers," she called out, her voice ringing with triumph and celebration. "I present to you Bree and Molly Tanner, our newest members, bound to us in love and magic forevermore!"

The barn erupted in cheers and applause, the solemnity of the ritual giving way to jubilation. The circle broke as witches surged forward to embrace the new initiates, their faces alight with happiness and welcome.

Bree found herself passed from one warm embrace to another, receiving kisses on both cheeks, hearty handshakes, and murmured blessings in a dizzying succession. Through it all, she maintained a white-knuckled grip on her candle, determined not to let the precious flame extinguish amid the celebration.

Elaine Warren eventually noticed her predicament and approached with a knowing smile. "Here, my dear," she said, producing a small silver holder. "Your candle will be safe in this. It's traditional to keep it burning throughout the celebration and take it home with you afterward—a symbol of carrying the coven's light into your daily life."

As Bree secured her candle in the holder, she caught sight of her mother across the room. Mary Ann stood slightly apart from the general revelry, her expression a complex mix of pride, joy, and something else—perhaps wistfulness? Before Bree could make her way over to investigate, Lucy Warren's voice rose above the general chatter.

"Alright, everyone, gather round!" she called out, her voice bubbling with excitement. "I've got a special treat for our new sisters, something that's sure to put a little extra magic in your step!"

She stood beside a table that had been set up along one wall of the barn, now laden with an impressive array of food and drink. With theatrical flair, she whisked a cloth off a large, steaming cauldron at the center of the display, revealing what could only be her famous "Witches' Brew"—a spicy, aromatic concoction that filled the air with enticing scents of cinnamon, cloves, and something more exotic that Bree couldn't identify.

"Form an orderly queue, now," Lucy instructed with mock sternness as the coven members eagerly approached. "There's plenty for everyone, but our new sisters get the first taste!"

Bree and Molly were ushered to the front of the line, each presented with a delicate China cup filled with the steaming brew. Bree took a cautious sip and felt warmth spread through her body, a pleasant tingling sensation that seemed to heighten her awareness of the magical energies still buzzing in the air around them.

"It's delicious," she told Lucy, who beamed with pride.

"Family recipe," Lucy confided, leaning in conspiratorially. "With a few special additions of my own. Drink up—it'll help you process all the new energies you're experiencing tonight."

As the celebration continued, the barn filled with music from a quartet of musicians who had set up in one corner—a violin, a cello, a flute, and a small hand drum creating a harmony that was both earthy and ethereal. Witches began to dance, moving in a flowing circle that reminded Bree of the ritual they had just completed, but with a joyous, unfettered energy that contrasted with the ceremony's solemnity.

Molly was quick to join the dance, her white robe swirling around her as she was swept into the circle by the King sisters. Bree, content to observe for the moment, found a seat on one of the benches that lined the walls of the barn.

She was soon joined by Marcus Thornwood, the silver-haired elder who had greeted them earlier. Up close, she could see that his eyes weren't simply blue but contained flecks of grey that caught the light when he moved.

"Quite a night," he observed, his rich voice carrying easily despite the music and chatter around them. "How are you feeling, Bree?"

"Overwhelmed," she admitted, "but in the best possible way. It's so much to take in."

Marcus nodded, his expression understanding. "The initiation is just the beginning, you know. The real work—and the real joy—of being part of the coven starts tomorrow."

"Our training begins tomorrow," Bree said, a mixture of excitement and apprehension in her voice. "That's the next step, isn't it?"

"Indeed." Marcus studied her face with keen, perceptive eyes. "The formal instruction in the ways of the coven. Then, in seven and ten days, will come the Passing of the Hat ceremony.

Marcus clarified with a gentle smile. "The coven believes in proper preparation. One of you will take up Nancy's mantle, but not before you've had time to understand what that truly means."

Bree glanced across the room to where Molly was now engaged in animated conversation with several of the younger coven members, her face flushed with excitement and the effects of Lucy's brew.

"What if neither of us is ready?" she asked softly, voicing the fear that had been lurking at the edges of her consciousness.

Marcus's expression grew thoughtful. "Readiness is rarely something we feel," he said after a moment. "It's something we discover in the doing. Nancy wasn't 'ready' when she became High Priestess, but she grew into the role magnificently."

He leaned closer, his voice dropping to ensure their conversation remained private despite the surrounding festivities. "What matters is not whether you feel prepared, Bree, but whether you are willing to learn, to serve, and to keep an open heart. The hat contains wisdom accumulated over generations, but it needs a living mind—and a courageous spirit—to wield that wisdom effectively."

Before she could respond, they were interrupted by a burst of laughter from a group gathered near the refreshment table. Lucy Warren stood at the center, gesturing expressively as she recounted what appeared to be a hilarious anecdote.

"I believe Lucy is about to share the infamous goose story," Marcus observed with a twinkle in his eye. "This is not to be missed."

He stood, offering Bree his hand with old-world courtesy. "Shall we join them? Lucy's tales of magical mishaps are legendary, and this one in particular holds an important lesson for new witches."

Curious, Bree allowed him to lead her to the growing crowd around Lucy, who was now standing on a chair for better visibility, her turquoise dress shimmering in the candlelight.

"Alright, everyone, gather round," Lucy was saying, her voice pitched with barely contained laughter. "Our new sisters need to hear about my initiation and the little mishap that followed. I don't want them to make the same mistake."

The witches, their faces alight with anticipation, pressed closer. Many were already grinning, clearly familiar with the story but eager to hear it again. Lucy took a dramatic swig of her brew, cleared her throat, and began her tale.

"So, there I was, fresh-faced and eager, ready to take my place in the Andromeda Coven," she began, her hands gesturing expressively as she spoke. "I had studied, I had prepared, and I was determined to make a good impression on my new sisters."

She paused, taking another sip before continuing. "The ceremony went off without a hitch. I recited the oath, I lit my candle, and I felt the rush of magic and connection that comes with joining the coven. It was exhilarating, empowering, and I was on top of the world."

Her expression shifted, a rueful grin spreading across her face. "But then, in my excitement and my haste to celebrate, I may have gotten a little carried away with the post-initiation festivities. I was so eager to show off my newfound magical prowess that I decided to attempt a little spell of my own, something to add a little extra sparkle to the night."

The witches leaned in, their eyes wide with anticipation and knowing amusement. Elaine Warren, standing nearby, rolled her eyes but couldn't suppress a fond smile.

"I had this brilliant idea to conjure a flock of enchanted doves, to fill the room with grace and serenity," Lucy continued, her voice trembling with barely suppressed laughter. "But in my enthusiasm and inexperience, I may have slightly mispronounced one of the key words of the incantation."

She took a deep breath, her shoulders shaking with mirth. "Instead of summoning majestic, cooing doves, I accidentally conjured a gaggle of noisy, mischievous geese!"

The barn erupted in laughter, witches clutching their sides and wiping tears of hilarity from their eyes. Even those who clearly knew the story were laughing as hard as those hearing it for the first time.

"Oh, it was pandemonium!" Lucy exclaimed, her own laughter ringing out above the din. "The geese were everywhere, honking and flapping and causing all sorts of commotion. They were chasing people around the room, stealing food from the tables, and generally making a ruckus."

She shook her head, her face flushed with the memory. "Poor Mama got the brunt of it," she said, gesturing toward Elaine, who was now chuckling despite herself. "She was trying to shoo the geese away, to maintain some semblance of order, but they just wouldn't listen. One particularly bold goose even managed to snatch her hat right off her head and went parading around the room with it, like it was the crown jewel of the coven!"

The laughter intensified, the witches picturing the scene with a mix of sympathy and hilarity. Bree found herself laughing along, the image of dignified Elaine being harassed by a hat-stealing goose too funny to resist.

"In the end, it took a bit of magical wrangling and a lot of patient coaxing to round up all the geese and send them on their way," Lucy said, wiping tears of laughter from her own eyes. "And let me tell you, I got quite the lecture from Mama after that little stunt."

She grinned, her expression a mix of sheepishness and pride. "But you know what? Even though it was a bit of a fiasco, even though I was embarrassed and chagrined, I wouldn't change a thing about that night."

Her voice softened, her eyes growing distant with the warmth of memory. "Because that mishap, that moment of utter silliness and joy, it bonded me to my sisters in a way that nothing else could. It showed me that even in the midst of mistakes and mayhem, the love and support of the coven would always be there, always ready to laugh with me and remind me not to take myself too seriously."

She raised her glass, her smile wide and infectious. "So, here's to the mishaps and the misadventures, to the moments that test us and the laughter that heals us. Here's to the magic of sisterhood, and the unbreakable bonds of the Andromeda Coven!"

The witches cheered, their voices rising in a joyous chorus as they clinked their glasses together, the sound of their laughter and their love echoing through the barn like a symphony of magic and sound that rose high into the night.

Bree, caught up in the wave of communal joy, found her glass suddenly recharged with Lucy's brew as people pressed forward to toast the sentiment. As she sipped, she caught sight of her mother and sister making their way toward her through the crowd.

Mary Ann's earlier reserve had melted away, replaced by a relaxed happiness that made her look years younger. Molly was practically glowing, her eyes bright with excitement and the magical energies still swirling through the barn.

"What do you think?" Molly asked, linking her arm through Bree's. "Everything you expected?"

Bree considered the question, looking around at the gathering—at the laughter and the light, the magic and the mundane mingled in such perfect harmony. She thought of the oath they had spoken, the commitment they had made, and the path that now stretched before them.

"No," she said finally, a smile spreading across her face. "It's so much more."

And as the celebration continued around them, as the witches danced and laughed and shared their stories, Bree and Molly Tanner knew with absolute certainty that they had truly found their place, their purpose, and their power, within the sacred circle of the Andromeda Coven.

What they couldn't know, as they basked in the warmth of their new magical family, was that far away in Louisiana, a darkness was stirring—a shadow from the past that would soon test the strength of their newly forged bonds and the depth of their commitment to the path they had chosen.

But that was a challenge for another day. Tonight was for celebration, for joy, and for the pure, unadulterated magic of belonging.

CHAPTER 12

THE FALL OF THE PALACE

The grand hall of the Eldorian palace—once the jewel of the capital where celestial diplomats had been welcomed and ancient peace treaties signed—had transformed into a final desperate battleground. Royal guards knelt behind overturned tables of millennium-old hardwood, the furniture that had hosted banquets for generations now serving as makeshift barricades. Soldiers crouched behind toppled statues of revered ancestors; their faces grim with the knowledge that they were likely the last line of defense their world would ever know.

Captain Elara Vos tightened her grip on her command staff, its crystalline tip pulsing with gathered energy. As leader of the palace guard, she had spent decades preparing for wars that never came, training exercises that seemed excessive in an era of peace. Now, as she surveyed her dwindling troops positioned throughout the hall, she silently thanked those years of relentless preparation.

"Hold steady," she called, her voice carrying the artificial calm of a leader who understands the direness of their situation. "Remember your oaths. Remember who we protect."

A young guard beside her—barely old enough for his position—trembled visibly, his weapon shaking in his hands. "Captain, they say the eastern wing has already fallen. The archives—"

"Focus on what's before you, Tallen," she cut him off firmly but not unkindly. "One moment at a time. That's all any of us have."

The massive double doors that separated the grand hall from the outer courtyard had been reinforced with every physical and magical barrier the palace defenses could muster. Enchanted metallic beams crisscrossed the entrance, glowing sigils of protection burned into their surface. Defensive spell-cores hummed at strategic points, ready to unleash concentrated arcane energy at the first sign of breach.

For several heartbeats, an eerie stillness descended over the hall. The sounds of distant fighting—energy weapons discharging, buildings collapsing, the occasional scream—filtered through like echoes from another world. Inside, there was only the ragged breathing of soldiers who knew they stood at the threshold of history.

Elara raised a hand to her comm unit. "Status report, eastern corridor?"

Static crackled, then a breathless voice: "They've broken through the secondary defenses, Captain. Drakorian heavy units advancing. We can't—" The transmission dissolved into weapons fire and screams before cutting out entirely.

"Western approach?" she tried next.

"Holding, but barely," came the strained reply. "Enemy battlemages attempting to dismantle the ward barriers. Estimate five minutes before breach."

Elara's jaw tightened. "Fall back to the grand hall. All remaining units converge here. We make our stand together."

As the last of her scattered forces filtered in, taking positions behind the barricades, Elara felt rather than heard a change in the air. A low vibration began in the floor, rising through her boots and into her bones. The chandelier crystals above tinkled against each other, a delicate counterpoint to the growing rumble.

"They're using phase disruptors," said Commander Rask, her second-in-command, his artificial eye whirring as it adjusted focus. "Standard Drakorian siege tactic. Destabilize the molecular structure of the barrier before—"

The rest of his assessment vanished in a thunderous explosion that seemed to compress time itself. The reinforced doors—fifteen feet of enchanted metal and wood that had stood for centuries—did not merely open or break. They atomized. A blinding flash turned night to day for one searing moment, followed by a concussive wave that threw the front line of defenders backward like rag dolls.

Through the swirling vortex of dust and debris, the first wave of Drakorian shock troops poured into the hall. Their armor—sleek black carapaces with pulsing purple energy lines—made them appear more machine than organic. Their movements held the precision of those who had enacted this same scenario on a hundred worlds before.

"HOLD!" Elara bellowed, raising her command staff. "On my mark!"

The palace guards tensed, energy weapons charged to maximum capacity, fingers hovering over triggers. The first wave of Drakorians advanced in perfect formation, their footsteps eerily synchronized.

"NOW!"

A horizontal curtain of crimson energy erupted from the defenders' position, each beam seeking the vulnerable joint sections of Drakorian armor. The front line of invaders faltered, several dropping to the marble floor with smoking holes in their carapaces. For a brief, hopeful moment, it seemed the defenders had scored a decisive first strike.

Then the second wave entered, and with them came General Malakai Drach.

Where his troops moved with mechanical precision, Malakai flowed like liquid shadow. His custom battle suit—a masterpiece of Drakorian war-craft—enhanced his already imposing height. Every plate and joint radiated malevolent purpose, the entire ensemble less armor than extension of the man's will. But it was his eyes that drew attention—molten amber orbs that surveyed the chaos with the dispassionate interest of a predator assessing prey.

"Is this truly the best defense Eldoria can muster?" His voice carried effortlessly across the cacophony of battle, deep and resonant with an unnatural harmonic that set teeth on edge. "How disappointing."

With a casual gesture that belied its devastating effect, he sent a wave of sickly green energy rolling toward the right flank of defenders. Where it touched, matter simply... unraveled. Guards who had served faithfully for decades were reduced to drifting particles, their expressions of horror the last thing to fade.

"Battlemages, forward!" Elara commanded, refusing to let shock paralyze her. "Containment protocol Zeta!"

Five robed figures stepped from behind the defensive line, their hands already weaving complex patterns. The air between them and the advancing Drakorians shimmered as competing magical forces clashed, creating a prismatic display of deadly energies, each holding their ground.

Commander Rask sidled up beside Elara, his voice low. "Captain, we need to consider the secondary contingency. The royal family—"

"Has already been evacuated to the sanctuary chambers," she finished for him. "Our priority now is buying time."

Rask's organic eye widened slightly. "Time for what? The city has fallen. Our orbital defenses are gone. What are we—"

"We are soldiers of Eldoria, Commander," Elara cut him off sharply. "We follow orders. High Priestess Zara and Grand Necromancer Xaloth required time for their ritual. We will give it to them."

Understanding dawned on Rask's weathered face. "The Sanctuary Protocol. It's actually been activated?"

Before she could respond, a Drakorian battlemage broke through the defensive spell barrier. The enemy caster—face concealed behind a helmet shaped like a snarling beast—sent arcs of purple lightning cascading across the hall. Two palace guards were caught in the discharge, their bodies convulsing before collapsing.

"Return fire!" Elara shouted, raising her command staff and sending a concentrated beam of white-hot energy directly at the Drakorian mage. The beam struck true, punching through the ornate helmet and dropping the caster instantly.

For a fraction of a second, Elara allowed herself the smallest spark of hope. Her troops were fighting with everything they had, their desperation lending them strength beyond their training. Perhaps they could hold long enough after all.

Then Malakai Drach stepped fully into the fray.

"Enough of these games," he said, his tone almost conversational as he strode forward. The air around him distorted with power, purple-black energy coalescing around his gauntleted hands. "I have a schedule to maintain."

With a two-handed thrust, he sent a wave of corrupted energy expanding outward in a perfect circle. Unlike his previous attack, this one didn't disintegrate—it paralyzed. Guards caught in its radius froze mid-motion, their bodies locked in place while their eyes remained terrifyingly aware.

"Much better," Malakai commented, walking casually between the paralyzed defenders. He stopped before one young soldier, studying him with clinical interest. "You Eldorians have always been so proud of your supposed moral superiority. Your magical ethics." He traced a finger along the soldier's frozen cheek. "Yet when faced with extinction, you fight with the same desperation as any other species."

Elara, who had managed to avoid the paralysis field by diving behind a fallen column, rose to her full height. "We fight to protect our world from monsters who would destroy it for power," she declared, her voice steady despite the fear coursing through her. "There is no shame in that."

Malakai turned to her, something like amusement glinting in those inhuman eyes. "Captain Elara Vos. Your reputation precedes you." He gave a small, mocking bow. "Your tactical acumen is impressive. In another life, you might have made an excellent Drakorian officer."

"I'd rather die," she spat.

"That can be arranged," he replied pleasantly. "But first, I'd like some information. Where are the witch and necromancer leaders conducting their ritual? The Nexus chamber, perhaps?"

Elara's momentary hesitation told him everything.

Malakai smiled, the expression grotesque on his scarred features. "Thank you, Captain. Your cooperation is noted." He turned to his officers. "Secure this hall. Execute the paralyzed—slowly. I want their screams to echo through every corridor of this palace. Let any remaining resistance understand the futility of their position."

"And you, General?" questioned one of his lieutenants.

"I have a ritual to interrupt." Malakai's gaze returned to Elara. "Captain Vos will escort me personally."

"Never," she hissed, raising her command staff for one final, desperate attack.

Malakai moved with supernatural speed, closing the distance between them before she could discharge the weapon. His hand closed around her throat, lifting her off the ground with inhuman strength.

"Your bravery is commendable but misplaced," he said, studying her like an interesting specimen. "You will take me to the Nexus chamber, Captain. Not because I'll torture you—though I would excel at that—but because I'm offering you a choice."

He lowered her slightly, allowing her feet to touch the ground but maintaining his grip. "Guide me, and I'll grant your remaining troops quick deaths. Refuse, and I'll ensure they suffer for days, preserved at the edge of life by Drakorian medical technology. Their agony will be legendary, their screams composed into a symphony that will echo through this palace until we reduce it to rubble."

Elara's eyes darted to her remaining soldiers—those not paralyzed were being systematically surrounded and disarmed. Young faces looked to her for guidance, for some miracle strategy that would save them. There was none to give.

"Well, Captain?" Malakai prompted. "What will it be? Mercy for your troops, or a lesson in true suffering?"

Elara closed her eyes briefly, decades of training and duty warring with the immediate reality. When she opened them again, they held the resignation of one who had calculated all possible outcomes and found no victories.

"The northwest corridor," she said, her voice hollow. "Behind the ancestral tapestry is a hidden passage that leads directly to the lower chambers."

Malakai released her throat, satisfaction evident in his posture. "Excellent choice, Captain. Lieutenant Vex, hold this position. Secure any stragglers. I'll proceed with Captain Vos to claim our prize."

"As you command, General," the brutish lieutenant acknowledged. "What of your promise regarding the prisoners?"

Malakai cast a cold glance at the captive palace guards. "Execute them quickly, as agreed. We are not savages, after all." His lips curved in a mockery of a smile. "We are merely inevitable."

As Malakai gestured for Elara to lead the way, she caught a glimpse of Commander Rask, still free but cornered, his eyes meeting hers in silent communication. The slight adjustment of his hand toward his emergency beacon told her that her final order had been transmitted—the warning to the ritual chamber that their position had been compromised.

It would have to be enough. Whatever Zara and Xaloth were attempting, they would now know time had run out. The Sanctuary Protocol would need to be accelerated.

"This way, General," Elara said, straightening her spine with the last shreds of her dignity. "Though I warn you, the chamber is heavily warded. Even with your power, breaking through will be difficult."

"My dear Captain," Malakai replied as they left the grand hall behind, the execution of her troops already beginning, "difficulty is merely an opportunity to demonstrate superiority. The ritual will fail. The Nexus will be mine. And Eldoria's power will serve as the foundation for a new order—my order."

As they walked through the once-magnificent corridors now stained with the evidence of war, Elara silently recited the ancient Eldorian prayer for the fallen. Not just for her troops, but for her world. For everything that was about to be lost.

And perhaps—though she scarcely dared hope—for whatever small flame of Eldoria might escape to burn elsewhere, beyond Malakai's reach.

Chapter 13
SHADOWS

Morning sunlight dappled the sidewalk of Willow Street as Bree and Molly made their way toward Main Street, both sisters energized despite the late night of celebration. The initiation ceremony had left them with a lingering sense of connection to something larger than themselves—a feeling that hummed just beneath their skin like electricity.

"I still can't believe we're actually members of the coven now," Molly said, adjusting the strap of her messenger bag. "I mean, I knew it would happen eventually, but it feels different than I expected."

Bree nodded, understanding exactly what her sister meant. "It's like... I always knew magic was real, but now I *feel* it. Does that make sense?"

"Perfect sense," Molly agreed. "Like we've been looking through a window all these years, and someone finally opened the door."

They walked in comfortable silence for a moment, each processing their own thoughts about the previous evening. The memory of reciting the oath still sent shivers down Bree's spine—the way the energy had surged through the barn when they'd spoken the final words, binding them to the coven.

As they approached Sam's house, Bree's steps unconsciously slowed. There he was, sitting on his porch swing with a notebook balanced on his knee, looking every bit the stereotypical writer. His dark hair fell across his forehead as he hunched over the page, pen moving rapidly. Sunlight caught on his wire-rimmed glasses, momentarily obscuring his eyes.

He must have sensed their presence because he looked up suddenly, a warm smile spreading across his face as he caught sight of them.

"Good morning, Bree, Molly," he called, raising a hand in greeting.

"Morning, Sam," they responded in unison, returning his smile.

Bree noticed how his eyes lingered on her for a moment longer than necessary, and she felt a flutter of something unfamiliar in her chest. She'd never been particularly interested in dating—her focus had always been on books and studies—but there was something about Sam Sorken that intrigued her on a level she couldn't quite explain.

"Beautiful day, isn't it?" Sam commented, closing his notebook. "Headed into town?"

"Yes, Bree's starting her new job at Infinitely Books today," Molly replied, a hint of pride in her voice.

Sam's eyebrows rose with interest. "Congratulations! That's a wonderful place—some of the best browsing I've done since moving to Ballad."

"Thanks," Bree said, finding her voice. "I'm really excited about it."

An awkward moment of silence followed, with Bree suddenly very aware of how she looked in her carefully chosen outfit—a blue blouse and black pants that she hoped struck the right balance between professional and approachable for her first day.

"Well," Sam said finally, "I won't keep you. Good luck today, Bree."

"Thanks," she managed again, mentally kicking herself for not being more articulate. "Have a good day with your writing."

As they continued down the street, Bree could feel Molly's eyes on her, practically burning with curiosity and mischief. She tried to ignore it, but her sister's silence was almost worse than whatever teasing comment was surely coming.

"What?" Bree finally asked, unable to stand it any longer.

Molly nudged her gently with an elbow, a mischievous glint in her eye. "So, little sister," she began, her voice low and conspiratorial, "what do you think about our mysterious neighbor?"

Bree felt heat rise to her cheeks. "What do you mean?"

"Oh, come on," Molly pressed. "You know exactly what I mean. The way he looks at you? The way you suddenly forget how to form complete sentences around him?"

"I do not!" Bree protested, though she knew it was partly true. "He seems nice enough," she said, her gaze fixed firmly on the sidewalk ahead. "I mean, he was friends with Grandma Nancy, so he can't be all bad, right?"

Molly grinned, her expression knowing. "Oh, I think he's more than just 'nice enough,'" she teased, her eyebrows waggling suggestively. "And I bet he thinks the same about you."

Bree, her blush deepening, swatted at her sister's arm. "Stop it," she mumbled, unable to suppress a small, pleased smile. "I barely know him."

"But you want to," Molly observed, her voice softening. "I can tell."

Bree sighed, unable to deny it. "Maybe. I don't know. There's something about him that feels... I can't explain it. Like I've known him before or something."

"Maybe you have," Molly suggested with a thoughtful expression. "In another life or something. The coven does believe in reincarnation, after all."

"Now you're just being ridiculous," Bree laughed, but the idea settled somewhere in her mind, a possibility she couldn't entirely dismiss.

"Well, maybe it's time to change that—the barely knowing him part, I mean," Molly suggested, her tone turning more serious. "I mean, he's obviously connected to our world somehow, even if we don't know how yet. And Grandma Nancy trusted him. That's got to count for something."

Bree considered this, remembering the way her grandmother had always spoken fondly of "that nice writer next door." Nancy had never explicitly said Sam was aware of magic or the coven, but there had been something in the way she talked about him that suggested a deeper connection than mere neighbors.

"Maybe you're right," she admitted, her voice soft and thoughtful. "But not today. Today, I need to focus on my new job."

As they approached the town square, the morning bustle of Ballad surrounded them. The café on the corner was doing brisk business, the scent of fresh coffee and pastries wafting onto the street. Across the way, the hardware store was just opening its doors, and a produce truck was making deliveries to the small grocery at the end of the block.

Infinitely Books occupied one of the most charming buildings on the square—a two-story brick structure with large display windows and an inviting blue door. The window display featured a collection of summer reading recommendations, artfully arranged around a miniature beach scene complete with tiny deck chairs and parasols.

"Speaking of your new job," Molly said as the bookstore came into view, her eyes sparkling with anticipation, "I can't wait to see what other secrets that loft holds. While you're getting settled in downstairs, I'm going to do a little more exploring, see what other treasures I might uncover."

Bree raised an eyebrow. "You're not planning to get me fired on my first day, are you? Sarah might not appreciate you rummaging through magical texts without supervision."

"I won't rummage," Molly promised, placing a hand over her heart. "Just a little... organized browsing. Besides, I'm a member of the coven now too, remember? I have a right to learn."

Bree, her own excitement rising to match her sister's despite her concerns, nodded eagerly. "Just be careful," she cautioned, her protective instincts kicking in. "And don't get too lost in those books. Some of them looked really old and valuable."

"And potentially dangerous?" Molly suggested with a raised eyebrow.

"That too," Bree admitted. "Magic isn't something to take lightly. You saw what happened to Lucy with the geese."

They both laughed at the memory of Lucy's story from the previous night.

"Don't worry about me," Molly said, giving her sister a playful wink. "I'll be fine. You just focus on making a great first impression and learning everything you can."

Bree paused, her hand on the door handle, as a sudden thought occurred to her. "You know, maybe you should ask Sarah if there's a job opening for you, too," she suggested, her eyes lighting up at the idea. "I mean, you love books just as much as I do, and it would be amazing to work together."

"In a place where we could also study magic between customers?" Molly added, her expression brightening. "That's actually brilliant."

"Right?" Bree agreed. "And with your organizational skills, you'd be perfect for inventory management or something."

Molly's expression turned thoughtful, running a hand through her auburn hair. "That's not a bad idea," she admitted, a smile tugging at the corners of her mouth. "I'll definitely bring it up with Sarah. But for now, let's just focus on getting you settled in."

With a final, encouraging squeeze of her sister's hand, Molly pushed open the door to Infinitely Books, the tinkling of the bell above the entrance announcing their arrival.

The bookstore was quiet at this early hour, the morning sunlight streaming through the windows to illuminate dust motes dancing in the air. The familiar scent of books—paper and ink, leather bindings and the faint hint of vanilla that came from aging pages—enveloped them in a comforting embrace.

Sarah looked up from behind the counter, where she was arranging a display of bookmarks. Her face broke into a warm smile at the sight of the sisters.

"There you are!" she exclaimed, coming around to greet them. "I was starting to wonder if last night's celebration might have left you sleeping in." She gave each of them a quick hug. "How are you both feeling this morning? Any lingering effects from the initiation?"

"I feel..." Bree searched for the right words. "Connected. Like I can sense things I couldn't before."

Sarah nodded knowingly. "That's perfectly normal. The ritual creates pathways for magical energy that weren't fully open before that you weren't aware of. You'll both find your senses heightening over the next few days."

"I dreamed about stars," Molly said suddenly. "Not just looking at them but being among them. It was... intense."

"The Andromeda connection," Sarah said with a smile. "Our coven is named for the constellation for a reason. Many members report similar dreams after their initiation. It's a good sign—it means the coven has accepted you on a deep level."

Bree felt a surge of relief and belonging at these words. The experience had been so strange and wonderful that part of her had wondered if she was imagining things.

"Now," Sarah said, clapping her hands together, "are you ready for your first day, Bree? And Molly, what are your plans while your sister works?"

Molly glanced toward the back of the store with poorly concealed eagerness. "I thought I might browse a bit, if that's okay. Maybe look at some of those special books we saw yesterday?"

Sarah's eyes twinkled with understanding. "The loft is open to all coven members, though I'd appreciate it if you'd let me know before handling anything particularly old or delicate. Some of those volumes require special care."

"Of course," Molly agreed quickly. "I just want to learn more about what we're getting into with all this."

"A wise approach," Sarah approved. "Knowledge is the foundation of responsible magic. Why don't you start with the 'Beginner's Guide to

Magical Theory'? It's a slim volume with a green cover, on the leftmost shelf as you enter the loft."

Molly's face lit up. "Perfect! Thank you!"

"And no spellcasting up there alone," Sarah added firmly. "Reading only for now."

"I promise," Molly said, already edging toward the back of the store. "Have fun with your training, Bree!"

As Molly disappeared toward the staircase, Sarah turned to Bree with a warm smile. "Well then, shall we begin? There's quite a bit to learn about running a bookstore, especially one that serves as both a business and a haven for magical knowledge."

Bree nodded eagerly, the excitement of her new job momentarily eclipsing even the wonder of her recent initiation into the coven. "I'm ready. Where do we start?"

"With the basics," Sarah replied, leading Bree behind the counter. "The register, inventory system, and customer service approach. Then we'll move on to the more... specialized aspects of Infinitely Books."

For the next hour, Bree followed Sarah through the bookstore, absorbing information with eager attention. The store, with its towering shelves and countless volumes, seemed to hold an endless array of knowledge and magic, just waiting to be discovered. There was something comforting about the ordered chaos of a well-stocked bookstore—each volume in its place, yet thousands of worlds and ideas coexisting in the same space.

Sarah proved to be a patient teacher, explaining the intricacies of the store's organization system with clarity and enthusiasm. She had a story for almost every section, anecdotes about particularly memorable customers or special orders that had led to unexpected discoveries.

"The young adult section is over here," she said, gesturing to a nearby shelf filled with colorful spines and eye-catching covers. "It's one of our busiest areas, especially during summer break. The teens in Ballad are quite the readers."

"I would have lived in this section at their age," Bree commented, running her fingers along the spines. "I used to devour fantasy series especially."

Sarah smiled knowingly. "Many witches start their journey through fiction, you know. The imagination is a powerful magical muscle—the more you exercise it by reading about magical worlds, the more prepared your mind is to work with actual magic."

"That explains a lot about Molly and me," Bree said thoughtfully. "We've always been bookworms."

"Nancy encouraged that, I'm sure," Sarah replied. "She was quite strategic about preparing you both, even from a distance."

They continued through the store, with Sarah pointing out the different sections and sharing insights about the regular customers who frequented each area.

"And the non-fiction titles?" Bree asked, her gaze drifting to the far wall where neatly organized shelves displayed books on everything from astronomy to zoology.

"Arranged by subject," Sarah confirmed, a hint of pride in her voice. "With the biographies and memoirs taking up the majority of the space. You'd be amazed at how many incredible life stories are just waiting to be told."

She lowered her voice, glancing around to ensure no ordinary customers were within earshot. "Some of the biographies contain hidden magical knowledge, you know. Accounts of historical figures who were secretly practitioners, coded so that only those with the right perspective would recognize the magical elements."

"Really?" Bree's eyes widened. "Like who?"

"Benjamin Franklin, for one," Sarah said with a mischievous smile. "His experiments with electricity were partly magical in nature. And Marie Curie—her work with radiation had a magical component that the scientific community couldn't recognize."

Bree was about to ask for more examples when a sudden chill ran down her spine—an inexplicable feeling of being watched, of some unseen presence lurking just beyond her awareness. The sensation was so strong and unexpected that she actually shivered, rubbing her arms instinctively.

Sarah, her own senses honed by years of magical practice and a deep connection to the energies of the store, stiffened, her eyes narrowing as she scanned the aisles. Bree, attuned to her mentor's sudden shift in demeanor, followed her gaze, her own intuition prickling with a sense of unease.

"Do you feel that?" Bree whispered, not wanting to attract attention if there were any customers browsing nearby.

Sarah nodded, her expression tense. "Someone's here. Someone with power, but not from our coven."

There, in the shadows of the far corner, they caught a fleeting glimpse of movement, a flash of dark hair and brown skin that vanished almost as quickly as it had appeared. Bree and Sarah, their hearts pounding with a sudden surge of adrenaline, moved quickly towards the spot, their eyes searching the surrounding shelves for any sign of the mysterious figure.

"Hello?" Sarah called, her voice firm but not unfriendly. "Can I help you find something?"

Silence answered them. As they reached the corner, they found only empty space, the lingering sense of a presence that had been there mere moments before now dissipated like smoke in the wind.

Bree, her brow furrowed in confusion and concern, turned to Sarah. "Did you see...?" she began, her voice trailing off as she struggled to put words to the strange sensation that had overcome them both.

"I did," Sarah confirmed, her gaze already scanning the rest of the store for any further signs of disturbance. "A young woman, I think. And whatever it was, whoever it was, I don't think they wanted to be seen."

"Could it have been just a normal customer?" Bree suggested, though she didn't believe it herself. The energy had been too distinct, too charged with something that felt like magic.

Sarah shook her head firmly. "No ordinary customer gives off that kind of energy signature. That was someone with power—untrained, perhaps, or differently trained than our tradition, but definitely magical."

As if in response to her words, the soft tinkling of the bell above the front door echoed through the store, drawing their attention to the entrance. Bree and Sarah, moving as one, hurried towards the sound, their footsteps echoing in the sudden stillness of the store.

But as they reached the door, they were met with only the sight of it swinging shut, the briefest glimpse of long, black hair disappearing into the bright sunlight beyond.

"Should we follow her?" Bree asked, already reaching for the door handle.

Sarah caught her wrist gently. "No. If she wanted to speak with us, she would have. Pursuing her might be seen as aggression, and we don't want to provoke a confrontation when we don't know what we're dealing with."

Bree, her heart still racing and her mind whirling with questions, turned to Sarah, her eyes wide with a mix of confusion and apprehension. "What do you think it means?" she asked, her voice barely above a whisper.

Sarah, her own expression one of grave concern, shook her head. "I don't know," she admitted, her hand coming to rest on Bree's shoulder in a gesture of reassurance. "But I have a feeling that this is just the beginning, that there are forces at work here that we don't yet understand."

She glanced toward the back of the store. "I'm concerned for Molly. Let's make sure she's alright."

They moved quickly toward the "Employees Only" door at the rear of the shop. Sarah reached for the knob, but before she could turn it, the door swung open and Molly emerged from the back room, a green book tucked under her arm. Her expression was excited rather than alarmed—clearly she had been too absorbed in her reading to notice anything amiss.

"Oh!" Molly said, startled to find them standing right outside the door. "I was just coming to find you both! This book is absolutely fascinating—I've never seen anything like these ancient magical techniques before!"

"Molly," Sarah said, her voice carefully neutral to avoid alarming her unnecessarily. "Did you notice anyone else in the back room or up in the loft while you were there?"

Molly looked surprised by the question. "No, I was alone the whole time. Why? Did something happen?"

Sarah and Bree exchanged a meaningful glance before Bree explained, "We think someone was in the store—someone magical who isn't from the coven. We caught a glimpse of them, but they left before we could talk to them."

"Oh!" Molly's eyes widened. "That's... concerning. Do you think they were looking for something specific?"

"That's what worries me," Sarah admitted. "The timing seems significant—just after your initiation, and with the Passing of the Hat ceremony approaching."

Bree, her resolve hardening with each passing moment, squared her shoulders and met Sarah's eyes with a look of determination. "Whatever it is," she said, her voice ringing with the strength of her conviction, "we'll face it together."

Sarah, a smile of pride and affection tugging at the corners of her mouth, nodded in agreement. "You're right," she said, giving Bree's shoulder a final, reassuring squeeze. "But I think it's important that we don't take this lightly. I'm going to speak with my mother about what happened here today. It could be nothing, but the coven should be made aware, just in case."

Molly moved closer, forming a tight circle with her sister and Sarah. "Should we tell Mom too? She's been in the coven longer than we have—she might have insights."

"Absolutely," Sarah agreed. "Mary Ann needs to know about any potential threats, especially with..."

She trailed off, but Bree filled in the blank. "Especially with the Passing of the Hat ceremony coming up. That's what you were going to say, isn't it?"

Sarah nodded; her expression solemn. "The transition of power is always a vulnerable time for any magical organization. When Nancy passed, the coven lost not just its High Priestess but also centuries of accumulated knowledge and power that's now contained solely in the hat."

Bree, her brow furrowing with a sudden thought, asked, "Do you think it could have something to do with the ceremony? I mean, with Grandma Nancy gone and the leadership of the coven in transition..."

"It's possible," Sarah admitted, her gaze drifting towards the door where the mysterious figure had disappeared. "The Passing of the Hat is a significant event, and there are always those who might seek to take advantage of a moment of vulnerability or uncertainty. But that would only be from someone who even knows about it."

She turned back to Bree and Molly, her expression serious. "The coven should definitely be informed about this. We need to be vigilant during your training period and especially as we approach the ceremony."

"So, we're still proceeding as planned?" Molly asked. "With the full training period before the ceremony?"

Sarah nodded. "Absolutely. Marcus was clear about the importance of proper preparation, and we shouldn't let an unexplained visitor—concerning as it may be—rush such an important transition. We still have the next week or so to prepare you both properly."

"But we should be careful," Bree added, her voice thoughtful. "Maybe increase security around the hat?"

"A wise suggestion," Sarah agreed. "I'll speak with the elders about setting protective wards, just as a precaution. The hat is safest in your home for now, but we should take no chances."

Bree felt a new sense of responsibility settling onto her shoulders. "I'll talk to Mom when we get home," she said, her voice steady and determined. "We'll make sure that everything is secure, and that the coven is aware of what happened today."

Sarah reached out to squeeze Bree's hand, her expression warm with affection. "You're already thinking like a coven member," she said with approval. "Cautious but not fearful. The Andromeda Coven is lucky to have both of you. Never forget that."

As they separated, the bell above the door jingled again, and all three women turned sharply, still on edge from their earlier encounter. This time, however, it was Sam Sorken who stepped through the doorway, his tall frame silhouetted against the bright sunlight outside.

"Good morning, ladies," Sam said with a friendly smile, glancing around the store before his gaze settled on Bree. "Hope I'm not interrupting?"

"Not at all," Sarah replied smoothly, recovering quickly from their tense conversation. "Just showing Bree the ropes on her first day. What brings you to Infinitely Books?"

Sam stepped fully into the store, closing the door behind him. He wore a casual button-down shirt over jeans, and his hair looked slightly windblown, as if he'd been working outside. "I'm looking for a reference book for my new novel. Something about Middle Eastern mythology, specifically the Jinn."

"The Jinn?" Molly repeated, perking up with interest. "As in genies from Arabic folklore?"

"That's the popular conception," Sam agreed, "but they're much more complex than the simplified Western idea of wish-granting spirits in lamps. In various Middle Eastern traditions, they're a whole separate category of beings—not quite angels, not quite demons, but something in between. Created from smokeless fire, according to some accounts."

Bree noticed Molly watching her with barely concealed interest, no doubt analyzing her every reaction to Sam. She tried to maintain a professional demeanor but couldn't help feeling a flutter of excitement at his unexpected appearance.

"That sounds fascinating," Bree said, genuinely interested despite her self-consciousness. "Do you have a specific title in mind?"

"No, not really," Sam admitted. "Just looking for something that is comprehensive. The older the better, preferably something with authentic folklore rather than pop culture interpretations."

Before Bree could respond, Kristy emerged from the back office, carrying a stack of new releases to be shelved. "Morning, everyone! Oh, hello Sam," she added with a friendly nod.

"Kristy," Sam acknowledged with a smile. "How are things?"

"Busy as always," Kristy replied, setting down the books on the counter. "Especially with the fair starting tomorrow night. Everyone's been coming in for reading material to enjoy between carnival rides and cotton candy."

"The fair?" Bree asked, momentarily distracted from their book search. "I didn't realize it was that time of year already."

"Annual Ballad Spring Fair," Kristy confirmed. "Rides, games, food stands—the whole traditional small-town experience. They set up in the old field at the edge of town each year. It's actually quite fun, even for us grown-ups."

Sam's expression brightened. "That's right, I'd forgotten all about it." He hesitated for a moment, then turned to Bree. "I don't suppose... would you be interested in going? Maybe tomorrow evening, after your shift?"

The question hung in the air for a moment. Bree was acutely aware of Molly suddenly becoming very interested in a nearby bookshelf, though she was clearly straining to hear every word. Sarah and Kristy, both busied themselves with inventory tasks that conveniently kept them within earshot.

"I, um..." Bree felt her cheeks warm as she realized everyone was waiting for her answer, despite their poor attempts to pretend otherwise. "Yes, that sounds fun. I'd like that."

Sam's smile widened, genuine pleasure lighting his features. "Great! I could pick you up here after closing? Around six?"

"Perfect," Bree agreed, trying to ignore Molly's not-so-subtle thumbs up from behind a display of bestsellers.

Sarah cleared her throat. "Now, about that book on the Jinn—I think I know just what you're looking for, Sam. Let me check the back room."

As Sarah disappeared into the rear of the store, Kristy suddenly remembered a display that needed arranging on the complete opposite side of the shop, and Molly became intensely fascinated with the spines of the mystery novels—all thinly veiled attempts to give Bree and Sam a moment of privacy.

"They're not exactly subtle, are they?" Sam commented in a low, amused voice.

Bree laughed softly, feeling some of her nervousness dissolve. "About as subtle as a carnival barker."

"So," Sam said, leaning against the counter, "how's your first day going? Aside from everyone's apparent interest in your social life."

"It's been... eventful," Bree replied carefully, not wanting to mention the mysterious visitor. "But good. I've always loved books, so working here feels right somehow."

"I can see that," Sam said, his voice warm. "You have that look people get when they're exactly where they're meant to be."

Before Bree could respond to this unexpectedly perceptive comment, Sarah returned from the back room, a thick, leather-bound tome clutched in her hands.

"Found it!" she announced, holding up the book. "The Complete History and Mythology of the Jinn, by Dr. Cyrus Alamut. This should have everything you're looking for, Sam."

Sam, momentarily distracted from Bree, reached for the book with evident delight. "This is perfect," he said, examining the embossed cover with its intricate geometric patterns. "Exactly what I needed for my research."

He turned toward the door, the book tucked securely under his arm. "Thank you for your help. And I'm looking forward to tomorrow, Bree."

Bree called after him, suddenly remembering something rather important. "Sam?"

Sam stopped, his hand holding the door open, turning back with a questioning look. "Yes?"

Bree waved him back inside where she stood with Sarah, trying to suppress a smile. "I'm sorry, Sam, but you're going to have to pay for the book."

Sam's head dropped slightly between his shoulders and his eyes widened in mortification. "Oh! Yes, of course! I, uh..." he handed the book back to Sarah to ring up, his face flushing with embarrassment. "I'm not usually... I didn't mean to..."

Sarah cut him off with a good-natured laugh as she moved behind the counter. "That's OK, Sam. You were mentally preoccupied." She turned to Bree with an approving smile. "Well done! Maybe you'll be the employee of the month!"

As Sarah rang up the purchase, Sam looked at Bree with a rueful smile that made her heart skip a beat. "Whatever I can do to help your career advancement," he told her, his voice warm with humor.

"That'll be thirty-eight fifty," Sarah announced, sliding the book into a paper bag with the store's logo.

Sam pulled out his wallet and handed over two twenties. "Keep the change," he said. "Consider it a contribution to the continued excellence of Infinitely Books—and its newest employee."

"Thank you," Bree said, feeling oddly touched by the gesture.

"I'll see you tomorrow," Sam said with a final smile before heading out the door, this time with his properly purchased book tucked securely under his arm.

The moment the door closed behind him, Molly abandoned all pretense of browsing and rushed over to Bree.

"Did that just happen?" she demanded, her eyes wide with excitement. "Did Sam Sorken just ask you to the fair? And did you just say yes?"

"I believe she did," Sarah confirmed, her eyes twinkling with amusement. "And I believe someone has questions about inventory that urgently need answering in the back office, don't they, Molly?"

"What? Oh! Right," Molly said, not fooled for a second. "Very important inventory questions. But this conversation isn't over," she added to Bree with a grin before following Sarah to the back of the store.

Bree shook her head, laughing softly at her sister's enthusiasm. Despite the unsettling encounter with their mysterious visitor earlier, she couldn't help feeling a flutter of excitement about tomorrow evening. A night at the fair with Sam Sorken—the prospect filled her with a sweet, ordinary kind of anticipation that provided welcome balance to the weightier magical concerns now filling her life.

As customers began to trickle in for the afternoon rush, Bree found herself occasionally glancing at the door, her body twisting from side-to-side, half expecting—or perhaps hoping—that Sam might return with some excuse to continue their conversation. The mysterious visitor from earlier still troubled her, but for the moment, the prospect of the fair tomorrow evening provided a bright counterpoint to the shadows that seemed to be gathering at the edges of her new magical life. After all, even witches needed moments of ordinary joy—Ferris wheels, cotton candy, and perhaps, if she was lucky, a first kiss beneath the carnival lights.

CHAPTER 14
THE CONQUEROR

General Malakai Drach moved through the ruins of the Eldorian palace like a shadow given form. His massive frame, encased in obsidian battle armor inlaid with pulsing veins of purple energy, seemed to devour what little light remained in the devastated corridors. Each calculated step echoed with terrible finality—the sound of one who had witnessed the fall of a hundred worlds and found it routine.

The palace's once-pristine marble floors were slick with blood beneath his boots. Tapestries that had chronicled Eldorian history for millennia now burned, their ashes drifting like black snow through shattered halls. To others, this destruction might seem senseless waste. To Malakai, it was merely the necessary prelude to rebirth.

He paused at a broken window, surveying the panorama of devastation. From this vantage point, he could see the entirety of Lumina spread before him—a city of legendary beauty now transformed into a landscape of fire and ruin. Drakorian war machines methodically reduced ancient spires to rubble while squadrons of shock troops secured strategic locations with mechanical efficiency.

The twisted mass of scar tissue that was Malakai's face shifted into what passed for a smile in the dim light. His eyes—obsidian orbs that reflected nothing and seemed to absorb all surrounding darkness instead—took in the chaos with cold satisfaction. The Eldorians had always been proud of their magical prowess, their advanced civilization, their supposed moral superiority. Now they died like any other race he had conquered—confused, terrified, and ultimately insignificant beneath the crushing weight of his unstoppable power.

"Beautiful, isn't it?" he mused aloud, though no one was present to hear. "The moment when a civilization realizes its own mortality."

An unexpected disturbance in the debris behind him caused Malakai to turn slightly, though he showed no sign of alarm. His enhanced senses had already identified the approaching figure by the cadence of its footsteps—the uneven gait of Lieutenant Vex.

The lieutenant emerged from a cloud of dust and smoke, his enormous frame nearly filling the corridor. Where Malakai was precision and calculated cruelty, Vex was brute force embodied—a mountain of muscle and crude cybernetic enhancements with a face that appeared to have been chiseled from granite with a blunt instrument.

"General," Vex growled, his voice like stones grinding together. The lieutenant slammed his fist against his chest in salute, the impact producing a metallic echo from beneath his armor. "Our forces have breached the central courtyard. The main contingent of royal guards has been neutralized."

Malakai turned fully to face his subordinate, his movement unnaturally fluid. "And the Eldorian Council?"

"Most confirmed eliminated," Vex reported with evident satisfaction. "The King and Queen were executed publicly as you ordered. Maximum psychological impact achieved."

"Yet resistance continues," Malakai observed, less a question than a statement.

Vex's expression darkened, the crude implants at his temples pulsing with irritation. "The defenders retreat with each engagement, but they fight for every inch. The witches have established healing stations throughout the palace complex. Our casualties are... higher than projected."

The temperature in the corridor seemed to drop several degrees as Malakai's displeasure manifested physically. The purple energy lines in his armor brightened ominously.

"Higher than projected," he repeated, his voice deadly soft. "After I personally provided the defensive schematics? After our agent disabled their primary wards? After three months of meticulous planning?"

Vex took an involuntary step backward, primal self-preservation overriding military discipline. "The Eldorian spirit is... resilient, General. They fight with the desperation of those who know they have nothing to lose."

"They fight because they still have hope," Malakai corrected, his scarred hand rising slowly. Dark energy coalesced around his gauntleted fingers, crackling with malevolent purpose. "Hope is a disease that must be excised. Thoroughly. Painfully."

He closed his fist suddenly, and the energy condensed into a pulsing orb of pure destructive potential. "Return to the front lines, Lieutenant. I want the remaining pockets of resistance crushed without mercy. No prisoners. No survivors. Make examples of the leaders—the slow deaths, the ones that linger in memory."

The massive lieutenant bowed his head, a cruel anticipation lighting his eyes. "As you command, General. I'll oversee the executions personally."

"One more thing," Malakai added as Vex turned to leave. "What news of the Nexus chamber? Have our forces secured it?"

Something like unease flickered across the lieutenant's craggy features. "Not yet, General. A combined force of necromancers and witches has established a defensive position there. Our initial assault teams were... repelled."

Malakai's eyes narrowed to obsidian slits. "Repelled? By academics and healers?"

"They've erected some kind of barrier," Vex explained hastily. "Our mages report it's unlike anything they've encountered before—a fusion of death magic and life energy. Three assault teams have been completely annihilated attempting to breach it."

Instead of the expected outburst, Malakai fell eerily still. After a moment of silence that stretched Vex's nerves to breaking point, the general nodded slowly.

"So, old Xaloth has finally learned to work with his witch counterparts," he mused, something almost like respect coloring his tone. "A pity such cooperation comes only at the end. Their combined power might have been formidable if cultivated earlier."

With sudden decision, Malakai strode past his lieutenant. "Continue the elimination of resistance. I will deal with the Nexus chamber personally. This ends tonight."

As Vex hurried back toward the main battle, Malakai proceeded deeper into the palace complex. The sounds of fighting grew more distant behind him as he entered areas that had been largely abandoned during the initial assault. Here, the destruction was less complete—ghostly reminders of Eldorian life remained in the form of half-eaten meals on tables, children's toys abandoned in corridors, the mundane detritus of lives interrupted.

Turning a corner, he came upon an unexpected scene. A group of Eldorian witches had established a makeshift field hospital in what had once been a grand reception hall. Wounded defenders lay on improvised pallets while witches moved among them, their hands glowing with the soft, pulsing light of healing magic.

Malakai paused in the shadows, observing. None had noticed his presence yet—their attention fixed entirely on saving those they could. The dedication was almost admirable. Even knowing their world was ending, they struggled to preserve individual lives, to ease suffering, to maintain their principles until the very last.

Such foolishness. Such weakness.

Yet as he watched, prepared to eliminate this pocket of resistance with a single devastating spell, Malakai's attention fixed on one particular witch. Unlike the others focused on healing, she appeared to be reinforcing the magical defenses around the makeshift hospital. Her hands wove complex patterns in the air, creating shimmering webs of protective energy that crackled with surprising potency.

Her copper hair caught the flickering light of enchanted lamps, creating the illusion of living flame cascading down her back. When she turned slightly, Malakai glimpsed a profile of striking beauty—not the fragile prettiness common among Eldorian nobility, but a fierce, wild beauty tempered by intelligence and determination.

Something about her triggered a response in him that Malakai had thought long excised—a flicker of recognition, perhaps even respect. In her movements, he sensed not just power but purpose. Not just skill but vision.

As if sensing his scrutiny, the young witch suddenly turned, her emerald eyes locking directly with his across the chamber. Where others would have shown fear, confusion, or denial upon facing Eldoria's destroyer, her gaze held only clear-eyed defiance.

In that moment of connection, Malakai perceived something that disturbed him far more than any weapon could have—she saw him. Not just the scarred exterior or the mantle of power, but something deeper. Something true.

The moment stretched between them; a silent communication more profound than words. Then, deliberately, she turned away—not in retreat, but in dismissal. As if he, for all his terrible power, was ultimately irrelevant to what truly mattered.

Malakai felt an emotion he had not experienced in decades: uncertainty. His hand, raised to unleash catastrophic destruction upon his enemies, hesitated for a crucial moment. The witch had already moved on, hurrying down a narrow, torch-lit side corridor that Malakai knew led toward the heavily guarded Nexus chamber.

Curiosity overcame his initial impulse to obliterate the hospital and everyone in it. Instead, he followed the young witch, moving like a shadow along the parallel corridor, observing through gaps in the damaged walls.

She moved with purpose, navigating the chaotic palace with the confidence of one following a connection rather than a map. When she reached the antechamber of the Nexus, she paused briefly at the threshold, her gaze falling upon the circle of necromancers within.

At the edge of the formation stood a young man Malakai recognized from intelligence reports—Sameril, Xaloth's most promising student. The one whose understanding of necromantic theory had impressed even Drakorian mages who had studied intercepted communications.

For a heartbeat, Sameril and the copper-haired witch locked eyes across the chamber. Something passed between them—something profound and intensely personal that transcended the horror surrounding them. The connection was so palpable that Malakai could almost see it manifest physically—a golden thread of light binding two souls across the arbitrary divisions of their magical disciplines.

In that moment of witness, Malakai experienced a rare insight. These two young practitioners—one of death, one of life—represented something his meticulous planning had not accounted for. Their connection was not just romantic affection or physical attraction, but a fundamental harmony between opposing forces. A balance that, if fully realized, might pose a genuine threat to his ambitions.

The witch moved on, joining her coven sisters in forming a secondary circle around the necromancers, their combined magic visibly strengthening the barrier that protected the Nexus. Sameril returned to his work, but Malakai noted the renewed vigor in his movements, the straightening of his shoulders—as if the brief contact had transferred vital energy between them.

Fascinating. And potentially problematic.

Malakai retreated from his observation point, recalculating his approach. The barrier protecting the Nexus was clearly stronger than his lieutenants had reported. Direct assault would be costly, perhaps even risky for one of his powers. A more strategic approach was required.

As he strode toward the main chamber entrance, Malakai activated his communication implant. "Lieutenant Vex, redirect our elite mage units to my position. And bring the phase disruptors—all of them."

"At once, General," came the immediate response. "Estimated arrival: four minutes."

Malakai positioned himself in the shadows near the main entrance to the Nexus chamber, patient as only an immortal could be. The young witch and Sameril were now variables in an equation he had thought solved. Their connection represented an unknown factor—one that prudence demanded he eliminate before proceeding.

The universe had taught Malakai many lessons over his centuries of conquest, but one stood above all others: true power required not just strength, but the elimination of all opposition. All resistance. All alternatives.

As his elite forces assembled silently around him, Malakai's scarred lips pulled back in what passed for a smile. The barrier, for all its impressive construction, would fall. The Nexus would be his. And if these two young lovers represented some cosmic balance that might threaten his plans—well, balance had never been particularly difficult to disrupt.

One simply needed to remove a crucial piece.

With a gesture, he signaled the attack to begin. The phase disruptors activated with an ominous hum; their specialized magic designed specifically to unravel complex enchantments. The barrier would hold for a time—perhaps even longer than his calculations predicted if the connection he had witnessed continued to strengthen it.

But in the end, it would fall. They always did.

And when it did, Malakai would ensure that neither Sameril nor his copper-haired witch would live to witness the new order he would create from the ashes of their world.

Chapter 15
Lights of the Fair

The afternoon sun slanted through the windows of Infinitely Books, casting long golden rectangles across the wooden floor. Bree shelved the final stack of new arrivals, her mind only partly on the task as she recalled yesterday's unsettling encounter with the mysterious stranger.

"Did you talk to your mother about our visitor?" Sarah asked, approaching with a cup of tea in each hand. She offered one to Bree, who accepted it gratefully.

"I did," Bree confirmed, leaning against the bookshelf. "She was concerned but not panicked. She said she'd reach out to Elaine Warren and some of the other elders."

Sarah nodded, stirring her tea thoughtfully. "My mother said the same. The coven's setting up some additional protective wards around key locations, especially your house where Nancy's hat is kept."

"Do they have any idea who it might have been?" Bree asked, lowering her voice though the store was empty of customers at the moment.

Sarah shook her head. "Nothing definitive. Mom mentioned there are a few possibilities—perhaps a witch from another tradition passing through, or someone with latent abilities who was drawn to the magical energy here without fully understanding why."

"Or someone with less benign intentions," Bree added quietly.

"Always a possibility," Sarah acknowledged. "But the coven's been protecting Ballad for generations. Your grandmother put particularly strong wards around your family before she passed, and now the elders are reinforcing them."

Molly emerged from the back room, carrying a box of bookmarks. "Mom also said not to let it ruin our reintegration into Ballad," she reminded Bree. "Specifically, she said you should still go on your date tonight."

Bree felt her cheeks warm. "She did not say that."

"Not in those exact words," Molly conceded with a grin, "but she definitely implied it when she said we shouldn't let uncertainty stop us from living our lives."

Sarah laughed softly. "Mary Ann always did have a practical approach to magical concerns. She's right, though. The coven will handle the investigation, and you two should continue your training and, yes, even social engagements."

"Speaking of which," Kristy called from the register, where she was counting the day's receipts, "someone should probably start getting ready for a certain carnival date with a certain handsome neighbor."

"It's just the fair," Bree protested, though she couldn't help glancing at the clock.

"Which is exactly why you've checked the time twelve times in the last hour," Molly teased. "Go on. Sarah said you could leave early to get ready."

"I did say that" Sarah confirmed with a smile. "We're almost closed anyway, and Molly and Kristy can handle the last few minutes."

Bree hesitated, then relented. "If you're sure..."

"Very sure," Sarah said firmly. "Go have fun. The coven will handle the mysterious visitor situation, and we'll update you if there's anything you need to know."

"But not tonight," Molly added, shooing her sister toward the back room to collect her things. "Tonight is for Ferris wheels and cotton candy and maybe a little romance."

"Molly!" Bree protested, but she was already heading to get her purse, her sister's laughter following her.

Sam stood before the mirror in his bedroom, adjusting the collar of his navy button-down shirt for the third time. The shirt was simple, casual even, yet he'd changed his outfit twice already. His usually steady hands fumbled slightly with the buttons, betraying a nervousness he rarely experienced.

"Ye look fine, lad," came a gruff voice from the corner of the room. "Stop yer fussin' like a wee bairn on his first day o' school."

Sam glanced in the mirror to see Ezekiel's translucent form lounging in the reading chair by the window. The Scottish soldier's eighteenth-century uniform was as crisp as the day he'd died, though the spectral blood stain on his chest served as a permanent reminder of his violent end.

"I'm not fussing," Sam replied, though he immediately straightened his collar again. "I'm just making sure I look... appropriate."

A lilting feminine laugh drifted through the doorway as Margaret's ghostly figure floated into the room. The Victorian woman's high-necked dress and elaborately pinned hair were a stark contrast to Ezekiel's military attire, but both spirits shared the same silvery translucence that marked them as inhabitants of a realm beyond the living.

"Look at 'im, Ez," Margaret teased, circling Sam with an appraising eye. "All nerves for a simple carnival! Never seen 'im like this before, have we?"

"Because it's not 'simple,'" Sam muttered, reaching for his watch on the dresser. "It's Bree Tanner."

The name hung in the air between them, charged with meaning. Both spirits exchanged knowing glances.

"Aye," Ezekiel said more gently. "We know who she is to ye, lad."

Sam paused, his eyes meeting Ezekiel's in the mirror. "She doesn't remember. And she might never remember. That's not why I'm doing this."

"Course not," Margaret said, her tone softening. "But still special, ain't she? Even without knowin' what came before."

Sam nodded, unable to argue the point. Whether Bree remembered her past life as Briella or not, he was drawn to her in this life too—her intelligence, her curiosity, her gentle compassion for others, and the captivating way her eyes lit up when she talked about books or ideas that excited her passionate mind.

"Don't go rushin' things," Ezekiel cautioned, standing and adjusting his spectral uniform out of ancient habit. "The lass deserves proper courtin', not some scoundrel with presumptions."

"I know how to behave, Ez," Sam said with a hint of exasperation. "I'm taking her to the fair, not proposing marriage."

"Sam'll be a perfect gentleman," Margaret insisted, floating protectively between the two men. "Won't ya, Sam? Just remember to bring 'er back at a decent hour. Girl's got a protective family, she does."

"More than she knows," Sam murmured, thinking of Nancy Tanner and the protective spells she'd woven around her granddaughters—spells he could sense but never mentioned to the old witch during their long friendship.

He checked his watch—5:30. He'd need to leave soon to pick Bree up from the bookstore at six. With a final glance in the mirror, he grabbed his leather jacket from the bed and headed for the door.

"Don't wait up," he called over his shoulder to the spirits, who both laughed at the old joke between them.

"We ain't goin' nowhere," Margaret called after him, throwing her arm up into the air. "Never do!"

"And mind yer manners!" Ezekiel added. "A proper gentleman keeps his hands to himself on a first outing!"

Sam shook his head, smiling despite his nervousness. His unusual housemates had been with him for years, ever since he'd discovered his ability to see—and eventually summon—the dead. They were family now, annoying and overprotective as they might be.

As he climbed into his old blue pickup truck, he glanced back at the house, catching glimpses of both spirits watching from the upstairs window. They waved, Margaret with enthusiasm and Ezekiel with military precision, and Sam felt a surge of affection for them both.

The drive to Infinitely Books took only minutes in Ballad's light early evening traffic. Sam pulled up outside just as Sarah was turning the sign to "Closed" and Bree emerged from the doorway.

She looked beautiful in a simple dress of deep green under a light jacket, her dark hair loose around her shoulders. Sam felt his breath catch as she spotted his truck and smiled, waving as she said a quick goodbye to Sarah.

"Right on time," Bree said as she climbed into the passenger seat. "I thought I might be keeping you waiting. Sarah had some last-minute inventory questions."

"Perfect timing," Sam assured her, trying not to stare. "You look... really nice."

A slight blush colored Bree's cheeks. "Thanks. So do you."

An awkward moment of silence followed both of them, suddenly shy despite their easy conversation in the bookstore the day before.

"So," Sam said, putting the truck in gear, "ready for cotton candy and questionable carnival rides?"

Bree laughed, the tension breaking. "Absolutely. I haven't been to the Ballad Fair since I was a teenager. Is it still set up in the old field on Route 16?"

"Same place," Sam confirmed, pulling away from the curb. "Some traditions never change in this town."

As they drove through Ballad's quiet streets toward the outskirts of town, Bree asked, "How's the research going? Did you find what you needed in that book on the Jinn?"

"It's fascinating," Sam said, genuinely enthusiastic. "The folklore is much richer than most Western accounts suggest. The Jinn are complex beings with their own societies, moral codes, even religious beliefs. Did you know they're considered to be made from 'smokeless fire' while humans were created from clay?"

"I didn't," Bree admitted. "Though it reminds me of some other creation myths I've read. Is this research for your next novel?"

Sam nodded, careful not to reveal too much. "I'm exploring the idea of beings that exist alongside humans but in a different... state of being, I guess you could say. Visible sometimes, invisible others. Powerful but bound by their own rules and limitations."

"That sounds absolutely fascinating," Bree said, and he could hear the genuine intellectual interest in her voice, her curiosity clearly piqued by the concept. "Will you let me read it when it's done? I'd love to be one of your first readers."

"You'll be the first," Sam promised, feeling a pleasant warmth at her interest in his work.

They crested a small hill, and suddenly the fairgrounds came into view, a riot of colored lights against the deepening twilight. The Ferris wheel rose above the rest, its slow rotation creating a mesmerizing pattern of movement and light. Even from a distance, they could hear the distant music and the mingled sounds of laughter and excitement.

As Sam pulled into the makeshift parking area in an adjacent field, Bree leaned forward in her seat, eyes bright with anticipation. "It looks even better than I remembered!"

"The magic of nostalgia," Sam suggested with a smile. "Things from childhood always seem more magical in memory."

Something flickered in Bree's expression at the word "magical," but it passed so quickly that Sam wondered if he'd imagined it.

They walked from the parking area to the entrance, where a banner proclaimed "103rd Annual Ballad Spring Fair" in bold red letters. The ticket booth was manned by a cheerful elderly woman.

"Two wristbands, please," Sam said, smoothly changing the subject as he handed over some bills.

Armed with neon orange wristbands that would grant them access to all the rides, they entered the fairgrounds. The sensory experience was immediate and overwhelming—the sweet scent of funnel cakes and cotton candy, the mechanical whir and cheerful music of the rides, the colorful lights that transformed the ordinary field into a wonderland of excitement.

"Where should we start?" Sam asked, watching Bree take it all in with evident delight.

She pointed to a row of game booths. "How's your aim? I bet you can't win me one of those ridiculous oversized teddy bears."

Sam grinned at the challenge. "Questioning my carnival game skills already? I'll have you know I once won three goldfish in a single night."

"And how long did these champion goldfish live?" Bree asked skeptically.

"About three days," Sam admitted. "But that was the fault of my cat, not my fish-keeping abilities."

They headed for the game booths, where Sam paid for three attempts at a ring toss. His first two tries fell short, but the third landed perfectly around the neck of a bottle.

"Not bad," Bree said, accepting the small stuffed penguin that was his prize. "Though I notice it's not quite the oversized bear I was expecting."

"That just means we have to keep playing," Sam replied. "By the end of the night, you'll need a truck just to get your prizes home."

They moved from game to game, their competitive spirits emerging as they challenged each other. Bree proved surprisingly skilled at the balloon dart throw, popping enough balloons to win a medium-sized unicorn with rainbow hair that she immediately presented to Sam.

"For your writing desk," she said solemnly. "Every serious author needs a rainbow unicorn for inspiration."

Sam accepted it with equal solemnity. "It'll go right next to my computer. My muse in plush form."

As they wandered through the fair, their initial awkwardness gradually melted away, replaced by an easy camaraderie that felt both new and somehow familiar. They shared stories of their childhoods—Sam's in a small town in Oregon, Bree's split between Ballad and the city where she'd moved with her mother and sister. They discovered shared tastes in books and movies, debated the merits of various musical artists, and found themselves laughing more than either had expected.

After trying several games, they decided to explore the food options. The fair offered every imaginable indulgence—corn dogs, funnel cakes dusted with powdered sugar, caramel apples, and deep-fried concoctions that defied nutritional logic.

"I'm not sure I've ever seen a deep-fried Oreo before," Bree said, examining the food stand's menu with fascination.

"Fair food exists in its own culinary dimension," Sam explained. "Normal rules of health and digestion are suspended for the duration of the event."

Bree laughed. "In that case, I'll have one of everything."

They compromised on sharing a selection—nachos covered in bright yellow cheese sauce, a funnel cake, and cotton candy in electric blue. Finding a bench near the carousel, they sat to enjoy their feast while watching children circle on painted horses that rose and fell to the tinny carnival music.

"I used to love carousels when I was little," Bree said, tearing off a piece of the cotton candy and watching it dissolve on her tongue. "My grandmother would take me and Molly every summer. I always chose the black horse because I thought it looked magical."

"Did you believe in magic as a child?" Sam asked, the question casual despite his intense interest in her answer.

Bree looked thoughtful. "I think all children do, don't they? That sense that the world is full of possibilities beyond what adults tell you is real." She paused, then added, "Nancy—my grandmother—she encouraged that kind of thinking. She'd tell us stories about witches and spirits and powers beyond the ordinary world. Made it seem like magic might be just around the corner if you knew where to look."

"And now?" Sam pressed gently. "Do you still believe in those possibilities?"

Something flickered in Bree's eyes—caution, perhaps, or careful consideration of how much to reveal. "I think," she said carefully, measuring each word as if testing its weight, "that the world is more complex than most people realize. That there are things we don't understand, mysterious forces we can't always explain through conventional science or reason."

Before Sam could respond to this intriguingly diplomatic answer, a voice called out from nearby.

"Sam! Is that you?"

They turned to see a short, bald man with a prominent nose and thick glasses approaching. He wore khaki shorts despite the cool evening air, paired with a polo shirt tucked in with military precision.

"Arthur," Sam greeted him, rising to shake the man's hand. "Good to see you. Enjoying the fair?"

"Oh, you know me," Arthur Denim said with a dismissive wave. "Just checking that they've got proper safety protocols in place. These rides need regular inspection, you know. Can't be too careful with public safety."

His eyes landed on Bree, curious and assessing. "And who's this?"

"This is Bree Tanner," Sam introduced her. "She's just moved back to Ballad, into her grandmother's house next door to me. Bree, this is Arthur Denim, my across-the-street neighbor."

"Nancy Tanner's granddaughter?" Arthur's eyebrows rose above his glasses. "Interesting family, the Tanners. Your grandmother had quite the... unusual gardening practices."

"She was knowledgeable about herbs," Bree replied smoothly. "Many people came to her for natural remedies."

"Yes, quite the community herbalist," Arthur said, his tone suggesting he found this less than conventional. "Always had strange visitors at odd hours. And those gatherings! Once a month like clockwork, cars all up and down Willow Street."

Sam intervened, recognizing the territorial gleam in Arthur's eye that usually preceded a lengthy complaint about neighborhood activities. "Arthur works for the city planning department," he explained to Bree. "Keeps us all in line with the local ordinances."

"Somebody has to maintain standards," Arthur sniffed. "Speaking of which, Sam, your hedges are getting rather unruly. Approaching the sixteen-inch height limit stipulated in the Ballad Residential Greenery Code."

"I wasn't aware. I'll trim them this weekend," Sam promised, having had this exact conversation at least monthly for the past three years.

"See that you do," Arthur said, apparently satisfied. "Well, I should continue my inspection. The Tilt-A-Whirl looks distinctly under voltage." He nodded to Bree. "Nice to meet you, Ms. Tanner. Do remind your mother about the noise ordinance if she's planning any... gatherings like your grandmother used to host."

With that, he marched off toward the rides, clipboard in hand though he held no official position with the fair.

"Sorry about that," Sam said once Arthur was out of earshot. "He's harmless, really, just extremely... particular."

Bree was smiling. "Every neighborhood has one, I guess. The self-appointed guardian of propriety."

"Arthur elevates it to an art form," Sam assured her. "But he's actually helped me a few times when packages were delivered to the wrong address, so I can't complain too much."

"Just keep those hedges in check," Bree teased, mimicking Arthur's officious tone.

Sam laughed. "Sixteen inches exactly. I measure with a ruler to avoid citations."

They finished their carnival treats and decided to try some of the rides. The Ferris wheel was first, its slow revolution offering expansive views of Ballad and the surrounding countryside. As their car reached the top, the fair spread out below them in a tapestry of lights and movement, the noise temporarily muted by height and distance.

"It's beautiful from up here," Bree said, gazing out at the panorama. "Like its own little universe."

Sam watched her profile in the colored lights that illuminated their car, struck again by how familiar she seemed despite their limited interactions in this life. Did some part of her soul recognize him too? Was there an echo of their past connection still resonating between them?

"Sam?" Bree turned to find him watching her. "Everything okay?"

"More than okay," he said softly. "Just enjoying the view."

Something in his tone made her blush slightly, though she didn't look away. For a moment, as the Ferris wheel held them suspended between earth and sky, there seemed to be a current of understanding flowing between them, something deeper than their brief acquaintance could explain.

The spell was broken as the wheel began to move again, carrying them back toward the ground. But something had shifted between them, a tentative bridge formed across the gap that separated their worlds.

After the Ferris wheel, they tried several more rides—the carousel for nostalgia's sake, where Bree insisted on riding the black horse and Sam took the white one beside her; the scrambler that spun them dizzyingly and had them both laughing from the sheer childish joy of it; and even the haunted house, which was more cheesy than scary but gave Bree an excuse to grab Sam's arm at a particularly sudden mechanical ghost.

As they emerged from the haunted house, still laughing at the spectacularly unconvincing vampire that had dropped from the ceiling, they nearly collided with two familiar figures.

"Bree!" Molly exclaimed with exaggerated surprise that didn't quite mask her obvious intentions. "What a *completely unexpected* coincidence to run into you here!"

Beside her stood Kristy, the blonde assistant from the bookstore, who gave Sam a knowing smile and barely suppressed a laugh at Molly's poor acting.

"Wow, Molly," Bree said dryly. "Such a surprise to see you at the exact fair where you heard Sam ask me to come yesterday."

"You must be psychic," Bree teased her sister. "Showing up at the exact same place we mentioned we'd be yesterday."

Molly had the grace to look slightly embarrassed. "Pure coincidence, I swear. Kristy mentioned wanting to check out the fair, and I thought, why not?"

"Of course," Bree said, clearly unconvinced. "Just happened to be in the neighborhood of the only entertainment option in town."

Kristy laughed. "Busted. But in my defense, the fair only comes once a year, and Sarah mentioned how good the funnel cakes are."

"They're excellent," Sam confirmed. "Worth the annual pilgrimage."

"So..." Molly looked between Sam and Bree with poorly concealed interest. "Having fun?"

"We are," Bree answered, giving her sister a look that clearly said *behave yourself*. "What about you two? Tried any rides yet?"

"We just got here," Kristy explained. "Still getting our bearings."

"The Ferris wheel gives the best overview," Sam suggested. "Though I'd avoid the corn dogs from the blue stand. I have my suspicions about their meat source."

"Noted," Molly said with a laugh. "We'll stick to funnel cakes and cotton candy. Safe territory."

An awkward pause followed, with Molly clearly wanting to ask more questions and Bree equally clearly hoping to avoid an interrogation.

"Well," Kristy said finally, taking Molly's arm, "we should let you two get back to your evening. There's a ring toss with my name on it somewhere around here."

"Good luck," Bree said gratefully. "Those games are rigged, you know."

"Challenge accepted," Kristy replied with a grin. "See you tomorrow, Bree. Nice seeing you, Sam."

As they walked away, Molly glanced back over her shoulder, giving Bree an exaggerated thumbs-up that made her groan.

"Sisters," she explained to Sam. "Equal parts wonderful and mortifying."

"She seems nice," Sam said diplomatically. "Protective of you."

"Molly's always looked out for me," Bree agreed. "She's technically supposed to be the responsible older sister. She was so excited when I said yes to tonight. I think she worries I don't have enough fun."

"And do you?" Sam asked. "Have enough fun?"

Bree considered this. "I've always been the serious one. Books, studies, planning for the future. But since coming back to Ballad, I've been thinking that maybe I've been missing something. That there's more to life than just... preparing for it."

"It's never too late to start living it," Sam said softly.

Bree met his eyes, a smile playing at the corners of her mouth. "That's exactly what I'm trying to do."

They continued through the fair, trying a few more games and rides before deciding to call it a night as the crowd began to thin. The drive back to Willow Street was comfortable, their conversation flowing easily between topics, punctuated by comfortable silences that felt natural rather than awkward.

As Sam pulled into his driveway, he was acutely aware that the evening was coming to an end. He hadn't felt this kind of connection with someone in longer than he could remember—perhaps not since Briella herself, centuries ago in another life.

"I had a really nice time tonight," Bree said as they got out of the truck. "Thank you for suggesting it."

"Thank you for saying yes," Sam replied, coming around to walk her to her door. The night air was cool, stars visible above the streetlights that illuminated Willow Street.

They walked slowly, neither seemingly in a hurry to end the evening. When they reached the Tanner house's front porch, Bree turned to face him, backlit by the porch light.

"So," she said, a hint of playfulness in her tone, "this is where I live."

"It is," Sam agreed, suddenly feeling like a teenager again despite his centuries of experience. "It's a nice place. Historic."

Bree laughed softly. "Are we really making small talk about architecture right now?"

Sam smiled, caught in his awkwardness. "Apparently we are. I'm better at writing dialogue than delivering it, it seems."

"You're doing fine," Bree assured him, her eyes warm in the soft light.

Taking a breath for courage, Sam leaned forward and placed a gentle kiss on her cheek, a gesture that felt both too bold and not bold enough.

Bree looked at him with a mixture of amusement and challenge. "That's it?"

"Well... I..." Sam stammered, caught off guard by her directness.

Before he could overthink it, he leaned forward again, this time pressing his lips gently against hers in a kiss that was brief but unmistakably meaningful.

When he pulled back, Bree was smiling, her eyes sparkling. "I had a great time tonight, Sam!"

"Me, too," he replied, feeling a warmth that had nothing to do with magic or past lives, and everything to do with the remarkable woman standing before him.

With a final smile, Bree turned and entered her house, leaving Sam standing on the porch with the memory of their kiss still lingering.

He walked back to his own house slowly, hands in his pockets, a smile playing at his lips despite his attempt to maintain his usual composure. The night had gone better than he'd dared to hope—not because of any connection to the past, but because of the very real connection forming in the present.

As soon as he closed his front door behind him, he sensed them before he saw them—the expectant presence of his spectral housemates hovering just inside the entryway.

Margaret materialized first, practically vibrating with curiosity, her ghostly form flickering with excitement. Ezekiel appeared beside her, attempting to maintain his military dignity but clearly just as eager for details.

"So..." Ezekiel began, a knowing grin spreading across his translucent features.

Sam held up his hand, index finger raised. "Nope!"

"But we just—" Margaret started to protest.

"No!" Sam repeated more firmly, though he couldn't keep the smile from his face as he headed for the stairs. "Not tonight."

"The lad's all flustered," Ezekiel observed with satisfaction. "Must've gone well indeed."

"Told ya she'd remember 'im somehow," Margaret said confidently. "Some things, death itself can't erase."

"I can hear you both," Sam called from the stairs, not bothering to correct Margaret's assumption. Whether Bree remembered him from before didn't matter tonight. Tonight was about new beginnings, not ancient history.

And as he closed his bedroom door on the specters' continued speculation, Sam allowed himself to hope—for the first time in longer than he could remember—that perhaps this time, things might work out differently for them both.

Chapter 16

THE NECROMANCER'S LAST STAND

The inner sanctum of the palace—a chamber never meant to see battle—now served as Eldoria's final bulwark against annihilation. Most of the ancient artifacts and sacred texts had been hastily removed, leaving only the essential ritual components surrounding the Nexus. At the center of this sanctified space, Xaloth stood before his assembled disciples, his weathered face lined with a master's determination.

The barrier they had created—a shimmering curtain of spectral energy that pulsed between silver and midnight blue—undulated gently along the perimeter of the chamber. Beyond it lay the Nexus itself, the point where the boundaries between life and death grew thin enough to touch. For millennia, necromancers had drawn upon this wellspring of power, always with reverence, always maintaining the delicate balance between realms.

Xaloth surveyed the faces before him—some young acolytes wide-eyed with fear, others seasoned practitioners grim with understanding. Most of his finest students had already been sent away as part of the Sanctuary Protocol. Those who remained had chosen to stay, knowing what awaited them.

"My brothers and sisters," he began, his voice carrying a resonance that seemed to echo from somewhere beyond the physical plane. "Since the founding of our order, we have been entrusted with the most solemn of responsibilities—to maintain the boundary between the realms of the living and the dead."

He gestured toward the shimmering barrier. "Throughout our history, we have honored that trust, have dedicated our lives to ensuring that the natural order remains undisturbed, that the balance between life and death remains intact."

A violent tremor ran through the ancient stone chamber as another devastating explosion rocked the crumbling palace complex above them. Fine crystalline dust sifted down from the ornately carved ceiling in choking clouds, momentarily obscuring the eerie, pulsating light of the magical barrier protecting the desperate survivors.

"Today," Xaloth continued, undeterred, "we face our greatest challenge. Not just the defense of our world, but the protection of knowledge that, in the wrong hands, could unravel the very fabric of existence itself."

His gaze swept over the assembled necromancers, meeting each pair of eyes in turn. "I will not deceive you. Many of us will not survive this day. But in our sacrifice, we preserve something greater than ourselves—the sacred trust that has been passed down through generations of our order."

He raised his staff—an ancient artifact of twisted bone and gleaming silver, topped with a crystal that seemed to contain a galaxy of stars within its depths. "Pour everything you have into the barrier. Hold fast against the darkness. Remember your oaths, and know that even in death, you serve the balance!"

The necromancers responded in unison, their voices merging into a rhythmic chant that pulsed in harmony with the barrier's fluctuations. The air in the chamber grew thick with power, the boundaries between realms becoming almost tangible as they channeled their collective will into the protective shell around the Nexus.

Xaloth moved among them, his presence bolstering their efforts, his own considerable power flowing seamlessly into the working. Despite his outward confidence, he harbored no illusions about their chances. The moment Sameril and the others had been sent away with the crystallized knowledge of their order, Xaloth had accepted his fate. This was not a battle to be won, but a delaying action—buying precious time for the seeds of Eldoria to take root elsewhere in the cosmos.

The sudden silence above was more ominous than the explosions had been. The fighting had stopped, which could mean only one thing—the palace's outer defenses had fallen. The remaining royal guards and battle mages would have been overwhelmed.

"Prepare yourselves," Xaloth warned, sensing the shift in energies beyond their sanctuary. "They come."

The massive doors to the chamber—fifteen feet of enchanted hardwood reinforced with spells laid down by the founders of their order—shuddered under an impact that defied natural explanation. A second blow followed, and then a third, each more powerful than the last. On the fourth strike, fractures appeared in the ancient wood, spiderwebbing across its surface like frozen lightning.

The fifth blow shattered the doors completely.

Through the swirling dust and debris strode a figure of terrible purpose. General Malakai Drach entered the chamber with the casual confidence of a predator who knows its prey is cornered. His black battle armor absorbed what little light reached it, creating the impression of a moving void. The only color came from the pulsing purple energy lines that traced arcane patterns across the carapace and the molten amber of his eyes.

Behind him flowed his elite guard—twelve towering warriors in obsidian armor etched with ancient forbidden runes that seemed to writhe in the shifting light, their movements unnaturally synchronized like a single organism with many limbs, their faceplates featureless save for vertical slits that emanated the same sickly purple glow as their master's formidable armor.

"So," Malakai's voice carried effortlessly across the chamber, a deep resonance that seemed to vibrate in the bones of all who heard it. "This is where you've hidden it. The Nexus of Eldoria—the wellspring of your vaunted necromantic tradition."

He surveyed the chamber with the practiced, calculating eye of a ruthless interplanetary conqueror, noting the strategic positioning of each exhausted necromancer, the concerning fluctuations in the weakening barrier, the subtle but exploitable weaknesses in their hastily assembled defensive formation.

"I'm disappointed. I expected something more impressive," he continued, voice deep, his tone conversational despite the circumstances both sides faced. "After all the trouble we've gone through to reach this place."

Xaloth stepped forward, positioning himself between Malakai and the barrier. "You've gone to considerable trouble for nothing, Malakai. No matter how many of us you kill, you will never reach the Nexus. We've seen to that."

For the first time, a flicker of genuine emotion crossed Malakai's scarred features—a momentary uncertainty quickly masked by contempt.

"The great Xaloth Sytrig," he mocked, spreading his arms in a grandiose gesture. "Champion of necromancers and defender of the realm. How fitting that we should meet here, at the culmination of my greatest conquest."

"This is no conquest," Xaloth replied, his weathered face impassive. "This is desecration. You seek not to rule Eldoria but to drain it of its vital essence. To corrupt the natural order for your own twisted ambitions."

Malakai's lips twisted in what might have been a smile on a more human face. "Natural order? Such quaint terminology from one who communes with the dead. You've hoarded the power of the Nexus for millennia, restricting its use with your precious 'ethics' and 'balance.' Under Drakorian guidance, its true potential will finally be realized."

"It's true potential would mean the end of all life as we know it," Xaloth countered, his voice rising with barely contained fury. "The barrier between realms exists for a reason, Malakai. Breach it completely, and you doom not just Eldoria but countless worlds to a fate worse than mere destruction."

The Drakorian general's amber eyes narrowed, genuine curiosity evident in his expression. "You actually believe that don't you? That your order serves some greater cosmic purpose rather than simply monopolizing power?"

He took a step forward, and the necromancers tensed, their chanting intensifying as they reinforced the barrier.

"I offer you one chance, Xaloth—not out of mercy, but efficiency," Malakai stated, his tone suddenly businesslike. "Surrender the Nexus. Share the full knowledge of your order. Do this, and I will grant your remaining disciples a quick death rather than the educational experiences my interrogators have planned."

Xaloth's response was immediate and unflinching. "You may have breached our walls, Malakai, but you will never breach our spirit. The secrets of necromancy are not commodities to be traded or stolen—they are a sacred trust we would die to protect."

"As you wish." Malakai's artificial calm dissolved into something far more dangerous—a cold, calculating rage that radiated from him like waves of freezing darkness, turning the very air brittle around him. With a sharp, decisive gesture to his elite guard, his fingers tracing ancient symbols of death that glowed momentarily with crimson energy, he commanded: "Secure the perimeter. Kill the lesser practitioners without mercy or hesitation. Leave Xaloth to me."

The chamber erupted into chaos, panic spreading through defenders' ranks like wildfire. The Drakorian elites moved with inhuman speed, their blades gleaming with malevolent energy as they targeted the necromancers maintaining the barrier. Despite their magical prowess and desperate incantations, the defenders were no match for these engineered warriors whose very existence defied the natural laws necromancers held sacred.

Xaloth raised his staff, and a wave of spectral energy erupted from the crystal at its peak. Three of Malakai's guards were caught in the blast, their armored forms suddenly encased in a ghostly blue light that seemed to freeze them in place.

"Impressive," Malakai acknowledged, drawing his own weapon—a dark-bladed sword that hummed with corrupt energy. "But futile."

He lunged forward with supernatural speed, his blade arcing toward Xaloth's throat in a strike that would have decapitated a lesser opponent. The necromancer barely managed to deflect the blow with his staff, the impact sending him staggering backward.

"You fight well for a relic of a bygone age," Malakai taunted, pressing his advantage with a flurry of strikes. Each blow resonated with dark energy that threatened to shatter Xaloth's defenses through sheer corrupt force. "But you cannot hope to stand against the might of the Drakorian Empire. Surrender now, and I may yet show mercy."

Around them, the battle for the Nexus intensified. Half the necromancers had already fallen, their bodies crumpled on the ancient stones. The barrier flickered dangerously; its integrity compromised as fewer practitioners remained to maintain it.

Xaloth parried another devastating strike, countering with a spell that momentarily distorted the space between him and his opponent. "I would sooner die than submit to the likes of you," he snarled, his normally controlled demeanor giving way to raw defiance. "You and your kind are a blight upon the galaxy—a cancer that must be excised before it consumes all that is good and true."

Malakai's laughter was a harsh, grating sound that seemed to scrape against the very air. "You speak of corruption, old fool, yet it is you and your pathetic order who hoard the secrets of death like misers clutching gold. The power of true necromancy—unrestrained by your outdated morality—could elevate my race to godhood!"

Their duel intensified, magic and blade creating a deadly dance at the center of the dying chamber. With each passing moment, more necromancers fell, and the barrier weakened further.

Malakai leaned in close during a momentary deadlock, his amber eyes boring into Xaloth's. "Give me those secrets, Xaloth. Reveal to me the core mysteries of your dark arts, and I may spare your remaining disciples. Refuse, and I will ensure they experience deaths so prolonged and agonizing that they will beg for oblivion long before I grant it."

For a heartbeat, something like doubt flickered across Xaloth's weathered features—not fear for himself, but concern for those who had chosen to remain with him. Then his expression hardened into granite resolve.

"You speak of power, Malakai," he responded, his voice dropping to a near whisper that nonetheless carried throughout the chamber, "but you understand nothing of its true nature. The secrets of necromancy are not weapons to be wielded by the unworthy. They are a burden we bear for the sake of all life."

With a sudden, unexpected motion, Xaloth disengaged from their deadlock and stepped backward—not in retreat, but with purpose. In the heartbeat of space this created, he slammed his staff against the chamber floor with such force that the crystal at its peak shattered.

"And I will die a thousand deaths before surrendering them to the likes of you."

The released energy surged outward in a concussive wave that momentarily staggered even Malakai. In that crucial moment, Xaloth turned toward the failing barrier and the handful of surviving necromancers still maintaining it.

"NOW!" he commanded, his voice carrying the full weight of his authority as Grand Necromancer.

The survivors responded immediately, abandoning the barrier maintenance to join their power with Xaloth's in a final, desperate ritual. Their voices rose in a chant unlike any heard before—not to maintain separation between realms, but to trigger a catastrophic collapse of the barrier itself.

Understanding dawned in Malakai's eyes, too late. "STOP THEM!" he roared, lunging toward Xaloth with murderous intent.

But the ritual had already reached its critical point. The barrier didn't simply fail—it imploded, drawing all energy toward the Nexus in a rapidly contracting sphere. Necromancers and Drakorians alike were pulled inexorably toward the center point as reality itself began to warp and fracture around them.

"What have you done?" Malakai demanded, genuine fear breaking through his arrogant facade for the first time.

Xaloth, standing at the eye of the metaphysical storm, smiled with grim satisfaction. "Ensured that the Nexus will never be yours. If we cannot protect it, we will destroy it—along with everyone in this chamber."

The implosion accelerated, space and time distorting as the fundamental forces holding reality together began to unravel around the destabilized Nexus. Malakai fought against the pull with inhuman strength, his armor's systems overloading as they struggled to counteract the forces threatening to tear him apart.

"This isn't over, Xaloth!" he snarled, even as his elite guards were reduced to their component atoms around him. "I will find your precious students! I will hunt down every last fragment of your knowledge across the stars! This is not victory—it is merely delay!"

Xaloth, already beginning to dissolve as the uncontrolled energies of the Nexus consumed him, regarded his enemy with calm acceptance. "Perhaps. But delay is all we needed. A new generation carries our legacy now, beyond your reach. The balance will be maintained, with or without us."

As the chamber collapsed inward, as reality itself fractured around the destabilized Nexus, Xaloth closed his eyes. His final thoughts were not of fear or regret, but of hope—hope that Sameril and the others would find safety among the stars, that the knowledge and traditions of Eldoria would take root on distant worlds.

His last conscious sensation was a fleeting awareness of Malakai somehow tearing free of the implosion's grip—the Drakorian's corrupted technology and dark magic creating a pathway to escape what should have been inescapable.

Then there was light—blinding, purifying light as the Nexus released its accumulated energy in one cataclysmic eruption.

And then there was nothing.

The heart of the palace—and half the capital city with it—vanished in an apocalyptic explosion that momentarily outshone Eldoria's twin suns, transforming day into blinding, unnatural night. Where the sacred Nexus had stood for millennia, untouched by time and conflict, there remained only a perfect hemispherical crater, its smooth surface vitrified into glass by temperatures that defied measurement.

At the crater's edge, barely alive and horribly wounded, Malakai Drach pulled himself from the rubble. His armor was shattered, his body broken, yet still he lived—sustained by technology and magics that defied the natural order.

As he gazed upon the devastation, at the ruin of his ambitions, a cold fury took root in what remained of his heart. The Nexus was gone, the direct path to power lost. But somewhere among the stars, the heirs of Eldoria had fled with their precious knowledge.

He would find them. No matter how many centuries it took, no matter how many worlds he had to scour. The secrets of necromancy would be his.

And when they were, the entire galaxy would tremble.

Chapter 17
STREET FIGHT

As the afternoon sun climbed high in the sky, Mary Ann Tanner and Susan Fond moved with practiced efficiency through the Tanner house, preparing for the arrival of their fellow coven members. The anticipation in the air was palpable, hovering like a subtle enchantment in every corner of the warm, inviting home.

Mary Ann, her dark auburn hair pulled back in a loose bun and an herbal-infused apron tied snugly around her waist, arranged trays of freshly baked cookies and delicate porcelain teacups with deft, confident hands that moved with practiced grace. The rich aromas of cinnamon and vanilla mingled with the delicate fragrance of wildflowers strategically placed throughout the house for both beauty and magical protection.

"Do you remember," Susan began, looking up from her platter of sandwiches, her short blonde hair catching the golden kitchen light, "the first time we attended the county fair together? It must have been, oh... thirty years ago now."

Mary Ann's eyes crinkled with fond remembrance. "Of course I do. We were just teenagers then, so full of dreams and possibilities." She placed another cookie on the tray, perfectly aligned with the others. "I remember how we saved up all our money for weeks, just so we could ride the Ferris wheel and eat cotton candy until we felt sick."

Susan's laughter rang through the kitchen, bright and melodious. "And do you remember how Elaine got so dizzy on the Tilt-A-Whirl that she nearly threw up all over poor Trudie?"

"Poor Trudie," Mary Ann laughed, shaking her head. "She was always such a good sport, even when we were young and foolish."

Their voices blended with the ambient sounds of preparation—the clink of teacups, the soft rustle of napkins, the gentle hum of the refrigerator—creating a symphony of domesticity that seemed to breathe life into the very walls of the house.

The living room awaited the gathering, its overstuffed couches and cozy armchairs arranged in a welcoming circle. Family photographs chronicled generations of Tanners, while carefully tended plants and gleaming candles adorned the fireplace mantel, silent witnesses to the magic and mystery that had always been part of the family's legacy.

Upstairs, the bedrooms belonging to Bree and Molly carried the sweet, earthy scent of lavender and sage, drying herbs hanging from the corners in carefully bundled rituals arrangements. Handcrafted tapestries and intricate dream catchers adorned walls painted in soothing blues and greens, each meaningful item a testament to the girls' growing connection to the natural world and their magical heritage.

Outside, the neighborhood seemed to pulse with its own quiet energy. Gardens overflowed with fragrant blooms and lush greenery, humming with bees and birdsong. Golden afternoon light dappled the sidewalks, promising adventures and secrets yet to be discovered.

"I think we're just about ready," Mary Ann said, surveying their handiwork with satisfaction. "The others should be arriving any minute now."

As if on cue, the doorbell chimed, and the first of their coven sisters arrived, bringing with them waves of laughter and conversation that filled the Tanner home with warmth.

The evening progressed in a haze of companionship and shared purpose. Mary Ann, Molly, and Bree greeted each guest with genuine affection, their faces alight with the joy of reunion.

Susan and Sarah moved through the living room with graceful familiarity, distributing treats and pouring fragrant tea as conversation flowed around them, punctuated by bursts of laughter and the soft music from an old record player spinning in the corner.

"And then," Aunt Carol declared from her position in an overstuffed armchair, her fiery red hair gleaming like copper in the lamplight, "he had the audacity to suggest that I was being 'too intense' for a second date!"

Trudie Catshill's round face split into a wide grin. "What did you say to that?"

"I told him," Carol replied with a theatrical flourish, "that if he thought this was intense, he should see me during a full moon."

Jasmine Davis leaned forward; dark eyes sparkling. "And his reaction?"

"Let's just say there won't be a third date," Carol winked, setting off another round of laughter.

Outside, across the street, Arthur Denim stood on his front porch, wire-rimmed glasses perched on his nose as he observed the comings and goings at the Tanner house. Middle-aged with the first signs of balding,

Arthur appeared unassuming, but those who knew him understood that beneath his mild exterior lay a keen, observant mind and insatiable curiosity.

For years, he had watched the women gather for their mysterious meetings, coinciding with inexplicable events that left him puzzled and intrigued. Though he knew nothing of witchcraft or covens, he couldn't shake the feeling that something extraordinary bound these women together, setting them apart from the sleepy, ordinary town.

The sound of a car pulling up the street drew his attention, breaking the evening's quiet. Elaine and Lucy Warren emerged from their expensive dark blue sedan, moving with unusual synchronicity to the trunk to retrieve what looked like mysterious supplies and covered dishes for the gathering. Their purposeful movements and secretive glances around the neighborhood only deepened Arthur's fascination and growing suspicion.

A flicker of movement at the other end of the street caught his eye. Squinting into the gathering dusk, he made out a shadowy figure lurking just beyond the reach of the streetlights. The figure seemed to melt deeper into the darkness, as if aware of his scrutiny and intent on avoiding detection.

Acting on impulse, his heart racing with nervous excitement and investigative determination, Arthur hurried to his cluttered garage and returned with a weathered folding lounge chair. With deliberate, cautious strides that betrayed his amateur surveillance attempt, he positioned himself beside a large oak tree surrounded by concealing bushes in his front yard, settling in to watch the mysterious proceedings unfold.

"What exactly are you looking for?" he murmured to himself, eyes fixed on the spot where the mysterious figure had vanished.

The warm, humid air pressed around him as evening descended, bringing with it a sense of anticipation that matched his own mounting curiosity. Arthur scanned the shadows, searching for any sign of the strange, inexplicable forces that seemed to gather around the Tanner house.

Sam Sorken walked up the sidewalk with a bag of groceries clutched in his arms. His dark hair tousled by the evening breeze, he noticed Arthur seated on his tree lawn, intently watching the Tanner house next door to Sam's own home.

"Good evening, Arthur," Sam called out as he approached, his tone friendly and casual. "Enjoying the night air?"

Arthur started, turning toward Sam with surprise. "Oh, hello, Sam." His eyes darted back to the Tanner house before lowering his voice conspiratorially. "Just checking for potential code violations. Those monthly gatherings of theirs tend to overflow the street parking capacity stipulated in section 5.3 of the Ballad Residential Assembly Ordinance."

Sam shifted his groceries to one arm and moved closer, having endured three years of Arthur's obsession with local regulations. "Is that the only reason you're hiding behind a bush with a lawn chair, Arthur?"

Arthur hesitated, adjusting his wire-rimmed glasses. "It's just... there's something not right about those people living in that house," he said in a low, urgent voice. "I've seen things... strange things... happening around there. Unusual visitors at odd hours, just like with old Nancy Tanner. I couldn't tell anyone else in the neighborhood—they'd think I was crazy. Or worse, they'd accuse me of improper surveillance techniques."

"I see," Sam replied neutrally. "And what kind of strange things have you noticed... if you don't mind me asking?"

Arthur leaned forward; eyes gleaming. "Lights flickering in the windows at odd hours," he whispered excitedly. "People coming and going at all times, like they're attending some kind of secret meeting. And the energy, the feeling in the air... it's incredible if you've never experienced it before."

Sam nodded gravely, his heart quickening at the confirmation of his suspicions. "That does sound... unusual."

For a moment, both of them sat in contemplative silence. Then Sam spoke again, his voice deliberately casual despite his growing curiosity. "Do you mind if I join you? I'd love to see for myself what's got you so intrigued."

"Of course, of course!" Arthur exclaimed, trying to contain his excitement. "Wait here just one second." He hurried back to his garage, returning after a moment with another lawn chair, setting it up beside his own. "Here, make yourself comfortable. Something's going to happen, I can feel it. You'll see..."

The evening air settled around them as they watched and waited, each harboring their own secrets and motivations, each sensing they stood on the threshold of something profound.

For Arthur, it was the thrill of sharing his suspicions with another, finding a kindred spirit who understood the strange pull of the Tanner house.

For Sam, it was an opportunity to observe the coven from a new perspective, gathering information that might prove invaluable in his own secret pursuits.

As they settled into their vigil, footsteps drew their attention back to the Tanner house. Elaine and Lucy Warren approached the front door, arms laden with bags and boxes of food.

Just as the women reached the entrance, a strange flicker of energy rippled through the air, causing the streetlights to dim momentarily. Arthur leaned forward, breath catching in his throat.

Elaine stepped inside, her cheerful greeting audible from where they sat. Lucy, however, paused at the threshold, her hand still on the doorknob as her gaze swept the street with visible unease, as if sensing unseen presences lurking in the shadows.

For a heartbeat, her eyes seemed to linger on their hiding spot. Then the moment passed, and Lucy disappeared inside, her laughter joining the excited chatter drifting into the night air.

"Did you see that?" Arthur whispered, words tumbling out in a rush. "The lights, the way they flickered... and the way she looked, like she knew something was out here, watching..."

"Yes, I saw it," Sam confirmed quietly. "There's definitely something... unusual about this place, about the people who live here." He paused, gaze returning to the Tanner house. "But I wonder if there might be more to it than just strange coincidences and odd happenings. If there might be a deeper meaning, a purpose behind it all..."

Arthur leaned closer, voice dropping to a conspiratorial whisper. "What do you mean? Do you think... do you think they might be involved in something... supernatural?"

Sam shrugged, a hint of a smile playing at his lips. "Who can say? But one thing's for sure... there's more to this neighborhood, and to these people, than meets the eye. And I have a feeling that we're only just beginning to scratch the surface."

Sam studied Arthur from the corner of his eye, amused by how this bureaucratic stickler for rules had inadvertently become the neighborhood's most attentive observer of supernatural activities. For all his fussing about hedge heights and noise ordinances, Arthur Denim was the only ordinary human in Ballad who had noticed the coven's regular gatherings—even if he had no idea what they actually were.

Inside the Tanner house, warmth and camaraderie filled the living room as the Andromeda coven members conversed, their voices rising and falling in a harmonious blend of sisterhood and shared purpose.

"I swear," Aunt Carol exclaimed, gesturing expressively, "it's like the universe is conspiring against me. Every time I think I've found the perfect man, he turns out to be a dud."

"The universe isn't conspiring against you," Trudie said reassuringly. "It's just making sure you're available when the right one finally shows up."

"Well, the universe needs to hurry up," Carol retorted. "I'm not getting any younger, and neither are my—"

Her words cut off abruptly as the lights began to flicker, steady illumination replaced by an unsettling, intermittent dimness. The bulbs sputtered and died, plunging the room into a strange half-light, softened only by the glow of already burning candles.

"What's happening?" Jasmine whispered, an edge of concern in her voice.

Molly rose from her seat, exchanging worried glances with Bree, Lucy, and Sarah. "Let's check outside," she suggested, her tone calm despite the tension visible in her shoulders. "See if it's just us or the whole street."

The four women made their way to the front door and stepped onto the porch. The warm evening air enveloped them, carrying a sense of anticipation that set their nerves on edge. The streetlights had gone dark, their usual steady glow replaced by an eerie blackness that seemed to swallow the familiar contours of the neighborhood.

"Power outage?" Bree suggested, but her tone indicated she didn't believe it.

Lucy shook her head. "This doesn't feel like a normal outage. Something's... off."

From their hiding place, Sam and Arthur watched the scene unfold with rapt attention, eyes fixed on the four women silhouetted against the warm glow emanating from within the Tanner house.

For Arthur, the darkness and strange behavior of the lights added another piece to his puzzle, another hint at the mysteries behind the drawn curtains of the enigmatic house.

For Sam, the moment carried deeper significance. As a necromancer attuned to subtle disturbances in the fabric of reality, he couldn't shake the feeling that something ominous approached—that the darkness blanketing the street heralded a greater mystery yet to be revealed.

They watched as the women descended from the porch and moved down the driveway, steps cautious and measured, eyes scanning the shadows for signs of movement or threat.

Sarah's gaze fixed on a spot just beyond her house. "Who is that?" she whispered tensely, pointing toward the end of the street where a shadowy silhouette loomed in the darkness, barely visible in the faint moonlight.

The distance and darkness made details impossible to discern, but the figure's stillness—its silent, watchful presence—sent shivers down the spines of the four women.

Lucy stepped forward onto the sidewalk, her voice ringing clear and strong in the heavy silence. "Can we help you?" she called, words carrying a hint of challenge.

The figure remained motionless, as if considering her question. Then, with sudden fluid motion, it raised an arm, hand extending toward the women in a gesture both commanding and threatening.

Before anyone could react, a bolt of sickly green energy erupted from the stranger's outstretched hand, crackling through the air as it hurtled down the street. It struck Lucy's arm, sending her spinning sideways with a cry of pain and surprise as the energy left a searing, blistering wound.

"Lucy!" Molly cried, rushing to her side with Bree and Sarah.

Lucy pushed away their supportive hands, face contorted with pain and fury. "Oh, no! No, no, no," she muttered, words spilling out in an angry rush. "You did not just do that to me!" She began pulling up her shirtsleeves, eyes blazing. "Honey, when I get ahold of you, you're gonna get your ass spanked Southern style by a witch with a switch!"

Behind them, the front door burst open as other coven members spilled onto the porch, drawn by the commotion and the unsettling wrongness permeating the air.

Lucy ignored them, focus locked on the shadowy figure as she stepped into the road. "YOU," she yelled, finger jabbing accusingly, "are about to get a whooping!"

Her words echoed through the stillness, bouncing off silent houses like a challenge and warning combined.

The figure hesitated momentarily, seemingly taken aback by Lucy's defiance and the unyielding force of her presence. Then, before Lucy could begin her own attack, it raised both hands, palms facing outward in a gesture of unleashed power.

Twin bolts of green energy erupted from the stranger's hands, streaking down the street with devastating speed. They struck Lucy square in the chest, lifting her off her feet and sending her flying through the air like a rag doll.

She landed heavily with a sickening thud on the hood of a nearby car, back slamming against the windshield with force enough to shatter the glass and trigger a piercing alarm that wailed through the night like a scream.

For a moment, Lucy lay motionless, body sprawled across crumpled metal. Then, with a pained groan and stubborn determination, she raised her head, eyes struggling to focus on the shadowy figure.

"OK... I'm done," she muttered, voice thin and strained as she laid her head back on the shattered glass.

"Lucy!" Elaine cried, rushing into the street with a mother's desperate speed. She skidded to a halt beside the car, hands cradling her daughter's face, eyes frantically searching for signs of life.

Lucy looked up at her mother. "I'm fine, mama."

Aunt Carol emerged from the house, mouth hanging open in shocked disbelief as she took in the scene—the shattered windshield, crumpled metal, and Lucy's still form draped across the hood.

With sharp movements, she pulled a key fob from her pocket, fingers fumbling until she found the right button. With a loud chirp, the car alarm fell silent, leaving a heavy, oppressive quiet in its wake.

Carol turned to the others, her expression a mixture of shock, outrage, and disbelief. "I just paid that damn thing off!" she exclaimed, voice rising with frustration and anger. "Sixty payments! Sixty! And I finally made the last one on Tuesday!"

Her gaze shifted to the figure at the end of the street. With purposeful strides fueled by rage, she stepped into the road, body language radiating power and determination. Her fiery red hair seemed to glow with an inner light of its own as she pointed a manicured finger at the shadowy attacker.

"Do you have ANY idea how hard it is to find a good financing rate with my credit history?" she shouted.

She had barely taken a dozen steps when another blast of green energy erupted from the stranger's hands. It struck Carol square in the chest, the impact lifting her off her feet and sending her flying through the air.

By sheer chance, she landed on top of Arthur Denim, who had risen from his hiding place at the first sign of trouble, moving with surprising agility for his age and unassuming appearance.

They tumbled through bushes and crashed to the ground in a tangle of limbs and gasping breaths, the impact knocking the wind from their lungs and sending shockwaves of pain through their bodies.

For a moment, they lay stunned and unmoving. Then Arthur pushed himself onto his elbows, eyes meeting Carol's with concern.

"Are you alright?" he gasped, voice thin but carrying a hint of quiet strength.

Carol nodded once; jaw clenched against the scream of rage threatening to burst from her throat. As the shock faded, she became increasingly aware of Arthur's body beneath her own, of his arms wrapped protectively around her.

With a sharp intake of breath, Carol felt her anger and fear transform into something warmer, something fluttering she couldn't quite name. She relaxed slightly, gaze locking with his.

"You saved my life," she whispered, voice filled with wonder.

Arthur's cheeks flushed. "Well, I happened to be in the right place at the right time, and according to the Good Samaritan clause of the Ballad Civic Responsibility Code, section 4.2, any citizen who witnesses—"

Before he could finish reciting the municipal code, Carol's lips found his in a fierce, hungry kiss filled with desperate need. Arthur froze momentarily, mind reeling from the sudden intimacy. His clipboard, which he'd somehow managed to keep hold of through the entire ordeal, slipped from his fingers. Then, with a soft sigh that seemed to release decades of pent-up adherence to proper procedure, he melted into the kiss, arms tightening around her waist.

When they finally broke apart, Carol's eyes shone with fierce intensity. "Are you married?" she asked urgently.

"No, I'm not," Arthur whispered, heart pounding with excitement and trepidation.

With a low, throaty growl of desire, Carol captured his lips once more in a searing kiss that left no room for hesitation.

Nearby, Sam watched with growing impatience, mind racing with the need to confront the shadowy figure and end the chaos. With decisive motion, he rose and began walking up Arthur's side of the sidewalk, gaze locked on where the stranger had last been seen. Reaching the next house, he crossed a neighbor's driveway to the other side of the street.

Bree's heart pounded with sudden dread as she noticed Sam's movements. Without hesitation, she broke away from the group surrounding Lucy and Elaine, racing toward Sam with desperate speed.

"Sam, wait!" she called out, though not loudly enough for him to hear.

She couldn't bear the thought of him facing the shadowy figure alone, of him being hurt by the raw power emanating from the stranger. Now he was walking straight into supernatural danger. Though unsure how much help she could provide without exposing her powers, she had to try to protect him.

Just then, the figure at the end of the street vanished, melting into shadows as if it had never existed. The street fell into heavy silence, broken only by ragged breathing as everyone struggled to process what had happened.

With a sudden blinding flare, power returned—streetlights flickering back to life with a hum that filled the air with relief.

"She's gone," Bree said as she reached Sam at the spot where the figure had stood.

"Yes," Sam replied, careful to sound appropriately surprised and confused. Despite his necromantic intuition telling him exactly what sort of entity had just attacked them, he maintained his cover as an ordinary neighbor. The attack confirmed what he had long suspected about the increasing supernatural activity around the Andromeda coven. "I've never seen anything like that before." He turned to Bree with genuine concern, knowing full well she was a witch but pretending to be unaware of her abilities. "Are you alright?"

"Yes, I think so," she answered, though her voice trembled slightly.

Sam scanned the area carefully, noting the faint trace of otherworldly energy that lingered in the air—something he couldn't mention without revealing his own supernatural abilities. "I think we should head back and check on the others. That was one hell of a second date, huh?"

Bree managed a small smile despite the circumstances. "I don't think this counts as a date."

"Fair enough. Rain checks on that movie, then?"

As Bree nodded in agreement, her thoughts shifted to her grandmother's hat and the upcoming ceremony. An uncomfortable suspicion formed—could there be a connection between the hat and this attack? Without thinking, she reached out and took Sam's hand in hers, drawing comfort from his steady presence. She had no idea that her neighbor already knew her secret identity as a witch, just as she remained completely unaware of his necromantic abilities. Two supernatural beings, each keeping their true nature hidden from the other, connected by the simple, human gesture of holding hands in the aftermath of danger.

Chapter 18

THE APPRENTICE'S CHOICE

From a short distance away, Sameril and the other young necromancers watched the unfolding duel with a mix of awe and terror. They maintained their positions behind the barrier they had helped create—a shimmering curtain of spectral energy that separated the Nexus from the rest of the chamber. Though they were participating in the ritual to maintain this protective shield, their eyes never left the deadly dance between their master and the Drakorian general.

Sameril knew that Xaloth was the greatest of their order, a master of the necromantic arts who had stood against the forces of darkness for longer than any of them had been alive. The fluid grace with which he wielded his staff, the complex spells he wove with seemingly effortless precision—these were the hallmarks of a lifetime dedicated to the perfection of his craft.

But they also knew that Malakai's power was vast and terrible. The Drakorian general had delved into the darkest depths of forbidden magic in his relentless pursuit of conquest and domination. His corrupted version of necromancy violated every principle their order held sacred, twisting the natural balance for his own gain.

"He's absorbing the life force of those he kills," whispered Talien, horrified understanding dawning on his face as he watched another defender fall to Malakai's elite guard.

"An abomination," Sameril agreed grimly, his grip tightening on his own staff.

The young necromancers redoubled their efforts, their voices rising and falling in the eerie, otherworldly chant that sustained the barrier between the realms. But even as they fought to maintain the fragile balance that held the dark energies at bay, they couldn't help but feel a creeping sense of despair, a gnawing fear that their efforts would all be for naught in the end.

For Malakai's power seemed to grow with every passing moment, his dark magic surging and swelling like a rising tide of shadows. And Xaloth, for all his skill and strength, was beginning to falter, his movements growing sluggish and his spells losing their potency as the toll of the battle began to wear him down.

Through the carnage, Sam's eyes sought out Xaloth, watching his mentor and friend with growing concern. The old necromancer's staff was flashing and whirling in a dizzying display of skill and power, but even from his position, Sameril could see the toll the battle was taking. Xaloth's movements were growing slower, his counters less precise with each passing moment.

"We're losing ground," murmured Elsira, the youngest of their group, her voice tight with fear as more of their fellow necromancers fell to the Drakorian onslaught.

Sam, his heart pounding against his ribs, knew that the time was fast approaching when they would have to make a choice. To stand and fight to the last, pouring their every last ounce of strength into the defense of their world and their way of life? Or to break and run, to seek some distant refuge where they could preserve the secrets of their order and live to fight another day?

It was a choice that tore at his very soul, a decision that would haunt him for the rest of his days. He felt the weight of the memory crystal Xaloth had given him earlier that day, hidden beneath his robes—the crystallized knowledge of fifteen generations of necromancers, entrusted to him in case the worst should happen.

"The Sanctuary Protocol," Talien said softly, naming what they were all thinking. "Master Xaloth prepared us for this possibility."

"But to leave him—to leave all of them—" Elsira's voice broke with emotion.

Sameril said nothing, his eyes never leaving his mentor's increasingly desperate battle. Then, in a single, heart-stopping instant, he saw the light of realization dawn in Xaloth's eyes. The old necromancer knew that the battle was lost, that the forces of Eldoria were being pushed back and overwhelmed on every front. But more than that, he knew that the true danger lay not in the loss of the city, but in the risk that the secrets of necromancy might fall into Malakai's hands.

For a brief moment, Xaloth's eyes met Sam's across the chaos of battle—a final, wordless communication between master and apprentice. Sameril read the message clearly: *Be ready.*

"Prepare yourselves," he told the others quietly. "Master Xaloth is going to create an opening for us."

"To do what?" asked one of the younger apprentices.

"To fulfill our duty to the order," Sameril replied, his hand instinctively touching the hidden crystal. "To ensure our knowledge survives, even if we do not."

As they watched, Xaloth seemed to gather his remaining strength, his form straightening despite the exhaustion that clearly plagued him. Around them, the barrier they maintained was growing dangerously thin as more of their fellow practitioners fell to the Drakorian forces.

Sameril steeled himself, his grip tightening around the staff that had been passed down to him upon completing his advanced training. He drew in a deep, shuddering breath, and prepared to face whatever fate the gods had in store for him, for his order, and for the world that he had sworn to defend with his very last breath.

And still, the battle raged on, with Malakai pressing his advantage with ever-increasing ferocity, his dark blade slashing through the air with impossible speed as he sought to land the final, decisive blow against the Grand Necromancer of Eldoria.

Chapter 19
Aunt Carol

As Bree and Sam made their way back to the others, the scene before them was one of controlled chaos. Lucy remained sprawled across the hood of Aunt Carol's car, with Elaine hovering anxiously beside her. The other women of the coven had gathered in a protective circle, their expressions a mixture of concern and barely contained fury.

"Is she going to be okay?" Sam asked, his voice low with genuine worry as they approached the group.

Mary Ann turned to him, her face softening slightly at his concern. "We'll take care of her," she assured him, placing a gentle hand on his arm. "Thank you for your help, but we can handle things from here."

Trudie stepped forward; her round face set with determination. "Yes, we've dealt with... accidents before. Lucy will be just fine with us looking after her."

Sam glanced between the women, noticing their protective stances and the way they had subtly positioned themselves between him and Lucy. Though he knew exactly what they were—a coven of witches preparing to use healing magic once he was gone—he carefully maintained his facade of innocent concern.

"Are you sure? I could call an ambulance, or—"

"No ambulance," Elaine said quickly, perhaps too quickly. "It's not as bad as it looks. Family remedies will take care of it."

Jasmine nodded, her dark eyes watching Sam carefully. "We appreciate your concern, but this is a family matter now."

Molly approached, offering Sam a grateful smile that didn't quite reach her eyes. "Really, it's getting late. You should head home and get some rest. We've got this covered."

Sam hesitated, playing the part of the concerned neighbor while inwardly noting how efficiently they were removing him from the situation to protect their secret. "If you're certain..."

"Completely certain," Mary Ann said firmly. "We women will take good care of our own."

Bree stepped closer to Sam, gently touching his arm. "I'll walk you to your door," she offered, giving the others a meaningful look. "Be back in a few minutes."

As they walked away from the group, Bree felt a twinge of guilt for the secrets she was keeping from him. "I'm sorry about all this. Not exactly how I pictured our evening going."

Sam smiled down at her. "I don't think anyone pictures energy bolts and car crashes as part of their evening plans."

"Thanks for trying to help. It was brave of you to go after that... whatever it was."

They reached Sam's front door, and he turned to face her. "Just being neighborly," he said with a gentle smile, though inside he was calculating how soon he could begin his investigation into the entity that had attacked them. "Will you be okay?"

"I'll be fine," Bree assured him, thinking of the healing spells the coven would soon be working on Lucy. "We'll talk tomorrow?"

"Count on it," Sam promised. He watched as Bree hurried back across the street, waiting until she was safely inside before closing his door. Only then did he allow his casual expression to fade, replaced by one of intense concentration as he considered what this attack meant for his own plans regarding the Andromeda coven.

As the members of the Andromeda coven filed back into the Tanner house, their faces etched with a mix of shock and confusion, the atmosphere was one of barely contained chaos and urgency. The events of the past few minutes had shaken them all to the core, leaving them reeling with the realization that their world, their very way of life, was under attack from a powerful, unknown enemy.

Inside the living room, the elder witches gathered around Lucy, their hands gentle but firm as they examined her injuries, their voices low and soothing as they murmured words of comfort and reassurance. Elaine, her face pale and drawn with worry, hovered nearby, her eyes never leaving her daughter's face as she watched the healing process unfold.

"How bad is it?" Elaine whispered, her fingers twisting anxiously in the fabric of her sweater.

Jasmine, who had taken the lead in examining Lucy's wounds, looked up with a grim expression. "I didn't recognize the energy signature. It's left a residue that's resisting our standard healing approaches."

"What does that mean?" Lucy asked through gritted teeth, wincing as Jasmine's fingers probed the angry red mark on her arm.

"It means," Trudie interjected, reaching for her bag of healing herbs, "that we'll need to get creative." She pulled out several small pouches, opening them one by one and sniffing their contents. "Sarah, could you bring me the mortar and pestle from the kitchen? And Mary Ann, do you still keep chamomile and yarrow in the cabinet by the stove?"

Mary Ann nodded, already moving toward the kitchen. "Fresh or dried?"

"Both, if you have them," Trudie called after her. "And any St. John's wort, if there's any left from last season."

Under the soft, golden glow of the lamps, the witches worked their magic, their fingers tracing intricate patterns in the air as they channeled the energy of the earth and the sky, the power of the elements and the strength of their own indomitable spirits. Slowly, gradually, the angry, blistering wound on Lucy's arm began to fade, the skin knitting together until only a faint, silvery scar remained, a testament to the incredible resilience and power of the young witch's body and mind.

"That's remarkable," Bree whispered, having returned from seeing Sam home. She watched in awe as the last of the wound closed before her eyes.

"Not my first magical injury," Lucy said with a weak smile, flexing her arm experimentally. "Though definitely the most dramatic."

"How are you feeling?" Elaine asked, kneeling beside her daughter and brushing a strand of hair from her face.

Lucy sat up slowly, grimacing slightly. "Like I got hit by a bus. A magical, glowing green bus with serious anger issues."

"You were lucky," Sarah observed, clearing away the remnants of the healing ritual. "A direct hit like that could have been much worse."

"Lucky?" Lucy raised an eyebrow. "I was thrown onto the hood of Aunt Carol's car. My back feels like one giant bruise."

"And we'll take care of that too," Trudie promised, already preparing another poultice. "But first, maybe you should lie down somewhere more comfortable than the dining table."

As Lucy was helped to the couch, her face still pale but her eyes shining bright, the conversation turned to the mysterious figure in the street, to the raw, unleashed power that had nearly brought their world crashing down around them.

"I've never seen anything like it," Trudie Catshill murmured, her voice low and troubled. "The way they threw that energy, the way it seemed to come out of nowhere... it was like nothing I've ever encountered before."

"Did anyone get a good look at them?" Molly asked, leaning forward with intense curiosity. "Height, build, any distinguishing features?"

Sarah shook her head. "Too dark, and they stayed in the shadows."

"They knew what they were doing," Jasmine pointed out. "Cutting the power first, staying at a distance... this wasn't random. They came prepared to attack us specifically."

Jasmine Davis, her dark eyes narrowed in thought, nodded slowly. "Historically," she said, her voice calm and measured, "a witch can only do that outside with the help of the weather, the atmosphere, and the lightning. It's a rare and dangerous feat, one that requires immense skill and control."

"Are we certain it was a witch?" Bree asked, wrapping her arms around herself as a sudden chill crept up her spine. "Could it have been... something else?"

The room fell silent as the women exchanged uneasy glances. They all knew there were other magical practitioners in the world—some benign, others decidedly not—but few had ever directly encountered anything outside their own tradition.

"What else could generate that kind of targeted energy?" Elaine wondered aloud. "Demons require summoning and binding. Fae wouldn't use such direct attacks. And most other magical creatures lack the precision we witnessed."

A murmur of agreement rippled through the room, the witches exchanging glances of unease. They all knew the stories, the legends of witches who had harnessed the power of the storms and the skies, who had brought down lightning and thunder with a wave of their hand and a whisper of their will. But to see it done in the middle of a quiet, suburban street, with no warning and no apparent source of power... it was enough to send a shiver of fear down even the most seasoned witch's spine.

"But how did they do it?" Molly asked, her voice small and uncertain in the heavy, oppressive silence of the room. "Where did that energy come from, if not from the sky or the earth?"

"Could they have been using a focus object?" Bree suggested. "Something that stores energy, like a charged crystal or an enchanted artifact?"

Trudie shook her head. "Even the most powerful focus objects have limitations. What we saw tonight went beyond what any normal magical item should be capable of."

For a moment, no one spoke, the question hanging in the air like a tangible thing, a weight that seemed to press down on them all with an almost physical force. And then, with a sudden, sharp intake of breath,

Susan's eyes widened, her face draining of color as a terrible, sickening realization dawned on her.

"The power lines," she whispered, her voice barely more than a breath. "They must have used the energy from the electrical lines to fuel their attack. That's why the power went out, why the whole neighborhood was plunged into darkness. They drained the grid, siphoning off the energy they needed to unleash their magic."

"Is that even possible?" Sarah asked, her brow furrowed in disbelief. "Converting electrical energy into magical force?"

"Theoretically," Jasmine mused, her academic mind already exploring the possibilities. "Electricity is just another form of energy. If someone found a way to harness and transform it..."

"That would require incredible skill," Mary Ann pointed out. "And knowledge that goes far beyond traditional witchcraft."

A stunned, horrified silence followed her words, the witches exchanging glances of disbelief. The implications of what Susan had just said were staggering, the realization that their enemy possessed a level of power and control that went beyond anything they had ever encountered before.

"But who are they?" Molly asked, her voice trembling. "Who would do something like this, who would attack us in our own homes, on our own streets?"

"And why target us specifically?" Lucy added from the couch, her face still pale from her ordeal. "What have we done to warrant this kind of aggression?"

"Perhaps it's not what we've done," Elaine suggested grimly, "but what we have."

No one had an immediate answer. The witches looked at each other, all faces etched with worry and each of them grappling with the magnitude of the threat they now faced.

Suddenly, Mary Ann spoke up, her voice cutting through the tense silence. "What about Nancy's Hat?" she asked, her eyes widening with a sudden, terrible realization. "Is it possible that whoever this person is, they know about the hat and its power?"

A ripple of unease passed through the room, the witches exchanging glances of alarm and dismay. The Hat, they all knew, was more than just a symbol of Nancy's leadership and wisdom. It was a conduit of power, a vessel for the ancient magic that had been passed down through generations of Andromeda witches.

"Grandmother's Hat?" Bree repeated, her voice catching. "You think that's what they're after?"

"It would make sense," Jasmine said slowly. "The Hat contains centuries of accumulated magical knowledge and power. In the wrong hands..."

She didn't need to finish the thought. They all understood the devastating potential of the Hat if it were ever to fall into the possession of someone with malicious intent and the dark knowledge to unlock its ancient, catastrophic powers.

"If they know about the Hat," Elaine said, her voice tight with fear and anger, "then they know about the coven, about our traditions and our ways. They must have been watching us, studying us, waiting for the right moment to strike."

"But how could they know?" Sarah asked, her voice rising with distress. "We've always been so careful, so discreet in our practices."

"Knowledge has a way of spreading," Trudie said grimly. "Old texts, lapsed members, careless talk... there are countless ways our secrets could have leaked over the generations."

"But why now?" Trudie asked, her brow furrowed in confusion. "Why attack us on the very night we were going to discuss who the Hat would be passed to?"

Susan's eyes widened, a sudden, sickening realization dawning on her. "Because they knew we would be vulnerable," she whispered, her voice barely more than a breath. "They knew that without a Priestess, without Nancy's power to guide and protect us, we would be weaker, more easily defeated."

"Which means they've been watching us closely," Elaine concluded, her expression hardening. "Closely enough to know about tonight's meeting, about our plans for the succession."

"We should search the perimeter," Sarah suggested, already rising to her feet. "Check for any signs of surveillance, magical or otherwise."

"And strengthen our wards," Jasmine added firmly. "Every house, every property belonging to a coven member needs additional protection immediately."

A heavy, oppressive silence fell over the room, the witches grappling with the implications of Susan's words. They all knew that the coven needed a leader, a Priestess who could wield Nancy's power and guide them through the dark times ahead.

"We can't wait any longer," Mary Ann declared, her voice cutting through the anxious murmuring. "We need to perform the Passing of the Hat ceremony," she said, her voice firm and determined. "We need to choose a new Priestess, someone who can take up Nancy's mantle and lead us in the fight against this new enemy."

"Mary Ann is right," Elaine agreed, her earlier fear now replaced with resolve. "Without a Priestess, we're vulnerable. The Hat needs a bearer, and the coven needs a leader."

All eyes turned to Molly and Bree, the two young witches who had been chosen as potential successors to Nancy's legacy. They sat side by side, their hands clasped tightly together, their faces pale but resolute in the flickering candlelight.

"I know this is a heavy burden to bear," Mary Ann said softly, her gaze locked on her daughters' faces. "But one of you must take up the Hat, must accept the responsibility and the power that comes with being our Priestess."

"Tonight?" Bree asked, her voice barely audible, her eyes wide with apprehension. "After everything that's happened?"

"Not tonight," Trudie interjected calmly. "The ceremony requires preparation, and besides, we're all exhausted from this evening's ordeal. But soon. Very soon."

Molly and Bree exchanged a long, searching look. They had always known that this moment would come, that one day they would be called upon to lead the coven, to take up the mantle of their ancestors and carry on the legacy of the Andromeda witches.

But now, faced with the reality of the task before them, with the weight of their family's history and the fate of their entire world resting on their shoulders, they couldn't help but feel a flicker of doubt, a whisper of uncertainty that threatened to undermine their resolve.

"What exactly is involved in the ceremony?" Bree asked, her voice steadier now as she struggled to process the enormity of what was being asked of them.

"It's an ancient ritual," Jasmine explained, her academic tone offering a small measure of comfort in its familiarity. "The Hat chooses its wearer as much as the wearer chooses the Hat. There's a communion of energies, a binding of purpose between the witch and the artifact."

"And once it's done?" Molly inquired softly.

Elaine's expression softened. "Once it's done, you'll be changed. The knowledge, the wisdom, the power of all the Priestesses who came before you—including your grandmother—will become accessible to you. Not all at once, but gradually, as you learn to commune with the Hat."

"I'll do it," Molly said suddenly, her voice ringing out clear and strong in the stillness of the room. "I'll take up the Hat, I'll accept the responsibility of being our Priestess."

Bree turned to her sister, her eyes wide with surprise and concern. "Molly, are you sure?" she asked, her voice trembling slightly. "This is a huge undertaking, a burden that will change your life forever."

"Are you certain, Molly?" Mary Ann asked, her voice gentle but probing. "The Hat is not a responsibility to be taken lightly. Once bound, the connection cannot be easily severed."

Molly nodded; her expression solemn but determined. "I know," she said softly, her hand reaching out to squeeze Bree's own. "But I also know that this is what I was meant to do, what I was born to do. I can feel it in my bones, in the very core of my being."

"Molly has always had the stronger connection to the traditional aspects of our craft," Bree admitted, her initial shock giving way to a sense of rightness. "Her intuition for ritual and connection to our ancestral knowledge is... remarkable."

She turned to face the rest of the coven, her eyes shining with a fierce, unyielding light. "I may not have all the answers," she said, her voice ringing with conviction. "I may not know exactly what lies ahead or how we're going to defeat this new enemy. But I do know that together, we are stronger than anything that seeks to tear us apart. Together, we have the power to face any challenge, to overcome any obstacle, and to emerge victorious, no matter the cost."

A murmur of agreement rippled through the room, the witches nodding their heads in approval and support. They knew that Molly was right, that the strength of their sisterhood, the power of their magic and their love, was the key to their survival and their success.

"Then it's decided," Mary Ann declared, her voice steady despite the emotion shining in her eyes. "Molly will undergo the Passing of the Hat ceremony and become our new Priestess."

"When should we hold the ceremony?" Sarah asked practically. "After tonight's attack, we'll need time to prepare and strengthen our defenses."

"And we'll need everyone present," Jasmine added. "The full coven must witness and participate for the ritual to reach its full potency."

"What about Lucy?" Elaine asked, glancing at her daughter who was still recovering on the couch. "She'll need time to heal properly."

As the witches of the Andromeda coven huddled together, their voices rising and falling in a chorus of planning and preparation, the sound of the front door opening and closing echoed through the house. Moments later, Aunt Carol appeared in the doorway of the living room, her usually immaculate appearance slightly disheveled, her fiery red hair tousled and her clothing askew.

"Did I miss anything important?" she asked breezily, as though she hadn't been conspicuously absent for the past hour.

The coven members turned to stare at her, momentarily dumbfounded by her casual entrance after all that had transpired. Lucy was the first to break the silence with a weak laugh.

"Oh, nothing much," she said sarcastically from her position on the couch. "Just a mysterious magical attack, me getting thrown onto your car, and Molly agreeing to become our new Priestess."

Carol's eyebrows shot up in surprise. "Well, that certainly sounds eventful." Her gaze swept over to Lucy. "Are you alright, dear? You look like you've been through the wringer."

"I'll live," Lucy assured her dryly. "No thanks to your sudden disappearance during the crisis."

With a heavy sigh, Carol crossed the room and plopped herself down on the couch next to Lucy, her body sinking into the soft cushions as if she couldn't quite muster the energy to hold herself upright. The other witches, momentarily distracted from their discussion of the Passing of the Hat ceremony, continued to stare at her, their faces showing a mix of concern and curiosity.

Susan, ever the motherly figure, was the first to break the silence. "Carol, where have you been?" she asked, her voice gentle but firm. "I think we forgot about you in all of the excitement."

Carol looked up at Susan, a small, secret smile playing at the corners of her mouth. "I think I found myself a man," she said, her voice barely above a whisper, as if she couldn't quite believe the words herself.

For a moment, the room was silent, the witches struggling to process the unexpected revelation. And then, as if a dam had burst, they all exclaimed in unison, their voices rising in a chorus of shock and disbelief. "What?!"

"During a magical attack?" Sarah asked incredulously. "You were... what exactly?"

Carol's smile widened, her eyes sparkling with satisfaction. "You remember that nice man from across the street? The one who broke my fall when that awful creature attacked us?"

"Arthur Denim?" Bree clarified, her eyes widening in disbelief. "The neighborhood busybody who's always complaining about our hedge height and measuring our mailbox distance from the curb?"

The witches nodded, their minds trying to piece together the events of the night, the blur of fear and adrenaline that had consumed them all.

"Well," Carol continued, her voice taking on a dreamy, faraway quality, "let's just say that we got to know each other a little better in the aftermath of the battle."

"By 'a little better,' you mean...?" Jasmine asked, leaving the question hanging in the air.

Elaine, her eyebrows raising in a silent question, leaned forward, her voice low and conspiratorial. "Carol, are you saying what I think you're saying?"

Carol's grin turned positively wicked, her eyes dancing with barely suppressed glee. "Let's just say that Arthur Denim is a man of many talents," she said, her voice dripping with innuendo. "And that I'm very much looking forward to exploring those talents in greater depth."

"Arthur Denim?" Lucy repeated, momentarily forgetting her injuries as she sat up straighter. "The same Arthur Denim who filed a formal complaint about our wind chimes being 'sonically disruptive to the neighborhood ambiance'?"

"The very same," Carol confirmed with a satisfied smirk. "Though I assure you, he wasn't filing any complaints tonight. Quite the opposite, in fact."

The witches erupted in a chorus of gasps and giggles, their faces flushing with a mix of shock and delight. They had always known Carol to be a free spirit, a woman who lived life on her own terms and never apologized for her desires. But to hear her speak so openly, so unabashedly, about her conquest... it was a side of her they had never quite seen before.

"Carol!" Mary Ann exclaimed, her voice a mix of reproach and admiration. "I can't believe you! In the middle of a fight, with the fate of the coven hanging in the balance..."

"You disappeared to... to..." Trudie couldn't even finish the sentence, her round face pink with embarrassment.

But Carol just shrugged, her smile never wavering. "What can I say?" she said, her voice filled with a carefree, unapologetic joy. "Sometimes, life throws you a curveball. And sometimes, that curveball comes in the form of a handsome, mysterious stranger who sweeps you off your feet and makes you forget all about the danger and the chaos swirling around you."

"Arthur Denim is hardly mysterious," Sarah pointed out with a snort. "The man's daily schedule is so predictable you could set your watch by it."

"That's what makes it all the more exciting," Carol countered with a mischievous grin. "All that buttoned-up precision hiding such... unexpected depths."

"I'll never be able to look at him the same way again," Molly muttered, shaking her head in disbelief.

"Just wait until the next time he complains about our garden gnomes being improperly positioned," Bree added with a laugh. "How are you going to keep a straight face?"

The witches shook their heads, their laughter ringing out through the room like a balm, a moment of levity and light in the midst of the darkness that threatened to consume them all.

"Well, while you were... getting acquainted with Mr. Denim," Jasmine said, steering the conversation back to more pressing matters, "we've been deciding on the Passing of the Hat ceremony. Any input on timing?"

Carol, still radiating post-tryst satisfaction, considered the question. "My schedule is fairly open this week, except for Thursday evening—I have tickets to the community theater production of 'Cats.'" She paused, a sly smile spreading across her face. "And perhaps I should keep my weekend evenings flexible, in case Arthur would like to continue our... civic discussions."

"Too much information, Carol," Elaine groaned, though she couldn't entirely suppress her smile. It had been a long time since any of them had seen Carol so animated, so genuinely happy.

As the witches of the Andromeda coven continued their discussions late into the night, a consensus slowly began to emerge. With so many members juggling the demands of work, family, and their own personal lives, it was clear that finding a time for the Passing of the Hat ceremony that would allow everyone to attend would be no easy feat.

"What about next Tuesday?" Sarah suggested, consulting her phone calendar. "I could rearrange my client meetings."

"I have a dental appointment that morning," Trudie said with a frown.

"Thursday afternoon?" Jasmine proposed.

Elaine shook her head. "Lucy has physical therapy sessions on Thursdays, and after tonight's injuries, she definitely shouldn't miss them."

"Saturday is no good for me," Bree added. "I promised to help Sam with his garden redesign." She blushed slightly as several knowing looks were directed her way. "It's just neighborly," she insisted, though her pink cheeks suggested otherwise.

"Neighborly, hmm?" Carol waggled her eyebrows suggestively. "Is that what the kids are calling it these days?"

"Not everyone moves at your speed, Carol," Mary Ann said with a laugh, coming to her daughter's defense.

But after much deliberation and careful consideration of each member's schedule, a decision was finally reached. The ceremony would take place in one week's time, a date that would ensure the maximum possible attendance and allow the coven to come together as one, united in their purpose and their power while allowing for a full Moon and preparation of spells due to planetary alignments that would make the ceremony a success.

"One week from today, then," Mary Ann confirmed, looking around at the gathered women. "That gives us time to prepare properly and for Lucy to recover from her injuries."

"I'll be fine," Lucy insisted, though her still-pale face suggested otherwise. "Don't delay on my account."

"It's not just for you," Jasmine reminded her gently. "We all need time to gather our strength after tonight. And to prepare our defenses in case our mysterious attacker returns."

"And to research electrical-to-magical energy conversion," Trudie added grimly. "I'll start going through the archived grimoires tomorrow."

"I'll help," Bree offered, her mind already racing with possibilities. "There might be something in Grandmother's personal journals that could give us insight."

With the decision made and the plans set in motion, the witches began to take their leave, each of them departing the Tanner house with promises to stay vigilant and to begin preparations for the ceremony immediately.

Inside, Mary Ann turned to her daughters, "Good night, my darlings," she said softly, her voice filled with a deep, abiding love. "Get some rest, both of you. We have a big day ahead of us tomorrow."

She turned and made her way upstairs, her footsteps heavy with the weight of the day's events and the knowledge of the challenges still to come.

Bree, her own body aching with fatigue and her mind racing with the implications of all that had happened, nodded in agreement. "I think I'm going to wash up and try to get some sleep," she said, her voice sounding tired. "I have work in the morning, and I want to be at my best for whatever comes next."

"How are you feeling about all this?" Molly asked softly, studying her sister's face with concern. "About me taking the Hat, about the attack... everything."

Bree paused, considering the question. "Honestly? I'm terrified," she admitted. "But also... relieved, I think. I've always known the Hat wasn't meant for me, not really. And seeing you volunteer just felt... right, somehow."

"You're not disappointed?"

"Not at all," Bree assured her with a warm smile. "Proud, actually. My big sister, the next Priestess of the Andromeda coven. Grandmother would be so pleased."

Molly, her eyes bright, gave her sister a small, understanding smile. "I know what you mean," she said softly, her hand reaching out to give Bree's own a gentle, reassuring squeeze. "But I think I'm going to stay up a little longer, try to make some headway with the Compendium of Arcane Incantations. There's so much knowledge, so much power locked away in those pages... I feel like I'm just scratching the surface."

"Starting your studies already?" Bree teased gently. "The Hat hasn't even been passed yet."

"Better to be prepared," Molly replied with a small shrug. "Especially now, with this new threat emerging."

Bree nodded, her own eyes flickering with a hint of the same hunger, the same thirst for knowledge and understanding that burned within her sister's heart. "Just don't stay up too late," she said. "We're going to need all the strength and clarity we can muster in the days ahead."

"I won't," Molly promised. "Just an hour or so. There's a section on defensive wardcraft I've been meaning to review, and after tonight..."

"It seems particularly relevant," Bree finished for her. "I understand. Just remember—no practical applications without supervision. Some of those old spells can be tricky."

"Yes, mother," Molly replied with a roll of her eyes, though her smile took any sting from the words.

With a final, fierce hug, the two sisters parted ways, each of them retreating to their own rooms to seek the solace and the answers that only solitude and study could bring.

As Bree lay in bed, her body heavy with exhaustion, her mind drifted to Sam. What had he made of the night's strange events? Would he ask questions she couldn't answer? The thought of keeping secrets from him twisted uncomfortably in her chest, but she pushed the feeling aside. The coven's safety had to come first, especially now.

She thought of the shadowy figure at the end of the street, of the raw, destructive power they had wielded with such casual ease. Who were they? What did they want? And how could the coven hope to stand against such formidable magical might?

Questions without answers swirled through her mind, but as sleep began to claim her, one certainty remained: whatever challenges lay ahead, the Andromeda coven would face them together, bound by blood and magic and the unbreakable bonds of sisterhood.

With a deep, steadying breath and a silent prayer to the ancient gods of magic and mystery, Bree surrendered to the sweet oblivion of sleep, unaware of the watchful eyes that even now observed the Tanner house from the shadows, patient and calculating, waiting for the perfect moment to strike again.

Chapter 20
THE PORTAL TO EARTH

With a final burst of magic, Xaloth disengaged from his exhausting duel with the Drakorian general and turned to face the surviving young necromancers who huddled behind the faltering barrier. At that same moment, the reinforced doors at the far side of the chamber burst open with explosive force, admitting a small group of battle-worn young witches led by Briella of House Tanner, her copper hair singed and her once-pristine emerald robes torn.

"The western evacuation has fallen!" Briella announced breathlessly. "High Priestess Zara sent us here—she said you would know what to do, Master Xaloth."

The old necromancer's eyes flickered with grim satisfaction despite the dire circumstances surrounding them and the devastating losses they had suffered. The convergence of both types of magical practitioners—precisely as the ancient, long-dormant Sanctuary Protocol had specified in its most secretive final clause.

"Sam!" Xaloth cried, his voice ragged with exhaustion and determination. "You must gather the others and flee! Take the portal to the distant world of Earth, and there preserve the secrets of our orders! It is the only way!"

General Malakai, momentarily staggered by Xaloth's magical disengagement, recovered quickly. Understanding dawned on his scarred features as he noticed the young practitioners for the first time.

"No!" the Drakorian general roared, lunging forward with renewed fury. "Kill the apprentices! None must escape!"

Xaloth intercepted him with a barrier spell that momentarily halted even Malakai's corrupted power. "Now, Sam! There's no time!"

Sam's heart clenched with a sickening mix of fear and grief, but he knew that his mentor was right. The knowledge crystal pressed against his chest beneath his robes—the accumulated wisdom of generations of necromancers that must not fall into Drakorian hands.

"To me, brothers and sisters!" he shouted, turning to the combined group of young necromancers and witches. "We must make haste, before all is lost!"

The young practitioners rallied to his side—six necromancers including Talien and Elsira, and seven witches led by Briella. Their faces reflected the same terrible conflict Sameril felt—the anguish of abandoning their world and mentors against the solemn responsibility of preserving their sacred knowledge.

As Xaloth and the remaining defenders engaged the Drakorian forces in one final, desperate stand, Sameril raised his staff and began to trace an intricate pattern in the air before him. It was an ancient symbol, one that had been taught to him by Xaloth in the early days of his training—a key to unlock the hidden pathways between worlds.

"I need help stabilizing the portal," he called to Briella. "The energies are too chaotic with the barrier failing."

Without hesitation, Briella stepped forward, her hands weaving complementary patterns to Sam's. "Witches, lend me your strength," she commanded, and her companions joined their power to hers.

The convergence of necromantic and witch magic—so rarely attempted on Eldoria due to the traditional separation of their disciplines—created something new and unexpected. Where Sam's spell alone would have created a tenuous gateway, their combined working tore a permanent passage through the fabric of reality itself.

As he poured his power and will into the spell, the air began to shimmer and ripple, a vortex of swirling energy taking shape before their eyes. Within its depths, Sameril caught glimpses of an alien world—blue skies, green fields, and strange structures unlike anything on Eldoria.

"Earth," he breathed, recognition flowing from the knowledge Xaloth had implanted in the crystal. "Our new home."

Behind them, the battle reached its crescendo. Xaloth had engaged Malakai directly once more, but this time with no attempt at self-preservation. He was buying time with his life, and they all knew it.

"Necromancers, go!" Sameril ordered, maintaining the portal with one hand while gesturing toward the vortex with the other. "Talien, lead them through!"

His oldest friend hesitated only momentarily before nodding grimly. "May the balance guide you, Sam. Follow quickly." With that, he led the other necromancer apprentices into the shimmering portal, their forms dissolving into mist as they crossed the threshold between worlds.

"Witches, you're next," Sameril said, turning to Briella.

But she shook her head, her emerald eyes fierce with determination. "Not without you. I'll hold the portal from this side while you cross, then follow."

"That wasn't the plan—" Sameril began.

"Plans change," she interrupted, the authority in her voice belying her youth. "You carry the necromantic knowledge. I carry the witches' traditions. Neither can be risked unnecessarily."

Before he could argue further, an agonized cry tore through the chamber. They turned to see Xaloth driven to his knees, Malakai's dark blade embedded in his chest. The old necromancer's eyes met Sam's one final time, a silent command in their depths.

"Go!" Briella urged, physically pushing Sameril toward the portal. "I'm right behind you!"

With a final, anguished glance back at Xaloth and the brave defenders of Eldoria, Sameril stepped through the portal. The sensation was like being unmade—his physical form dissolving into pure energy as he traversed the vast distance between worlds.

Behind him, he heard Briella's voice raised in a final spell—not following immediately as promised, but sealing the portal from pursuit. Her sacrifice ensured their escape would not be tracked.

As the shimmering mists of the otherworld engulfed him, Sam's last glimpse of Eldoria was of Xaloth, broken but defiant, raising his hand toward the Nexus in a final, catastrophic spell that would deny Malakai his prize even in defeat.

Then there was light—blinding, purifying light—and Sameril knew no more until his consciousness re-formed on the surface of a new world, beneath the alien sun of Earth.

Chapter 21
SECRETS BEHIND CLOSED DOORS

The soft chime of the bell above the door barely registered as Bree placed another stack of books on the already crowded cart. Sunlight streamed through the front windows of *Infinity Books*, casting long shadows across the worn wooden floors. The shop smelled of old paper, binding glue, and a hint of the lavender sachets Sarah had tucked between shelves to ward off insects and negative energy alike.

"Excuse me," a woman's voice cut through Bree's distraction. "Do you have the new Marian Keyes novel?"

Bree blinked, focusing on the middle-aged customer standing before her. "Yes, of course. We just got it in yesterday." She gestured toward a display near the front counter. "They're right over there."

As the woman thanked her and walked away, Bree rubbed her temples. Focusing on work had been nearly impossible all day. Her mind kept replaying the events of the previous night—the shadowy figure at the end of the street, energy bolts, Lucy being thrown onto Carol's car. And then there was the decision about Nancy's Hat, with Molly stepping forward to take on the responsibility that would forever change her sister's life.

The store's phone rang, startling her from her thoughts.

"*Infinity Books*, this is Bree speaking."

"How are you holding up?" It was Molly's voice, warm with concern.

Bree sighed, leaning against the counter. "I'm fine. Distracted, but fine. How's the... study session going?"

They had agreed not to discuss coven matters explicitly over any potentially monitored phone lines, but Bree knew Molly was spending the day with Jasmine and their mother, Mary Ann, practicing complex defensive and offensive protective spells in preparation for the increasingly imminent Hat ceremony.

"It's intense," Molly admitted, lowering her voice. "I had no idea how much I didn't know. Jasmine is... thorough."

Bree smiled despite herself. Jasmine's academic approach to witchcraft was said to be legendary within the coven—equal parts brilliance and exhausting meticulousness.

"I'm sure you're doing great," Bree assured her. "Better you than me with all those theoretical frameworks and historical precedents."

Molly laughed softly. "You'd be surprised. Some of it's actually pretty fascinating." She paused. "Any word from... you know?"

Bree knew she meant their attacker. "No, thankfully. Everything's been quiet."

"Good. Listen, I should go. Jasmine is giving me that look. You know the one."

"The 'your recreational chatting is impeding any chances of serious advancement' look?"

"That's the one. I'll see you at home later?"

"Actually," Bree hesitated, thinking of Sam. She'd barely spoken to him since he'd walked her to his door last night. "I might be a little late. I want to check on Sam after work, make sure he's okay after everything."

"Sure," Molly replied, a hint of something—curiosity? concern? —in her voice. "Just... be careful, okay? After last night..."

"I will," Bree promised. "It's broad daylight, and I'm just going next door."

After they hung up, Bree turned her attention back to the bookstore. A few customers browsed the shelves, but the afternoon lull had settled in. Her gaze drifted to the small section in the back corner—books on mythology, folklore, and the occult. To most customers, it was just an eclectic collection of interesting titles. To those who knew what to look for, they contained subtle pointers to genuine magical knowledge, carefully disguised.

Sarah had maintained this special section for years, long before Bree had started working at Infinity Books. As a fellow witch and member of the Andromeda coven, Sarah understood the importance of keeping certain knowledge accessible yet protected.

Bree wondered if any of these books might contain information about an entity that could harness electrical energy for magical attacks. It seemed unlikely; such knowledge would be kept in the private libraries of covens, not on public bookshelves. Still, she made a mental note to ask Sarah if she might have any relevant texts in her personal collection.

The rest of the day passed in a blur of customers, inventory, and distracted thoughts. By closing time, Bree felt mentally exhausted despite having accomplished relatively little.

"I can finish up here if you want to head out early," Sarah offered, coming from the back room with a stack of new arrivals. Her blonde hair was pulled back in a loose tail, and her kind eyes studied Bree with the concern of someone who had witnessed the previous night's events firsthand.

"Are you sure?" Bree asked, grateful for the offer but not wanting to burden her boss and friend.

Sarah nodded. "You look like you could use some rest. We all could after last night." She lowered her voice, though the store was empty of customers. "Molly told me about her decision. That's a big step for both of you."

"It is," Bree agreed. "But it feels right. Molly's always had a stronger connection to the traditional aspects of..." she glanced around, lowering her voice further, "...our practices."

"Your grandmother would be proud," Sarah assured her with a warm smile. "Now go on, get some fresh air. I'll see you at the ceremony preparation tomorrow."

Bree thanked her, gathered her things, and stepped outside. She flipped the sign to 'Closed' as she left, hearing Sarah lock the door behind her.

Outside, the late afternoon air carried the first hints of evening coolness. The sun hung low in the sky, not yet setting but beginning its descent. Bree adjusted her bag on her shoulder and started walking toward Willow Street, her mind still churning with unanswered questions about the attack.

It felt strange to be walking this route alone, Bree realized. Usually, she and Sarah would close up together and walk back to their neighboring houses on Willow Street, chatting about books or coven matters. Sarah had lived next door to the Tanners for as long as Bree could remember, a constant, reassuring presence throughout her childhood.

The neighborhood looked so normal, so peaceful. Children living near the corner of Main Street played in front yards, neighbors chatted across fences, and sprinklers created rainbow prisms in the golden light. It was hard to believe that just hours ago, this same street had been the site of a violent magical attack.

Farther down, as she approached Sam's house, a slight movement caught her eye. One of the branches of the massive oak tree in his front yard was bouncing gently, almost imperceptibly, in a way that didn't match the afternoon breeze. Bree slowed her pace, curiosity piqued. Drawing closer, she realized with surprise that Sam was perched on one of the thick branches, his body stretched along its length as he gazed intently at his own house.

A mischievous smile spread across Bree's face. Sam was so focused on whatever he was watching that he hadn't noticed her approach. Moving as quietly as possible, she made her way to the base of the tree and began to climb, grateful for all the hours she'd spent scaling trees as a child. The rough bark pressed against her palms as she navigated her way up, careful not to rustle the leaves too much.

When she reached Sam's branch, she paused, holding back a laugh at his complete absorption in whatever he was observing. With playful stealth, she reached out and grabbed his ankle.

Sam jerked violently, nearly losing his balance as he twisted around, eyes wide with alarm. When he saw Bree grinning at him, his expression shifted from fear to exasperation in an instant.

"Bree!" he hissed in a harsh whisper, clutching the branch to stabilize himself. "What are you doing?"

"I could ask you the same thing," she whispered back, nodding toward his house. "What's so interesting that you're playing spy up here?"

Sam's jaw tightened. "Go home, Bree. Now."

The urgency in his voice caught her off guard, but before she could respond, movement in an upstairs window of Sam's house caught her attention. A shadow passed across the glass—large and oddly shaped.

"Sam," she whispered, her playfulness evaporating, "there's someone in your house!"

"I know," he muttered, his gaze darting between Bree and the window. "That's why you need to leave. Now."

But Bree's mind was already racing. A burglar. Sam was watching his house because someone had broken in, and instead of calling the police, he was hiding in a tree. What if they were dangerous? What if Sam tried to confront them and got hurt?

"Stay here," she whispered decisively, already beginning to descend the tree. "I'll handle this."

"No! Bree—" Sam reached for her, but she was already moving down the branches with surprising agility.

"Trust me," she called up softly. "I can take care of myself." *More than you know*, she thought, mentally reviewing defensive spells she could use without being too obvious about her abilities.

As her feet hit the ground, Bree darted toward Sam's front door, ignoring his increasingly desperate whispers behind her. The door was unlocked—odd for a break-in—but she didn't stop to question it, slipping inside and closing it quietly behind her.

The interior of Sam's house was dimly lit, with the fading daylight creating long shadows across the hardwood floors. Bree stood perfectly still, listening for any sounds of movement. The house had a strange smell—musty and organic, like damp earth and something else she couldn't identify.

In his haste to follow her, Sam fell from the tree, his body seen through the glass window of the door behind Bree. She winced, hoping he wasn't hurt, but remained focused on the task at hand. Her eyes adjusted to the dim light as she moved cautiously through the front room, scanning for any sign of the intruder.

The living room seemed normal enough—bookshelves lined the walls, a comfortable-looking couch faced a small fireplace, and a writing desk stood beneath the window, covered in papers and notebooks. Everything looked like what she'd expect from a writer's home, yet something felt... off. Some of the books on the shelves seemed unusually old, with bindings that appeared centuries rather than decades old.

Bree approached the kitchen door, noticing a sliver of light beneath it. She placed her hand on the doorknob, preparing a simple stunning spell in her mind—one that would appear to be just a lucky shove if anyone was watching.

The moment her fingers touched the knob, a deep, guttural growl emanated from the other side of the door.

Bree froze, her heart hammering against her ribs. That was not a human sound. It wasn't even a normal animal sound. It was something primal and threatening that made every instinct in her body scream *danger*.

Slowly, she removed her hand from the knob. The growling subsided momentarily, then the door began to edge open on its own, pushing outwards in her direction.

In the narrow opening, two glowing red eyes appeared, floating about four feet off the ground. They fixed on Bree with malevolent intelligence, and another growl—deeper, more menacing—filled the air.

Bree stumbled backward as the door swung open wider, revealing a massive, dark shape. It wasn't fully visible in the dim light, but she could make out a hulking form with matted fur, unnaturally long limbs, and those burning crimson eyes.

The creature let out a roar that shook the picture frames on the walls and lunged forward.

Bree screamed, slamming the kitchen door shut just as the beast reached it. The impact made the entire wall shudder, and Bree threw her weight against the door, feeling it bulge inward as the creature rammed it from the other side.

Claws scrabbled against the wood, and the growling intensified into a furious barking that sounded nothing like any dog Bree had ever heard. It was deeper, more articulate somehow, as if the sounds were almost forming words.

The door cracked, a jagged line splintering the wood near the hinges.

Bree screamed as she backed away from the disintegrating door.

Strong hands suddenly gripped her shoulders from behind. Bree yelped, spinning around to find Sam, his expression a mixture of fear and irritation.

"There's something in there!"

"I know!" he shouted over the creature's barking, grabbing her wrist and pulling her toward the stairs. "Come on!"

They had barely reached the staircase when the kitchen door exploded into the family room, fragments of wood spraying across the floor. The creature bounded into the large room, stopping after impacting the couch, its massive form filling the space as it oriented on them.

Bree caught only glimpses as they raced up the stairs—slavering jaws filled with needle-sharp teeth, patches of coarse fur interspersed with scaly skin, and those burning eyes that seemed to pierce right through her.

"What is that thing?" she gasped as they reached the second floor.

"Later!" Sam pulled her down the hallway, the creature's claws scrabbling on the wooden stairs behind them.

They burst into what appeared to be a bedroom, and Sam slammed the door, turning the lock for all the good it would do. Bree looked around frantically, noticing the sparse furnishings—a bed, a desk, a chair, and a large wooden wardrobe against the far wall.

"That door isn't going to stop it," she panted, backing toward the window. Maybe they could climb out onto the roof...

"I know." Sam crossed to the wardrobe and pulled open its doors. "In here. Quickly!"

Bree stared at him in disbelief. "You want us to hide in a closet? That's your plan?"

A thunderous crash from the hallway—followed by more splintering wood—made the decision for her. She darted into the wardrobe, expecting to find hanging clothes and a cramped space. Instead, she found herself in what appeared to be a dark, narrow corridor lined with shelves.

"How deep is this thing?" she asked as Sam followed her in, pulling the wardrobe doors closed behind them.

"Just keep going," he urged, once again taking her wrist and leading her deeper into the impossible space.

Bree stumbled over a pair of dress shoes but stayed upright with Sam still holding on to her.

The passage twisted once, then again, before ending at another door—this one made of dark wood with an ornate brass handle. Outside the passage, Bree could hear the beast tearing the bedroom apart, furniture crashing and wood splintering as it searched for them.

Sam opened the door and gently pulled Bree through.

She stepped into the space beyond and gasped, momentarily forgetting the danger behind them. They stood at the entrance of an enormous library, far larger than could possibly fit inside Sam's modest house. Towering bookshelves stretched toward a vaulted ceiling at least thirty feet high. Ornate iron spiral staircases connected multiple levels, and reading nooks with comfortable chairs and small tables were scattered throughout. Globes, astronomical instruments, and glass display cases containing curious objects dotted the space between shelves.

The air smelled of old parchment, leather bindings, and something subtly magical that Bree couldn't quite identify. Soft golden light emanated from wrought-iron chandeliers and wall sconces, casting the vast room in a warm glow.

"What..." Bree began, but words failed her as she tried to process the impossibility of what she was seeing.

Sam closed the door behind them, and the sounds of destruction immediately ceased, as if the door separated them from reality itself rather than just another room.

"Come on," Sam said quietly, taking hold of her hand as he led her deeper into the library.

Bree followed in stunned silence, trying to take in the countless volumes on the shelves they passed. Many of the spines bore titles in languages she didn't recognize, and some seemed to shift and change as she looked at them, as if the letters were alive.

She had just begun to grasp the enormity of the space when she abruptly stopped walking, causing Sam to halt as well.

"What's wrong?" he asked, still holding her wrist.

Bree held up a finger to her lips and tilted her head slightly. "Do you hear someone?"

From deeper in the library, the sound of voices raised in argument drifted toward them—high-pitched, raspy, and definitely not human.

Sam smiled, apparently relieved. "Yes, they work for me."

"They? Who's 'they'?"

Instead of answering, Sam continued leading her through the labyrinthine shelves until they reached a small clearing. Two figures sat at a large wooden table covered in open books, scrolls, and curious instruments. They were arguing heatedly, their strange voices echoing slightly in the cavernous space.

Bree stopped with a gasp as she got her first clear look at them.

The smaller of the two had dark reddish-brown skin that looked almost like bark, stretched over a thin frame. His face was long and pointed, with a pronounced chin and nose, and tiny spectacles perched precariously on the bridge. Straight, wispy hair the color of autumn leaves hung around his face, and his hands ended in long, spindly fingers that looked perfect for turning delicate pages. He sat rigidly at the desk, glaring at his companion.

"So, you're telling me that you read 'Bacrua'?" he demanded, his voice carrying the nasal quality of someone perpetually unimpressed.

The second figure was his physical opposite in almost every way—stocky and round where the first was thin and angular. His skin was a deeper brown with greenish undertones, and his head seemed too large for his body, dominated by bushy eyebrows that nearly obscured his eyes. He didn't bother looking up from the book he was examining.

"That's exactly what I am saying, yes," he replied, his voice deeper and gravellier than his companion's. His gaze flicked briefly toward the smaller figure before returning to his book.

The thin one squinted through his glasses, his expression skeptical. "And how, may I ask, did you ever find such a book?"

"I found it at Rizocs school in Keez," the larger one answered matter-of-factly, running a thick finger along the inside of the book's front cover.

"Rizocs!" the smaller one squeaked in disbelief. "How exactly? The earthly labyrinths don't even go there!"

The larger creature finally lifted his head from his book and turned his bulky body toward his colleague. "I had the help of Ulk and his family.

They all live in the woods near the area, and they are all quite familiar with the school and the book."

"Are they now?" the thin one replied, his tone dripping with skepticism. "I never knew they could even read."

It was at this point that the larger creature noticed Sam and Bree watching them from across the room. "Well, our boss returns with dinner."

The thin one swiveled in his chair, his gaze locking onto Bree with an expression of alarm. "Dinner?"

"What?" Bree whispered, taking a half-step backward. She turned to Sam with wide eyes.

Sam laughed, squeezing her hand reassuringly. "They're joking."

The larger creature raised his bushy eyebrows. "That's what he thinks. Goblins don't live on bread alone."

"Goblins," Bree repeated weakly, her mind struggling to process everything she was seeing. "Those are... goblins."

"Librarian goblins, to be precise," Sam corrected, leading her toward the table. "Bree, I'd like you to meet Tord and Glenken. They help me maintain the collection here."

Tord, the smaller goblin, stood and gave a stiff, formal bow. "Charmed, I'm sure," he said, though his tone suggested he was anything but. "I see our employer has finally decided to reveal our existence to his... companion."

Glenken snorted, his massive eyebrows twitching with amusement. "About time, too. We were beginning to think he was ashamed of us."

"I'm not ashamed," Sam protested. "I'm cautious. There is a difference."

"Cautious, secretive, paranoid," Glenken listed, ticking the words off on his thick fingers. "The distinctions blur after a while."

Bree found her voice at last. "I don't understand. Sam, who are you? What is this place? And what was that... *thing* in your house?"

The three males exchanged glances.

"Perhaps," Tord suggested primly, "this conversation would be better conducted somewhere more private?" He shot a pointed look at Glenken. "Some of us have actual work to complete, rather than fabricating implausible tales about mythical libraries."

"Rizocs is not mythical," Glenken growled, his bushy eyebrows drawing together. "Just because your knowledge is limited to what can be found in your precious earthly catalogs—"

"My catalogs are meticulously maintained and comprehensive," Tord interrupted, his voice rising. "They include every significant magical text from Andoria to Zephyria!"

"Except, apparently, 'Bacrua,'" Glenken retorted with a smug smile.

Tord's face darkened to a deep plum color. "That's because 'Bacrua' is a fabrication! A myth perpetuated by irresponsible scholars who—"

"I think," Sam cut in firmly, "we should continue this discussion another time." He turned to Bree, whose head was swiveling between the goblins like she was watching a tennis match. "Let me show you something."

Without waiting for a response, he guided her away from the bickering goblins toward a smaller room branching off from the main library.

"They're always like that," he explained as they walked. "Occupational hazard of librarians, I suppose. Each convinced they know more than the other."

"Do they?" Bree asked, still trying to process the existence of goblin librarians.

Sam laughed. "They're both brilliant in different ways. Tord is methodical, organized, traditional. Glenken is more... unconventional. He finds connections others miss, paths others don't see."

The smaller room that Sam led her to was a cozy study with a fireplace, a polished wooden desk, and walls lined with more bookshelves. Unlike the main library, which seemed to contain ancient tomes and magical texts, this room held a mixture of modern books, old volumes, and personal items—photographs, mementos, and what looked like research notes.

Sam closed the door behind them, then turned to face Bree, his expression serious.

"You want to know who I really am."

It wasn't a question, but Bree nodded anyway. "I think I deserve some answers after being chased by a monster and introduced to goblins who saw me as a menu item."

Sam ran a hand through his hair, a gesture of nervous habit that seemed strangely normal amid the extraordinary circumstances. "You're right. You do deserve answers." He paused. "But I can't give them all to you today."

"Why not?"

"Because there are... complications. Things I need to verify first." He took a deep breath. "I asked you to come back tomorrow evening for a reason. There's something I need to do tonight, something that will make my explaining all of this easier."

His eyes darted briefly toward the main library, where the goblins were still arguing, then back to Bree. She could sense he was weighing how much to tell her now, if anything, versus later.

Bree folded her arms across her chest. "So, I'm supposed to just go home and pretend none of this happened? That I didn't see a monster in your kitchen or an impossible library with goblin librarians?"

"I know it's a lot to ask," Sam admitted, rubbing the back of his neck. "But I promise you, tomorrow I'll explain everything. Who I am, what I do, this place—" he gestured around them, "—all of it."

"And the monster?" Bree pressed.

Sam's expression darkened, all traces of amusement vanishing. "That... that's part of why I need time. It shouldn't have been here. It wasn't supposed to be able to find this place."

"What do you mean?" Bree asked, suddenly alert to the genuine concern in his voice. "What was it?"

"A hellhound," Sam said quietly, his voice tense. "Not mine. Sent by someone who shouldn't know where I live. That's why I was in the tree watching the house—I sensed something had breached my wards, but I couldn't see what until it manifested physically."

Bree felt a chill run down her spine. Hellhounds weren't just monsters from mythology—they were powerful supernatural trackers, often bound to a specific master. If someone had sent one after Sam...

"Who sent it?" she asked, her mind racing with possibilities. Could it be connected to the figure that had attacked her coven?

Sam shook his head. "I have suspicions, but I can't be certain yet. That's why I need tonight—to confirm who's behind this and why." He paused, seeming to debate with himself before continuing. "I've already sent Morden—my third librarian goblin—to find an old friend of mine. Someone who might be able to help with this situation."

"Another goblin?" Bree asked.

"No," Sam replied. "A... colleague with expertise I may need in the coming days." He looked at her intently. "Especially after what happened on your street last night."

Bree stiffened. "What do you know about that?"

Sam hesitated again. "Not enough yet that I can explain right now. But I promise, by tomorrow evening, I'll be able to tell you everything—including how it might be connected to the hellhound."

Bree stared at him, trying to reconcile the Sam she knew—her friendly, somewhat dorky neighbor who wrote science fiction and helped her with heavy lifting at the bookstore—with this mysterious figure who spoke of hellhounds and wards and sent goblin messengers to find unnamed "colleagues." Whatever Sam Sorken really was, she was beginning to understand it was far more complicated than she'd ever imagined.

"Are you..." she hesitated, unsure how to ask. "Are you human?"

Sam smiled, though it didn't quite reach his eyes. "Yes, I'm human. Just a human with some... unusual interests and abilities."

Bree almost laughed at the irony. Here she was, a witch from a long line of witches, concerned about whether *he* was human. If he only knew...

"I don't suppose those unusual abilities and interests have anything to do with what happened last night? The attack on the street?"

Something flickered in Sam's eyes—recognition, concern, calculation. "Why do you ask that?"

"Just curious," Bree said, trying to sound casual. "It was pretty weird, and now I find out my neighbor has a giant secret magical library that doesn't fit inside his house. Seems like quite a coincidence."

Sam was quiet for a moment, studying her face. "The attack last night and this hellhound today... I don't believe in coincidences of this magnitude. Someone is making moves that affect both of us, and I need to understand why." He straightened his shoulders. "Once my friend Talien arrives—if Morden can find him—we'll have a better chance of getting answers."

"And you think this Talien can help?" Bree asked, wondering what kind of person Sam would trust with something like this.

"He's one of the few people I would trust with this situation," Sam replied, confirming her thoughts. "He has... specialized knowledge that could prove invaluable."

Bree considered pushing further but recognized the determined set of Sam's jaw. Whatever his secrets were, he wasn't ready to share them all yet.

"Fine," she conceded. "Tomorrow evening. But I expect the complete truth, Sam. No more evasions."

"The complete truth," he agreed, looking both relieved and apprehensive. "I promise."

"So... how do I get out of here? I'm assuming not back through the hellhound's territory?"

"No, there's a safer way out." He moved to a wall that appeared solid except for a small iron ring set into the stone. When he pulled the ring, a section of the wall swung inward, revealing a narrow staircase descending into darkness.

"This leads down to my backyard," he explained. "You can cut through to your house from there. I've checked—the hellhound is confined to the main house for now. My wards are holding it there."

Bree peered down the staircase, which was dimly lit by small lamps set into the wall at regular intervals. "This shouldn't exist, you know. Your house isn't big enough for all of this."

"I know," Sam agreed. "That's part of what I'll explain tomorrow."

"I'll hold you to that," Bree warned, taking a step toward the staircase. She paused, looking back at him. "One more question before I go. The hellhound—do you know who sent it? You mentioned suspicions."

"That," Sam said with a wry smile that didn't reach his eyes, "is the most complicated question of all. And one I hope to have a better answer for by tomorrow."

Bree nodded, then started down the stairs, her mind swirling with questions. Behind her, Sam called out, "Bree?"

She turned back. "Yes?"

"Be careful tonight. After what happened yesterday... just be on your guard. The hellhound was likely sent to find me, but I can't be certain it's the only threat out there right now."

The concern in his voice seemed genuine, deepening the mystery of who Sam really was and what he knew about the attack on her coven.

"I will," she promised, then continued down the stairs, each step taking her further from the impossible library and closer to home—but not, she suspected, closer to any real answers.

As the wall closed behind her, Bree felt she was leaving with far more questions than she'd arrived with. Who was Sam Sorken really? Why would someone send a hellhound after him? What kind of "colleague" was this Talien he'd sent his goblin to find? How did an ordinary-looking home contain an enormous magical library?

And most importantly, what did any of this have to do with the attack on her coven?

She would have to wait until tomorrow for answers. In the meantime, she needed to decide how much of this to share with Molly and the others. Without understanding Sam's role in all of this—whether he was a potential ally or another threat—it was hard to know what to do with the information she'd uncovered.

One thing was certain: Willow Street was becoming the center of something much larger and more dangerous than she'd ever imagined. First the attack on the coven, now a hellhound sent after her neighbor...

Tomorrow couldn't come soon enough.

CHAPTER 22

THE OATH OF VENGEANCE

As the portal winked out of existence, the last flickers of its otherworldly light fading into nothingness, Malakai stood amidst the ruins of the once-grand palace. His battle armor, once pristine obsidian, now bore the scars of Xaloth's final, desperate assault. The Nexus chamber had been utterly destroyed, its ancient stones reduced to little more than dust and scattered fragments. Of the Nexus itself—the wellspring of necromantic power he had coveted—nothing remained but a perfectly smooth depression in the ground, vitrified by energies beyond mortal comprehension.

Malakai's face twisted into a mask of rage, his amber eyes burning with an intensity that caused even his most hardened lieutenants to keep their distance. All around him lay the shattered remnants of Eldoria's capital, the bodies of the fallen strewn across blood-soaked ground like broken dolls. The sky above was choked with smoke and ash, the once-vibrant lavender heavens now a sickly gray that matched the desolation below.

"General," Lieutenant Vex approached cautiously, keeping a respectful distance from his commander's palpable fury. "The city is secured.

The remaining Eldorian forces have either been eliminated or taken prisoner."

Malakai barely acknowledged the report. His gaze remained fixed on the spot where the portal had closed—where his true prize had escaped his grasp.

"And what of the witches?" he asked, his voice unnaturally calm despite the storm raging within. "Were any of their leaders captured alive?"

"No, General," Vex replied, unable to completely disguise his unease. "High Priestess Zara was confirmed killed in the western sector. Most of their senior practitioners fell defending the civilian evacuation points."

"And the necromancers?"

"Master Xaloth and all senior members perished in the Nexus explosion. But..." Vex hesitated, knowing the next words would only feed his master's rage. "Intelligence confirms that a small group of apprentices escaped through the portal before it collapsed."

A low, dangerous sound emerged from Malakai's throat—something between a laugh and a growl. "So, despite our complete military victory, despite the utter destruction of their world and the death of their leaders, they still managed to deny me what I came for."

He turned slowly, surveying the carnage with eyes that saw not victory but failure. Yes, Eldoria had fallen. Yes, its once-proud civilization lay in ruins, its people scattered or enslaved. But even as he reveled in the complete and utter destruction of his enemies, Malakai couldn't shake the gnawing sense of dissatisfaction that clawed at his heart.

The necromancers—those cursed guardians of the secrets he so desperately sought—had escaped his clutches, fleeing to some distant, unknown realm where they could continue to hoard their precious knowledge. And with them, they had taken the key to unlocking the true potential of the Drakorian race, the power to conquer death itself and reign supreme over all the galaxy.

Malakai's fists clenched at his sides, his rage momentarily boiling over into the physical realm as pulses of dark energy radiated from his form, cracking the already damaged floor beneath his feet.

"General," Vex ventured, "despite this... setback, the campaign has been a resounding success. Eldoria's resources are now ours. Their technology, their cultural artifacts—"

"Trinkets," Malakai spat. "Baubles and scraps. I did not come here for resources, Lieutenant. I came for transformation."

He strode forward, stepping over the bodies of fallen warriors without a second glance. At the far end of the ruined hall, a squad of his elite guards held two broken figures at gunpoint—King Aldric and Queen Isadora, somehow still alive despite the devastation of their world. Their once-regal attire was now tattered and blood-stained, their proud bearing reduced to the slumped posture of the utterly defeated.

Malakai approached them slowly, savoring the look of despair in their eyes, the knowledge that all their efforts, all their sacrifices, had been for naught in the face of his overwhelming might.

"Your Majesties," he mocked, offering an exaggerated bow. "How kind of you to await my arrival. I had feared you might have joined your people in their cowardly flight."

King Aldric raised his head with effort, his grey hair matted with blood and dust. "Our place was here," he said simply, his voice hoarse but dignified even in defeat. "With our world, to the end."

"Noble," Malakai observed. "Foolish, but noble. And now you will witness the final death of your civilization, knowing that everything you built, everything you cherished, was ultimately meaningless."

Queen Isadora, her face lined with the grief of witnessing her world's destruction, nonetheless met Malakai's gaze without flinching. "You have won nothing this day, Malakai. Eldoria is more than stone and soil. Our knowledge, our traditions—they will live on through those who escaped."

A cruel smile spread across Malakai's scarred face. "For now, perhaps. But make no mistake, Your Majesty—I will find them. Every last one. No matter how far they've run, no matter how well they hide, I will hunt them to the ends of the universe itself."

"Why?" Aldric asked, genuine confusion breaking through his bone-deep exhaustion and visible despair. "You have conquered worlds beyond counting, extinguished entire civilizations without remorse. Is your blood-soaked empire not vast enough? Is your power not absolute enough to satisfy your insatiable, boundless ambition?"

Malakai's smile faded, replaced by an expression of terrible intensity. "This was never about conquest, Your Majesty. This was about transformation. The secrets of necromancy are the key to transcending the limitations of mortality itself. With the Nexus, I could have remade the very fabric of existence, could have elevated the Drakorian race to godhood."

"And destroyed the balance between realms in the process," Isadora said softly. "Some powers were never meant to be wielded, Malakai. Some boundaries were never meant to be crossed."

"Boundaries," Malakai sneered, "are for lesser beings."

With a casual gesture, he signaled to his guards. Without hesitation, they raised their weapons and fired, ending the royal line of Eldoria in a heartbeat. Malakai watched dispassionately as the bodies of the king and queen crumpled to the floor, joining the countless others who had fallen in defense of a lost cause.

But even that fleeting moment of satisfaction paled in comparison to the burning, all-consuming hunger that gnawed at his very soul. The hunger for power, for dominion, for the chance to remake the very fabric of the universe in his own image.

With a final, contemptuous glance at the ruins of Eldoria, Malakai turned his back on the conquered world. "Lieutenant Vex," he commanded, "begin extraction of any remaining artifacts of value. Establish occupation protocols for the surviving population. And assemble our finest trackers and mages in my war chamber."

"At once, General," Vex acknowledged. "And... the portal location?"

"Have our scientists analyze every particle of residual energy. I want to know which world they fled to, what defenses they might possess, everything." Malakai's eyes glittered with malevolent purpose. "The hunt begins now."

As he strode through the corridors of his flagship, Malakai allowed his rage to cool, transforming into something far more dangerous—a cold, implacable determination that would not be denied. The necromancers and witches had won this small victory, had denied him his prize at the moment of triumph. But they had merely delayed the inevitable.

The universe was vast, but not infinite. Resources were plentiful, but not limitless. Eventually, he would find them. Eventually, he would claim what was rightfully his. And when he did, the descendants of Eldoria would learn the true meaning of vengeance.

For Malakai Drach had tasted the bitter ashes of defeat this day, had seen his ultimate victory snatched away at the very moment of his triumph. And he would not rest, would not know a moment's peace, until he had avenged himself upon those who had dared to defy him, and claimed his rightful place as the undisputed master of life and death itself.

As the great engines of his warship rumbled to life, preparing to lift the massive vessel from the broken surface of Eldoria, Malakai gazed out at the stars—countless pinpricks of light in the endless void of space. Among them, somewhere, the survivors of Eldoria were establishing a new foothold, believing themselves safe from his reach.

A thin smile curved his scarred lips. Let them build. Let them grow comfortable. Let them believe they had escaped. It would make their eventual discovery all the more devastating, their ultimate defeat all the more complete.

Time was on his side. After all, he had engineered his own version of immortality through forbidden arts. He could afford to be patient in his hunt.

"Enjoy your reprieve, necromancers," he murmured to the distant stars. "Cherish these moments of false security. For I am coming. And when I find you, the fall of Eldoria will seem a mercy by comparison."

CHAPTER 23
MORNING REVELATIONS

Sunlight filtered through the curtains of Bree's bedroom, casting dappled patterns across the quilt her grandmother had made years ago. The familiar patterns of interconnected moons and stars, stitched with thread that seemed to shimmer with its own inner light, had always brought her comfort. This morning, however, even the sight of Nancy Tanner's handiwork couldn't calm the storm of questions swirling through Bree's mind.

She'd barely slept. Every time she closed her eyes, she saw the hellhound's burning red gaze or the impossible expanse of Sam's hidden library. Her dreams, when she did manage to drift off, were filled with goblin librarians arguing over obscure texts while shadowy figures with glowing green hands lurked at the edges of her vision.

With a sigh, Bree pushed back the covers and padded to her bathroom. The face that greeted her in the mirror looked as tired as she felt—dark circles under her eyes, her usually vibrant black hair hanging limp around her shoulders. She splashed cold water on her face, hoping to wash away some of the fatigue along with the remnants of restless dreams.

As she went through her morning routine, Bree's thoughts kept circling back to Sam. Who was he really? A writer with a secret magical library was certainly strange enough, but one who had voodoo witches sending hellhounds after him and mysterious, unseen friends like Talien who might be able to help protect the coven? It seemed impossible that she could have lived next door to him for so long without suspecting there was more to him than met the eye.

By the time Bree made her way downstairs, the aroma of coffee and freshly baked scones filled the air. She followed the scent to the kitchen, where she found her mother and sister huddled over a large piece of parchment spread across the table.

Mary Ann looked up when Bree entered, her smile warm but her eyes reflecting the same weariness Bree felt. "Morning, sweetheart. There's coffee in the pot and scones in the basket."

"Thanks," Bree murmured, making a beeline for the caffeine. The first sip of rich, dark coffee brought a small measure of clarity to her foggy brain. "What are you two working on so early?"

Molly, who had barely glanced up from the parchment when Bree entered, pushed a stray lock of hair behind her ear. Unlike Bree, who favored their father's darker coloring, Molly had inherited Mary Ann's auburn hair, though she kept hers in a practical bob while their mother's often flowed past her shoulders.

"Ward configurations," Molly answered, her finger tracing a complex geometric pattern on the parchment. "Jasmine found these in one of Grandmother's old journals. They're designed specifically for protection against directed energy attacks."

Bree moved closer, peering over her sister's shoulder. The diagrams on the parchment resembled the protective sigils their grandmother had taught them to draw, but with subtle differences that made them seem somehow more... substantial. More potent.

"These look intense," Bree observed, taking a scone from the basket and biting into its buttery softness. "Are they difficult to implement?"

Mary Ann nodded; her expression serious. "They require specific materials and precise placement. That's why we're heading to the old barn this morning—we need to gather some supplies from the coven's storage, and Jasmine wants to check a few references in the grimoires we keep there."

The old barn at the edge of town had belonged to the Warren family for generations and had been used by the coven for just as long. From the outside, it looked like nothing special—a weathered structure that most townspeople assumed was used for agricultural storage. Inside, however, was another story. The barn housed the coven's ceremonial space, a library of magical texts too powerful or sensitive to keep in their homes, and storage for rare herbs, crystals, and other magical supplies.

"Will you need help setting up the wards?" Bree asked, thinking of her workday ahead at Infinity Books.

"No, we should be fine," Mary Ann assured her. "Elaine and Trudie are meeting us at the barn and then coming back here to help implement the protections. Sarah mentioned she might stop by during her lunch break, too."

Molly finally looked up from the parchment, her green eyes meeting Bree's. "We're not taking any chances after what happened the other night. These wards won't just alert us to an intruder—they'll actively repel magical attacks."

"That's good," Bree said, an image of the shadowy figure at the end of the street flashing through her mind. "Very good."

"What about you?" Mary Ann asked, studying her youngest daughter with a perceptive gaze that made Bree feel like she could see every secret thought. "You look like you barely slept."

Bree shrugged, trying for nonchalance. "Just processing everything, I guess. It's not every day your street becomes a magical battleground."

She considered telling them about her adventure in Sam's house—about the hellhound and the impossible library and the goblin librarians. But something held her back. Until she knew more about Sam's connection to everything that was happening, it seemed wiser to keep what she'd discovered to herself. Besides, she'd promised to meet him that evening to get the full explanation.

"I should get going," Bree said, checking the time. "Sarah's expecting me at the store."

"Be careful today," Mary Ann cautioned, rising to give her daughter a quick hug. "Stay aware of your surroundings, and if you see anything unusual—"

"I'll call immediately," Bree promised, returning the embrace. "And I'll be straight home after work. I want to hear all about these new wards."

Molly looked up again, something unreadable flashing in her eyes. "Actually, do you think you could pick up dinner on your way home? We're likely to be working on the wards most of the day, and cooking might be the last thing on our minds."

"Sure," Bree agreed easily. "Pizza from Pizzeria Rustica?"

"Perfect," Mary Ann and Molly said in unison, then laughed at the synchronicity.

Bree smiled, grateful for the moment of normalcy amid all the chaos and uncertainty. She finished her coffee, grabbed another scone for the road, and kissed her mother and sister goodbye before heading out the door.

The morning air was crisp and clear, carrying the sweet scent of the flowering trees that lined Willow Street. Birds chirped in the branches overhead, and sprinklers hissed rhythmically across neatly manicured lawns. It was hard to believe that just two nights ago, this peaceful neighborhood had been the scene of a violent magical attack.

As Bree walked past Sam's house, she slowed, eyes scanning the property for any sign of her enigmatic neighbor. Usually, Sam would be on his front porch at this hour, laptop open and coffee at his side as he worked on his latest manuscript. The porch, however, was empty, the chairs unoccupied and no steaming mug in sight.

Bree hesitated, wondering if she should check on him. What if the hellhound had broken free from his wards? What if whoever had sent it had come themselves, or sent something worse?

But no—Sam had seemed confident in his ability to handle the situation, at least until his friend Talien arrived. And she would be seeing him that evening for the promised explanation. Whatever Sam was doing now, it likely involved gathering information about both the hellhound and the attack on her coven. The thought that these two events might be connected sent a chill down Bree's spine despite the warm morning sun.

Had Sam's goblin messenger found Talien yet? Bree tried to imagine what sort of person this mysterious colleague might be. Someone with "specialized knowledge," Sam had said. Knowledge of what? Hellhounds? Magical attacks that harnessed electrical energy?

Lost in these thoughts, Bree almost walked past Infinity Books. She caught herself just in time, turning toward the cheerful blue storefront with its display windows filled with colorful book covers and hand-lettered signs announcing upcoming author events.

Sarah Fond had already opened for the day, as evidenced by the "Open" sign hanging in the door and the lights glowing welcomingly inside. Bree pushed open the door, the familiar chime announcing her arrival.

The bookstore smelled of paper, coffee, and the subtle hint of the protection sachets Sarah discreetly tucked among the shelves—lavender and sage for general protection, rosemary to enhance mental clarity, and tiny traces of other herbs known only to practitioners. To ordinary customers, they simply made the store smell pleasant and somehow soothing. To those with magical sensitivity, they created an atmosphere of safety and welcome.

"There you are!" Sarah's voice called from the back of the store. She emerged from between the towering shelves, a stack of books in her arms and a welcoming smile on her face. In her late twenties, Sarah Fond had a warm, approachable presence that made customers of all ages feel comfortable in her store. Her blonde hair was pulled back in a tail, and her warm brown eyes sparkled with intelligence and humor.

"Sorry if I'm running late," Bree apologized, moving to take some of the books from Sarah's arms.

"Not at all," Sarah assured her, relinquishing half the stack. "I just got here a bit early. Had trouble sleeping and decided I might as well come in and update the new arrivals display."

Bree followed Sarah to the front of the store, where a large table awaited the fresh inventory. "Seems to be going around," she commented. "I didn't sleep well either."

Sarah glanced at her sharply, her bookkeeper's hands never pausing in their efficient arrangement of the display. "Understandable, after everything that happened." She paused briefly, her expression softening. "I think Molly will do wonderfully as our new Priestess. She has the perfect temperament for it."

"I think so too," Bree confirmed, handing Sarah another book. "It feels right. Molly's always had more of a connection to the traditional aspects of our craft."

"Your grandmother would be pleased," Sarah said, her voice softening with memory. "Nancy always said Molly reminded her of herself at that age—curious about everything, hungry for knowledge, eager to understand the deeper mysteries."

They worked in companionable silence for a few minutes, arranging books and tidying displays. Bree's mind drifted back to her childhood, when Nancy Tanner would bring her granddaughters to visit Sarah at the bookstore. While the adults talked, Bree and Molly would explore the shelves, always somehow finding their way to the special section in the back corner where the books on mythology, folklore, and the occult resided.

Sarah had been her grandmother's closest friend in the coven, Bree realized. If anyone might have insight into Sam—especially if he'd known Nancy—it would be Sarah.

"You seem distracted this morning," Sarah observed, breaking into Bree's thoughts. "Is everything alright? Besides the obvious, I mean."

Bree hesitated, then made a decision. "Can I tell you something in confidence? Something I haven't told Mom or Molly yet?"

Sarah's expression grew serious. "Of course. What is it?"

Bree glanced around the empty store, then lowered her voice anyway. "It's about Sam Sorken."

"Your neighbor? The writer?" Sarah's eyebrows rose slightly. "What about him?"

"He's..." Bree struggled to find the right words, twisting a strand of hair nervously between her fingers. "Not what he seems. Or at least, not *only* what he seems. There's something ancient about him."

Sarah's face remained carefully neutral, though her eyes revealed a flicker of knowing concern. "Go on. Tell me everything you've discovered."

Bree took a deep breath and told Sarah everything—about finding Sam mysteriously perched in the tree watching the coven meeting, the terrifying hellhound she'd unexpectedly encountered in his ordinary-looking house, the impossible, seemingly endless magical library with its strange goblin librarians who treated Sam with unusual deference, and Sam's cryptic mention of a powerful friend called Talien who might be able to help protect the coven from Kestrel's growing threat.

As she spoke, Sarah's expression shifted from initial surprise to intense concentration, her hands growing still on the dusty leather-bound books she'd been methodically arranging. When Bree finally finished her extraordinary account, Sarah remained silent for a long moment, her gaze distant as if seeing something far beyond the wooden walls of the bookstore.

"Sarah?" Bree prompted finally. "Should I be worried? About Sam, I mean?"

Sarah seemed to come back to herself, her focus returning to Bree with sharp clarity and thoughtful consideration of these new revelations. "If Sam wanted to harm the coven or steal magical artifacts, he's had ample opportunity over many seasons of rituals," she said slowly, weighing each word carefully. "He's lived next door to your family for three years, watching quietly from the shadows, and as far as I know, he's never shown any sign of ill intent or interference with our magical practices."

"That's what I thought too," Bree agreed, relieved to hear her own reasoning confirmed. "Besides, he was friends with Grandma Nancy, wasn't he?"

A strange expression flickered across Sarah's face so quickly Bree almost missed it. "They knew each other," she said carefully. "I wouldn't have characterized them as friends, exactly, but they... respected each other."

"What does that mean?" Bree asked, sensing there was more to the story.

Sarah sighed, moving toward the front counter where she kept a special blend of tea for private conversations. She filled an electric kettle with water and set it to boil before answering.

"Nancy never discussed Sam much with the rest of the coven," she explained, taking two delicate porcelain mugs from a shelf beneath the wooden counter. "But she did mention him to me once or twice in private, confidential conversations. She seemed to think he was... useful to have nearby, though she never fully elaborated on why despite my careful questioning."

"Useful?" Bree repeated, frowning. "That's an odd way to put it."

"Nancy could be cryptic sometimes," Sarah reminded her with a small smile. "Especially about matters she felt were sensitive or potentially divisive within the coven."

Sarah hesitated, then added thoughtfully, "You know, based on what you've described—the magical library, the ability to create spaces that shouldn't physically exist, controlling a hellhound with magical wards—he might be a witch himself. Perhaps from another coven with different traditions than ours."

"That would make sense," Bree nodded, considering the possibility. "Though I wonder why he wouldn't have made himself known to us. The Andromeda coven has several male witches—it's not like we'd have excluded him."

"Some practitioners prefer to keep to themselves," Sarah pointed out. "Especially if they follow different magical traditions. Not everyone wants to be part of a larger community."

The kettle clicked off, and Sarah poured the steaming water over sachets of her special blend consisting of a mixture of chamomile, lavender, and other herbs that were known to promote clarity and calm. She handed one mug to Bree, who accepted it gratefully, taking a deep inhale of the aroma.

"So, you don't think Sam is a threat?" Bree asked after taking a sip of the soothing tea.

"I think," Sarah said carefully, "that you should hear him out tonight, as planned. If Nancy saw value in having him nearby, there must be a reason." She paused, her expression growing more serious. "But I also think you should share what you learn with the coven as soon as possible. Especially now, with this new threat and Molly about to become Priestess."

Bree nodded. "That's fair. I was planning to tell everyone once I understood more about Sam's connection to everything that's happening."

"Good," Sarah approved. "No more secrets than absolutely necessary, especially within the coven. Secrecy has its place in our craft, but too much of it between sisters can lead to misunderstandings and division—exactly what we don't need right now."

"I promise I'll tell them everything after I talk to Sam tonight," Bree assured her. "I just want to have the full picture first."

Sarah studied her for a moment, then nodded. "I trust your judgment, Bree. Just be careful. Even if Sam himself isn't a threat, it sounds like he has powerful enemies. And sometimes the most dangerous place to be is between two opposing magical forces."

The bell above the door chimed, announcing the arrival of the day's first customer. Sarah smoothly transitioned from concerned friend and fellow witch to welcoming bookstore owner, greeting the elderly man who entered with a warm smile and an inquiry about whether he'd enjoyed the mystery novel he'd purchased the previous week.

Bree took her tea and moved toward the back of the store, her mind still churning with questions. The conversation with Sarah had been both reassuring and unsettling. On one hand, it seemed unlikely that Sam was an enemy, given Nancy's apparent respect for him. On the other hand, Sarah's cautious phrasing and the revelation that Nancy had kept her knowledge of Sam mostly to herself only deepened the mystery surrounding her neighbor.

What had Nancy known about Sam that she hadn't shared with the rest of the coven? Why had she considered him "useful to have nearby"? And most importantly, how was he connected to the attack on the street and the threat now facing the Andromeda coven?

Bree sipped her tea, gazing absently at the books surrounding her. Somewhere in this store, there might be information that could help her understand what was happening—clues about hellhounds or magical attacks that harnessed electrical energy. But without knowing what to look for, searching seemed futile.

She would just have to wait until evening, when Sam had promised to tell her everything. Until then, all she could do was help customers, organize books, and try not to let her imagination run wild with possibilities too fantastic—or too frightening—to contemplate.

Chapter 24
New World Dawn

The portal's energy dissipated in a final flash of spectral light, depositing Sameril and his companions onto soft earth. The transition was jarring—one moment surrounded by the chaos of battle and death, the next engulfed in pristine silence broken only by the rustle of wind through unfamiliar trees.

Sameril staggered to his knees, the world spinning around him as his body adjusted to the alien environment. His lungs burned with the first breath of Earth's atmosphere—subtly different from Eldoria's, richer somehow yet lacking the natural magical resonance he had known since birth. The light felt wrong too—harsh and singular, emanating from a single yellow sun that hung in a sky of startling blue.

"Is everyone here?" he managed, his voice sounding strange even to his own ears. "Count off!"

One by one, the survivors called out, their voices weak and disoriented. Five necromancers besides himself had made it through—Talien, Elsira, and three younger apprentices. Of the witches, only twelve had emerged from the portal, their emerald robes now dirty and torn.

"Briella?" Sameril called, scanning the unfamiliar landscape. "Where's Briella?"

Silence answered him, heavy with implication. A young witch with dark skin and tightly braided hair—Nivea, he thought her name was—stepped forward.

"She stayed behind," Nivea said, her voice breaking. "To seal the portal. She said someone had to ensure Malakai couldn't track us."

The knowledge hit Sameril like a physical blow. Briella of House Tanner—the fiery-haired witch whose fierce intelligence had matched his own, whose brief connection had sparked something profound despite the traditions that separated their disciplines—gone. Just like Xaloth. Just like everything else from their world.

He closed his eyes, allowing himself one moment of grief before the weight of responsibility forced him back to his feet. They were stranded on an alien world with no resources, no shelter, and the knowledge of two magical traditions resting on their shoulders. There was no time for personal sorrow.

"We need to find shelter," Talien said, reading Sam's thoughts as he often did. "And assess our surroundings."

Sameril nodded, scanning the landscape with more purpose now. They had emerged in a small clearing surrounded by ancient forest. In the distance, rugged mountains rose against the horizon, their peaks capped with white. The air was cool and crisp, suggesting either high elevation or a temperate climate in its colder season.

No signs of civilization were immediately visible—no structures, no roads, no evidence of intelligent life. Whether that was blessing or curse remained to be seen.

"Form a circle," Sameril instructed, slipping naturally into the leadership role despite his youth. "We need to take stock of what we have."

The survivors gathered around him, their faces pale and drawn but resolute. Each emptied their pockets and pouches, creating a small pile of resources in the center of their circle—a few spell components, personal talismans, small tools, and survival items that had been on their persons when they fled.

Most importantly, each of the senior students carried knowledge crystals like the one Xaloth had given Sam—smaller, more specific repositories of their respective traditions. Between them, they had the essentials of both necromancy and witchcraft preserved.

"Not much to rebuild a civilization," Talien observed grimly.

"We're not here to rebuild Eldoria," Sameril replied, his voice strengthening as he spoke. "We're here to preserve its knowledge. To ensure that what makes our traditions valuable survives."

As he spoke the words, Sameril felt the image of Xaloth's final stand flash vividly before his mind's eye. He could still see the old necromancer's face as he faced down the overwhelming might of the Drakorian forces, could still hear the echo of his mentor's final words ringing in his ears:

"Preserve the secrets, Sam. Protect them with your life and pass them on to the generations yet to come. For in them lies the hope of our people, and the key to the salvation of the galaxy."

Sameril reached into his robes and withdrew the memory crystal Xaloth had entrusted to him. In the light of Earth's sun, it pulsed with an inner radiance, seeming to respond to his touch and intention.

"Before we do anything else," he said, "we need to ensure this knowledge is secure. If something happens to us—to any of us—these secrets must survive."

Nivea stepped forward, producing a similar crystal from within her own robes. "High Priestess Zara gave us the same instruction. The knowledge of both our traditions must be protected, no matter the cost."

Sameril nodded, a sense of kinship forming with this witch despite their different backgrounds. They were no longer separate orders with separate purposes—they were the last children of Eldoria, bound by a shared responsibility.

"The first thing we need to do," Elsira said practically, "is learn about this world. Its dangers, its resources, its inhabitants—if any."

"We should split into small groups," Talien suggested, "scout the immediate area, then reconvene before nightfall."

Sameril nodded his agreement. "Pairs—one necromancer, one witch in each. Our magics may work differently here, so we'll need to discover what's changed, what's possible."

"Different how?" asked one of the younger necromancers, fear evident in his voice.

"I'm not sure," Sameril admitted. "But I can feel it already—the magical currents here are...muted compared to Eldoria. We may need to adapt our techniques."

As the group organized themselves into pairs and prepared to explore their new surroundings, Sameril found himself standing apart, the weight of leadership settling uncomfortably on his shoulders. The crystal in his hand seemed to grow heavier with each passing moment, a physical manifestation of the burden he now carried.

Nivea approached him, her dark eyes reflecting a similar weight. "Briella spoke of you," she said quietly. "Before we came to the chamber. She said if anyone could preserve our knowledge in a new world, it would be you."

Sam's throat tightened. "I barely knew her."

"She knew you," Nivea replied simply. "She recognized something in you that matched what she carried within herself—a commitment to knowledge that transcends the boundaries we created between our traditions."

Before Sameril could respond, Talien called from the edge of the clearing. "Sam! There's something you should see."

Moving to join his friend, Sameril followed Talien's pointing finger to a distant curl of smoke rising above the tree line—evidence of fire, and perhaps of intelligent life. Earth was not uninhabited after all.

"What do we do?" Talien asked. "Make contact? Observe from a distance?"

Sameril considered the question carefully. The inhabitants of this world would know nothing of Eldoria, nothing of necromancy or witchcraft, nothing of the cosmic balance their traditions maintained. They would be primitive by comparison, perhaps even fearful of magic.

Yet they would be essential allies if the refugees were to survive long-term. They would need to learn Earth's languages, its customs, its territories.

"We observe first," Sameril decided. "Learn what we can without revealing ourselves. Then we decide how best to integrate."

"And our magic?" asked Elsira, joining them. "Do we hide it completely?"

Sameril stared into the distance, considering the question that would shape their entire future on this world. But before he could answer, a small, choked sob drew his attention.

A young girl—no more than twelve years old, with haunted eyes that had witnessed unspeakable horrors beyond her tender years—stood slightly apart from the other battle-weary witches, her emerald robes too large for her slight, trembling frame, auburn hair falling in tangled, smoke-scented waves over tear-streaked cheeks. He hadn't noticed her before in the chaos of their desperate arrival and the frantic preparations for defense, but now that he looked closely, he saw the unmistakable familial resemblance in her determined jawline and piercing gaze.

"You're thinking of my sister, aren't you?" she asked, her voice small but determined.

Sameril approached her slowly, kneeling to meet her eyes. "You're a Tanner," he said, not a question but a realization.

The girl nodded. "Elara Tanner. Briella is—was—my eldest sister. She pushed me through the portal before staying behind."

The revelation hit Sameril with unexpected force. He had thought the Tanner line ended with Briella's sacrifice, but here was its continuation—a child, bearing the legacy of one of Eldoria's most respected witch families. Thirteen families had made it through the portal, not twelve.

"I'm sorry," he said, genuine emotion breaking through his carefully maintained composure. "Your sister saved us all."

Elara straightened, wiping her tears with a determined gesture that reminded him painfully of Briella. "The Tanners have always protected the balance. That's what our mother taught us. Briella did what she had to do."

Nivea came forward, placing a gentle hand on the girl's shoulder. "I'll look after her," she told Sameril quietly. "House Tanner's traditions will continue."

Sameril nodded gratefully, then turned back to the group to answer Elsira's question. "Our magic is who we are," he said. "But we must be cautious. This world has its own rules, its own balance. We'll practice in secret, teach in secret, until we understand how our abilities fit into the natural order here."

As the day wore on, the survivors established a temporary camp in the clearing, using their limited magic to create basic shelters and wards of protection. The forest around them bustled with unfamiliar wildlife—creatures neither threatening nor friendly, simply going about their existence in a world untouched by the war that had consumed Eldoria.

That night, as Earth's single moon rose above them—a pale, singular orb so unlike the triple moons of their home—the survivors gathered around a small fire. The flames cast dancing shadows across faces lined with exhaustion and grief, yet determined nonetheless.

Sameril noticed young Elara sitting close to Nivea, watching the proceedings with solemn intensity. Despite her youth, there was a strength in her gaze that spoke of generations of witch heritage. The Tanner line would endure, he realized. Would adapt and grow on this new world, just as all of them must.

"We should formalize our purpose," Sameril said, looking at each face in turn. "What we are now, what we must become."

"Guardians," suggested Talien. "Keepers of the old ways."

"Teachers," added Nivea, with a meaningful glance at Elara. "For future generations who will never know Eldoria except through us."

Sameril nodded, feeling the crystal warm against his chest as if responding to their intentions. "All of these. But most importantly, we are the balance. Two traditions, once separate, now united by circumstance and purpose."

He stood, raising his staff. "I propose a new covenant. No longer strictly necromancers or witches, but Eldorian mages—practitioners who honor both traditions while adapting to this new world."

One by one, the survivors rose to their feet, forming a circle around the fire. Even young Elara joined them, her small hand clasped firmly in Nivea's, her face set with determination beyond her years.

"We vow to preserve the knowledge entrusted to us," Sameril began, his voice carrying through the still night air.

"To protect it from those who would misuse it," continued Nivea.

"To pass it on to those worthy of its power," added Talien.

"To maintain the balance between life and death," Elsira contributed.

"And to remember those who sacrificed everything so that we might stand here today," said Elara, her clear voice ringing with unexpected strength.

"And to honor their memory by building something new," concluded Sam, his thoughts turning to Xaloth and Briella, to High Priestess Zara and the countless others who had fallen defending Eldoria.

As if summoned by their words, a gentle breeze stirred the flames, sending sparks spiraling upward toward the alien stars. For a brief, transcendent moment, Sameril could almost believe that the spirits of those they'd lost were with them, blessing this new beginning.

But the moment passed, leaving only the harsh reality of their situation—fourteen survivors on an unfamiliar world, carrying the last remnants of a once-great civilization. The path ahead would be difficult, fraught with challenges they could scarcely imagine.

Yet as Sameril looked around at the determined faces of his companions, his gaze lingering on young Elara Tanner, he felt something unexpected bloom within his chest—hope. Not the desperate hope of the doomed, but the quiet, resolute hope of those who carry a purpose greater than themselves.

"We begin anew," he said simply, lowering his staff. "Here on Earth, we will build something that would make our mentors proud. Something that preserves what was best about Eldoria while embracing what this world has to teach us."

The others nodded their agreement, a solemn pact formed beneath the stars of their new home. Sameril knew that the future was uncertain, that danger might yet follow them across the vastness of space. Malakai had vowed to hunt them to the ends of the universe itself.

But for now, they were safe. For now, they had survived. And in that survival—particularly in the continuation of bloodlines like the Tanners—lay the seed of eventual triumph. Not through conquest or domination as Malakai sought, but through preservation, adaptation, and growth.

As the fire burned low and the survivors settled into their first night on Earth, Sameril remained awake, his eyes fixed on the unfamiliar constellations above. The crystal pulsed gently against his chest, a reminder of all that had been lost and all that must now be protected.

"I will not fail you, Xaloth," he whispered to the stars. "I will keep the flame alive."

And somewhere in the vast darkness of space, across the unbridgeable gulf between worlds, he imagined his mentor might hear him. Might know that their sacrifice had not been in vain. That Eldoria's legacy would continue, here on this distant shore, for as long as the stars themselves endured.

Chapter 25

BEYOND THE DOOR

The afternoon sun cast long shadows through the windows of Sam's library, illuminating dust motes that danced between towering shelves of ancient books. Sam stood at his desk, poring over a weathered tome bound in midnight-blue leather, his brow furrowed in concentration.

"I dinna see why ye're so troubled," came a gruff voice from near the window. "The lass already knows about the library and the hellhound. The hard part's done."

Sam looked up to see Ezekiel's ghostly form perched on the windowsill, his translucent military uniform catching the fading sunlight. "The hard part," Sam replied, closing the book, "is explaining who I am and what I do without scaring her away completely."

"Bree Tanner isna some delicate flower that'll wilt at the first mention of necromancy," Ezekiel countered, folding his spectral arms. "She's got backbone, that one."

"She's also a witch whose entire tradition views communing with the dead as dangerous and unnatural," Sam said, running a hand through his hair. "Not to mention the Andromeda coven has historical reasons to be wary of necromancers."

"Then perhaps don't lead with 'Hello, I raise the dead for conversation and the occasional favor,'" suggested another voice as Margaret's pearlescent form drifted through the bookshelf. "Start small. Work your way up to the more... controversial bits."

Sam gave her a wry smile. "Helpful as always, Margaret."

"I do try." The Victorian ghost adjusted her spectral lace collar. "Though I must say, you're overthinking this entire situation. Just tell her the truth. After what she witnessed the other night, she deserves that much."

"That's the problem," Sam sighed, leaning against his desk. "I'm not entirely sure what the truth is regarding that attack. The use of electrical energy as a magical conduit isn't common practice, and the target being the Andromeda coven specifically—"

"Suggests someone with knowledge of their inner workings," Margaret finished, her expression thoughtful. "Someone who knew they'd be gathered that night."

"Or someone trackin' the Hat," Ezekiel added grimly. "Powerful artifacts tend to draw unwanted attention."

"Which is precisely why I need Talien's perspective on this." Sam straightened while reaching into his jacket, checking his pocket watch. "Morden should have found him by now. With his contacts in the esoteric community—"

The click of a door latch interrupted Sam's train of thought. All three turned to see one of the library's many doors swing open, revealing not a closet or hallway, but a swirling mist tinged with an otherworldly purple light. Through this supernatural fog stepped Morden, closing the door firmly behind him.

The goblin librarian looked immaculate as always in his tailored suit, though a slight dishevelment of his usually perfect hair suggested he'd encountered some difficulty during his mission. He adjusted his small spectacles and gave a precise bow.

"Master Sorken, I have located Talien," he announced, his voice formal yet carrying a hint of urgency that was unusual for the composed goblin.

"Excellent," Sam replied, moving toward him. "Where is he? Why didn't he return with you?"

Morden cleared his throat delicately. "Master Talien is currently... indisposed. He appears to be engaged in a game of chance with several members of the Winter Court of Faerie."

"The Winter Court?" Sam groaned, pinching the bridge of his nose. "That idiot. What's he wagering this time?"

"I was unable to ascertain the precise nature of the stakes," Morden replied, removing a folded handkerchief from his pocket to polish his spectacles. "However, judging by the intensity of the proceedings and the rather alarming presence of the Queen's Huntsman, I suspect they are significant."

"You've got to be jesting," Ezekiel exclaimed, floating closer. "The Huntsman himself? What in blazes is Talien thinking?"

"Bold of you to assume he's thinking at all," Margaret remarked dryly.

"I would normally agree with your assessment, Madam Margaret," Morden said with a slight incline of his head toward the spirit, "but Master Talien appeared quite deliberate in his actions. He claimed his participation was, and I quote, 'a necessary evil for the greater good.'"

"That sounds ominously familiar," Sam muttered, moving to a cabinet and pulling open a drawer. "Did he elaborate on what 'greater good' he's supposedly serving this time?"

"He indicated it was related to your inquiry regarding the attack on the witches," Morden replied, watching as Sam removed several items from the drawer—a silver knife with runes etched along its blade, a pouch of what appeared to be fine powder, and a collection of chalk sticks in various colors.

"And you couldn't convince him to leave?" Sam asked, tucking the items into his pockets.

Morden straightened his already impeccable tie. "My presence was... not welcomed by certain elements of the Court. I deemed it prudent to withdraw before causing a diplomatic incident that might compromise Master Talien's position further."

"Smart thinking," Margaret nodded approvingly. "The Fae aren't known for their tolerance of goblin-kind."

"Historical prejudices die hard, even among immortals," Morden agreed with a slight grimace. "Hence my return to request your assistance, Master Sorken. I believe your extraction of Master Talien is now a matter of some urgency."

"Samuel," Margaret's tone turned serious as she drifted between Sam and the door. "Remember you promised Bree answers tonight. She'll be here soon."

Sam checked his watch again. "We should have time. The Winter Court is only a short jump through the right doorway, and Talien can't afford to drag this out much longer." He looked at the spirits. "If we're not back when Bree arrives—"

"We'll make ourselves invisible," Margaret assured him. "We know the drill."

"And perhaps find a way to delay her?" Sam suggested, gathering a few more items from his desk.

"Ye want us to scare the poor lass?" Ezekiel crossed his translucent arms disapprovingly.

"Not scare," Sam clarified quickly. "Just... create a minor distraction if necessary. Nothing traumatic."

"Leave it to us," Margaret said. "Though I'd suggest you hurry. The Fae aren't known for their patience, especially when they suspect they're being cheated."

"Is Talien cheating?" Sam asked Morden sharply.

The goblin's expression remained carefully neutral. "I couldn't possibly comment on Master Talien's strategic approach. However, I did observe him manipulating his sleeve in a manner that seemed... mechanically suspicious."

"Of course he is," Sam sighed, moving to the door Morden had entered through. "That means we have even less time than I thought."

Sam placed his fingertips on the door frame and began to trace intricate patterns. As his fingers moved, glowing blue lines appeared in their wake, forming complex sigils that pulsed with magical energy.

"The last time ye tangled with the Winter Court, ye came back missing two fingers and sporting a rather nasty curse," Ezekiel reminded him, hovering nearby.

"I got the fingers back," Sam replied without pausing in his work.

"After three weeks of regeneration potions that made ye smell like rotten eggs," Margaret pointed out.

"And the curse is still active on the third Tuesday of every month," Ezekiel added.

"I'm aware of my history with the Fae," Sam said, completing the final sigil. The entire door frame now glowed with an ethereal blue light. "But Talien has information we need, and I'm not leaving him to the mercy of the Winter Court."

"Such as it is," Morden murmured.

Sam turned to the spirits one last time, his expression betraying unusual anxiety despite his centuries of experience with dangerous situations. "If anything happens—"

"Nothing's going to happen to you, dear," Margaret cut him off firmly, her translucent form flickering with maternal concern. "You'll go in, find that troublemaking friend of yours hiding in his magical sanctuary, drag him out by his pointy ear if necessary, and be back before the kettle boils for Bree's tea. Trust me on this."

"Just mind yer manners with the treacherous Fae and their twisted words," Ezekiel warned, crossing his spectral arms defensively. "No accepting gifts, no making promises that'll bind yer soul, and for the love of all that's holy, don't eat or drink anything they offer, no matter how tempting it appears."

"This isn't my first crossing into their realm, Ez," Sam said with a small, patient smile that didn't quite reach his worried eyes.

"No, but we're hoping it won't be yer last, lad," the Scottish spirit replied gruffly, genuine concern evident beneath his harsh tone.

Sam nodded to Morden. "Ready?"

The goblin straightened his waistcoat and gave a precise nod. "As ever, sir."

With a deep breath, Sam grasped the door handle and pulled. The door swung open to reveal not a closet, but a misty twilight landscape where impossibly tall trees stretched toward a starless purple sky. The air that wafted through carried the scent of frost and wild magic, along with distant, haunting music.

"After you," Sam gestured to Morden, who stepped through the doorway with surprising confidence for one entering the dangerous realm of the Fae.

Sam followed; the door swinging shut behind them with a soft click that seemed far too final in the suddenly quiet library.

Ezekiel drifted closer to Margaret, his translucent form flickering with concern in the fading light of the sigils.

"I hope the lad know's wha' he's doin'," he said softly.

Margaret sighed, the sound like autumn leaves rustling. "When has that ever been the case?" She gazed at the door, its frame still glowing faintly with Sam's magic. "But he always manages to muddle through. Somehow."

The spirits faded into the shadows as the library grew darker, the sigils on the door frame providing the only illumination as evening approached and with it, Bree Tanner's promised visit.

Chapter 26
WHAT WAS LOST

B ree glanced at the clock hanging above the register at Infinity Books. Ten minutes to closing, and the store was blissfully empty. She'd spent most of the afternoon shelving new arrivals and helping the occasional customer, all while her mind kept drifting to her upcoming meeting with Sam. What would he reveal? How would it connect to the attack on the street?

Sarah emerged from the back room, carrying a small box of special-order books.

"You know what?" Sarah said, setting the heavy box of rare antiquarian books on the counter with a decisive thud. "Why don't you head out early and beat the evening traffic? I can close up the shop myself without any trouble."

"Are you sure?" Bree asked, grateful for the offer but reluctant to leave her boss with all the closing duties.

Sarah waved a dismissive hand, her silver bracelets jingling softly with the casual movement. "Absolutely. You need to pick up dinner for everyone waiting back at the house, and I know you're anxious about meeting with Sam later to discuss his mysterious discoveries." She raised an eyebrow knowingly, a hint of amusement playing across her features. "Unless there's something else keeping you here that you haven't told me about yet?"

Bree smiled, untying her apron. "No, I'm going. Thank you."

"Don't forget, I want a full report tomorrow on what Sam tells you," Sarah reminded her. "As long as it's not... you know, something private between the two of you."

"Sarah!" Bree felt her cheeks warm. "It's not like that."

"If you say so." Sarah's eyes twinkled with amusement. "Either way, I'm curious about what our mysterious neighbor has to say."

Bree gathered her things and headed out, the bell above the door chiming as she stepped into the late afternoon air. The sky was beginning to shift from bright blue to the soft gold of approaching evening. She walked briskly toward Pizzeria Rustica, mentally calculating how much time she had before she needed to be at Sam's.

The pizza shop was busy with the dinner rush, the scent of baking dough and spices filling the warm interior. Bree waited her turn, absently studying the chalkboard menu though she already knew what she was ordering.

"Next customer, please!" called the cashier, a teenage boy with a dusting of flour on his black t-shirt.

Bree stepped forward. "Hi, I'd like to order two large pizzas for pickup. One veggie supreme and one pepperoni. And a small order of garlic chicken wings."

"Name for the order?"

"Tanner."

The boy punched in her order and gave her the total. As Bree paid, she found herself glancing at the clock above the register. Just enough time to get the pizzas home, have dinner with her family, and then make it to Sam's for their talk.

Twenty minutes later, Bree emerged from Pizzeria Rustica balancing two pizza boxes and a small paper bag containing the wings. The savory aroma made her stomach growl as she made her way down Willow Street toward home.

The Tanner house looked peaceful in the evening light, windows aglow with warm illumination from within. The protection sachets hanging from the porch railings swayed gently in the breeze, their subtle magic a comforting presence that had defined Bree's childhood home.

She juggled the food as she unlocked the front door, pushing it open with her hip. "I'm home!" she called, kicking off her shoes in the entryway.

"In here!" Molly's voice answered from the family room.

Bree followed the sound to find her sister sitting cross-legged on the floor, surrounded by various small objects—crystals, herbs tied with twine, small bottles of oils, and what appeared to be a hand-drawn diagram of the house. Molly's dark hair was pulled back in a messy bun, and she had a smudge of something that looked like crushed sage on her cheek.

"Dinner," Bree announced, holding up the pizza boxes and bag. "Veggie supreme, pepperoni, and wings."

Molly looked up from her work, her eyes lighting up at the sight of food. "Perfect timing. I'm starving. Just let me finish setting this ward and I'll be right there."

"What exactly are you working on?" Bree asked, peering at the diagram.

"Enhanced protection ward," Molly explained, carefully placing a small crystal at what appeared to be the corner of the house on her drawing. "After what happened the other night, we need every layer of security we can get. This one ties into the foundation of the house itself, making it harder for hostile energy to penetrate."

"Impressive," Bree said, genuinely meaning it. Molly had always had a talent for protective magic.

"I'll be done in five minutes, tops," Molly promised. "Don't let Mom eat all the wings before I get there."

Bree laughed. "No promises."

She continued to the kitchen, where she found not just her mother, but also Susan Fond and Elaine Warren gathered around the large wooden table. Various bottles, jars, and bundles of herbs were spread out before them, along with a large, weathered book that Bree recognized as one of her grandmother's grimoires.

"Look what I found," Bree said, holding up the pizza boxes.

Mary Ann looked up from the book with a smile. "Perfect timing, sweetheart. We were just about to wrap up here."

"Hi, Bree," Susan greeted warmly. "Sarah mentioned you'd be stopping by Pizzeria Rustica. Smart thinking—none of us were in the mood to cook after all this preparation."

"Is that garlic I smell?" Elaine asked, sniffing appreciatively. "Please tell me you got wings."

Bree held up the paper bag. "Small order of garlic chicken wings, as requested."

"Bless you," Elaine said with feeling. "After the day we've had, I need protein."

"What have you all been working on?" Bree asked, setting the food on the counter and moving to gather plates from the cabinet.

"Protective potions," Mary Ann explained, closing the grimoire. "Some to be mixed with paint for the doorframes, others to be sprinkled at entry points around the property."

"And this," Susan added, holding up a small bottle filled with luminescent blue liquid, "is for emergencies only. It creates a temporary barrier that nothing—magical or mundane—can cross for about five minutes."

"Enough time to escape if needed," Elaine clarified, helping Bree distribute the plates.

Mary Ann began clearing the potion-making supplies from the table. "Molly still working on her ward?"

"Almost done," Bree confirmed, opening the pizza boxes. The savory aroma filled the kitchen, drawing an appreciative sigh from all three women.

"I'll get drinks," Susan offered, moving to the refrigerator. "Water? Tea?"

"Water's fine," Bree said. "Molly made a fresh pitcher of sweet tea this morning too."

As Susan poured drinks and Mary Ann finished clearing the table, Elaine leaned closer to Bree. "So," she said in a low voice, "Sarah mentioned you've been spending time with your neighbor. The writer."

Bree felt her cheeks warm. "It's not what you think. Sam and I are just... talking."

"Mm-hmm," Elaine hummed skeptically, a knowing smile playing at her lips.

"Really," Bree insisted. "I'm going over there after dinner because he promised to explain some things. About his house, and... other things."

Elaine raised an eyebrow but didn't push further. "Well, he's certainly easy on the eyes, I'll give him that."

"Mom," Bree warned, glancing at Mary Ann, who thankfully seemed absorbed in arranging napkins.

Elaine winked and moved to help Susan with the drinks.

Molly entered the kitchen, dusting her hands off. "All done. The ward is set and active." She sniffed appreciatively. "Oh, that smells amazing."

"Wash your hands first," Mary Ann instructed automatically. "You're covered in sage and salt."

Molly rolled her eyes good-naturedly but complied, scrubbing her hands at the sink. "The ward should hold against most magical intrusions," she explained over the running water. "It's tied to the house's foundation stones and the old oak out front. Anything with harmful intent will basically hit a brick wall."

"Good work," Susan said approvingly. "Between your ward, our potions, and the additional protection charms we'll set tomorrow, this house should be as secure as it can be before the ceremony."

As the women prepared to sit down, none of them noticed the faint shimmer in the air upstairs, or the subtle flicker of the lights that accompanied it. The air rippled and parted as Nissa Drach materialized, her lean frame wrapped in a dark shawl, her boots making no sound on the aged oak flooring.

Downstairs, the witches settled around the table, the earlier tension momentarily forgotten as they enjoyed the simple pleasure of sharing a meal. Conversation flowed easily, touching on preparations for the ceremony, town gossip, and the latest shipment of books at Infinity.

As Bree reached for another slice of pizza, she glanced at the clock. "I should probably text Sam that I'll be a bit late. I promised I'd stop by this evening."

Mary Ann nodded. "Just be careful when you do go over, sweetheart. After what happened..."

"I know, Mom," Bree assured her. "It's just next door, and I won't stay long." She hesitated. "Actually, there's something I should probably tell you all about Sam's house first."

Four pairs of eyes turned to her with interest.

"I was going to wait until after I talked to him tonight, but..." Bree took a deep breath and began to recount her adventure in Sam's impossible library, the hellhound, and the goblin librarians.

By the time she finished, the pizza was forgotten, and everyone was staring at her with expressions ranging from concern to fascination.

"Goblins?" Elaine repeated. "As in, actual goblins?"

"Librarian goblins," Bree confirmed.

"And the space inside his house—it's bigger than should be physically possible?" Susan clarified.

Bree nodded. "Much bigger. The library alone was the size of a cathedral."

Molly leaned forward, eyes bright with interest. "That would take incredible spatial manipulation magic. Most witches can't even create a pocket dimension large enough to store extra kitchen supplies, let alone an entire library."

"Which means Sam is... what, exactly?" Mary Ann asked, her brow furrowed with concern.

"I don't know," Bree admitted. "That's what I'm hoping to find out tonight."

"A witch, surely," Susan suggested. "Perhaps from a different tradition than ours."

"Maybe," Bree agreed. "Sarah thought the same thing."

"Wait," Mary Ann interrupted. "Sarah knows about this?"

"I told her this morning," Bree explained. "I needed someone to talk to about it, and she knew Grandma had some kind of relationship with Sam."

"Relationship?" Molly echoed, eyebrows rising.

"Not that kind of relationship," Bree clarified. "Sarah said they 'respected each other' and that Grandma thought Sam was 'useful to have nearby,' whatever that means."

Elaine and Mary Ann exchanged a look that Bree couldn't quite interpret.

"What?" she asked. "Do you know something about Sam and Grandma?"

"Not specifically," Mary Ann said carefully. "But your grandmother did mention a neighbor once or twice. Said she trusted his judgment in certain matters."

"Nancy was always selective about who she shared information with," Susan added. "Even within the coven."

"So you think Sam is... what? An ally?" Bree pressed.

"I think," Mary Ann said, "that you should hear what he has to say tonight. And then share it with us."

Their increasingly urgent conversation was interrupted by a faint sound from upstairs—a slow, deliberate creak of ancient floorboards that would normally go unnoticed if not for the sudden, attentive stillness that fell over the vigilant witches.

Molly set down her slice of pizza, head tilted slightly. "Did you hear that?"

Mary Ann frowned. "The house settling, maybe?"

Another creak followed, more distinct than the first.

"That's not the house settling," Elaine said quietly, her hand moving instinctively to a protective amulet at her throat.

Molly stood, wiping her hands on a napkin. "I'll check it out. Probably just a window left open." Despite her casual words, the set of her shoulders betrayed tension.

"I don't like it," Susan murmured. "Not after what happened on the street."

"My wards should be active," Molly reminded them. "Nothing with harmful intent should be able to get in." She moved toward the kitchen doorway. "I'll be right back."

Bree watched her sister disappear into the hall, an uneasy feeling settling in her stomach. The women at the table continued eating, but the earlier easy conversation had evaporated, replaced by a hyperawareness of every sound in the old house.

Upstairs, Nissa's eyes darted to the faded photos lining the hall wall—a watercolor of Ballad's fairgrounds, glimpses of the Tanner family through the years—before settling on Nancy's partially open bedroom door. Kestrel's orders burned in her mind: "Get the hat—break their power."

Her fingers brushed the voodoo talisman hanging around her neck, a bone shard that pulsed with its own energy, ready to aid her escape once the task was done. She pushed the bedroom door wider, revealing a four-poster bed with a sagging mattress, a cluttered dresser, and—her heart quickened—a cedar box on the bedside table, glowing faintly with the distinctive shimmer of a magical ward.

Nissa knelt before the box, hands trembling slightly as she traced the outline of the lock. All of Kestrel's lessons on ward-breaking flashed through her mind.

"It's not just a hat," Kestrel had hissed at her in the bayou shack, green fire flaring in the hearth. "It's their craft—every witch's life, stored when they die. Nancy's knowledge, Molly's too when her time comes—take it, and we wield centuries of power."

Guilt gnawed at Nissa's conscience about stealing such a legacy, but the memory of Kestrel's whip scars ached on her back, and fear was a powerful motivator. "Just the hat," she whispered to herself, beginning the chant that would unravel the ward. The glowing protection around the box flickered, then dissolved.

With trembling fingers, she lifted the lid. Inside, nestled on velvet, sat a black felt hat, unremarkable to the untrained eye but humming with power to Nissa's magical senses. It practically vibrated with stored knowledge, alive with the secrets of generations. She reached for it, breath hitching at the weight of what she was about to steal.

On the stairs, Molly paused, head cocked to one side. There it was again—a voice, faint but unmistakable, coming from her grandmother's old room. Her protective instincts flared. Whatever—whoever—was in Nancy's room shouldn't be there.

Molly moved silently down the hall, drawing magic to her fingertips, ready to defend her family's home. She reached the doorway just as Nissa lifted the hat from its velvet nest.

"Hey—who're you?" Molly's voice cut through the room, steady and sharp.

Nissa spun around, eyes wide with panic, the hat clutched in her hands. Molly stood in the doorway, hands raised, a flicker of witch-light sparking at her fingers.

"Put that down," Molly said, stepping closer, "and we can talk."

Nissa's heart raced—Kestrel's wrath or this girl's mercy? In the end, panic won. "Stay back!" she snapped, thrusting a hand out—a voodoo blast erupted, wild and green, meant only to stun.

It hit Molly square in the chest. She gasped, stumbling backward, eyes widening in shock—not meant to kill, not meant to kill. The force slammed her into the corner of the dresser, a sickening crack as her head struck the solid wood. She crumpled to the floor, still, the witch-light fading from her fingertips.

Nissa froze, breath hitching—no, no, no. Blood pooled beneath Molly's dark hair, stark against the oak floorboards. The hat slipped from Nissa's grip, landing beside her—she hadn't meant this, hadn't wanted death.

Downstairs in the kitchen, the minutes stretched on without Molly's return. Bree set down her glass, a sense of foreboding growing stronger.

"She's been gone a while," she said, trying to keep her voice casual.

Susan and Elaine exchanged glances. "Perhaps we should check," Susan suggested.

Bree was already rising from her chair. "Moll?" she called up the stairs. "You okay up there?"

Silence was her only answer.

"I'm going to go see what's keeping her," Bree said, moving toward the stairs. Mary Ann nodded, her own expression tight with concern.

Bree's boots hit the stairs, her pace quickening with each step, dread clawing up her spine. "Molly?" she called again, louder now.

Upstairs, Nissa heard the approaching footsteps. Panic surged anew. She snatched up the fallen hat, fingers shaking, and clutched her talisman. "Legba, take me," she whispered, her voice breaking. Green smoke swirled around her feet, rising quickly to envelop her entire body.

Nissa vanished just as Bree burst into the room, the air snapping shut behind her with a sound like a thunderclap.

Bree stopped dead in her tracks. Molly lay sprawled on the floor, eyes open but unseeing, a thin trickle of blood staining the floorboards beneath her head. Her sister, her rock, gone.

"Molly?" she whispered, voice breaking. Bree dropped to her knees beside Molly's still form. "No—Moll, wake up!" Her cries tore from her throat, grief drowning her as she pulled Molly's body close, rocking back and forth. Tears soaked into Molly's hair as Bree's world collapsed around her.

The air in the room shimmered, and Molly's spirit bloomed into existence—translucent, peaceful, a gentle echo of the vibrant young woman she had been. "Bree," she said, her voice like a distant breeze.

Bree's head snapped up, hope and pain warring in her tear-filled eyes. "Moll? You're here?"

Molly's spirit knelt beside her, a ghostly hand brushing Bree's cheek. "I'm alright, Bree—it's okay." Her touch was unfelt, only a slight coolness in the air, which shattered Bree further.

"No!" Bree sobbed, clutching Molly's physical body tighter. "You can't go, I need you!"

Molly's spirit smiled, sad but steady. "I'm not leaving; not really. The hat—she took it. It's got me in it—everything I learned, everything Grandma knew. You've got to get it back—its power's yours now."

Bree shook her head, tears streaming down her face. "I don't care about power, I want you!"

Molly's voice softened, her form growing fainter. "You're stronger than you know; my backup, now the front. The hat's our line—Nancy's craft, mine—wear it, and I'm with you. Stop her, Bree—I love you, always."

The glow wavered, Molly's spirit beginning to fade. "No... stay!" Bree cried, reaching through the air where her sister's ghost hovered.

"Get it back—stop her," Molly whispered as she vanished completely, leaving Bree alone with her body and a mission forged in loss.

Bree's wails filled the room, echoing down the hallway. She rocked back and forth, clutching Molly's cooling body, the blood staining her hands and clothes. Outside, the wind began to howl, dogs barked frantically down the street, and Sam's oak tree swayed violently—a storm breaking, inside and out. The hat was gone, Molly was gone, and Bree's grief was a fire she couldn't quench; not yet.

The sound of pounding footsteps came from the staircase, followed by Mary Ann's voice, tight with panic. "Bree? What's happened?"

Mary Ann reached the doorway first, Susan and Elaine right behind her. They froze in the frame of the door, the scene before them stopping their hearts.

Bree knelt on the floor, rocking back and forth, Molly's limp body cradled in her arms. Blood pooled around them both, dark against the wood, soaking into Bree's jeans. Molly's face was ashen, her eyes vacant, while Bree's was twisted in anguish, tears streaming unchecked down her cheeks.

"No," Mary Ann breathed, the word barely audible, a mother's denial in the face of the unthinkable. "No, no, no..."

She stumbled forward, dropping to her knees beside her daughters, hands reaching out but hesitating, as if afraid to confirm what her eyes were telling her.

Susan pressed a hand to her mouth, a choked sob escaping as Elaine gripped her arm for support, her own face draining of color.

"What happened?" Mary Ann finally managed, her voice breaking as she gently touched Molly's cold cheek.

"Someone was here," Bree gasped between sobs. "A woman. She took the hat. Molly tried to stop her and—" She couldn't continue, fresh grief overwhelming her.

"The hat?" Elaine whispered, horror dawning on her face. "Nancy's hat?"

Bree nodded, unable to form words, clinging to Molly as if she might yet return.

Mary Ann gathered both her daughters in her arms, one living, one gone, her own tears falling into Molly's dark hair. "My baby," she whispered. "My brave girl."

Susan approached slowly, kneeling beside them, one hand reaching out to squeeze Bree's shoulder. "Bree," she said gently, "did you... did you see her? Molly's spirit?"

Bree looked up, her face tear-streaked and devastated. "Yes," she whispered. "She... she's in the hat now. With Grandma. She said I have to get it back."

The four women huddled together around Molly's body, grief and determination mingling in the air around them. Outside, the wind continued to rise, branches scratching against the windows like mourners seeking entry. The storm was coming, both literal and figurative, and at its center lay a hat bearing the accumulated knowledge of generations—and now, the fresh spirit of Molly Tanner.

Chapter 27
The Winter Court

The transition between worlds was instantaneous yet disorienting. One moment Sam and Morden stood in the warm, book-lined library; the next, they were surrounded by towering silver birches whose naked branches clawed at the purple twilight sky. A thin blanket of pristine snow covered the forest floor, glowing with an inner luminescence that cast more light than the starless sky above.

Despite the snow, the air wasn't particularly cold—it was more the idea of winter than winter itself, as if the concept had been distilled into pure sensory experience without the discomfort. Every breath Sam took tasted of pine and frost and something indefinably wild.

"The settlement is just ahead," Morden said, his voice barely above a whisper yet carrying clearly in the strange acoustics of the Fae woodland. "Beyond that ridge."

Sam nodded, treading carefully along a path so narrow it seemed more suggestion than reality. Snow crunched beneath his boots, each step leaving a temporary imprint that slowly filled itself in after he moved on. The forest watched them—not metaphorically, but literally. Sam could feel the weight of countless invisible gazes tracking their progress.

"Remember," he murmured to Morden, "the Winter Court values decorum above all else. No matter what happens, maintain absolute politeness."

"You need not concern yourself with my manners, Master Sorken," the goblin replied with dignified affront. "I am well-versed in the protocols of Faerie. It is Master Talien's behavior that should concern us."

Sam couldn't argue with that. As they crested the ridge, the elven settlement came into view below them. It wasn't the rustic woodland village that human imagination might conjure; the Fae had no interest in mimicking mortal limitations. Instead, the structures appeared to have grown organically from the forest itself—soaring spires of living wood and ice that twisted impossibly upward, connected by crystalline bridges that sparkled in the sourceless illumination of the realm.

At the center of the settlement stood what could only be described as a palace, though calling it such felt woefully inadequate. It was a monument of ice and silver and living wood, its architecture defying mortal physics, towers spiraling in directions that made the eye water if observed too long.

"The Winter Palace," Morden observed unnecessarily. "Her Majesty must be in residence."

"Wonderful," Sam muttered. "Just what we need—royal attention."

They descended toward the settlement, following a path that widened as they approached the outer buildings. Lanterns hung from tree branches, filled not with mundane flame but with dancing motes of Fae magic that cast a cool, silvery light across the snow.

As they reached the outskirts of the settlement, Sam stopped and turned to Morden. "Wait here," he instructed. "The fewer of us who enter, the less likely we are to cause offense."

Morden nodded, though his expression betrayed mild disappointment. "A prudent decision, though I had hoped to observe the Court in session."

"Another time, perhaps," Sam said, knowing full well he'd never willingly bring any of his goblin librarians into the heart of Faerie again. "If I'm not back within an hour—"

"I shall return to the doorway and await you there," Morden finished. "And if you have not returned within three hours, I shall inform the spirits of your predicament."

Sam clapped the goblin on his small shoulder. "Let's hope it doesn't come to that."

He continued alone down the path toward the settlement's main entrance—an arched gateway formed by two living trees that had grown together, their branches intertwining to create an intricate canopy overhead. The trunks were wrapped in delicate silver chains that chimed softly in a breeze Sam couldn't feel.

Two sentries stood on either side of the arch, so still they might have been statues if not for the occasional blink of their almond-shaped eyes. They were tall and impossibly slender, clad in armor that appeared to be made of silver frost. Their pointed ears peeked through straight white hair that fell past their shoulders.

As Sam approached, both sentries shifted in perfect unison, their spears crossing to block his path. Though their movements were fluid, something about their synchronicity felt distinctly inhuman.

"Samuel Sorken," one of the sentries said, though neither of their lips appeared to move. "Necromancer. Last admitted to the Winter Court seven years past, when you departed under... contested circumstances."

Sam winced internally at the reminder. "I've resolved those misunderstandings," he said carefully. "All debts are paid."

"New debts are ever eager to be born," replied the other sentry, a faint smile playing at the corners of its mouth. "What brings you to the Court of Her Frostborne Majesty?"

"I seek only to retrieve my friend and colleague, Talien, who I believe is currently engaged in entertainment at one of your establishments," Sam said, choosing his words with precision. "My intention is to collect him and depart without disturbing the Court's proceedings."

The sentries exchanged a glance that seemed to communicate volumes.

"The one called Talien has provided much... amusement this evening," the first sentry said. "Her Majesty's Huntsman has taken particular interest in his games."

That wasn't good news. The Huntsman was notorious for his love of high-stakes gambling and his creative interpretation of the rules when he lost.

"I merely wish to speak with Talien briefly," Sam persisted. "Then we shall both take our leave. I have no intention of interfering with any ongoing entertainments."

The sentries considered this for a moment, then withdrew their spears in the same unsettling unison with which they had crossed them.

"You may proceed, necromancer," they said together. "But be warned—the laws of hospitality protect you only so long as you observe proper etiquette. Any perceived slight will be answered threefold."

"I understand and accept the terms of entry," Sam replied with a formal nod.

As he passed between them, the air shimmered slightly, as if he'd walked through an invisible curtain. The sensation wasn't unpleasant, but it left a tingling across his skin that reminded him he was being marked—the Court would know his location at all times now.

The settlement's interior was even more beautiful and disorienting than it had appeared from the ridge. Fae of various ranks and stations moved through the winding pathways with the languid grace of predators who had no need to hurry. Most paid Sam no attention, though a few noted his passage with calculating eyes or amused smiles.

Sam didn't need directions to find Talien. The loudest establishment would inevitably be where his friend had chosen to tempt fate. He followed the sound of ethereal music and raucous laughter until he reached a structure that resembled a tavern, if a tavern could be grown rather than built and was designed by someone with only a passing acquaintance with Euclidean geometry.

The entrance was a twisted spiral of wood that opened as Sam approached, admitting him to a space that was simultaneously cavernous and intimate. Tables of living wood dotted the room, each one unique in shape and surrounded by Fae in various states of merriment. The ceiling overhead shifted constantly, sometimes appearing to be a canopy of leaves, other times a field of stars, occasionally opening to reveal glimpses of landscapes that couldn't possibly exist outside.

Musicians played in one corner on instruments made of ice and bone, producing music that made Sam's teeth ache with its beauty and wrongness. The melodies seemed to slide between his thoughts, rearranging them slightly before moving on.

He scanned the room, looking for Talien's familiar figure among the otherworldly patrons. He spotted him at the back of the tavern, seated at a round table with four Fae nobles—evident by their elaborate attire and the way other patrons gave their table a wide berth.

Talien hadn't changed much in the years since Sam had last seen him. His dark hair was still pulled back in a ponytail, though perhaps with a few more silver strands than before. His lean face was clean-shaven, and his eyes—when he glanced up and spotted Sam—still held that characteristic gleam of perpetual amusement at some private joke.

What concerned Sam was not Talien's appearance, but rather the expression on the faces of his Fae companions. The tallest of them, a male with antlers sprouting from his temples—unmistakably the Queen's Huntsman—was watching Talien's hands with narrowed eyes. The others exchanged glances that communicated suspicion and growing irritation.

Whatever game they were playing, Talien appeared to be winning. And in the Winter Court, unexplained winning streaks were often interpreted as cheating, whether evidence existed or not.

Sam moved carefully through the tavern, nodding respectfully to any Fae whose gaze he met, but otherwise making himself as unobtrusive as possible. As he neared Talien's table, he could see the game more clearly—cards made of what appeared to be thin sheets of ice lay on the table, each one etched with symbols that shifted and changed even as he watched.

Talien glanced up again, meeting Sam's eyes with a barely perceptible nod before returning his attention to the game. The acknowledgment had been brief, but Sam had known Talien long enough to read the message in it: *Wait. Almost done.*

Sam positioned himself near the wall, close enough to observe but not so close as to appear involved. The Huntsman laid down a card that flashed with crimson light, causing several nearby Fae to murmur appreciatively. Talien studied it for a moment, then placed one of his own cards beside it. The symbol on Talien's card seemed to devour the Huntsman's, growing more complex as it did so.

The Huntsman's face darkened, his antlers lengthening slightly as his composure slipped. "A fortunate play," he said, his voice like ice cracking. "Your luck has been... remarkable this evening."

"Fortune favors the observant," Talien replied with an easy smile that didn't quite reach his eyes. He gathered the small pile of tokens at the center of the table—objects that appeared to be carved from moonlight. "Shall we call it a night? I've imposed on your hospitality long enough."

"One more hand," the Huntsman insisted, his tone making it clear this wasn't truly a request. "Double stakes."

Talien hesitated, glancing briefly toward Sam. "I really should be on my way. A prior engagement, you understand."

"Surely your friend can wait," said one of the female Fae, her skin the blue-white of glacier ice, her smile sharp as a blade. "The night is yet young."

Sam recognized the dangerous undercurrent in their voices. The Fae were no longer amused, and Talien's continued winning had transformed him from entertaining diversion to insulting anomaly. It was time to intervene.

He stepped forward with careful, measured movements that respected fae etiquette, bowing deeply and respectfully to the ornately carved table where the powerful entities sat watching. "My sincerest apologies for the unexpected interruption of your esteemed gathering," he said formally, his voice adopting the ancient cadence required for addressing fae nobility. "I am Samuel Sorken, seventh-circle necromancer of Ballad and guardian of its mortal boundaries. I've come to collect my wayward colleague on a matter of urgent business concerning what I believe to be imminent magical danger."

The Huntsman's piercing, inhuman gaze shifted to Sam, cold and assessing like winter frost, recognition dawning in his ancient eyes. "The arrogant death-speaker returns to our realm after all these centuries," he said, thin lips curling slightly into a predatory smile that revealed unnaturally sharp teeth. "Last we met in the Crystal Forests, you departed rather hastily with fewer fingers than you arrived with, as I recall with pleasure."

"A regrettable misunderstanding that has since been fully resolved through proper magical channels," Sam replied smoothly, his scarred hand subtly flexing at his side as ancient memories surfaced. "I hold no lingering grudges for past transactions fairly concluded according to the ancient laws binding our realms, unlike some who nurse centuries-old slights." His steady gaze never wavered from the Huntsman's predatory eyes, silently communicating both respect and unwillingness to be intimidated by the powerful fae.

"And yet," the Huntsman continued, his cold voice dripping with barely contained malice and ancient suspicion, "you arrive at a most... convenient moment for your impudent friend, who has been enjoying an unusual, unprecedented streak of good fortune at our considerable expense and diminished honor."

"Purely coincidental, I assure you," Sam said. "Though I must insist that Talien accompany me now. A mutual acquaintance awaits us, and the hour grows late in our realm."

Talien began gathering his winnings, moving with deliberate casualness. "It's been a pleasure, as always," he told his companions. "Perhaps we can continue another evening."

The Huntsman placed a hand on Talien's arm, his long fingers wrapping entirely around Talien's wrist. The tavern grew suddenly quiet, the musicians faltering in their playing.

"Before you depart," the Huntsman said, his voice soft but carrying in the silence, "perhaps you might empty your sleeves? Only as a courtesy, of course."

Talien's smile didn't waver, though Sam noticed a tightening around his eyes. "Of course," he agreed. "Though I assure you, my attire contains nothing untoward."

With his free hand, Talien turned back first one sleeve, then the other, demonstrating they were empty. The Huntsman released his grip, but his suspicious expression remained.

"Your boots, perhaps?" suggested the glacier-skinned Fae woman.

"Or your thoughts?" added another with a predatory smile, knowing the abilities of his guest. "The necromancer could extract those for examination, I'm sure."

This was rapidly deteriorating. Sam stepped closer to the table. "We've imposed on your hospitality long enough," he said firmly. "Talien has demonstrated his good faith, and we both have pressing matters to attend to in our realm."

The Huntsman rose to his full height—considerably taller than either human—his antlers nearly scraping the shifting ceiling. "Very well," he said after a tense moment. "Take your friend and go. But know this, necromancer—the Winter Court has long memories. Debts unpaid have a way of... compounding interest."

"I understand completely," Sam replied with another bow. "We thank you for your indulgence and bid you good evening."

Talien stood, pocketing his winnings with a flourish that Sam thought unnecessarily provocative under the circumstances. With a final bow to the table, Talien moved to join Sam, and together they made their way toward the exit.

"Not a word until we're clear of the settlement," Sam muttered under his breath as they walked through the tavern. Several Fae watched their departure with expressions ranging from amusement to disappointment to calculating interest.

The spiral entrance unwound to allow them passage back into the main pathways of the settlement. They walked at a measured pace—neither too slow to suggest lingering nor too quick to imply fear—toward the gate where the sentries still stood in perfect stillness.

"Departing so soon, necromancer?" one asked as they approached.

"Our business is concluded," Sam replied simply.

"For now," the other added with a knowing smile.

The sentries stepped aside, allowing them to pass through the archway. Only when they had put several hundred yards between themselves and the settlement did Sam allow himself to release the breath he'd been holding.

"Are you trying to get yourself killed?" he demanded as soon as they were out of earshot, knowing full well what might have happened. "The Huntsman? Really, Talien?"

Talien grinned, the expression transforming his serious face into something boyish and mischievous. "Good to see you too, Sam. It's been what, five years?"

"Seven," Sam corrected. "And you haven't changed a bit. Still courting disaster like it's your one true love."

"Says the man who just walked willingly into the Winter Court," Talien countered. "Where's Morden? I assume he's the one who fetched you?"

"Waiting ahead," Sam replied, gesturing toward a large boulder where the goblin's small form was barely visible in the perpetual twilight. "And you're lucky he found me. The Huntsman was about to turn that game into something far less pleasant."

"I had it under control," Talien insisted, patting his pocket where the moonlight tokens clinked softly. "Besides, I needed these."

"For what?"

"I'll explain everything in precise detail once we're safely back in your mortal realm away from curious entities," Talien whispered urgently, his normally jovial expression uncharacteristically serious. "It's not safe to discuss certain sensitive matters here where words have binding power." Talien tapped his pointed ear meaningfully, his eyes darting to the shimmering foliage surrounding them, reminding Sam that in Faerie, the very trees could be listening and reporting their conversations to interested parties with ancient grudges.

They reached the boulder where Morden waited, the goblin rising to his feet upon seeing their approach, showing evident relief at their appearance.

"Master Talien," he greeted with a formal nod. "I am pleased to see you unmaimed and still in possession of your soul."

"Your confidence is touching as always, Morden," Talien replied with a grin. "Did you miss me?"

"The library has been notably quieter in your absence," the goblin observed diplomatically.

"We need to move," Sam interrupted. "The doorway should still be stable, but I'd rather not linger here longer than necessary."

They set off through the silver birch forest, retracing the narrow path that would lead them back to the doorway between realms. The eyes of the forest followed their progress, more intense now, as if the very essence of Faerie was watching to see if they would escape its clutches.

"So," Talien said as they walked, "I hear you finally revealed your library to Bree Tanner. About time."

Sam shot him a warning look. "Not now."

"Fine, fine," Talien raised his hands in mock surrender. "But you and I are having a long conversation once we're back. There are things happening that you need to know about."

"That's why I sent Morden to find you," Sam replied. "After the attack on the coven—"

"You said not now," Talien cut him off, glancing meaningfully at the trees around them. "Patience, old friend. All will be revealed in due time."

The snow still glowed with its inner light, illuminating their way toward home and the explanations that awaited.

Chapter 28
Revelations

Gradually, Bree's sobs subsided, replaced by a tightness in her chest that felt like her grief was crystallizing into something harder, sharper. She drew a ragged breath and gently laid Molly's body back on the floor, arranging her sister's limbs with tender care. When she looked up, her face was tear-streaked but set with determination, her eyes burning with a newfound resolve.

"This wasn't an accident," she said, her voice rough from crying but steady. "Someone did this. Someone took the hat and killed Molly."

Mary Ann remained kneeling beside Molly's body, her face a mask of shock, one hand still stroking her daughter's hair as if she might somehow coax life back into her.

Bree turned to Susan and Elaine. "Can you stay with Mom? Help her... help her take care of Molly." Her voice caught on her sister's name, but she pushed through. "She shouldn't be alone right now."

Susan nodded, her own eyes red-rimmed. "Of course. We'll stay as long as needed."

"Where are you going?" Elaine asked, noting the determined set of Bree's shoulders.

"Next door," Bree replied, rising to her feet. "To talk to Sam."

"Sam?" Mary Ann looked up, momentarily pulled from her grief. "Why—"

"He knows things, Mom. About magic, about different traditions. Maybe about who might want Grandma's hat." Bree's hands clenched into fists at her sides. "He was supposed to tell me everything tonight. Well, I'm not waiting for an invitation anymore."

"Bree," Susan started, concern etching her features, "are you sure that's wise? After what just happened—"

"I'm done with being careful," Bree cut her off. "Molly's dead. The hat is gone. And I'm going to find out what Sam knows."

Without waiting for further discussion, Bree strode from the room, her footsteps heavy on the stairs as she descended. The front door slammed behind her, the sound reverberating through the house like a gunshot.

Outside, the wind had picked up, whipping Bree's hair around her face as she marched next door. Her mind raced with questions, each one burning hotter than the last. What did Sam know about this? Had he known something like this might happen? Who was he, really? Why had her grandmother considered him "useful to have nearby"?

The short walk to Sam's house felt both endless and instantaneous, her fury propelling her forward. The blood on her hands and clothes had dried to a rusty brown, but she barely noticed. She pounded on Sam's front door, the impact sending jarring pain up her arm that she welcomed as an anchor to reality.

No answer.

She knocked again, harder this time. "Sam! Open the door!"

Silence greeted her.

Bree tried the handle and found it unlocked. For a split second, caution whispered in her ear—walking uninvited into someone's home was crossing a line. But the memory of Molly's unseeing eyes drowned out that whisper, and she pushed the door open.

"Sam?" she called, stepping into the entryway. The house was quiet, still. Not the peaceful stillness of an empty home, but the tense quiet of a space holding its breath.

Bree moved through the rooms on the main floor, finding no sign of Sam. The kitchen was spotless, no evidence of the hellhound she'd encountered before. The living room was undisturbed, books neatly arranged on shelves, a half-empty coffee mug on a side table the only indication someone had been there recently.

Her search led her upstairs to the bedroom where she and Sam had fled from the hellhound. The room looked ordinary now—a neatly made bed, a dresser, a desk with a laptop closed on its surface. And the wardrobe that had contained the impossible passage to the library.

Bree approached it with determination, pulling open its doors to reveal hanging clothes—shirts and jackets, nothing out of the ordinary. She pushed them aside, feeling along the back panel of the wardrobe. There had to be a way through, a hidden latch or—

The back panel slid sideways at her touch, revealing the narrow corridor beyond, just as she remembered it. Bree stepped into the passage without hesitation, leaving the normality of Sam's bedroom behind.

The corridor twisted and turned, leading deeper into a space that couldn't possibly exist within the confines of Sam's house. Finally, it opened onto the vast expanse of the library she'd glimpsed before—towering shelves filled with ancient tomes, spiral staircases connecting multiple levels, reading nooks scattered throughout the cavernous space.

Bree spotted Tord and Glenken at a large table near the center of the room, engaged in what appeared to be a heated discussion over an open book. They didn't notice her at first, allowing her to catch a snippet of their argument.

"—clearly states the transference requires a living vessel," Tord was saying, his thin finger jabbing at a page.

"Only if the original binding was improperly—" Glenken broke off as he spotted Bree approaching. "Miss Tanner! This is... unexpected."

Tord's head snapped up, his tiny spectacles sliding down his long nose. "Indeed. Most unexpected. Master Sorken did not inform us you would be visiting again so soon."

"Where is he?" Bree demanded, skipping any pretense of politeness.

The goblins exchanged glances. "Master Sorken is not currently present," Tord replied carefully.

"I can see that," Bree said, her patience wearing thin. "Where did he go?"

"He had urgent business elsewhere," Glenken offered, his bushy eyebrows drawing together as he studied her more closely. His eyes widened as he noticed the dried blood on her clothes. "Miss Tanner, are you injured?"

"It's not my blood," Bree said flatly. "My sister is dead. Someone killed her and stole my grandmother's hat. So I'll ask again—where is Sam?"

The goblins' reactions were immediate and genuine—shock and distress crossing their inhuman features.

"Dead?" Tord whispered. "But how—"

"We don't know when Master Sorken will return," Glenken interrupted, his tone more gentle than before. "He left some hours ago with Morden to locate an old associate."

"Morden?" Bree questioned.

"Our colleague," Tord explained. "The third librarian."

Bree felt her anger shifting, not diminishing but redirecting. Sam wasn't here. He hadn't been here when Molly was killed. Which meant he likely didn't know about it yet, couldn't have prevented it.

"Then who else is here?" she asked. "Who else might know something useful?"

Another uncomfortable exchange of glances between the goblins.

"Perhaps..." Tord began hesitantly.

"Perhaps the archivists might speak with you," Glenken finished. "Though they don't typically interact with visitors."

"Take me to them," Bree demanded.

Tord sighed, setting down his quill. "Follow me, Miss Tanner. Though I make no promises about their willingness to engage."

He led her deeper into the library, past shelves that seemed to bend in ways that defied physics, beneath arches carved with symbols that shifted when viewed directly. They arrived at a reading area with comfortable armchairs arranged around a fireplace that burned with flames that gave off light but no heat.

The space appeared empty at first glance, but as Bree looked more carefully, she noticed a subtle shimmer in the air near two of the chairs—like heat waves rising from hot pavement, but more defined, more purposeful.

"Ezekiel, Margaret," Tord called, his tone formal. "Miss Tanner wishes to speak with you."

The shimmer intensified, condensing into two translucent figures—a Scottish soldier in an eighteenth-century uniform, complete with a bloodstain on his chest, and a Victorian woman in a high-necked dress with elaborately pinned hair.

"Well now," the soldier said, his accent thick and rolling, "this is a wee surprise. The lass has returned, and without our Sam tae escort her."

"Ezekiel," the woman chided gently, "do mind thy manners, I pray thee." She turned to Bree with a gracious nod. "I am Margaret, dear child. 'Tis a most pleasant acquaintance to make properly."

Bree stared at the spirits, momentarily distracted from her grief and anger. "You're ghosts," she said flatly.

"Spirits, if ye please," Ezekiel corrected, his Scottish brogue pronounced. "Ghosts are just echoes. We're the genuine article—full consciousness, memories intact, personality undiminished, ye ken?"

"You work for Sam?"

Margaret's translucent form drifted closer. "We prefer to think of it as a mutually beneficial arrangement, if thou wilt. Master Samuel provideth us with continued purpose and connection to the mortal realm. We, in turn, provide him with companionship and, upon occasion, insights from our considerable experience."

Tord cleared his throat. "I shall leave you to your discussion. Should you require anything, Miss Tanner, Glenken and I will be at our table."

The goblin retreated, leaving Bree alone with the spirits.

"Thou hast been weeping, child," Margaret observed softly. "Or thou wert, until most recently."

Bree brought a hand to her face, feeling the tight, salt-stained tracks of dried tears on her cheeks. "My sister is dead," she said, the words still raw and painful. "Someone killed her tonight. She was trying to stop them from stealing our grandmother's hat."

The spirits exchanged a significant look.

"The Tanner hat?" Ezekiel asked sharply, his spectral form flickering with agitation. "Nancy's hat, ye mean?"

Bree nodded, surprised. "You knew my grandmother?"

"Sam has known thy family for generations," Margaret said gently. "And by extension, so have we been acquainted with thy line."

"Nancy was a force tae be reckoned with," Ezekiel added, a note of admiration in his voice. "One o' the few mortals who earned Sam's complete trust. A formidable witch, yer grandmother."

"And now someone hath stolen her hat," Margaret murmured, troubled. "'Tis grave news indeed, most grave."

Bree's gaze drifted past the spirits to a small writing desk nearby. On it lay an open book, different from the ancient tomes that filled most of the library shelves. It looked newer, its leather binding supple and unmarked by time. The pages were covered in handwriting that she recognized as Sam's.

She moved toward it without thinking, drawn by the possibility of answers.

"That is Master Samuel's private journal," Margaret said, a note of warning in her voice, although she made no attempt to stop her. "Most personal, I assure thee."

Bree ignored her, reaching for the book. "My sister is dead. I need answers. Now."

"Lass," Ezekiel began, floating closer with concern, but Margaret shook her head, silencing him.

"She deserveth to know, Ez," the Victorian spirit said softly. "Master Samuel was to tell her this very night regardless of circumstance."

Bree picked up the journal, her eyes scanning the open page. Her brow furrowed in confusion at what she read—references to places she'd never heard of, names that seemed unpronounceable, events that made no sense in the context of the world she knew.

"What is this?" she asked, looking up at the spirits. "What am I reading?"

The spirits exchanged another long look, some unspoken communication passing between them.

"The truth," Margaret finally said. "About Master Samuel. About who he is and from whence he came."

"And what is that truth?" Bree pressed, her patience threadbare.

Ezekiel drifted closer, his spectral form rippling with what might have been a sigh. "Samuel Sorken isna from this world, lass. He was born on a planet called Eldoria, in a city named Luminara."

Bree stared at the spirit, momentarily speechless. "A... planet? He's an alien?"

"He is human," Margaret clarified. "Or mostly so, if thou wilt. Eldorians are physically indistinguishable from Earth humans, though their inherent magical capabilities tend to be... more pronounced, most assuredly."

"And he's a necromancer," Ezekiel added, the Scottish lilt in his voice deepening.

"A necromancer?" Bree repeated, the word feeling strange on her tongue. She'd heard of necromancy, of course—most witches had. It was considered a dangerous, often forbidden branch of magic, dealing with death and the spirits of the deceased.

"Aye, that's why he can see us, speak with us," Ezekiel explained, gesturing between himself and Margaret. "The lad has the ability tae commune with the dead, tae see beyond the veil that separates yer world from ours. It's a gift his people cultivated for generations."

Bree looked back down at the journal, reading more carefully now. "It says something about destruction, about someone named Malakai Drach?"

The spirits grew visibly agitated at the name.

"Malakai Drach was a tyrant," Ezekiel growled, his form darkening with emotion, his accent thickening. "A power-hungry monster who brought ruin tae Eldoria."

"Master Samuel's world," Margaret's spectral form shimmered with emotion as she spoke, "Eldoria was a most beautiful, thriving planet—until this Malakai Drach launched his terrible attack."

"Malakai sought the Nexus," Ezekiel explained, his ghostly features hardening. "A sacred site that served as the barrier between the realm o' the living and the realm o' the dead. He believed controlling it would give him power over death itself."

"Grand Master Xaloth, leader of the necromancers, made an impossible choice," Margaret continued, her voice carrying the formality of a history lesson. "Rather than permit the Nexus to fall into Malakai's hands, he destroyed it—a safeguard of most desperate resort. But the consequences were most catastrophic indeed."

"While Xaloth's action prevented Malakai from gainin' control o' death magic," Ezekiel said grimly, "it couldnae stop Malakai's armies from layin' waste tae Eldoria. Cities fell. Millions perished. An entire civilization was bein' systematically destroyed."

"In the final moments," Margaret said, "as Malakai's forces overwhelmed the last strongholds, Grand Master Xaloth, the leader of the necromancer's guild, created one last portal. Sam and his friend, Talien were among the five necromancers chosen to protect and guide a group of thirteen young witches—the last hope for their people's knowledge and traditions."

"The youngest of the witches was Elara Tanner," Ezekiel added, watching Bree's face carefully. "Yer ancestor. She was sister tae Briella, who sacrificed herself tae close the portal behind them, preventing Malakai's forces from following immediately."

"Elara... Tanner?" Bree repeated, the pieces suddenly clicking into place. "Are you saying my family isn't even from Earth originally?"

"Just one branch of thy family tree," Margaret clarified. "Elara married into the Earth Tanner family—witches from this world who had already established themselves in this world. The bloodlines merged, creating a most powerful magical lineage that incorporated both traditions, quite extraordinary."

"Times?" Bree questioned.

"The passages they traveled through didn't just connect worlds," Margaret explained. "They connected moments—different points in history. The portal Grand Master Xaloth created brought Sam's group to America in the late 1600s, shortly before the Salem witch trials."

"And what does this have to do with my family?" Bree asked, struggling to process everything she was hearing. "With the Andromeda coven?"

"The Andromeda coven was formed tae protect the survivors," Ezekiel said, his ghostly uniform rippling as he moved. "The Earth witches who took in Elara and the others recognized the danger Malakai Drach posed—not just tae the Eldorian refugees but tae all magic practitioners on Earth. They formed a sisterhood dedicated tae preservin' both Earth and Eldorian magical knowledge, and tae watchin' for signs of Malakai's eventual arrival.

"The Andromeda coven was created by the original thirteen witches who survived the journey to earth, tae start over."

"Master Samuel made a solemn pledge as leader of the necromancers on this planet," Margaret continued, her voice taking on a formal, almost ceremonial quality. "To protect the coven of witches for as long as the threat of Malakai Drach remained. Thy ancestors sheltered the Eldorian refugees, and in return, the necromancers vowed to be their guardians through the generations, a most sacred oath."

"Nancy knew," Ezekiel added. "She discovered Sam's true nature decades ago, an' rather than fearin' it, she embraced the alliance. She understood the value o' havin' a necromancer nearby, especially one with knowledge from another world."

Bree sank into a nearby chair, the journal still open in her hands. "This is... this is impossible," she whispered, though she knew it wasn't. The library itself was impossible. The goblins were impossible. And yet, here they were.

"No less impossible than witchcraft," Margaret said gently, adjusting her spectral lace collar. "'Tis merely a different kind of magic from a different world, child."

"And Malakai Drach?" Bree asked, a terrible suspicion forming in her mind. "What happened to him?"

The spirits exchanged another significant look.

"No one knows for certain," Ezekiel said grimly, his Scottish accent thick with emotion. "Sam believes Malakai survived an' wouldnae stop until he found his own way tae Earth eventually. That he'd never stop huntin' those who escaped his purge."

"Master Samuel has spent centuries watching," Margaret added, her voice soft with old sorrow. "Waiting most vigilantly for signs that Malakai had found his way to our shores. Protecting the coven that sheltered the refugees with utmost dedication."

"You think whoever killed my sister and stole the hat is connected to him?" Bree asked, the pieces starting to fit together in her mind.

"Och, lass," Ezekiel's ghostly features twisted with genuine sorrow. "If Malakai's people have found the earth or the Andromeda coven, then I fear the danger is far greater than even Sam anticipated."

Chapter 29

THE NECROMANCERS RETURN

The fascinating, revealing conversation between Bree and the centuries-old spirits halted abruptly as the ornately carved door frame at the far end of the vast magical library began to glow with increasing supernatural intensity. The ancient blue sigils of protection that had previously faded to a dull, barely perceptible shimmer suddenly blazed to life with blinding brilliance, pulsing with renewed magical energy that cast eerie, dancing shadows across the towering mahogany bookshelves filled with forbidden knowledge.

"They've returned," Margaret announced, her translucent form drifting toward the door. "Rather sooner than I expected, I must say."

Ezekiel nodded, floating alongside her. "Aye, the lad must've had an easier time with the Fae than we feared."

The door swung open of its own accord, and three figures stepped through—Sam first, followed by a third goblin who could only be Morden, dressed in an impeccable three-piece suit that made Tord and Glenken look positively disheveled by comparison. Behind them came a tall, lean man with dark hair pulled back in a ponytail, streaked with silver at the temples. Unlike Sam's casual attire, he wore what appeared to be a tailored charcoal waistcoat over a crisp white shirt, the sleeves rolled up to reveal forearms covered in intricate tattoos that seemed to shift and move in the library's magical light.

"—just a matter of speaking their language," the newcomer was saying, his hands gesturing animatedly as they entered. "The Fae are easy enough to deal with if you've had enough dealings with them. All those formal rules actually make them predictable, once you understand the underlying patterns."

"Says the man who nearly lost his shadow in a game of chance last spring," Sam replied dryly, though there was fondness in his voice.

The tattooed man—Talien, Bree presumed—threw his arms wide, taking in the vast expanse of the library with obvious delight. "I always said this place was amazing, Sam! That's why you were chosen to lead!" His voice carried through the cavernous space, echoing slightly off the distant ceiling. "The other Sanctuaries are impressive, sure, but none of them compare to this. You've taken what Xaloth taught us and elevated it beyond anything we could have imagined back home."

Talien spotted Ezekiel and Margaret hovering near a reading nook and his face lit up with genuine pleasure. "Ezekiel! Margaret! It's been too long—nearly a decade, by my count. I've missed your particular brand of judgment and disapproval."

It was then that Talien noticed the third person in the group. Bree had risen from her chair and stepped forward between the spirits, the journal still clutched in one hand.

Talien froze mid-step, his exuberant expression giving way to shock. His hand came up almost reflexively, a single finger pointing at Bree while his head swiveled toward Sam. He looked back at Bree, his finger still extended, then slowly raised his hand to cover his mouth. When he finally spoke, his voice was barely above a whisper.

"She looks just like her."

Sam's response was quiet, resigned. "I know."

The atmosphere in the library seemed to thicken with unspoken history as Bree stepped forward, her eyes fixed on Sam. The grief and anger that had momentarily receded during her conversation with the spirits came rushing back, hardening her voice.

"So? I need to hear it from you. What's going on? Who and what are you, and what happened to my sister?"

Sam's expression shifted from surprise to concern. He glanced at the spirits, understanding dawning in his eyes.

"The child hath already seen thy journal, Master Samuel," Margaret said, adjusting her spectral lace collar with a prim gesture. "Most unavoidable, given the circumstances."

"Aye, we told the lass as much as we knew," Ezekiel added, his Scottish brogue thick with apology. "She came here lookin' for answers, Sam. Her sister's dead."

"Dead?" Sam echoed, the color draining from his face. "Molly?" He turned back to Bree, really seeing her for the first time since he'd entered—the dried blood on her clothes, the raw grief etched into her features, the determined set of her jaw.

"Tell me," Bree demanded, refusing to be sidetracked. "All of it. Now."

Sam drew a deep breath, seeming to center himself. "Talien and I come from a world called Eldoria," he began, his voice steady despite the obvious tension in his shoulders. "A world of magic that was destroyed centuries ago, at least from our perspective. We were part of a small group that escaped—five necromancers and thirteen young witches, the last hope for our people's knowledge and traditions."

He gestured to include the library around them. "My life's mission since then has been to ensure the survival of both groups—the coven of witches and the remaining necromancers. To keep the coven safe, to help it prosper and grow in membership, to preserve the knowledge and traditions that would otherwise have been lost forever."

"And Briella?" Bree asked, her voice softening slightly at the name of her ancestor. "Ezekiel and Margaret mentioned her. They said she was my ancestor's sister."

Sam lowered his head for a moment, an old pain flashing across his features. When he looked up again, his eyes held a depth of sorrow that transcended ordinary grief.

"Briella was... a friend. Someone I cared for deeply." His voice grew rough with emotion. "She was supposed to follow me through the portal to Earth, but instead, she sent her younger sister, Elara, and then closed the portal behind them. She sacrificed herself to keep General Malakai and his forces from following us."

A heavy silence fell over the library. Even the goblins, who had been pretending not to eavesdrop from their table, had abandoned any pretense of disinterest.

Bree turned to Talien, who had been watching the exchange with an unreadable expression. "What did you mean, 'She looks just like her'?"

"Briella," Talien answered simply, studying Bree's face with open fascination. "You could be her double. Perhaps you are the reincarnation of her." He shrugged, as if this were a perfectly ordinary possibility. "That does happen, you know," he added matter-of-factly.

Sam's attention had shifted back to Bree's appearance, his eyes tracking over the dried blood staining her clothes. "What happened?" he asked quietly. "You said Molly is dead?"

The blunt question cut through Bree's momentary distraction. "Yes," she said, her voice cracking slightly. "Someone broke into our house tonight. They were stealing Grandma Nancy's Hat. Molly caught them, and..." She couldn't finish the sentence.

Sam turned abruptly and placed his hands on a nearby desk, his head bowed, knuckles white with tension. "I'm sorry," he whispered, the words barely audible. "I'm so sorry, Bree."

Talien took a step forward, his earlier exuberance completely gone. "It's my fault," he said, addressing both Sam and Bree. "If Sam hadn't come looking for me, he might have been here to defend her."

Bree looked between the two men, a strange calm settling over her despite the tumult of emotions still raging inside. Neither of them was at fault—she could see that clearly. They couldn't have known what would happen, couldn't have predicted that tonight of all nights, someone would come for the Hat.

"Molly is gone," she said simply, her voice steadier than she would have thought possible. "Her spirit... it appeared to me, right after it happened. She said the Hat contains her now, along with Grandma Nancy." She fixed Sam with a direct gaze. "Do you know who could have done this? Who would want the Hat badly enough to kill for it?"

Sam straightened, turning back to face her. The grief in his eyes had hardened into something colder, more dangerous—a look that reminded

Bree that for all his gentle demeanor, this was a man who had survived the destruction of his world and centuries of life afterward.

"I have a terrible suspicion," he said quietly. "One I've been dreading for a very long time."

Chapter 30
An Unexpected Confession

The heavy, tension-filled silence that followed Sam's devastating revelation was broken suddenly by an unexpected sound that startled everyone present—three sharp, deliberate knocks at the front door of the house, the sound somehow echoing with supernatural clarity all the way down to the subterranean library despite the impossible physics of the magically expanded space and the many floors between.

Sam's head jerked up instinctively, his tear-stained expression immediately shifting from profound grief to alert wariness with practiced speed. He exchanged a quick, meaningful glance with Talien, some unspoken communication of ancient understanding passing between the two supernatural allies.

"Stay here with Bree," he instructed, already moving toward the door that would lead back to the normal confines of his house. "It could be nothing, but after what's happened..."

"Or it could be exactly what we fear," Talien finished, nodding grimly. He moved closer to Bree, his earlier fascination replaced by protective vigilance. "Go. We'll be fine here."

"I'll accompany ye," Ezekiel declared, his spectral form already drifting after Sam. "Two sets o' eyes are better than one, even if one set belongs tae a dead man."

Sam didn't argue, his footsteps quickening as another series of knocks, more urgent this time, echoed through the passage. Bree watched them go, feeling strangely disconnected from the moment, as if all of this—the impossible library, the necromancers from another world, her sister's death—were happening to someone else.

Morden stepped forward, his impeccable suit somehow unwrinkled despite their adventure in the Fae realm. "Perhaps the young lady would care for some refreshment?" he suggested, his formal tone at odds with the tension in the air. "We have an excellent tea selection."

Before Bree could respond, Margaret drifted closer. "The child is in shock, Master Morden. 'Tis hardly the time for social niceties, however well-intentioned."

Talien's eyes never left the door through which Sam had disappeared. "Let her be," he said quietly. "Some griefs can't be soothed with tea and sympathy."

Sam reached the front door of his house, the normal world feeling oddly constrained after the vast expanse of the library. He peered through the small window beside the door, tension evident in every line of his body.

Standing on his porch was a young Black woman, perhaps in her early twenties, with straight hair that fell past her shoulders. She was shifting from foot to foot, her eyes darting nervously up and down the street as if expecting to be followed. There was something about her posture—a combination of terror and resignation—that made Sam's centuries-old instincts prickle with warning.

"She looks scared out o' her wits," Ezekiel observed, floating beside him. "No' the look of someone with ill intent, generally speakin'."

"Appearances can be deceiving," Sam murmured, though he reached for the doorknob nonetheless. Years of experience had taught him to trust his instincts, and right now, they were telling him this frightened young woman posed no immediate threat.

He opened the door just wide enough to present a barrier while still being able to speak with her. "Yes?" he asked, his voice carefully neutral.

The young woman looked up at him, her dark eyes wide with a mixture of fear and something else—determination, perhaps, or desperation. She swallowed hard before speaking.

"My name is Nissa Drach," she said, the words tumbling out in a rush. "I'm the one who killed the girl next door."

Sam went very still, his mind processing the implications of that name—*Drach*—even as the confession itself struck him like a physical blow.

"Bloody hell," Ezekiel whispered beside him, his Scottish brogue thickening with shock.

Nissa clutched something to her chest—something Sam hadn't noticed at first, wrapped in a cloth bundle. "I was only trying to steal this hat," she continued, her voice trembling. "But I don't want it. I couldn't do it."

Sam studied her face, searching for deception but finding only fear and a desperate sort of honesty. The name Drach echoed in his mind like a warning bell. Could she be a descendant? After all these centuries, had Malakai's bloodline finally tracked them down?

"Would you... would you like to come inside?" he asked carefully, opening the door wider.

Nissa hesitated, clearly terrified but also seemingly determined to follow through with whatever decision had brought her to his doorstep. She nodded once, then stepped over the threshold, the bundle—which must be Nancy Tanner's hat—clutched tightly against her.

"I canna believe it!" Ezekiel exclaimed, moving to circle around Nissa, studying her from all angles as if she were a particularly puzzling artifact. "She came willingly! And brought the hat!"

Nissa's eyes widened as they landed on Ezekiel's translucent form. "You can see spirits," she whispered, addressing Sam. "You're like him, aren't you? A necromancer."

Sam closed the door behind her, his mind racing. "Like who?" he asked, though he feared he already knew the answer.

"Malakai," she answered, confirming his worst fears. "My grandfather."

Sam exchanged a look with Ezekiel. This changed everything.

"Let's continue this conversation somewhere more private," he suggested, gesturing toward the stairs that would lead back to the library. "I think there are others who need to hear what you have to say."

Nissa followed Sam through the house, her steps hesitant but determined. When they reached the bedroom with the wardrobe, she paused, confusion evident on her face.

"Through here," Sam explained, opening the wardrobe doors and revealing the passage beyond. "It's safe, I promise."

Nissa's eyes widened as she stepped into the narrow corridor, her fear momentarily overridden by wonder. "How is this possible?" she breathed, gazing at the impossible space that stretched before them.

"Magic," Ezekiel answered simply, floating ahead. "Different from yers, lass, but magic all the same."

As they emerged into the vast expanse of the library, Nissa's breath caught audibly. She turned in a slow circle, taking in the towering shelves, the impossible architecture, the soft magical light that seemed to emanate from everywhere and nowhere at once.

"It's beautiful," she whispered, seemingly despite herself.

Their entrance had not gone unnoticed. Talien had positioned himself protectively near Bree, his earlier joviality completely absent as he assessed the newcomer with narrowed eyes. Margaret and Morden hovered nearby, while Tord and Glenken watched curiously from their table.

Bree's attention, however, was fixed entirely on the cloth bundle in Nissa's arms. "That's the hat," she said, her voice tight with emotion. "That's my grandmother's hat."

Nissa's composure, already fragile, shattered completely at Bree's words. Her knees seemed to give way, and she sank to the floor, tears streaming down her face as her body shook with barely contained sobs.

"I'm sorry," she gasped between ragged breaths. "I'm so sorry. I had no choice. My mother—Kestrel—she ordered me to take it. I've already endured so many beatings, so many whippings. To fail her would mean my death."

She looked up at Bree, her eyes pleading for understanding. "The magic I used—it wasn't meant to kill. It was just supposed to stun. I didn't mean for your sister to die." Her voice broke on the last word. "But after it happened, after I saw what I'd done, I knew I couldn't give the hat to my mother. She would only use it for evil, for destruction. So I decided to return it, regardless of what Kestrel might do to me when she finds out."

The room fell silent as everyone processed this unexpected confession. Bree's face remained impassive, but her eyes burned with a mixture of grief, rage, and confusion.

"How do we know you're telling the truth?" she finally asked, taking a step toward Nissa. "How do we know this isn't some trick?"

Without waiting for an answer, Bree marched forward, took Nissa firmly by the arm, and turned her sideways. Before anyone could react, she grabbed the hem of Nissa's shirt and lifted it, exposing her back.

The collective gasp that filled the library was entirely justified. Nissa's back was a tapestry of cruelty—old, silvery scars crisscrossed with newer wounds, some still swollen and bruised, others barely healed. It was the kind of systematic abuse that couldn't be faked or inflicted for a ruse.

"Saints preserve us," Ezekiel breathed, his spectral form flickering with distress. "Yer mother did this tae ye, lass?"

Nissa nodded, her face averted in shame as Bree lowered her shirt.

Bree took a step back, her expression softening slightly though the wariness remained. "Is that all?" she asked. "You just wanted to give back the hat?"

Nissa turned to face her, wiping tears from her cheeks with trembling hands. "I'm sorry for what I did. I can't go back to Kestrel now. She'll kill me as soon as I arrive. She is pure evil, unlike anything you've ever seen before." She drew a shaky breath. "I can't bring back Molly. But I can help you fight Kestrel, if you'll let me."

"Oh, the poor dear child," Margaret murmured, drifting closer with maternal concern evident in her translucent features. "'Tis most terrible, what she hath endured. No mother should inflict such cruelty upon her own flesh and blood."

Talien had been patiently watching the exchange with calculating eyes. He moved to Sam's side, speaking low enough that only Sam could hear. "She could be useful," he suggested. "If she's really Malakai's granddaughter, she might have some hidden memories or inside knowledge we desperately need."

"Or she could be a trap," Sam countered, though without much conviction. The wounds on Nissa's back had been all too real, as was the terror in her eyes. "Malakai has never been above sacrificing his own people to achieve his goals."

"True," Talien acknowledged. "But my instincts say she's genuine. And either way, she's our first real lead in decades. We can't ignore that."

Sam nodded slowly, then addressed Nissa directly. "You said Kestrel is your mother, and Malakai is your grandfather. Do you know what they're planning? Why they want the hat so badly?"

Nissa looked up, her expression haunted. "My mother has been preparing for something she calls 'the Great Working' for as long as I can remember. She needs powerful magical artifacts to complete it—the hat was just one of several she's been seeking."

"The Great Working?" Talien repeated, alarm evident in his voice. "Sam, that sounds like—"

"I know," Sam cut him off, his expression grim. He turned back to Nissa. "Do you know what this 'Great Working' is supposed to accomplish?"

Nissa shook her head. "Only that it requires immense power, and that it's connected to something called 'the Nexus.'"

Sam and Talien exchanged a look of pure dread.

"If Kestrel is trying to recreate the Nexus here on Earth..." Talien began.

"Then we're facing a catastrophe beyond imagination," Sam finished. He ran a hand through his hair, a gesture of frustration and fear. "Do you know what we're up against, Talien? Have you seen anything like this in your travels?"

Talien nodded grimly. "Yes, but I think we need to confirm our suspicions before we act. There's someone we should consult, someone who might have more insight into Kestrel's current capabilities."

"You mean—" Sam started.

"Yes," Talien confirmed. "I do."

Sam was quiet for a long moment, clearly weighing their limited options. "I don't think we have a choice," he finally agreed. "We need to find out for sure."

Bree, who had been listening intently to this exchange, stepped forward. "Find out what?" she demanded. "And who are you talking about consulting?"

Sam and Talien exchanged another meaningful look before he answered.

"The Great Working that Nissa mentioned—if it's what we think it is, it threatens not just the coven, but potentially this entire world."

He gestured to Talien. "There's someone who might be able to tell us more, to confirm what we suspect. Someone Talien and I knew back on Eldoria."

"Another necromancer?" Bree guessed.

"Not exactly," Talien replied, his usual levity completely absent. "Someone with a broader perspective."

"Someone who's been dead for centuries," Sam clarified. "Which is why we need to consult them together. One necromancer alone couldn't sustain contact with a spirit from our world—the connection is too tenuous across such vast distances, both physical and metaphysical."

Bree's brow furrowed. "But you already have spirits here," she pointed out, gesturing to Ezekiel and Margaret.

"They're from Earth," Talien explained. "Their spirits were already here when they died. What Sam's talking about is reaching across the void to contact a spirit that never existed in this world while alive."

"It's incredibly difficult," Sam added. "And potentially dangerous. But if anyone would know Malakai's true plans, perhaps passed down to his daughter, it would be this person."

Throughout this exchange, Nissa had remained kneeling on the floor, the hat still clutched in her arms. Now she looked up, her expression a mixture of hope and trepidation.

"Are you going to help me?" she asked quietly. "Will you protect me from my mother?"

Before Sam could answer, Bree stepped forward and held out her hands. "The hat," she said, her voice firm but not unkind. "May I have it back, please?"

Nissa immediately offered up the bundled hat, unwrapping it with careful hands. The black felt hat looked deceptively ordinary, though Bree could feel the power emanating from it—a subtle vibration in the air that spoke of accumulated knowledge and magic spanning generations.

As Bree took the hat, her fingers brushed against its brim, and for a fleeting moment, she thought she heard Molly's voice whispering her name. She clutched the hat to her chest, fighting back a fresh wave of tears.

"Thank you," she said to Nissa, her voice thick with emotion. "For bringing this back."

Nissa nodded, her own eyes welling with tears again. "I wish I could undo what I did. I'd give anything to take it back."

"I know," Bree said softly, surprising herself with the words. The rage and grief were still there, raw and painful, but alongside them was a growing understanding of the broken young woman before her. "But you can't. None of us can change what's already happened. All we can do now is try to stop more people from getting hurt."

She turned to Sam and Talien. "Whatever you need to do, whatever spirit you need to contact—do it. But I'm not leaving. This involves my family, my coven, my sister. I have a right to be here."

Sam nodded, accepting her decision without argument. "Of course. But Bree..." He hesitated, then continued. "What we're about to attempt is necromancy in its purest form. It's not something most witches are comfortable witnessing."

"I'm not 'most witches,'" Bree replied steadily. "And after everything I've seen today, I doubt much else will shock me."

Talien laughed, a short, surprised sound that lightened the heavy atmosphere for a brief moment. "She really is just like Briella," he remarked to Sam. "Same spirit, same steel."

Sam didn't respond directly, but the look he gave Bree was filled with a complex mixture of admiration, concern, and something deeper, more personal.

"Alright," he said finally. "Then let's prepare. We'll need a suitable space, and specific materials." He turned to Nissa, who was still kneeling on the floor. "And we'll need your help too. If you're truly willing to stand against your mother and grandfather, we'll protect you. But in return, we'll need everything you know about them—their plans, their capabilities, their weaknesses."

Nissa nodded, a glimmer of hope breaking through her fear for the first time. "I'll tell you everything I know. I swear it."

"Good," Sam said, offering her a hand to help her up. "Because I suspect we're going to need every advantage we can get."

Chapter 31
PREPARATIONS

As Sam and Talien began to discuss preparations for the spiritual contact, Bree stood apart, the hat still clutched to her chest. So much had changed in the span of a few hours—her sister was dead, her understanding of her family's history had been upended, and she had discovered a world of magic beyond anything she'd previously imagined.

And yet, as she watched Sam organizing the various components they would need, she felt an unexpected sense of clarity cutting through her grief. Whatever came next, whatever dangers they might face, she would face them head-on. For Molly. For her family. For the legacy contained within the hat she now held.

The time for tears had passed. Now was the time for action.

"We'll need a focusing circle," Sam was saying to Talien, his tone becoming more professional, more focused. "Something that can anchor a connection across dimensional barriers."

Talien nodded, already moving toward one of the many cabinets that lined the walls of the library. "I'll get the silver dust and the quartz crystals. Do you still have the obsidian mirror?"

"East cabinet, third shelf," Sam confirmed, before turning to Morden. "We'll need the ceremonial space prepared. Full containment protocols."

The goblin nodded with grave understanding. "Of course, Master Sorken. I shall attend to it immediately." He paused, glancing at Nissa who still looked uncertain and frightened. "And what of our... unexpected guest?"

Sam considered the question. "She stays with us. If she's genuinely broken with Kestrel and Malakai, she may have insights that could be valuable during the communion."

"And if she hasna?" Ezekiel asked, floating closer with obvious concern. "If this is some kind of trap?"

"Then we'll be prepared," Sam assured him, his expression hardening momentarily. "I've dealt with Malakai's tricks before."

Bree watched this exchange with growing curiosity that momentarily overshadowed her grief. "What exactly are you planning to do?" she asked. "And who are you trying to contact?"

Sam exchanged a meaningful look with Talien before answering. "We're going to attempt to commune with Grand Master Xaloth."

"But you said he's been dead for centuries," Bree pointed out. "And that he died on Eldoria, not Earth."

"That's what makes this difficult," Talien explained, returning with an ornate wooden box inlaid with strange symbols. "Contacting Earth spirits like Ezekiel and Margaret is relatively straightforward for a trained necromancer. Contacting spirits from another world entirely—especially one that may no longer exist in any recognizable form—is exponentially more challenging."

"It's like trying to make a phone call to another galaxy," Sam added, seeing Bree's confusion. "Except the phone lines were never connected in the first place, and you're not entirely sure the number you're dialing still exists."

"Then how can you possibly reach him?" Bree asked.

Sam's expression grew solemn. "Because Talien and I were both there during Malakai's attack. Master Xaloth... we witnessed some of his final moments, heard some of his final words. That creates a connection, a tether of sorts that transcends ordinary barriers."

"And as his students," Talien continued, "we carry echoes of his energy signature within our own magical cores. It gives us something to aim for in the void."

Margaret drifted closer, her spectral form shimmering with concern. "I must caution thee, Master Samuel. Such magics you perform are most perilous. To reach across the veil between worlds requires energy most profound. The toll upon thy physical form could be considerable."

"Margaret's right," Ezekiel agreed, his Scottish brogue thickening with worry. "The last time ye attempted something like this, ye were bedridden for a fortnight. And that was just tryin' tae contact someone from Eldoria who'd died on Earth."

"We don't have a choice," Sam replied firmly. "If Kestrel is truly attempting to recreate the Nexus here, we need to understand exactly what we're up against. And no one knew more about the Nexus than Xaloth."

Throughout this exchange, Nissa had remained quiet, watching the proceedings with fascination. Now she spoke hesitantly, her voice still rough from crying.

"My grandfather—he often spoke of someone called Xaloth. With hatred, but also... respect, maybe? He said Xaloth was the only one who ever truly understood what could be achieved through death magic."

All eyes turned to her.

"Your grandfather?" Sam asked carefully. "You speak of him in the past tense."

Nissa nodded. "Malakai died five years ago. At least, his physical form did. My mother Kestrel believes his spirit still exists in the Realm of the Dead, retaining all his knowledge and power."

"Malakai is dead?" Talien repeated, shock evident in his voice. "After all this time, after everything we feared..."

"His body may be gone," Sam said grimly, "but I'm not convinced that means we're safe from his influence. What else can you tell us, Nissa? Why did your mother want the hat?"

Nissa took a shaky breath. "The hat is just one of several powerful magical artifacts she's been gathering. My mother plans to use them to open a doorway into the Realm of the Dead."

"Why?" Bree asked, clutching the hat tighter protectively. "What could she possibly want there?"

"Power," Nissa said simply. "She intends to enter the Realm of the Dead and consume the memories and knowledge from the accumulated spirits of the witches—all the generations contained in artifacts like the hat. She believes she can absorb their combined power, as well as tap into something she calls the Tower of Souls."

"The Tower of Souls?" Sam exchanged an alarmed glance with Talien. "That's not possible."

"She thinks it is," Nissa continued. "And once she's gathered all that power, she plans to return to the living Realm to conquer and rule over it. She's obsessed with finishing what my grandfather started."

Sam and Talien exchanged a look of deep concern.

"That aligns with what I've feared she might attempt," Sam said grimly.

"And explains why she would need powerful magical artifacts," Talien added, nodding toward the hat that Bree still clutched. "Each one connected to generations of magical practitioners, their spirits and knowledge preserved."

"But what exactly does your mother intend to do?" Bree asked, frustration evident in her voice. "You're talking about the Realm of the Dead, but what does that even mean?"

"It's the place where spirits go after death," came a new voice from the doorway.

Everyone turned to see Tord standing there, his small form somehow dignified despite his stature. The goblin librarian adjusted his tiny spectacles before continuing.

"According to the texts I've cataloged over the centuries, the Realm of the Dead exists in parallel to our own world—a dimension where the spirits of the deceased naturally migrate after their physical bodies expire."

"And if someone were to physically enter this realm?" Bree asked, though she had already begun to guess the horrifying answer.

"Then they would have direct access to every spirit that has ever existed," Sam explained, his voice grave. "Not just to communicate with them, as necromancers like Talien and I can do in limited ways, but to manipulate and potentially consume their essence."

"Imagine it," Talien said quietly. "Every witch, every magical practitioner who has ever lived, their knowledge and power harvested by a single entity. No peaceful rest for any soul."

"And Kestrel would wield that power," Sam finished. "A level of magical might never before seen on Earth."

The enormity of this threat settled over everyone like a physical weight. Bree found herself unconsciously tightening her grip on the hat, as if its familiar presence could somehow anchor her in this new reality where the stakes had suddenly become apocalyptic.

"Now do you understand why we must contact Xaloth?" Sam asked her gently. "Why we're willing to take the risk?"

Bree nodded slowly. "Yes. But I'm coming with you—not just in the room, but part of the ritual. If this involves my family, my coven, I want to be fully engaged." She raised the hat slightly. "Besides, I have this now. If it contains a spiritual connection and knowledge of my ancestors, including my sister, maybe it can help strengthen your connection between here and there."

Sam started to protest, but Talien laid a hand on his arm.

"She has a point," he said, studying Bree with newfound respect. "The hat is a repository of ancestral magic, including the original Eldorian witches who came through with us. That connection might be exactly what we need to stabilize the channeling."

Sam hesitated, clearly torn between the potential benefit and his concern for Bree's safety.

"I don't know," he began. "The risks—"

"Are mine to take," Bree interrupted firmly. "My sister is dead, Sam. Her killer returned what she had stolen, and now we're facing someone who wants to harvest the souls of every witch who ever lived. I think we're well past the point of playing it safe."

Her words hung in the air, challenging anyone to contradict them. No one did.

Finally, Sam nodded. "Alright. But you follow our instructions exactly. No improvising, no experimenting. Necromancy at this level doesn't allow for error."

"Agreed," Bree said immediately.

"Then let's move to the ceremonial chamber," Sam decided, turning to Morden who had just returned. "Is it ready?"

The goblin nodded gravely. "Yes, Master Sorken. All is prepared as you specified."

Sam turned to Nissa, who had been watching the exchange with wide eyes. "You'll come with us, but you won't participate directly. I need you to observe and provide context if Xaloth mentions anything about your grandfather's current activities that you recognize."

Nissa nodded, clearly relieved to have a role, however peripheral. "I understand."

"Good." Sam gestured for everyone to follow Morden. "Then let's not waste any more time."

The goblin led them deeper into the library, past shelves and through archways carved with ancient symbols. Bree tried to memorize the path but soon gave up—the library seemed to rearrange itself as they walked, making any attempt at creating a mental map futile.

Finally, they reached a set of double doors made of what appeared to be solid silver, etched with intricate designs that seemed to pulse with their own inner light. Morden placed his small hand on a circular indentation at the center, and the doors swung open silently.

The chamber beyond took Bree's breath away. It was perfectly circular, with a domed ceiling that seemed to reflect the night sky—not as it appeared from Earth, but a vista of unfamiliar stars and celestial bodies that must have been the view from Eldoria. The floor was polished obsidian, glossy enough to reflect the starlight from above, creating the disorienting impression that they were suspended in space.

At the center of the room was a raised dais, upon which a complex geometric pattern had been laid out in what appeared to be silver dust. Five crystal pillars surrounded the pattern, each glowing internally of a different color—red, blue, green, white, and purple.

"Wow," Bree breathed, momentarily distracted from her grief by the sheer beauty and strangeness of the space.

"The ceremonial chamber," Sam explained, his voice taking on a more formal cadence as they entered. "Designed to amplify and focus necromantic energies while containing any... unexpected consequences."

"Unexpected consequences?" Bree echoed, suddenly remembering that for all its beauty, what they were about to attempt was potentially dangerous.

"Communing with the dead is never without risk," Talien said simply, moving to the edge of the silver pattern. "Especially when reaching across dimensional barriers."

Sam nodded. "The barrier between worlds isn't just physical—it's metaphysical, spiritual. Punching a hole through it, even temporarily, can have unpredictable results."

"Like what?" Bree asked, not entirely sure she wanted to know the answer.

"Best case scenario, nothing—we make contact, get the information we need, and close the connection cleanly," Sam explained. "Worst case..."

"Other entities might notice the opening," Talien finished when Sam hesitated. "Entities that would very much like to cross over into our world."

"Hence the containment protocols," Morden added from near the doorway, where he was carefully placing small, glowing crystals at regular intervals.

Bree swallowed hard, but her resolve remained firm. "Tell me what I need to do."

Sam studied her for a moment, then nodded, apparently satisfied with what he saw in her expression. "Stand here," he instructed, indicating a point at the edge of the silver pattern. "Talien and I will take positions at the other points of the pentagram."

As Bree took her place, Sam continued his instructions. "When we begin the ritual, focus on the hat. Try to connect with the spirits contained within it—particularly any with links to Eldoria."

"How do I do that?" Bree asked, suddenly aware of how little she knew about actually utilizing the hat's power.

"Just hold it and think of your sister," Talien suggested gently. "Of your grandmother. Of your connection to them. The hat will do the rest."

Nissa was directed to a small bench near the wall, where she could observe without interfering. Ezekiel and Margaret took positions near her, their spectral forms seeming more solid somehow in the strange light of the chamber.

"We'll be watchin'," Ezekiel assured Bree. "If anything goes awry, we'll alert ye immediately."

"Indeed," Margaret agreed. "'Tis a most serious undertaking, but thou art not alone in it, child."

Sam and Talien took their positions at two points of the pentagram, leaving two points empty—presumably for the spirits they hoped to channel. From a pouch at his belt, Sam withdrew a small obsidian mirror and placed it at the center of the pattern.

"Ready?" he asked, looking first at Talien, who nodded, and then at Bree.

She took a deep breath, clutching the hat firmly. "Ready."

Sam nodded, then raised his hands, palms outward. Talien did the same. When they spoke, it was in perfect unison, their voices resonating at a frequency that seemed to vibrate in Bree's very bones.

"Xaloth, Master of the Veil, Keeper of the Transition, we call to you across the void. By the bonds of student to teacher, by the witness of your final moments, by the shared blood of Eldoria, we seek your counsel."

The silver dust began to glow, the light spreading outward from the center until the entire pattern was illuminated. The crystal pillars pulsed in response, their individual colors blending into a swirling aurora that surrounded the three of them.

Bree felt a strange pressure building in her chest, as if the air itself was becoming thicker, harder to breathe. The hat in her hands grew warm, then hot, though not painfully so. She could feel a vibration emanating from it, resonating with the cadence of Sam and Talien's chanting.

Following Talien's advice, she closed her eyes and thought of Molly—her smile, her laugh, the fierce protective instinct that had ultimately led to her death. She thought of Nancy, the grandmother whose wisdom and strength had been a cornerstone of the Tanner family. She thought of all the generations of witches before her, stretching back to Elara, who had escaped a dying world to build a new legacy on Earth.

The hat grew hotter in her hands, and suddenly, Bree could feel them—not just Molly and Nancy, but dozens, perhaps hundreds of other presences, a chorus of voices just below the threshold of hearing. They swirled around her, through her, their collective knowledge and power like an ocean she could barely comprehend.

And then, from the depths of that ocean, something answered Sam and Talien's call.

The obsidian mirror at the center of the pattern began to glow with an eerie, greenish light. The air above it shimmered and distorted, as if reality itself was being warped by some unseen force. Slowly, a figure began to coalesce—not solid like Ezekiel and Margaret, but more like a collection of glowing particles arranged in a vaguely humanoid shape.

When it spoke, its voice seemed to come from everywhere and nowhere at once, each word carrying the weight of centuries.

"My students," it said, the glowing particles pulsing with each syllable. "After all this time, you reach across the void to summon me. The situation must be dire indeed."

"Master Xaloth," Sam said, his voice tight with effort as he maintained the connection. "We seek your wisdom. Malakai's daughter, Kestrel, plans to breach the Realm of the Dead."

The glowing figure seemed to pulse more intensely at this news. "So, the daughter follows the father's path. But where he failed, she believes she can succeed."

"This witch has the Tanner Hat," Talien added, nodding toward Bree.

"And according to Malakai's granddaughter," said Sam "the daughter is collecting other artifacts of similar power to the hat."

"To enter the Realm physically," Xaloth's spectral form shimmered with pulsating ethereal energy and ancient concern. "A dangerous, potentially soul-destroying endeavor, even for one as powerful as Kestral must be after decades of dark practice. The rules of that realm are not like those of the living world. Time, space, identity—all become fluid, malleable, unpredictable to mortal minds."

"Can it be done?" Sam asked. "Could she actually absorb the power of the Tower of Souls?"

"It has never been accomplished," Xaloth replied, "but that does not mean it is impossible. The Tower stands at the heart of the Realm, a repository of all who have passed. If one could reach it, harness its power..." The spirit paused. "The consequences would be catastrophic for both realms."

"How do we stop her?" Bree asked, finding her voice despite the overwhelming strangeness of addressing a being from another world, another time.

Xaloth's form seemed to turn toward her, though it had no discernible face. "You carry the legacy of Elara," it observed. "And now her descendants, including one very recently transitioned. The hat serves as both repository and gateway."

"Gateway?" Bree repeated, glancing down at the hat in her hands.

"Between realms," Xaloth confirmed. "It was designed to preserve the knowledge and power of each High Priestess, but it also maintains a connection to their spirits in the Realm of the Dead."

Sam and Talien exchanged a significant look. "You're suggesting we use the hat to follow Kestral," Sam said slowly. "To enter the Realm ourselves."

The glowing form was definitely fading now, the effort of maintaining contact across dimensional barriers taking its toll. "The Tower of Souls is guarded by forces beyond even my understanding," came the fading reply. "But there is one who might help... one who stands at the threshold..."

With those final words, the glowing form dissolved completely, the particles scattering into nothingness. The obsidian mirror cracked with a sharp report, and the silver dust pattern flared brilliantly before going dark.

Sam and Talien both staggered slightly, the effort of the ritual clearly taking its toll. Bree felt drained as well, though the hat in her hands continued to pulse with a gentle warmth, as if acknowledging its role in what had just transpired.

A heavy silence fell over the chamber as everyone processed what they had learned. It was Bree who finally broke it.

"So what do we do now?" she asked, looking between Sam and Talien. "How do we stop Kestral from reaching this Tower of Souls?"

Sam straightened, his expression resolute despite his evident exhaustion. "We need to speak with Papa Legba."

"Papa Legba?" Bree echoed. "Xaloth mentioned someone at the threshold, but who exactly is Papa Legba?"

"He's the guardian of the crossroads," Sam explained. "The keeper of the gates between the living world and the Realm of the Dead. Nothing passes from one realm to the other without his knowledge."

"You speak as if you know him personally," Nissa observed quietly from her place near the wall.

Sam nodded. "I do. I've met with him several times over the centuries."

This revelation seemed to surprise even Talien. "You never mentioned that."

"It wasn't relevant until now," Sam replied with a slight shrug. "When we first arrived on Earth, I needed to understand how death magic worked in this world. Our necromantic traditions from Eldoria didn't always translate perfectly. Papa Legba was... educational."

"Educational?" Talien raised an eyebrow.

"He has his own way of teaching," Sam said, a wry smile briefly crossing his face. "But he helped me adapt, helped me understand the rules of this world's afterlife."

"And you think he'll help us stop Kestral?" Bree asked.

"Papa Legba is dedicated to maintaining the balance between worlds," Sam explained. "If Kestral plans to drain the Tower of Souls, to harvest the spirits of the dead for her own power, that's a fundamental violation of the natural order. He won't stand for it."

"But will he intervene directly?" Talien asked, clearly skeptical. "The loa aren't known for their direct action in human affairs."

"Perhaps not," Sam conceded. "But he can advise us, guide us. At the very least, he can warn us what we're truly up against."

Talien nodded slowly, coming to a decision. "Then we need to speak with him, and soon. If Kestral is already preparing to cross over..."

"My mother works quickly," Nissa confirmed, her voice barely above a whisper. "Once she sets her mind to something, nothing stops her."

"Then it's settled," Sam said. "Talien and I will attempt to contact Papa Legba, warn him of what's coming, and seek his counsel on how to stop Kestral."

"I'm coming too," Bree said firmly, the hat still clutched in her hands.

Sam shook his head. "Communicating with Papa Legba isn't like what we just did with Xaloth. It's dangerous in different ways, especially for someone not trained in necromancy."

"My sister is in this hat," Bree countered, her voice tight with emotion. "Her spirit is one of the ones Kestral wants to consume. I'm not sitting this out."

Sam and Talien exchanged a look, some silent communication passing between them.

"You said the hat is a gateway," Talien said thoughtfully. "Perhaps having it—and Bree—with us would strengthen our connection to Legba."

Sam hesitated, then nodded reluctantly. "Alright. But you follow our instructions exactly. Papa Legba can be... unpredictable."

"I understand," Bree said, relief evident in her voice.

"We should begin preparations immediately," Talien suggested. "The ritual to contact Papa Legba requires specific components."

"I know what we need," Sam assured him, already moving toward one of the many cabinets that lined the walls of the ceremonial chamber. "And I know where to find him."

As Sam gathered the necessary items, Bree watched him with new eyes. This was not just her neighbor who wrote science fiction novels. This was a necromancer who had walked between worlds, who had conversed with the guardians of death itself. A man who had lived centuries, carrying secrets she was only beginning to glimpse.

And now, together, they would attempt to stop a madwoman from upsetting the balance between life and death itself.

The weight of the hat in her hands seemed to increase, as if the spirits within sensed what was coming and responded with their own urgency. Somewhere in that swirl of consciousness was Molly, and Bree silently promised her sister that she would not fail. Whatever came next, whatever dangers awaited in the shadows between worlds, she would face them.

For Molly. For the coven. For all the spirits that rested in the Tower of Souls, unaware of the threat that was coming for them.

Chapter 32
Bayou Betrayal

The Louisiana bayou stretched dark and endless under a moonless night sky, its stagnant waters a sluggish mirror reflecting twisted cypress knees and hanging moss draped like funeral shrouds. One day had passed since Nissa Drach had stolen the Andromeda Coven's hat for her mother, only to vanish with it into the night. The humid air hung heavy with the promise of a storm, mosquitoes whining in desperate clouds around the rotting shack that slouched at the swamp's edge.

Kestrel Drach's lair squatted like a diseased toad half-sunk in the mud, its warped planks sweating with moisture, rusted tin roof groaning with each gust of wind. The sagging porch listed dangerously into the mire, its broken steps leading to a door that hung crooked on leather hinges. Three lanterns flickered with unnatural green flame, casting sickly, writhing shadows over the surrounding waters where gator eyes reflected the eerie light before submerging into darkness.

Inside, the air was thick enough to choke on—a miasma of decay, herbs, blood, and power that clung to the skin like oil. Altars of bone and feather lined the walls, carefully arranged in patterns that made the eye skitter away if observed too long. Jars of blood, herbs, and things less identifiable cluttered a splintered table, their contents sloshing as Kestrel's movements shook the unstable floor. A voodoo circle glowed faintly in the packed dirt, etched with runes that pulsed like a heartbeat, each symbol carved with precision despite their seemingly chaotic arrangement.

The stolen hat should have been there, perched atop the main altar, its power ready to be harnessed. But Nissa's betrayal had upended everything, and the empty space where the hat should have rested burned in Kestrel's vision like an accusation.

"That ungrateful little *worm*," Kestrel snarled, her voice a raspy drawl that slithered through the stale air like a Cottonmouth in the swamp. "All these years, all my teachin', all my preparation, and she turns tail at the final moment."

Kestrel stood at the circle's center—tall and gaunt as a starving predator, her black hair wild and streaked with premature gray, her eyes glinting with an unhinged malevolence in the green light. She wore no cosmetics, no artifice—her power was raw, her appearance a testament to her disregard for anything but the magic that consumed her. Deep lines etched her face, not from age but from channeling energies that had taken their toll on her physical form.

Her hands gripped a staff of gnarled cypress, blackened as if charred though no flame had touched it. The wood twisted unnaturally, spiraling up to a crow's skull mounted at its peak, the beak open in a silent scream. Small objects—feathers, beads, tiny bones, and scraps of fabric—dangled from leather cords wrapped around its length. This was her conduit, alive with dark magic, an extension of her will made physical.

She wore a tattered robe, once white but now stained with mud, blood, and the residue of a hundred rituals. Around her neck hung a necklace of teeth—human, animal, and things less easily identified—each one a trophy from a conquered enemy, each one imbued with a specific curse. They rattled as she paced, a discordant percussion accompanying her rage.

"Nissa," she hissed, voice dropping to a venomous whisper. "You cowardly little rat. You thought you'd run with my prize? After everything I done for you?" A bitter laugh escaped her cracked lips. "I'll peel your soul apart—thread by thread—'til you beggin' for the dark. Won't be quick, no ma'am. Won't be clean neither."

She slammed the staff down on the dirt floor, and green fire flared from the runes etched there, a power crackling through the shack that set the hanging jars swinging and the bones on the altars rattling. The very air seemed to vibrate with her wrath, a low hum that ached in the teeth and made the eyes water.

A low chant spilled from her lips, words that no living tongue was meant to speak—a voodoo incantation, sharp and ancient, calling on powers that lurked in the spaces between worlds.

"*Legba, tande mwen... louvri chemen an*," she intoned, her Louisiana drawl lending the Creole words a unique cadence. "Hear me, Legba... open the way. That girl's treachery won't stop me none. Hat or no hat, I'll have it all."

Outside, the wind picked up, howling through the cypress trees as if the spirits themselves protested what was to come. Inside, Kestrel only grinned wider, knowing the disturbance for what it was—a sign that her words were being heard beyond the veil of the living world.

Her plan churned in her mind, vast and terrible in its ambition. The hat would have made things easier, yes—a direct connection to generations of witch spirits, a bridge between realms. But Kestrel Drach had spent decades preparing for this moment, and she would not be deterred by a single setback, not even the loss of such a powerful tool.

She would detach her soul from her body, send it across the threshold to the Realm of the Dead. There, she would confront Papa Legba, bend the guardian of the crossroads to her will through bribery or force. Beyond him lay her true prize—the Tower of Souls, where the spirits of every witch who had ever lived congregated, their knowledge and power accumulated across centuries.

She would drain them all, absorb their essence, their memories, their abilities. And when she returned to her body in the living world, she would wield a power unmatched by any practitioner who had ever drawn breath.

Kestrel knelt by the table, clawing through a pile of relics and artifacts—tools of her trade, each one steeped in the suffering of its acquisition. Her long fingers, tipped with nails filed to points and stained with substances best left unidentified, pushed aside bones and feathers until she found what she sought—a cracked mirror in a frame of blackened wood, her scrying glass.

The surface was cloudy, as if perpetually fogged by breath, though no one had blown upon it. Those with the sight might have noticed the faint faces that occasionally pressed against the glass from the inside, mouths open in silent screams—spirits trapped between reflections.

"Time to see what we're dealin' with now, ain't it?" she murmured to the mirror. She reached for one of the jars, uncorking it to release the metallic scent of blood—fresh, taken from a drifter who had made the mistake of seeking shelter too near her domain just days ago. With her thumb, she smeared a line of the viscous red liquid across the mirror's surface.

"Show me," she snarled, and the glass began to shimmer, the blood seeping into the surface rather than dripping down. The cloudy surface roiled like disturbed water, and then visions began to form, swirling and taking shape as Kestrel leaned closer, her eyes reflecting the unearthly light.

The Realm of the Dead unfurled before her inner eye, its landscape a misty gray expanse where distance and perspective seemed to shift with each passing moment. Distant echoes wailed across the void—the voices of the recently departed, confused and afraid as they adjusted to their new state of being. At the center of her vision, a crossroads materialized, five paths converging at a point that pulsed with shadow and light simultaneously.

There stood Papa Legba, tall and imposing in his top hat and coat, leaning on a cane adorned with symbols of power. His face was both ancient and ageless, dark skin creased with the wisdom of millennia, eyes sharp as obsidian knives as they seemed to stare directly at Kestrel through the vision. The gatekeeper, the trickster, the first obstacle between her and ultimate power.

"You lookin' right at me, ain't ya, old man?" Kestrel whispered, her lips curling into a smile that held no warmth. "See me comin', do ya? Well, you just wait. I got plans for you, Papa."

Beyond Legba, barely visible through the swirling mists, she could make out her true objective—the Tower of Souls. It loomed impossibly tall, a structure that seemed built of light rather than any physical material, stretching beyond what the eye could comprehend. Around it, countless tiny motes of luminescence swirled and danced—souls, each one a repository of memory and power, each one a piece of the feast she intended to consume.

Her grin widened, jagged and wild, her teeth gleaming in the green light. Her planning had been precise, her malice pure and undiluted by doubt or morality.

"Legba, you old fool," she said, her voice low and rich with anticipation. "You think you gonna bar my way? I've studied you for decades. I know what you want, what you can't refuse."

She pushed herself to her feet, moving to a shelf laden with small pouches and boxes. With careful deliberation, she selected several items—a pouch of small bones, polished coins from a dozen different eras, a lock of hair that could only have come from a child, and other objects less easily identified. These she gathered in a worn leather sack, which she then tossed into the center of the glowing circle.

"Offerings for the gatekeeper," she explained to the empty room, as if teaching an invisible student. "He'll take 'em too, greedy bastard that he is. Won't be able to help himself. And then he'll let my soul pass through, thinkin' I'm just another petitioner come to beg favors."

She chuckled, the sound like gravel underfoot. "But I ain't beggin', no sir. I'm takin'. Once I'm past him, it's straight to the Tower. Every witch who's ever passed over, every necromancer's trick, every shred of knowledge and power they accumulated in life—it'll all be mine for the takin'."

Kestrel's voice rose, a fevered edge creeping in as she paced the circle's perimeter. "Just imagine it—I'll know the craft of centuries, every hex, ward, and binding ever devised. Spells forgotten by the living will be mine to command. And when I walk back into my body, this world and everything in it will bend to my will."

The mirror on the table suddenly shifted, its surface rippling as the vision changed. Now it showed her daughter Nissa's face, flickering as if viewed through disturbed water. She wasn't alone—the image widened to reveal that she was in what appeared to be a library of impossible proportions, standing near a man that Kestrel recognized immediately.

"Samuel Sorken," she hissed, the name like a curse on her lips.

Her staff came down on the table with such force that the wood cracked, several jars toppling to shatter on the floor. Green liquid sizzled where it touched the dirt, sending up acrid smoke that coiled toward the ceiling.

"That necromancer thinks he can stop me?" Her voice rose to a shout that sent a nearby roosting crow flapping frantically from the rafters. "Nissa's run straight to him, has she? Spilled all my secrets? Let 'em come! The Realm of the Dead is my territory now. I've spent my whole life preparin' for this."

She moved back to the circle, tracing its edge with the tip of her staff, watching as the runes flared brighter at her touch. "The soul is the key to it all," she said, her voice calmer now, methodical as she refocused on her task. "Detach it from the body, send it across the threshold. The hat would've made it easier, provided a direct bridge. But I've got enough power without it."

From her robe, she produced a dagger of cold iron, its blade etched with voodoo symbols. With practiced precision, she pricked her palm, allowing several drops of blood to fall into the circle. Where they landed, the runes flared with green fire, a reaction that made her smile with satisfaction.

"Just a test run," she murmured. "Gotta make sure the circle's properly charged."

She began to chant again, her voice dropping to a guttural growl that seemed to come from somewhere deeper than her throat. The words were ancient, a language that had never been widely spoken even in its heyday, now preserved only in the oldest and darkest of voodoo practices.

"*Legba, pran ofrann mwen epi gide nanm mwen nan Pilye a,*" she intoned. "Legba, take my offering and guide my soul to the Tower. Them souls there—witches, warriors, fools—they don't know what's comin'. I'll rip 'em open, drink 'em dry, leave nothing but husks."

The shack began to tremble, dust sifting down from the ceiling as the hanging moss outside swayed without wind. The water of the bayou lapped at the stilts supporting the structure, as if some massive creature was moving beneath the surface.

And then something extraordinary happened—a shadow seemed to peel away from Kestrel's body, a dark silhouette that hovered just inches from her physical form, connected by tendrils of green light that pulsed like veins.

She laughed, a sound of pure, malicious triumph. "See that?" she crowed to the empty room, as if Nissa could hear her. "You can't stop this, girl! You gave me the start, showed me it could be done. The hat would've been nice, but I don't need it. I don't need you neither, 'cept maybe for some payback when I'm done."

The writhing, smoke-like shadow snapped back into her sweat-drenched body with an audible, bone-chilling crack that echoed through the ritual chamber, leaving her gasping painfully for breath but grinning wildly with malevolent triumph. "Just a necessary practice run to test the dimensional boundaries," she panted, her eyes glowing with unnatural green energy. "But it worked perfectly as I theorized. It actually worked beyond my expectations!"

Regaining her composure, Kestrel moved to another altar, this one dominated by a large crow's skull surrounded by smaller bones arranged in a spiral pattern. From a shelf above, she took a cracked bottle containing dark rum, which she poured carefully over the skull.

"Legba's favorite," she explained to the empty room. "He's got a taste for the good stuff. This'll be part of my offerin', get his attention right quick. He'll think I'm just another petitioner, wanting a favor, wanting to speak to some dead relative." Her laugh was sharp, cutting. "He'll open the gate, thinkin' I'm just passin' through. Then I'll make my move on the Tower."

She paused, fingers tracing the rim of the skull almost tenderly. "Even without the hat in hand, I can use its echo. Nancy's power, Molly's fresh arrival—they'll draw me to the right souls in the Tower. Every bit of witchcraft they ever knew, every spell, every secret—mine to take, mine to twist."

The bayou outside stirred with unnatural movement—gators splashing frantically away from the shack, birds taking wing despite the darkness, as if sensing the wrongness emanating from within. The wind picked up, howling through the cypress trees with a sound almost like voices wailing in pain.

Kestrel turned her attention to a small cage tucked in the corner of the room. Inside, a raccoon cowered, its eyes wide with a too-human understanding of its fate.

"Need me a little practice," Kestrel muttered, approaching the cage with her dagger drawn. "A little juice to get things started proper."

With quick, practiced movements honed through decades of sacrificial rituals and forbidden blood magic, she pulled the terrified, struggling creature from its rusted wire-mesh prison, slashing its exposed throat in one efficient, merciless motion with her ancient ceremonial obsidian blade that hungered for life energy. The warm, crimson blood pooled rapidly in a specially consecrated clay bowl marked with voodoo symbols she held strategically beneath the wound, not a precious drop wasted in the oppressive darkness. The raccoon's twitching, lifeless body she tossed carelessly aside onto a growing pile of small animal sacrifices needed for the powerful spell—its sole purpose now fully served, its essential life force now permanently part of her increasingly powerful magical working that would soon reach its devastating completion.

She carried the bowl to the circle, pouring the fresh blood along the innermost ring of runes. The reaction was immediate—the entire circle flaring with intense green light, the voodoo bridge between realms humming with power that set the teeth on edge and made the air taste of metal.

"Legba will bow to me," she whispered, her voice thick with anticipation. "The Tower will be mine. The souls will scream when I take what's rightfully mine."

She lifted the bloodied dagger to her lips, tongue darting out to taste the blade, her expression one of complete, consuming madness. With sudden violence, she kicked the scrying mirror from the table, sending it crashing to the floor where it shattered into a dozen pieces, each reflecting her wild eyes.

"Nissa's dead when I'm done," she promised the empty room. "Samuel Sorken too. Any who stand in my way. Hat or no hat, I'm comin' for what's mine."

Kestrel returned to the center of the meticulously constructed ritual circle, her carved obsidian staff planted firmly in the blood-soaked dirt, her elaborate magical preparations nearly complete after hours of painstaking work. All around her, the ancient voodoo symbols pulsed with sickly green light, responding to her will, her grim determination, her absolute certainty that nothing and no one would deny her the ultimate power she had coveted for decades.

Outside, the swamp seemed to hold its breath, a green mist rising from the dark waters as if the very environment reflected her will and purpose. Miles away in Ballad, the Andromeda Coven remained unaware of the magnitude of the storm brewing in the Louisiana bayou—a tempest centered on one woman whose ambition knew no bounds, whose madness had crystallized into terrible purpose.

Kestrel Drach stood amid her power, plans locked in place, wrath her only engine, ready to cast her soul into the realm beyond death and claim dominion over all who had passed before. The crossroads awaited. Papa Legba awaited.

And beyond them both, the Tower of Souls loomed, its bounty of power promised to the one with the will to take it, its fate.

Chapter 33
The Crossroads Guardian

The ceremonial chamber had transformed since their encounter with Xaloth's spirit. Gone were the silver dusted patterns and crystal pillars, replaced now with arrangements that seemed to blend multiple magical traditions into something uniquely suited to their current purpose.

Sam worked methodically, his movements precise as he arranged various items in a circle at the center of the obsidian floor. A bottle of dark rum, three hand-rolled cigars, a walking stick carved with intricate symbols, and several coins of various origins now formed points of a perfect circle. In the center, he placed a small wooden crossroads marker—two sticks bound together with red thread to form an X.

Talien was handling a different aspect of the preparation, drawing symbols in white chalk around the perimeter—veve designs that represented Papa Legba's domain and authority. The designs were complex, featuring crosses, stars, and spiraling patterns that seemed to shift if one looked at them too long.

"These will anchor the connection," Talien explained to Bree as he worked, his usual exuberance tempered by the gravity of their task. "The veve acts as both invitation and doorway—it acknowledges Legba's sovereignty over the crossroads while providing us the means to reach him."

Bree nodded, clutching the Tanner Hat close to her chest. She could still feel it pulsing gently with power, the spirits that were tied to it stirring within as if they were aware of what was about to happen and eagerly waited to assist.

On the far side of the room, Nissa sat with Margaret and Ezekiel hovering nearby. The young woman looked uncomfortable but determined, her hands clasped tightly in her lap as she listened to the spirits.

"If Kestrel succeeds in her endeavor," Margaret was saying, her Victorian propriety giving an odd formality to the horrific scenario she was describing, "the consequences would be most dire indeed. The Tower of Souls stands as the repository of all who have passed—every spirit, every memory, every fragment of knowledge accumulated across generations."

"And yer mother seeks tae consume it all," Ezekiel added, his spectral form rippling with agitation. "Tae drain the very essence of every witch, every practitioner who's passed intae the next realm."

"What would happen to those souls?" Nissa asked quietly, genuine concern in her voice. "If she... if she takes their power, what becomes of them?"

Margaret's translucent face grew solemn. "They would cease to be as they are, child. Their individuality, their memories—all would be absorbed into thy mother's being. 'Twould be a second death, most terrible and permanent."

"And not just witches," Ezekiel interjected grimly. "Once she starts, once she learns how tae consume spirits, what's tae stop her from expandin' her appetite? Every soul in the Tower could fall prey tae her hunger."

"Even our own existence might be threatened," Margaret admitted, adjusting her spectral lace collar in a nervous gesture. "Though we remain tethered to this realm through Master Samuel's magic, our essence still resides primarily in the Realm of the Dead. Should thy mother's corruption spread…"

She left the sentence unfinished, but her meaning was clear. Even the library's resident spirits weren't safe from Kestrel's ambitions.

"I'm sorry," Nissa whispered, her eyes downcast. "I should have realized sooner what she was planning. I should have stopped her before—"

"Ye cannae blame yerself for yer mother's madness," Ezekiel interrupted, his Scottish brogue softening with compassion. "Ye've done right by comin' here, by returnin' the hat."

"Indeed," Margaret agreed. "Thy courage in defying such cruelty is most commendable. Few would have had the strength to break free as thou hast done."

Across the room, Sam straightened, surveying his handiwork with a critical eye. "It's ready," he announced, turning to Bree. "Last chance to reconsider. Contacting Legba won't be like our communication with Xaloth. We won't just be speaking with him—we'll be crossing over, at least partially."

Bree stepped forward without hesitation. "My sister's soul is at risk. The entire coven is at risk. I'm coming."

Sam studied her for a moment, then nodded. "Alright. Bring the hat—it may help establish our intent when we meet Legba." He gestured to a spot between himself and Talien. "Stand here, and whatever happens, stay close to us. The crossroads can be... disorienting for the uninitiated."

Bree took her place in the circle, the hat held firmly in both hands. She could feel her heart pounding against her ribs, fear and determination warring within her.

"What do I need to do?" she asked, striving to keep her voice steady.

"Focus on the hat," Sam instructed. "On the connection it represents—to your sister, your grandmother, all the witches of your lineage. That connection will help anchor you when we cross over."

Talien moved to complete the circle, his usual levity completely absent now. "And stay silent unless directly addressed," he added. "Papa Legba is ancient and powerful, with his own rules and protocols. We're entering his domain as petitioners—it's best to let Sam lead the conversation."

Sam nodded in agreement, then closed his eyes, centering himself. When he spoke again, his voice had taken on a resonant quality that seemed to vibrate in the very stones beneath their feet.

"Legba, Master of the Crossroads, Guardian of the Gateway, we seek audience at your threshold. By rum and smoke, by wood and metal, we call to you across the divide."

He picked up the rum bottle, uncorking it and pouring a circle around the wooden crossroads marker. The obsidian floor seemed to absorb the liquid instantly, though the strong scent of alcohol remained, sharp and pungent in the still air.

"Papa Legba, open the way," Sam continued, his voice dropping to a rhythmic chant. "We come with respect, we come with purpose, we come with warning."

Talien joined in, his deeper voice harmonizing with Sam's in perfect counterpoint. "Legba, we stand at the crossing, seeking passage to your domain. Grant us safe journey, grant us your wisdom, grant us your ear."

The air in the chamber grew thick, heavy with more than just humidity. Bree felt a pressure building against her skin, as if the very atmosphere was condensing around them. The hat in her hands grew warmer, almost hot to the touch, though not painfully so.

Sam struck a match and lit the three cigars, placing them at specific points around the crossroads marker. Blue smoke curled upward, twisting into shapes that seemed almost deliberate before dissipating.

"Papa Legba, we come with offerings and respect. Open the gate between worlds, allow us passage to speak with you directly."

The chalk symbols around the perimeter began to glow with a soft, pulsing light. The crossroads marker at the center of their circle suddenly cast a shadow far longer than it should have, stretching across the obsidian floor and up the far wall.

And then something shifted—not a visible change, but a sensation like the world tilting beneath their feet. Bree felt dizzy, disoriented, as if she were spinning while standing perfectly still. She clutched the hat tighter, focusing on it as Sam had instructed, using it as an anchor against the vertigo.

When the sensation passed, they were... elsewhere.

Gone was the ceremonial chamber with its domed ceiling and obsidian floor. Instead, they stood at an actual crossroads—five dirt paths converging in a perfect star pattern, each leading off into different landscapes that shouldn't have been able to exist side by side. One path led into a misty swamp, another toward a sun-baked desert, a third into a snow-covered forest, a fourth toward what appeared to be a bustling city street from a bygone era, and the fifth into absolute, impenetrable darkness.

The sky above them was neither day nor night, but a strange twilight state where stars were visible despite a sun that hung perpetually on the horizon. The air felt charged with potential, as if this place existed in a permanent state of becoming rather than being.

And there, seated on a wooden stool at the very center of the crossroads, was Papa Legba.

He appeared as an elderly man—tall and lean, with skin the color of aged mahogany, deeply lined with the wisdom of centuries. He wore a straw hat atop gray-streaked hair, a weathered suit of indeterminate vintage, and leaned on a gnarled walking stick similar to the one Sam had placed in their circle. A lit pipe was clutched between his teeth, sending up curls of fragrant smoke that hung motionless in the still air.

His eyes, though—his eyes belied his elderly appearance. They were ancient beyond reckoning, glittering with a sharp intelligence and unfathomable depth. These were eyes that had witnessed the passage of countless souls, eyes that knew all the secrets of life and death.

For a long moment, he simply regarded them, smoke curling from his pipe. Then he broke into a broad grin that transformed his face from imposing to almost mischievous.

"Well, well, well," he drawled, his voice rich with a Louisiana cadence that reminded Bree of slow-moving rivers and cypress swamps. "If it ain't Sammy Sorken come callin' again after all these years. And you brought friends this time, cher! How generous of you to share ol' Papa's company."

Sam stepped forward, offering a respectful bow. "Papa Legba, it's been too long. Thank you for granting us passage."

Legba waved a dismissive hand, though his eyes remained sharp and evaluating. "Don't you try dat smooth talk wit' me, Sammy. You ain't never come visitin' just to pass the time, eh? Always some crisis, always some problem needin' ol' Papa's help."

He turned his attention to Talien, looking him up and down with open curiosity. "Another necromancer from your world, I see. Been a long time since I met one of your kind." His gaze shifted to Bree, and his expression softened slightly. "And a witch of the Tanner line, carryin' Nancy's hat, no less. The old lady finally passed it on, did she?"

Bree remained rigid, swallowing hard under that penetrating gaze. "My grandmother died recently," she said, surprised at how steady her voice sounded. "The hat came to me after my sister Molly was killed."

Something flickered in Legba's ancient eyes—a momentary sadness quickly masked. "Ah, Molly Tanner. Yes, she came through my crossin' recently. Bright spirit, that one. Strong. Refused my offer to guide her, said she had to stay with the hat, had responsibilities still." He tapped his pipe thoughtfully. "Now I'm wonderin' if that wasn't the wiser choice, given what's brewin'."

He leaned forward on his stool, suddenly all business. "So, what brings the three of you to my doorstep? Must be somethin' serious to risk crossin' over like this."

Sam stepped forward again. "It is serious, Papa. We've come to warn you. Kestral Drach, daughter of Malakai Drach, is planning to enter the Realm of the Dead."

Legba's expression didn't change, but the air around them grew noticeably colder. "Is that so?" he said softly, dangerously. "And what business might this Kestral have in my realm?"

"She seeks the Tower of Souls," Talien explained. "She believes she can physically enter your realm, bypass your authority at the crossroads, and reach the Tower."

"Once there," Sam continued, "she intends to consume the spirits of deceased witches, absorb their power and knowledge. Her ultimate goal appears to be the creation of a new Nexus, one she can control."

At the mention of the Nexus, Legba's easy demeanor vanished entirely. He rose from his stool in one fluid motion that belied his apparent age, his walking stick striking the ground with a crack like thunder.

"She plans to do WHAT?" he demanded, his voice echoing across all five paths of the crossroads. The twilight sky darkened perceptibly, and wind whipped suddenly around them, carrying whispers that sounded disturbingly like moans of pain.

Bree found herself taking an involuntary step backward, only Sam's steadying hand on her arm keeping her from retreating further.

"Tell me everything," Legba commanded, his Louisiana drawl now underscored with something older, something that had never been human. "Every detail, every plan you know of. How does this woman intend to enter my realm without my permission?"

Between them, Sam, Talien, and Bree laid out everything they knew—Kestral's voodoo practices, her collection of magical artifacts, the partial soul detachment she had already achieved according to Nissa, and her ultimate goal of draining the Tower of Souls.

As they spoke, Legba's anger seemed to condense around him like a storm cloud. When they finished, he paced the crossroads, his walking stick leaving smoldering impressions in the dirt with each strike.

"The audacity," he muttered, his accent thickening with his emotion. "The sheer, blasphemous audacity of this woman. To think she can jus' waltz into my realm, bypass my authority, and start consumin' souls like they some kind of all-you-can-eat buffet!"

He turned abruptly, fixing Sam with a piercing stare. "And her father—this Malakai—he's dead, you say?"

Sam nodded. "According to his granddaughter Nissa, he died physically about five years ago. But Kestral believes his spirit remains intact in the Realm of the Dead, possibly guiding her actions."

Legba's expression darkened further. "If that's true, then we got bigger problems than just the daughter. A spirit that powerful, that knowledgeable about the barriers between realms..." He shook his head grimly. "He could be helpin' her find ways around my crossroads."

"That's what we feared," Sam admitted. "Which is why we came directly to you. If anyone can strengthen the barriers between realms, secure the crossroads against unauthorized passage, it's you, Papa."

Legba's anger seemed to recede slightly at this acknowledgment of his authority. He resumed his seat on the stool, tapping his pipe thoughtfully.

"You right about that, Sammy. Ain't nobody crosses without my say-so—not supposed to, anyhow." He frowned, obviously troubled. "But voodoo magic, properly applied... it can bend rules that shouldn't be bendable. Especially if she's found a way to partially detach her soul already."

"We're offering our help," Talien said. "Sam and I are experienced necromancers. We understand the boundaries between worlds better than most."

"And I have the hat," Bree added, holding it up. "If Kestral wants the knowledge of generations of witches, she'll have to go through us to get it."

Legba studied them for a long moment, smoke curling from his pipe in contemplative whorls. Finally, he nodded, decision made.

"I appreciate the warnin', truly do. Not many would risk crossin' over just to bring news." He tapped his pipe against his palm, emptying it of ash that sparkled like tiny stars before vanishing. "I can handle this Kestral woman if she tries to force her way through my crossroads. Been guardin' this place since before her ancestors were even thinkin' about bein' born."

He stood again, leaning on his walking stick. "But if she's got alternate methods, ways of slippin' past my jurisdiction..." He frowned, clearly disliking the admission. "Well, I might be glad of your assistance after all, Sammy. You and your friends."

"Just say the word," Sam assured him. "We can return if needed."

Legba nodded, his expression grave. "Best you head back to your world for now. Shore up your own defenses, prepare your coven." He glanced at Bree. "The hat is powerful protection, cher, but it's also a target. Keep it close, keep it safe."

He turned to Sam and Talien. "I'll be watchin' the boundaries, strengthenin' the weak spots. If this Kestral tries to cross over, I'll know it." A grim smile crossed his weathered face. "And she'll find ol' Papa ain't as easy to get past as she might be thinkin'."

"And Malakai?" Sam asked. "If his spirit is guiding her, helping her find ways around your authority..."

Legba's expression hardened. "I'll be lookin' for him too. If he's in my realm, he's under my jurisdiction, powerful spirit or no." He tapped his walking stick against the ground, sending up a shower of golden sparks. "Ain't no spirit—not even one from another world—that can defy the Baron of the Crossroads in his own domain."

He made a sweeping gesture with his hand, and suddenly the crossroads seemed to shift around them, the five paths blurring at the edges. "Time for you to return, before your tether to the living world grows too thin. Remember what I said—prepare yourselves. If I need you, I'll send a sign."

As the world began to dissolve around them, Papa Legba's voice followed them, carried on a wind that smelled of rum and tobacco. "And Sammy—don't be such a stranger next time, yeah? Ol' Papa appreciates a social visit now and then, not just when the worlds are endin'..."

The crossroads vanished completely, and Bree felt that same disorienting sensation of spinning while standing still. She clutched the hat tightly, closing her eyes against the vertigo.

When she opened them again, they were back in the ceremonial chamber of Sam's library. The chalk symbols had burned away, leaving scorched marks on the obsidian floor. The rum, cigars, and other offerings were gone, consumed in the ritual.

For a moment, no one spoke, the weight of their experience settling over them like a heavy cloak. Then Sam staggered slightly, catching himself against a nearby table. Talien didn't look much better, his face drawn with exhaustion.

"Crossing over and back takes a toll," Sam explained, noticing Bree's concerned look. "We'll recover."

"What do we do now?" Bree asked, still clutching the hat close to her chest.

Sam straightened, moving with deliberate care to a chair. "Now we prepare. Papa Legba is powerful, but if Kestral has found alternative methods to enter the Realm of the Dead, we need to be ready to assist him."

"And what about Malakai?" Talien asked, his voice grim. "If his spirit is truly guiding Kestral from beyond the grave..."

"Then we're facing an enemy who knows as much about necromancy as we do," Sam finished. His expression hardened with determination. "But we have advantages too—a reformed insider in Nissa, the repository of generations of witch knowledge in the hat, and now Papa Legba as an ally."

He turned to Bree. "You should return home, tell the coven what's happening. Anyone who wants to help should meet back here in a few hours. The more magical practitioners we have on our side, the better our chances."

Bree nodded, understanding the gravity of the situation. "I'll bring as many as I can," she promised. With one last look at the scorched ritual circle, she left the chamber, the hat still clutched protectively in her hands.

After she had gone, a heavy silence fell over the library. Sam looked around at those who remained—Talien, the goblins who had been watching from a respectful distance, and the spirits hovering nearby, all waiting for instructions.

"We're facing a catastrophic crisis unlike any I've encountered in my countless centuries wandering the realms on Earth," he said quietly, his ancient eyes reflecting uncharacteristic fear. "If Kestral succeeds in her dark ritual, if she manages to consume even a fraction of the innocent souls trapped in the Tower of the Dead... the delicate balance between life and death will be irrevocably altered throughout all planes of existence."

"Can she really accomplish such a thing?" Morden asked, his impeccable suit somehow still pristine despite the tense atmosphere. "Consuming spirits, absorbing their power?"

"Theoretically, yes," Talien replied grimly. "It's forbidden knowledge, but it exists. If she's found the right rituals, combined with her voodoo practices..."

"'Tis most disturbing to contemplate," Margaret said, her Victorian composure finally showing cracks. "To think that our very essence might be... consumed by such a woman."

"Aye," Ezekiel agreed, his spectral form flickering with agitation. "Even in my worst battles, I never faced an enemy who could destroy not just my body, but my very soul."

Sam rose from his chair, exhaustion temporarily masked by determination. "Which is why we cannot—will not—let her succeed. The coven, the hat, our combined knowledge... we'll find a way to stop her."

His gaze swept over the gathered allies—necromancer, spirits, and goblins alike—their faces reflecting the same resolve he felt.

"The next few hours or the next few days will determine the fate of not just our world, but the Realm of the Dead as well. Whatever it takes, whatever sacrifices must be made... Kestral Drach must be stopped."

Outside the library, beyond the impossible physics of Sam's house, the real world continued its normal rhythms, oblivious to the crisis brewing in hidden realms. The deep darkness of night had given way to that hollow hour between 1 and 2 AM, when even the most determined night owls had surrendered to sleep. Soon, the first hint of dawn would creep over Ballad, a town that had no idea how precariously balanced the natural order had become.

The battle for the Tower of Souls was about to begin.

Chapter 34
THE COVEN GATHERS

B ree's hand trembled slightly as she inserted her key into the front door lock. The Tanner Hat was still clutched tightly under her arm, its presence a constant reminder of everything that had happened. Dawn was still hours away, but a soft glow from inside the house told her that someone was still awake.

She pushed the door open and stepped into the warmth of her home, immediately enveloped by familiar scents that now carried a bittersweet comfort. The living room lights cast gentle shadows across walls lined with family photographs—images of happier times that seemed impossibly distant after the events of the night.

Her mother, Mary Ann, looked up from where she sat on the couch between Susan Fond and Elaine Warren. All three women had the hollow-eyed look of those who had been crying but had temporarily exhausted their tears. A pot of tea sat on the coffee table, steam no longer rising from the untouched cups.

"Bree!" Mary Ann was on her feet in an instant, pulling her daughter into a fierce embrace. "We were so worried. Where have you been all this time?"

Susan and Elaine approached more slowly, their weathered hands clasped together for mutual support, their faces etched with deep concern and unmistakable grief for the coven's recent losses. Susan's short blonde hair caught the golden lamplight as she studied Bree's haunted expression with motherly intuition. "You've been through something profound today," she observed quietly, her voice barely above a whisper. "Something traumatic beyond what happened earlier at the bookstore."

Bree nodded, the weight of everything she'd learned and witnessed pressing down on her like a physical burden. "You have no idea," she whispered.

"Molly's body..." Bree began, her voice catching.

"We've taken care of her," Elaine said gently, her usually stern features softened by compassion. "She's at rest upstairs, prepared according to the old ways. Tomorrow—or rather, later today—we'll begin the formal rituals."

Bree clutched the hat tighter. "Molly's not just... gone," she said. "She's in here, with Grandma Nancy. I spoke with her spirit."

The three older women exchanged glances, not entirely surprised by this revelation. The Tanner Hat's properties were well-known within the inner circle of the coven.

"Come sit," Mary Ann urged, guiding Bree to the couch. "Tell us everything."

And so she did. The story spilled from her in a torrent—Sam's true identity as a necromancer from another world, the destruction of Eldoria, the historical connection between the Andromeda coven and the refugees, Nissa's betrayal and subsequent change of heart, Kestrel

Drach and her terrible plans for the Tower of Souls, and finally, their meeting with Papa Legba at the crossroads between worlds.

By the time she finished, the room had fallen completely silent. Even the usual creaks and settlings of the old house seemed to have paused, as if the very building was holding its breath.

"So, it's true," Susan finally said, her voice barely above a whisper. "The old stories about our coven's founding... they weren't just metaphors or myths."

"And Sam Sorken," Mary Ann breathed, her eyes wide with disbelief. "Our neighbor all this time... a necromancer from another world."

Elaine Warren stood abruptly, her practical nature asserting itself through the shock. "We need to call the others," she declared. "If what you're saying is true, Bree—and I believe it is—then we're facing a crisis unlike anything the Andromeda coven has encountered in generations."

Mary Ann nodded, already reaching for her phone. "How soon does Sam need us there?"

"He said to bring anyone willing to help back to his house in a few hours," Bree replied. "We need as many witches as possible if we're going to help Papa Legba defend the Realm of the Dead against Kestrel."

"Then we'll start making calls," Susan said firmly. "Even at this hour, this can't wait."

Bree glanced down at herself, suddenly aware that she was still wearing the same clothes from earlier—jeans and a blouse stained with Molly's dried blood. The rusty brown patches made her stomach turn.

"I need to shower," she said quietly. "And change out of these clothes."

Mary Ann nodded, eyes filling with fresh tears as she noticed the blood stains for the first time. "Of course, honey. Take your time."

Bree carried the hat upstairs and placed it carefully on her dresser before peeling off the stained clothes. Under the hot spray of the shower, she watched as her sister's blood swirled down the drain, a final physical reminder of the tragedy washing away. She pressed her forehead against the cool tile and allowed herself one brief moment of overwhelming grief before steeling herself again for what lay ahead.

Clean and dressed in fresh clothes, she rejoined the others downstairs, ready to face whatever came next.

The next few hours passed in a blur of activity. Despite the late hour, the women methodically contacted every member of the coven, providing brief explanations and requesting their presence at Sam's house by 7 AM. To their credit, not one witch declined the call—even those who responded with sleepy confusion agreed to come once they understood the gravity of the situation.

Bree finally retired to her room around 5 AM, intending to catch a brief hour of rest before the gathering. She placed the Tanner Hat carefully on her bedside table and lay down fully clothed, too exhausted to even consider changing. Sleep claimed her almost instantly, though her dreams were filled with shadowy crossroads and towers made of light.

When her alarm buzzed at 6 AM, she rose immediately, feeling as though she'd barely closed her eyes. After splashing cold water on her face and changing into fresh clothes, she returned downstairs to find her mother and Susan already preparing a simple breakfast for what promised to be a very long day.

"The others will start arriving soon," Mary Ann said, pushing a mug of strong coffee into Bree's hands. "Eat something while you can."

By 6:30, the first coven members had begun to arrive. Trudie Catshill came bearing baskets of muffins, her round face set with determination despite the early hour. Jasmine Davis arrived shortly after, dark eyes alert and focused as she helped set up additional chairs in the living room.

As 7 AM approached, the gathering had spilled out onto the front lawn and the street between the Tanner house and Sam's home. Women of various ages clustered in small groups, their voices a low murmur of concern and speculation. Some were dressed casually in jeans and sweaters, others more formally, but all carried the subtle markers of their craft—specific jewelry, particular colors, small pouches of protective herbs.

Across the street, Arthur Denim stood at his front window, coffee mug frozen halfway to his lips as he stared at the unprecedented gathering. He had seen the monthly meetings of what he assumed was some kind of neighborhood social club, but nothing like this—dozens of women converging before dawn, their expressions serious and purposeful.

His wire-rimmed glasses slid down his nose as he counted heads, mentally referencing section 7.2 of the Ballad Public Assembly Ordinance regarding unpermitted gatherings in residential areas. But his bureaucratic thoughts scattered when he spotted a familiar flash of copper-red hair among the crowd.

"Carol?" he murmured in surprise, spotting his new girlfriend's unmistakable copper-red hair among the gathering crowd.

The events of the previous night came rushing back—the attack, their unexpected first kiss, and the hours they'd spent talking afterward on his porch, sharing stories and discovering a genuine connection that neither had anticipated. They'd parted with another lingering kiss and plans for dinner that evening, but he certainly hadn't expected to see her involved in whatever was happening across the street.

Setting his coffee aside, Arthur slipped on his shoes and headed for the door. He needed to speak with Carol directly and find out what was going on.

The front door of the Tanner house opened, and Bree stepped onto the porch. She wore a simple navy sweater and jeans, the Tanner Hat clutched in one hand. Despite her exhaustion, there was a quiet authority in her bearing—something that hadn't been there before last night's events.

"It's time," she called to the assembled women. "Sam's waiting for us."

The gathered witches turned as one, their quiet conversations falling silent as Bree descended the steps and began walking toward Sam's house. Without hesitation, they fell into step behind her, a procession that spilled from the yard onto the street, moving with collective purpose.

Arthur hurried across his lawn, weaving between parked cars to intercept Carol as she walked between the two houses. "Carol!" he called.

She turned, copper-red hair catching the early morning light. Surprise flickered across her face, followed quickly by concern. "Arthur? What are you doing here?"

"I saw you from my window." He gestured toward the procession of women. "What's going on? Large gatherings in residential areas require a permit according to—"

"Not now, Arthur," Carol cut him off, glancing ahead at the group that continued moving toward Sam's house. "You should go back home. This doesn't concern you."

Arthur straightened, adjusting his glasses with one finger. "I'm concerned about you," he said, his voice softening. "Carol, I care about you, and after what happened last night... I just want to make sure you're safe."

Something in his tone made her pause. The fierce expression that had become her trademark softened momentarily. "This is important, Arthur. And complicated."

"Then let me help," he insisted. "Or at least understand."

Carol looked at him for a long moment, weighing options in her mind. Finally, she sighed. "You can follow at your own risk. But please don't interfere or be shocked by anything you see."

Arthur's brow furrowed. "Why, what am I going to see, exactly?"

Carol didn't answer. Instead, she took his hand, her fingers intertwining with his in a gesture that felt simultaneously protective and reassuring. Together, they hurried to catch up with the others, who had nearly reached Sam's front porch.

Sam Sorken stood in his doorway, dressed in dark clothes that somehow seemed more formal than his usual casual attire. His face was serious, his eyes scanning the crowd as they approached. When his gaze found Bree at the front, something passed between them—an understanding, a shared purpose.

"Thank you all for coming," he said, his voice carrying easily across the lawn. "Please, follow me inside."

He extended his hand toward Bree. Without hesitation, she stepped forward and took it, the gesture seeming both personal and ceremonial. Together, they turned and entered the house, leading the procession inside.

The witches filed in, filling Sam's living room and spilling into the adjacent kitchen and hallway. Many glanced around curiously—most had never been inside Sam's home, and they studied the bookshelves lined with science fiction novels, the tasteful but minimal décor, the subtle signs of a life lived alone.

"This way," Sam directed, still holding Bree's hand as he led the group up the stairs.

Carol tugged Arthur along, bringing up the rear of the procession. "Remember," she whispered, "not a word. Just observe."

Arthur nodded, too intrigued now to consider turning back. His mind was already cataloguing building code violations—the number of people surely exceeded the safe occupancy limit for a residential structure of this size.

At the top of the stairs, Sam led them down a hallway to what appeared to be his bedroom. It was sparsely furnished—a neatly made bed, a dresser, a desk with a closed laptop. And against one wall, a large wooden wardrobe that looked antique but well-maintained.

Sam released Bree's hand to open the wardrobe doors, revealing hanging clothes—shirts and jackets, nothing extraordinary. The witches exchanged confused glances, and a murmur of uncertainty rippled through the crowd.

Then Sam pushed the clothes aside and pressed his palm against the back panel. It slid sideways with a soft click, revealing a narrow corridor beyond that shouldn't have been possible given the positioning of the wardrobe against what should have been an exterior wall.

"Single file, please," Sam instructed, stepping aside to let Bree enter first. "The passage widens as you go."

One by one, the witches followed, their expressions ranging from awe to apprehension as they passed through the impossible doorway. Arthur, still clutching Carol's hand, found himself being pulled forward until they were about to step into the wardrobe.

"What is this?" he whispered, unable to contain himself any longer.

"Magic, Arthur," Carol replied simply. "Real magic."

Before Arthur could process this statement, they were stepping through the passage, which twisted and turned in ways that disoriented his sense of direction. The corridor seemed far longer than the few feet it should have taken to exit the back of Sam's house, and the quality of the light changed—becoming warmer, golden, emanating from no visible source.

And then they were emerging into a space that made Arthur stop dead in his tracks, his mouth falling open in complete astonishment.

The library was vast—impossibly, gloriously vast. Towering bookshelves stretched upward to a ceiling that had to be at least fifty feet high, with spiral staircases connecting multiple levels. Reading nooks with comfortable-looking chairs were scattered throughout the cavernous space. Globes that seemed to depict worlds Arthur had never seen rotated slowly on ornate stands, and maps covered walls that couldn't possibly exist within the confines of Sam's modest suburban home.

The witches spread out, their voices hushed with wonder as they took in the impossible space. Some reached out to touch the spines of ancient books, while others simply stared upward, tracing the patterns of constellations that seemed to move subtly across the domed ceiling.

Arthur, still holding Carol's hand in a grip that had tightened considerably, took a few more steps into the library. His bureaucratic mind struggled to reconcile what he was seeing with anything in his extensive knowledge of municipal regulations.

"I don't believe there's a code provision for this," he whispered to no one in particular, his voice faint with shock. "No building permit could possibly cover... this."

Carol gave his hand a squeeze, unable to suppress a smile despite the gravity of the situation. "I think we're a bit beyond Ballad's building codes now, Arthur."

Three small, green-skinned figures approached with purposeful, oddly graceful strides—goblins, if Arthur had been familiar with such mythological creatures, though his practical mind initially classified them as "unusually proportioned persons of indeterminate origin with peculiar anatomical features." They were dressed in what appeared to be perfectly tailored charcoal-gray suits of expensive fabric, with tiny golden-rimmed spectacles perched on their long, warty noses.

"Master Sorken," said the one in the lead, addressing Sam with a formal bow, "the preparations are complete, as you requested. We've arranged seating for your... numerous guests."

"Thank you, Morden," Sam replied. He turned to address the assembled witches, raising his voice to be heard throughout the vast space. "If everyone would please follow Tord and Glenken to the central reading area, we can begin."

The other two goblins—Tord and Glenken, apparently—gestured toward the heart of the library, where a large circular area had been cleared. Comfortable chairs, sofas, and cushions had been arranged in concentric rings, enough to seat everyone present.

"I know you all have questions," Sam continued as the group began to move. "And I promise, everything will be explained. But first, I think introductions are in order." He gestured to a tall man with dark hair streaked with silver who stood near one of the reading nooks. "This is Talien, my associate and fellow necromancer."

A ripple of whispers passed through the crowd at the word "necromancer." Some of the older witches looked alarmed, while others seemed merely curious.

"And these remarkable entities," Sam continued, gesturing with casual familiarity to two translucent figures that had silently materialized near a centuries-old stone fireplace adorned with arcane symbols, "are Margaret and Ezekiel, my longtime spiritual companions who assist in maintaining the vast interdimensional library and its precious magical contents."

The Victorian woman and battle-scarred Scottish soldier nodded in respectful greeting, their translucent spectral forms shimmering slightly in the golden afternoon light.

Arthur's grip on Carol's hand had become almost painful. "Are those—" he began, his voice a strangled whisper.

"Ghosts," Carol confirmed calmly. "Or spirits, as they prefer to be called."

To his credit, Arthur remained standing, though his face had gone pale beneath his wire-rimmed glasses. He swallowed hard, gaze darting from the spirits to the goblins to the impossible architecture surrounding them.

"And I thought your building code violations on Willow Street were extensive and worth documenting," he muttered weakly, his bureaucratic mind still functioning despite the supernatural shock, causing Carol to stifle a surprised, appreciative laugh.

As the last of the witches filed into the central area, Sam and Bree took positions at what appeared to be the focal point of the gathering. The Tanner Hat sat on a small table between them, its seemingly ordinary appearance belied by the soft glow that emanated from it—visible now to everyone with even the slightest magical sensitivity.

A young woman stood slightly apart from the others—Nissa Drach, though only Sam, Talien, Bree, and the spirits knew her identity or the role she had played in the unfolding crisis. She looked nervous, unsure of her place among so many witches, each one a potential enemy given her mother's plans.

Sam cleared his throat, and the murmur of conversations immediately died away. The assembled witches settled into their seats, faces turned expectantly toward him. Even Arthur found himself drawn forward, Carol guiding him to a seat at the outermost ring.

"Thank you all for coming on such short notice," Sam began. "Especially at this early hour. What I'm about to tell you will challenge everything many of you believe about your coven, your history, and the nature of magic itself."

He looked out at the sea of faces—some familiar from years of living in Ballad, others known only by reputation or not at all. But all were united by their connection to the Andromeda coven, a connection that, unknown to most of them, stretched back to another world entirely.

"The crisis we face," Sam continued, his voice growing grave, "threatens not just your coven, but the very balance between the worlds of the living and the dead."

CHAPTER 35

DARK CROSSING

N ight clung to the Louisiana bayou like a lover, reluctant to release its hold even as the first hint of dawn threatened the eastern horizon. The stagnant water reflected nothing but darkness, its surface occasionally broken by the silent movement of creatures best left unnamed. Cypress knees jutted from the murk like the knuckles of drowned giants, while Spanish moss hung from gnarled branches, swaying without wind.

At the edge of the swamp, Kestrel Drach's decaying shack seemed to pulse with an unholy light. Sickly green illumination seeped through the cracks between warped boards, casting elongated shadows across the fetid water. Inside, the air had grown thick enough to choke on—heavy with the metallic scent of blood, the acrid bite of herbs, and the unmistakable sweet-rot stench of death.

Kestrel moved through her sanctum with predatory grace, her gaunt frame silhouetted against the unnatural glow emanating from the voodoo circle etched into her dirt floor. The runes pulsed like a heartbeat, each throb sending fresh waves of power rippling through the cramped space. Her matted black hair, streaked with premature gray, hung wild around her face, framing eyes that gleamed with manic intensity.

"Almost time now," she murmured, her Louisiana drawl stretching the words into something musical yet menacing. "Almost time for ol' Papa to meet his match."

She knelt beside a rough wooden table crowded with the tools of her dark craft—clay bowls filled with mixtures best left undisturbed, bundles of herbs tied with strips of leather, feathers and bones arranged in patterns that hurt the eye to follow. Jars of murky liquid lined one side, their contents moving occasionally of their own accord.

With reverent hands, she opened a small carved box, revealing a collection of teeth—human, animal, and things less easily identified. Each one represented a conquered enemy, a binding curse, a soul bound to her will. She selected three: a canine incisor yellowed with age, a molar with a gold filling that caught the green light, and something that resembled a fang but curved in ways nature never intended.

"Y'all gonna help me cross over," she crooned to the teeth, dropping them one by one into a clay bowl filled with rum. "You gonna make sure Papa Legba can't keep me out. No sir, not this time."

Rising, Kestrel surveyed her domain with critical eyes. Animal carcasses—raccoons, possums, and less recognizable creatures—had been strategically placed around the circle, their blood long since drained to feed her workings. Black candles burned at precise intervals, their flames unnaturally still in the heavy air. Tobacco leaves and dried herbs formed complex patterns between the runes, ready to be ignited when the moment came.

"Need somethin' more," she muttered, stalking to a shadowed corner where a battered trunk sat beneath a shelf lined with cloudy jars. "Somethin' special for this journey."

She threw open the trunk, revealing layers of fabric, small boxes, and folded papers—relics and keepsakes accumulated through decades of dark practice. With unerring precision, she reached to the very bottom and withdrew a small bundle wrapped in faded red silk.

"There you are, darlin'," she whispered, unwrapping the silk to reveal a small, desiccated object that might once have been a human hand. The blackened digits had been curled into a specific gesture, locked in that position by death and dark arts. "My lucky hand. Took it off a necromancer who thought he could outsmart me, back in '97. Not too bright, that one."

Kestrel carried the mummified hand to her circle, placing it carefully at the northernmost point. "You know the way across," she told it, as if the severed appendage could hear. "You gonna help guide my soul to the Tower, just like you helped your previous owner cross over—'fore I sent him on permanent-like."

Standing, she reached for her staff—the gnarled cypress crowned with a crow's skull, its surface adorned with feathers, beads, and small bones dangling from leather cords. Power thrummed through the wood as her fingers closed around it, a connection to forces that had never been meant for human manipulation.

"One last thing," she said, moving to a cage tucked under a sagging shelf.

Inside, a small creature huddled in the corner—not animal, not insect, but something that seemed to be a horrifying amalgamation of both. Its many legs trembled as Kestrel approached, its too-aware eyes reflecting the green glow of the circle.

"Don't you worry none," she cooed, reaching into the cage and grasping the creature despite its frantic attempts to escape. "Your sacrifice is an honor. You gonna help me slip right past ol' Papa Legba like he ain't even there."

With practiced efficiency, she carried the struggling creature to the center of the circle. Holding it over the rum-filled bowl with the three teeth, she drew her iron dagger across its throat in one fluid motion. Dark ichor, thicker than blood should be, dripped into the bowl, sizzling when it made contact with the rum.

"Perfect," Kestrel breathed, her eyes widening as the mixture in the bowl began to glow with the same sickly green light as the runes in her circle. She discarded the creature's twitching body carelessly to the side, her focus entirely on the energies now building in her sanctum.

Moving methodically around the perimeter of the circle, she lit the tobacco and herbs with a candle, adding her voice to the rising power. The chant began low, a guttural growl that seemed to come from deeper than her throat, the words of a language that had never been meant for human tongues.

"Legba, m'ap vin sou gwo wout la," she called, her Louisiana accent giving the Creole words a unique, disturbing cadence. "M'ap vini, m'ap pran sa ki pou mwen. Pa gen anyen w ka fè pou kanpe m."

The flames consuming the herbs flared higher, changing from orange to green as they fed on the offerings. The runes pulsed faster, like the heartbeat of some vast, unseen creature growing more frenzied with each passing moment.

Kestrel placed her staff in the center of the circle, then knelt beside the bowl containing the rum, teeth, and dark ichor. With her iron dagger, she pricked her palm, allowing several drops of her own blood to fall into the mixture.

"Blood calls to blood," she intoned. "Spirit calls to spirit. Open the way between worlds. Let what's bound be unbound. Let what's tethered be free."

Taking a deep breath, she dipped her fingers into the mixture and drew a symbol on her forehead—a crude crossroads that pulsed with the same green light as the circle. Then she drank the remaining contents of the bowl, teeth and all, her throat working as the unholy mixture burned its way down to her core.

Immediately, her body began to convulse, her back arching at an impossible angle as the magic took hold. Her eyes rolled back, showing only whites that soon began to glow with the same sickly green light. A shadow seemed to pull away from her physical form—a silhouette that maintained her shape but was composed of darkness deeper than the night surrounding the shack.

"Free," the shadow-Kestrel hissed, her voice now layered with echoes and undertones that had never emerged from a human throat. "Free to walk the paths between."

Her physical body collapsed in the center of the circle, still breathing but utterly still, eyes staring sightlessly at the ceiling. The shadow-self stretched, testing its new form, reveling in the sensation of being untethered from flesh and bone.

"Now for you, Papa Legba," the shadow whispered. "Let's see how well you guard them gates when I come knockin'."

The shadow rippled, then dissipated like smoke in a strong wind, leaving only the empty shack, the glowing circle, and Kestrel's abandoned body waiting for her spirit's return.

Miles away, in the impossible library hidden within Sam Sorken's house, the assembled witches of the Andromeda coven had settled into an uneasy silence. Sam stood at the center of a ritual circle he and Talien had prepared, explaining the gravity of their situation, the threat posed by Kestrel Drach, and the nature of the Tower of Souls.

Many faces showed skepticism or outright disbelief. Others, particularly among the older witches, displayed growing concern as pieces of ancient coven lore suddenly aligned with Sam's incredible revelations.

"How do we know this isn't an elaborate hoax?" one woman asked, her voice cutting through the murmurs of the crowd. "You're asking us to believe in other worlds, in necromancers, in a realm of the dead that can be physically breached?"

Sam gestured around at the impossible library they all sat within. "I understand your skepticism. But consider where you're standing right now—a space that cannot exist according to the physical laws you understand, yet undeniably does exist."

Arthur Denim, still clutching Carol's hand like a lifeline, muttered something about "dimensional variances not covered by current zoning laws," earning himself an elbow to the ribs and a hushed "not now" from Carol.

"The hat," Mary Ann Tanner said suddenly, her voice steadier than it had been since Molly's death. "The hat has always been our connection to those who came before. When we commune with it, we speak with our ancestors." She looked at Sam, eyes narrowing slightly. "Are you suggesting those spirits are physically located somewhere? In this Tower of Souls?"

"Yes," Sam confirmed. "The hat acts as a conduit, allowing communication across the barrier between realms. It's why your grandmother Nancy protected it so fiercely, why it's been passed down through generations. It's not just a repository of knowledge—it's a bridge."

Talien stepped forward, his usual exuberance tempered by the gravity of the situation. "And right now, Kestrel Drach is attempting to cross into the Realm of the Dead physically, to reach the Tower and consume those spirits—not just commune with them, but absorb their essence entirely."

"Including Molly," Bree added quietly, her words landing like stones in still water. "And Grandma Nancy. And every witch who has ever been part of our coven."

A grim, heavy silence fell over the increasingly anxious gathering as the full catastrophic implications of Sam's warning sank in deeply. Even the most traditionally skeptical faces now showed undisguised concern and dawning horror. The protective spirits of Margaret and Ezekiel hovered nearby, their translucent, shimmering forms seeming more agitated than usual, flickering erratically at the edges like disturbed candleflames.

"We've contacted Papa Legba," Sam continued, gesturing to the ritual circle where various items had been arranged—rum, tobacco, coins, and a wooden walking stick placed at the center. "He guards the crossroads between worlds. If Kestrel attempts to enter his realm, he'll signal us through this connection."

"And then what?" asked Elaine Warren, ever practical. "What can we possibly do against someone who's found a way to cross between worlds?"

"We follow her," Talien replied simply. "Using the hat as our anchor and guide."

This announcement sent another wave of murmurs through the crowd. Bree stepped forward to stand beside Sam and Talien, her posture resolute despite the fear visible in her eyes.

"I'll be going with them," she said, her voice carrying clearly throughout the library. "It's my sister at risk. My family's hat. Our coven's legacy."

Mary Ann half-rose from her seat, protest evident on her face, but Susan Fond placed a gentle hand on her arm, murmuring something that made her reluctantly sit back down.

"We don't expect any of you to join us," Sam assured the gathered witches. "But we do need your help to stabilize the connection from this side. Your combined power, channeled through the rituals of your coven, could make the difference between success and—"

He broke off abruptly as movement caught everyone's attention. The wooden walking stick, which had been lying flat in the center of the ritual circle, suddenly rose on one end as if lifted by an invisible hand. It stood perfectly vertical for three heartbeats, then clattered back to the floor with a sound that echoed ominously through the vast library.

Sam's eyes met Talien's, a moment of silent communication passing between them. "That's our sign!" Sam announced, urgency sharpening his voice. "Kestrel has entered the Realm of the Dead. Papa Legba is calling for our assistance."

At the crossroads where five paths converged, Papa Legba stood sentinel. His ageless eyes surveyed each road with ancient vigilance—the swamp path with its clinging mists, the desert route shimmering with heat, the snow-covered forest trail, the bustling city street from a bygone era, and the fifth path leading into impenetrable darkness.

He leaned on his walking stick, pipe clenched between his teeth, weathered face set in lines of concentration. The air around him vibrated with tension, the crossroads itself seeming to hold its breath in anticipation.

"I feel you creepin', woman," he murmured, smoke curling from his lips. "Think you can slip past ol' Papa without payin' your respects? Without proper offerings and permissions?" He tapped his walking stick against the ground, sending ripples of power outward along all five paths. "We'll see about that."

From the swamp path came a disturbance—not a physical presence but a shadow slipping between the cypress knees, moving with purpose toward the crossroads. Green light pulsed within the darkness, a heartbeat of malevolent power that made even Legba's ancient eyes narrow with concern.

"Comin' in hot, ain't you?" he remarked, turning to face the approaching shadow. "And bringin' all kinds of nasty with you too. Voudou mixed with somethin' older, somethin' not from this world."

The shadow paused at the edge of the crossroads, seeming to assess the guardian who stood between it and its destination. Then it began to change shape, the darkness condensing and taking on more defined features until Kestrel Drach stood there—or rather, the spirit-form of Kestrel Drach, her body still lying inert in her Louisiana shack.

"Papa Legba," she drawled, her voice carrying echoes of the bayou even in this between-place. "Keeper of the Gates, Master of the Crossroads. I've come to pay my respects."

Legba regarded her with eyes that had witnessed the passing of countless souls, that had seen every form of deception since the dawn of death itself. "Have you now?" he replied, his own Louisiana cadence carrying undertones of something far older. "Funny way of showin' respect, sneakin' up the swamp road without proper invitation."

Kestrel's spirit-form smiled, the expression made grotesque by the green light that pulsed beneath her translucent skin. "I brought offerings," she said, gesturing with one hand. At her feet appeared spectral versions of the items she had sacrificed—rum, tobacco, even the strange creature whose life had fed her crossing.

"These ain't proper offerings," Legba said, contempt evident in his voice. "These are bribes, woman. Tainted with your intentions, corrupted by your methods." He took a step forward, suddenly seeming taller, more imposing than his elderly appearance would suggest. "You think I don't know what you're after? The Tower of Souls ain't for the likes of you."

Kestrel's smile didn't falter, though her eyes narrowed dangerously. "Now, now, Papa. Don't be like that. I'm just a humble practitioner seeking knowledge." Her form flickered, darkness bleeding through her human shape like ink through paper. "Besides, you know the rules. Everyone gets to cross eventually."

"Cross, yes," Legba agreed, tapping his walking stick against the ground again. "In their proper time, in their proper way. Not like this—not as a spirit with a living body waitin' back home. Not with intentions of disturbin' the natural order."

He touched his walking stick to the ground one final time, more firmly than before. In the world of the living, in Sam's impossible library, the corresponding stick rose and fell—a signal, a warning, a call for assistance.

"I've called for help," Legba informed her, satisfaction evident in his ancient eyes. "Friends who understand exactly what kind of threat you pose."

Kestrel threw back her head and laughed, the sound rippling across the crossroads like oil on water. "You think I came unprepared? You think I didn't account for interference?" Her form began to change again, the human shape dissolving into pure shadow once more. "I don't need your permission, Papa. I found another way in."

Before Legba could respond, the shadow that was Kestrel shot upward, expanding into a vast, writhing darkness that spread across the twilight sky of the crossroads. For a moment it hung there, a malevolent cloud pulsing with green energy. Then it plunged downward—not toward any of the five paths, but directly into the ground at the very center of the crossroads, bypassing the established routes entirely.

"NO!" Legba roared, lunging forward with speed that belied his apparent age. His walking stick struck the spot where Kestrel had disappeared, sending a shockwave of power rippling through the Realm of the Dead. But it was too late—she had found a sixth path, one that shouldn't have existed, one that led beneath the crossroads rather than through them.

Legba straightened, his weathered face grim with determination. "So that's how it's gonna be," he muttered. "Breakin' the rules, makin' your own paths." He looked up at the twilight sky, eyes focusing on something beyond ordinary perception. "Better hurry, Sammy. The woman's found a back door, and she's headed straight for the Tower."

Chapter 36
Through the Veil

The wooden walking stick lay motionless once more on the floor of the ritual circle, but its message had been delivered. The library fell silent, every pair of eyes fixed on Sam as he straightened, his face grim with determination.

"It's time," he announced, his voice carrying to every corner of the vast space. "Kestrel Drach has entered the Realm of the Dead, and Papa Legba has called for our assistance."

Murmurs rippled through the assembled witches, a mixture of fear, excitement, and disbelief. Sam raised his hands, calling for silence.

"We need your help now," he continued, directing his words to the entire coven. "Those of us sending our spirits across the veil will need your collective energy—a tether to our physical bodies and a shield against Kestrel's power."

Talien stepped forward, his usual playfulness replaced by focused intensity. "This isn't a theoretical exercise anymore. The boundary between realms has been breached by someone who means to consume the souls of your ancestors, to drain the Tower of Souls and return with power that would upset the balance of both worlds."

Mary Ann Tanner rose from her seat, her gaze steady despite the grief still etched in her features. "Tell us what to do," she said simply. "The Andromeda coven stands with you."

Around her, the other witches nodded in agreement, even those who had expressed skepticism earlier. The enormity of the threat had united them, decades of coven loyalty overcoming their initial doubts.

"Form a circle around us," Sam instructed, gesturing to the ritual space. "Focus your energy on strengthening the connection between realms. Think of it as creating a bridge—one that will allow our spirits to cross over safely and return to our bodies once we've confronted Kestrel."

"And create a protective shield," Talien added. "Visualize it surrounding our spiritual forms, a barrier that Kestrel cannot penetrate, that will defend against her dark magic."

Sam turned to Bree, who stood beside the table where the Tanner Hat rested. "Bree, I need you here," he said, indicating a point in the circle opposite from where he stood. "Your connection to the hat, to your sister's spirit, will help guide us to where we need to go."

Bree nodded, moving to take her position. The hat remained on the table, glowing faintly with its own inner light, a beacon that connected them to generations of witches whose spirits now resided in the Tower.

"The hat stays here," Sam explained, noting a few questioning glances. "It's too dangerous to bring it across, even in spiritual form. If Kestrel were to get her hands on it in the Realm of the Dead, her power would increase exponentially."

"Besides," Talien added, "it serves as an anchor, a fixed point connecting both realms."

The witches began to arrange themselves in concentric circles around the ritual space, guided by Morden and the other goblins. Some held hands, others closed their eyes in concentration, all focusing their energy on the task Sam had described.

As Talien took his position, completing the triangle with Sam and Bree, a movement from the outer ring caught everyone's attention. Nissa Drach rose from her seat and stepped forward, her face set with determination as she approached the ritual circle.

"What are you doing?" Sam asked, surprise evident in his voice. "We don't have time for—"

"I'm coming with you," Nissa interrupted, her voice steady despite the tension visible in her shoulders. "It's my mother who caused all of this. I should be part of stopping her."

Sam exchanged a concerned glance with Talien. "Nissa, this isn't about redemption or atonement. The Realm of the Dead is dangerous even for trained necromancers. For someone without your mother's voodoo training or our experience—"

"I know her," Nissa insisted. "I know how she thinks, how she fights. I've spent my entire life studying her methods, even when I hated every minute of it." She pulled back her sleeve, revealing the scars that testified to years of abuse. "No one has more reason to want her stopped than I do."

"She has a point," Talien said quietly to Sam. "And we could use an extra pair of hands. Someone who knows Kestrel's weaknesses."

"Or someone who could be a liability," Sam countered, though his resolve was clearly wavering. "If something happens to your spirit form—"

"Then it happens," Nissa said firmly. "I've made my choice. Please, let me help fix what my family has broken."

The seconds ticked by, precious time slipping away while Sam weighed the risks. Finally, he nodded. "Take position here," he said, indicating a spot that would turn their triangle into a square. "Follow our lead, do exactly as we say, and if I tell you to return, you return immediately. Understood?"

"Understood," Nissa agreed, moving quickly to the position Sam had indicated.

"We need to hurry," Talien urged, glancing at the walking stick that had delivered Papa Legba's signal. "Kestrel has already crossed over. Every moment gives her more time to reach the Tower."

Sam nodded, raising his hands to begin the ritual. Around them, the witches of the Andromeda coven had formed their circles, their collective energy already building like an electric charge in the air.

"Remember," Sam called out to them, "focus on protection and connection. Visualize a shield surrounding our spirit forms, a bridge guiding us safely across the void. And maintain your vigil around our physical bodies—they'll be vulnerable while our spirits journey to the Realm of the Dead."

With that final instruction, he began to chant, his voice dropping to a resonant bass that seemed to vibrate in the very stones beneath their feet. Talien joined in, their voices weaving together in perfect harmony, the words of a language none present had heard before—the necromantic tongue of Eldoria, preserved through centuries of exile.

Bree and Nissa remained silent as instructed, their eyes closed in concentration, feeling the power building around them as the chant continued. The air within the circle grew thick, charged with energy that made the hair on their arms stand on end.

Around them, the witches began their own incantation, a melodic counterpoint to the necromancers' deeper tones. The ancient words of the Andromeda coven—a blend of Earth magic and Eldorian traditions—rose and fell in a hypnotic rhythm. As they chanted, a faint shimmer became visible around the inner circle, a protective barrier taking form as dozens of witches poured their combined power into its creation.

Arthur Denim, who had been watching the proceedings with wide-eyed astonishment, found himself standing without conscious decision. Beside him, Carol continued her part of the incantation, her copper-red hair seeming to glow with an inner light as she channeled her power into the collective working.

"Remarkable," Arthur whispered, his bureaucratic mind struggling to categorize what he was witnessing. This wasn't just a violation of building codes or zoning regulations—this was a fundamental rewriting of reality itself, accomplished through the focused will of dozens of practitioners. Despite his complete lack of magical ability, even he could feel the power building in the library, a pressure against his skin like the air before a thunderstorm.

In the center of the circle, the ritual reached its climax. The walking stick began to glow with the same light that had illuminated it when Papa Legba's signal came through. The glow spread outward, enveloping Sam, Talien, Bree, and Nissa in a column of soft, golden radiance.

For a moment, nothing seemed to happen. Then, almost imperceptibly, a change came over the four figures in the circle. Though their bodies remained standing, eyes closed in deep trance, there was a subtle shift—as if something essential had departed, leaving behind only the physical shell. Their breathing slowed to barely perceptible, their faces relaxed into perfect stillness.

"They've crossed over," Susan Fond whispered, recognition in her eyes. "Their spirits have left their bodies behind."

Mary Ann nodded, her voice steady despite her concern. "Now we protect them until they return."

The witches continued their chant, maintaining the protective shield and the connection that would allow their friends' spirits to return. In the center of the circle, the Tanner Hat glowed brighter, its connection to the spirits in the Tower of Souls strengthened by the thinning of the veil between worlds.

The transition between realms was different this time—more abrupt, more disorienting. Bree felt as if she'd been turned inside out and back again in an instant, her senses momentarily overwhelmed by the sudden shift in reality.

When her vision cleared, she found herself once more at the crossroads where five paths converged beneath a twilight sky that was neither day nor night. Sam, Talien, and Nissa stood beside her, all of them looking slightly shaken by the journey.

Bree glanced down at herself, startled to see that while she appeared solid, there was a subtle translucence to her form—light seemed to pass partially through her, giving her a ghostly quality. The others appeared the same way, spiritual versions of their physical selves.

Nissa seemed to be having the hardest time adjusting, her spectral face pale as she struggled to maintain her equilibrium. "Is it... always like that?" she gasped, one translucent hand pressed to her temple.

"First crossing's always the roughest," came a familiar drawling voice. "Takes a minute for your spirit to remember it ain't attached to flesh no more."

Papa Legba approached from the center of the crossroads, his elderly appearance belied by the fluid grace of his movements. He leaned on his walking stick—the twin of the one they'd left behind in the ritual circle—his weathered face set in lines of grim determination.

"Welcome back, Sammy," he said, nodding to Sam. "Brought your whole crew this time, I see. Just the spirits, smart move. Safer to leave the meat behind when visitin' my domain."

"We came as quickly as we could," Sam replied. "Where is she? Has Kestrel reached the Tower yet?"

Legba shook his head, his expression darkening. "Not yet, but she's on her way. Found herself a path I didn't even know existed—somethin' beneath the crossroads, a tunnel of sorts that bypasses my jurisdiction entirely."

"How is that possible?" Talien asked, his usual confident demeanor slipping slightly. "The crossroads is the nexus of all paths in the Realm of the Dead. Nothing should be able to circumvent it."

"Shouldn't be possible," Legba agreed, his Louisiana accent thickening with anger. "But that woman's been mixin' her voodoo with somethin' older, somethin' from another world." His ancient eyes fixed on Sam. "Somethin' that reminds me of your kind of magic, Sammy. But twisted, corrupted."

Sam and Talien exchanged troubled glances. "Necromancy," Sam said quietly. "But not as we practice it. This sounds like the dark arts Malakai was developing before Eldoria fell—a perversion of our traditions."

"You said her father was educating her," Bree reminded them. "Teaching her his methods."

"And now she's applying those methods here," Talien concluded grimly. "Using a combination of voodoo and corrupted Eldorian necromancy to breach the Realm of the Dead in ways that shouldn't be possible."

Nissa had recovered somewhat from the disorientation of crossing over. "That sounds like my mother," she said, her voice bitter. "She's always searching for ways to blend different magical traditions, to find the cracks between established systems."

Legba regarded her with sudden interest, his ancient eyes narrowing. "And who might you be, child? You got the same blood as the troublemaker, I can smell it on you. But different choices, different path."

"I'm Nissa Drach," she replied, meeting his gaze steadily. "Kestrel's daughter. I'm here to help stop her."

Legba studied her for a long moment, seeming to peer beyond her spiritual appearance to something deeper. Finally, he nodded. "Good. Family can sometimes reach places others can't. Might be useful before this is done."

He turned, gesturing for them to follow as he began walking toward the fifth path—the one that led into absolute darkness. "Come on. If we're gonna catch her before she reaches the Tower, we need to move quick."

"This way leads to the Tower?" Bree asked, eyeing the impenetrable blackness with understandable apprehension.

"Not directly," Legba replied over his shoulder. "But it'll intersect with her path eventually. I can feel her movin' through my realm, leavin' a trail of corruption wherever she goes. Like oil on water, visible to those who know how to look."

As they approached the dark path, Legba paused, turning to face them once more. "Word of warnin' before we go deeper," he said, his expression grave. "The deeper we get into the Realm of the Dead, the stranger things become. Time, space, identity—all get a little fluid. Stay close, focus on why you came, and whatever you do, don't get distracted by what you might see or hear."

"What might we see?" Nissa asked, a tremor of uncertainty in her voice.

Legba's ancient eyes softened slightly. "Spirits of the dead, child. Some recently departed, some ancient beyond reckonin'. Some might look familiar to you—loved ones, ancestors, figures from your past. They can't harm your spirit form, but they can distract, confuse, delay. And in this chase, delay is the last thing we can afford."

Without waiting for further questions, he turned and stepped into the darkness of the fifth path. The blackness seemed to part around him like a curtain, revealing a narrow trail that glimmered faintly with an inner light.

Sam followed immediately, his spectral form passing easily into the darkness, then Talien. Bree hesitated just a moment, then stepped forward as well, feeling the strange cool embrace of the darkness as it closed around her translucent spirit. Nissa came last, her breathing quick but controlled as she fought back her fear of the unknown.

The path grew clearer as they progressed, illuminated by a soft phosphorescence that seemed to emanate from the ground itself. The landscape around them gradually took shape—not the swamp or desert or snow-covered forest of the other paths, but a shifting, nebulous environment that never quite settled into any recognizable form.

Mist swirled around their spiritual feet, occasionally taking shapes that hinted at faces or figures before dissolving again. Whispers surrounded them, too faint to make out individual words but carrying emotional tones that ranged from confused to desperate to peaceful.

"The newly dead," Legba explained quietly, noticing their reactions to the whispers. "Not yet settled, not yet ready to move deeper into the realm. They cluster near the crossroads, uncertain, afraid."

"Do they know they're dead?" Bree asked, her thoughts turning inevitably to Molly.

"Some do, some don't," Legba replied. "Some accept it quick, others take longer. Everyone finds their way eventually."

They walked in silence for what might have been minutes or hours—time, as Legba had warned, seemed to function differently here. The path descended gradually, the mist growing thicker around them, the whispers fading as they moved deeper into the realm.

Suddenly, Legba stopped, raising his walking stick as a signal for the others to halt as well. "Feel that?" he asked quietly.

Sam nodded, his expression troubled. "A disturbance. Like a wound in the fabric of this place."

"That's her," Legba confirmed grimly. "Tearin' through barriers that ought not be torn, leavin' damage in her wake." He gestured with his stick toward something ahead that the others couldn't yet see. "The

Tower of Souls lies that way, beyond the Valley of Reflection. If we cut across this way, we might intercept her before she reaches it."

He turned off the main path, leading them through the shifting mist toward what appeared to be a ridge overlooking a vast depression in the landscape. As they crested the ridge, a breathtaking vista opened before them.

The Valley of Reflection stretched for what seemed like miles, its floor covered in countless pools of still water that mirrored the twilight sky above. Between the pools, narrow paths wound like silver ribbons, connecting larger islands where spirits gathered in quiet communion.

But what drew their attention immediately was a streak of sickly green light cutting across the valley floor—a wound in the landscape that pulsed with malevolent energy. It moved steadily toward the far side of the valley, where a structure loomed against the horizon—a tower that seemed to be built of light rather than any physical material, stretching upward beyond what the eye could comprehend.

"The Tower of Souls," Sam breathed, a note of awe in his voice despite the dire circumstances.

"And that," Legba said, pointing to the moving streak of green, "is our quarry. Makin' a beeline for it, tearin' up my realm as she goes."

"Mother," Nissa whispered, her spectral face pale in the ethereal light.

Legba turned to face them, his ancient eyes reflecting the distant glow of the Tower. "This is where it gets tricky," he warned. "The Valley of Reflection ain't just a pretty view. Those pools show more than just your face—they reflect memories, desires, fears. Step in one by accident, you might find your spirit lost in your own past, unable to distinguish reality from reflection."

"How do we cross safely?" Talien asked, studying the intricate network of paths between the pools.

"Stay on the paths, keep your mind focused on why you're here, and don't—under any circumstances—touch the water," Legba instructed. "Ready yourselves. Once we start down this slope, we're committed."

They nodded their understanding, faces set with determination. The Tower of Souls gleamed in the distance, a beacon of accumulated knowledge and power that had stood since the beginning of death itself. And racing toward it was Kestrel Drach, her corrupted spirit form cutting a path of destruction through the sacred realm.

"Let's go," Sam said, taking the first step down the ridge toward the Valley of Reflection. "We have a Tower to defend."

Back in the library, the physical bodies of Sam, Talien, Bree, and Nissa remained standing in the ritual circle, motionless except for the slow rhythm of their breathing. Their eyes were closed, faces expressionless—empty vessels awaiting the return of their spirits.

Around them, the witches of the Andromeda coven maintained their protective circle, their chanting now quieter but no less focused. Some had taken seats on the floor to conserve their energy, knowing that maintaining the connection between realms might require hours of sustained concentration.

Mary Ann Tanner hadn't taken her eyes off her daughter's still form since the ritual began. Beside her, Susan Fond kept a steadying hand on her shoulder, providing silent support.

"They'll return," Susan whispered. "Bree is strong—stronger than any of us realized."

Mary Ann nodded, though worry still creased her brow. "I know. But she's facing something we can't even imagine."

In the center of the circle, the Tanner Hat continued to glow on its small table, a beacon connecting the physical world to the realm where the four spirits now journeyed. Its power remained untapped for the moment, waiting to be worn by the next High Priestess.

The descent was steeper than it had appeared from above, the terrain shifting subtly beneath their spectral feet as if reluctant to be pinned down to any fixed form. Legba led the way, his walking stick tapping out a rhythm against the ground that seemed to stabilize the path before them. Sam followed close behind, with Bree, Nissa, and Talien in a tight formation behind him.

As they neared the bottom of the ridge, the first of the reflection pools came into view. Up close, they were even more unsettling—perfectly still water that didn't ripple even in the ethereal breeze that occasionally stirred through the valley. Each pool was ringed with a pearlescent edge that seemed to pulse with inner light, marking the boundary between safe ground and dangerous waters.

"Mind your step now," Legba cautioned, his Louisiana drawl carrying easily in the strange acoustics of the valley. "Path gets mighty narrow 'tween some of these pools. One misstep, and your spirit gets trapped in memories it might never escape from."

The warning wasn't exaggerated. As they reached the valley floor, the path between pools sometimes narrowed to barely the width of a foot, forcing them to proceed in single file, placing each step with deliberate care. The reflections in the pools seemed to shift and change as they passed, glimpses of scenes and faces that tugged at the edge of awareness, trying to draw attention and focus away from the path.

"Don't look directly at 'em," Legba advised, noticing Bree's curious glances toward a pool they were passing. "Just a quick glimpse is all it takes for some folks to get pulled in."

They continued their careful progress, winding between pools of various sizes. The path twisted unexpectedly, sometimes doubling back on itself before continuing in the desired direction. Legba navigated with unerring certainty, never hesitating at forks or junctions.

"How much farther?" Bree asked after what felt like an eternity of careful steps and held breath.

"Halfway there," Legba replied. "Tower's closer now, but we gotta circle 'round a bit more to stay on solid ground. No direct path through here—that's by design."

A sudden flash of green light illuminated the valley, causing them all to duck instinctively. The sickly emerald glow came from behind a ridge of higher ground to their left—Kestrel's progress through the realm, marked by these periodic bursts of corrupted power.

"She's gettin' closer to the Tower," Legba muttered, his pace quickening. "Gotta hurry now, but stay careful. Rushin' in this place is how mistakes get made."

The path narrowed again as they rounded a sharp bend, with pools pressing close on either side. Talien had moved to the back of their line, with Nissa just ahead of him. The girl's spectral form seemed to shimmer with anxiety as the path constricted, her eyes fixed firmly on Bree's back as if afraid to look anywhere else.

"You're doing fine," Talien assured her quietly. "Just keep moving."

Nissa nodded, placing one foot carefully in front of the other. But as she took her next step, the edge of the path crumbled slightly beneath her spiritual foot. She let out a startled cry, arms windmilling as she fought to regain her balance. For a heartbeat, it seemed she would recover—then her foot slipped sideways, breaking the surface of the nearest pool with a silent ripple.

The effect was immediate. Nissa's eyes went wide, her spiritual form freezing in place as if suddenly paralyzed. Her gaze fixed on something visible only to her within the depths of the pool, her mouth opening in a silent 'oh' of recognition or terror.

"Nissa!" Talien lunged forward, grabbing her arm just above the elbow with one hand while bracing himself against solid ground with the other. With a powerful tug, he pulled her away from the pool's edge, dragging her spectral form back onto the path.

Nissa stumbled forward, collapsing into Talien's arms, her eyes unfocused and distant. "I saw..." she whispered, her voice faint and confused. "I was back home, before mother... before everything went wrong. Father was still alive, smiling at me. He was reaching out..."

"It ain't real, child," Legba said sharply, having turned back at the commotion. "Just reflections of what might've been, what you wish had been. Pool's showin' you shadows to keep your spirit trapped." He tapped his walking stick impatiently against the ground. "Shake it off now. We can't linger."

Talien helped Nissa to her feet, his hand remaining supportively under her elbow as her eyes gradually refocused on their surroundings. "I'm okay," she said after a moment, though her voice still trembled slightly. "It just... it felt so real."

"That's their power," Sam explained, his face grim with understanding. "The pools reflect what's deepest in your spirit—memories, regrets, desires. The longer you look, the more real they seem, until you can't tell reflection from reality anymore."

"And then you're stuck," Legba added bluntly. "Spirit trapped in a loop of its own makin', forgettin' all about the real world outside." He gestured impatiently for them to continue. "Why you think I warned y'all so clear? This ain't no place for sight-seein'."

They resumed their careful progress, now even more cautious than before. Nissa stayed close to Talien, her brief exposure to the pool's power having clearly shaken her. Bree cast occasional concerned glances back at them but kept moving forward, aware that time was their enemy in this strange realm.

Another flash of green light, closer now, spurred them to greater speed. The path began to rise gradually, leading them toward the far side of the valley. The pools became less frequent as they ascended, the ground more solid beneath their feet.

"Almost there," Legba announced, pointing ahead with his walking stick. "Just beyond that rise is the main path to the Tower."

They climbed the final slope with renewed determination, the Valley of Reflection falling away behind them. As they crested the ridge, a wide, straight path opened before them, leading directly to the base of the Tower of Souls.

Seen up close, the Tower was even more awe-inspiring than it had appeared from a distance. It soared impossibly high, its structure composed of what looked like solidified light in countless shades—each hue representing different eras, different traditions, different souls. The base was broad and strong, narrowing as it rose, culminating in a point that seemed to pierce the very fabric of reality above them.

Around the Tower's perimeter, spirits moved in complex patterns, some entering, others departing—the natural cycle of the afterlife continuing despite the threat that approached. These spirits appeared more defined, more settled in their identity than the confused whispers they had encountered near the crossroads. These were souls who had accepted their state, who had integrated into the community of the dead.

"There it is," Sam said quietly, a note of reverence in his voice despite the urgency of their situation. "The repository of all who have passed—every witch, every practitioner, every soul that has ever lived."

"And the source of power my mother wants to consume," Nissa added, her face hardening with resolve after her moment of weakness in the valley.

Legba moved to the center of the path, his walking stick planted firmly before him. "Now we wait," he said, his ancient eyes scanning the direction from which they had come. "She's comin' this way, tearin' through my realm like she owns it. When she reaches this point..."

"We'll be ready," Bree finished, taking position beside him.

From behind them came another flash of green light, far closer than before—illuminating the valley they had just traversed. A malevolent chuckle seemed to ride the air currents, carrying a Louisiana drawl twisted by cruelty and dark purpose.

"Hurry, hurry, little souls," Kestrel's voice taunted from somewhere just out of sight. "Run to your precious Tower. Won't make no difference in the end."

Legba's grip tightened on his walking stick, his weathered face set in lines of grim determination. "She doesn't know we're here," he said quietly. "Thinks she's just tauntin' random spirits. Let's keep it that way 'til she shows herself."

They arranged themselves across the path—Legba in the center, Sam and Talien to either side, with Bree and Nissa slightly behind them. A formidable barrier between Kestrel Drach and the Tower she sought to violate.

The green glow grew stronger, painting the landscape in sickly emerald light. The path before them darkened as a shadow approached—a corrupted spirit form moving with predatory grace, trailing tendrils of polluted power behind it like a toxic wake.

"Almost there," came Kestrel's self-satisfied drawl, closer now. "Almost time for the feast to begin. All them souls, all that power, all that knowledge—mine for the takin'."

Sam glanced at Legba, silently asking if they should reveal themselves. The ancient guardian shook his head slightly—not yet. Let her come closer, let her confidence build. The element of surprise might be their greatest advantage against such power.

And so, they waited, five spirits standing as the last line of defense before the Tower of Souls, as Kestrel Drach approached, unaware that her path to ultimate power was about to be blocked.

Chapter 37
Souls in Combat

The path before them rippled like disturbed water, the very fabric of the Realm of the Dead warping under unnatural pressure. A sickly green light pulsed from the distortion, casting eerie shadows across the five figures standing as sentinels before the Tower of Souls. The corruption spread outward, blackening the path where it touched, leaving scorch marks like acid burns on sacred ground.

"She's coming," Sam murmured, his spectral form tensing as he prepared for the confrontation.

Papa Legba nodded; his ancient eyes narrowed in concentration. "I feel her tearin' through the barriers. Breakin' rules older than humanity itself."

The distortion bulged upward, then split open like a wound. From within emerged Kestrel Drach, her spirit form rising through the ruptured path as if ascending from some deeper, darker realm. Unlike their translucent spectral bodies, Kestrel's form was a writhing shadow punctuated by flashes of that same sickly green light, as if whatever passed for her soul had been corrupted beyond recognition.

Her surprise at finding them blocking her path was evident—her shadowy form paused, fluctuating momentarily as if uncertain. Then a cruel laugh emerged from the darkness, a sound that seemed to scrape against the very air of the sacred realm.

"Well now," she drawled, her Louisiana accent thick with mockery, "ain't this a pretty little welcoming committee. Papa Legba himself, come to greet little ol' me."

Her gaze shifted, taking in the others. When she spotted Nissa, her form pulsed with what might have been anger or amusement—it was hard to tell through the darkness that consumed her.

"And my ungrateful daughter too. Should've known you'd scurry to hide behind these fools. Always were weak, just like your daddy."

"That's far enough, Kestrel Drach," Legba announced, his voice carrying the weight of eons, his own Louisiana cadence a pure counterpoint to her corrupted drawl. "You ain't welcome in my realm. You ain't been invited, you ain't been permitted, and you sure as hell ain't gonna go any further."

Kestrel's form solidified slightly, taking on a more human appearance—a gaunt woman with wild hair and eyes that glowed with that same unholy green light. She wore tattered robes that seemed to blend with the shadows around her, making it difficult to determine where her form ended and the darkness began.

"Your realm?" she mocked, spreading her arms wide. "Since when do the dead need your permission, Papa? We all come through eventually. I'm just... speedin' up the process a bit."

"You know that ain't how it works," Legba replied, tapping his walking stick against the ground. The impact sent ripples of golden light outward, reinforcing the path beneath them. "The living don't walk here in body or spirit 'less I allow it. And you—" he pointed the stick directly at her, "—you ain't got my blessing."

Kestrel's smile was a terrible thing to behold, too wide, too sharp, like something wearing a human expression without understanding its meaning. "Don't need your blessing, old man. Found my own way in, didn't I? And I'll find my own way to the Tower too."

She took a step forward, and Legba responded immediately. He slammed his walking stick down with enough force that the sound echoed like thunder. A barrier of golden light sprang up between Kestrel and the group, its radiating light spanning the width of the path.

"Turn back now," Legba warned, "while you still can. The Tower ain't for the likes of you."

Kestrel tilted her head, studying the barrier with predatory interest. "Protective as always, Papa. But you forgot somethin' important." Her voice dropped to a whisper that somehow carried to all of them. "I learned a few new tricks since comin' to this world."

With startling speed, she thrust both hands forward. Green lightning erupted from her fingertips, striking Legba's barrier with a sound like shattering glass. The golden light flickered, holding, but visibly weakening where the green energy connected.

"That all you got?" Legba taunted, though Sam noticed beads of sweat appearing on the ancient guardian's brow—a sign of effort that belied his casual tone.

Kestrel laughed again, the sound like broken glass being ground underfoot. "Just gettin' warmed up, sugar."

She redoubled her attack, the green lightning intensifying until it was painful to look at directly. Slowly, cracks appeared in Legba's barrier that were spreading outward like a spiderweb from the point of impact.

"Sam!" Legba called, never taking his eyes off Kestrel. "Lend me your strength, necromancer. She's usin' corrupted death magic—fight fire with fire!"

Sam stepped forward, joining his power to Legba's. A deep purple energy flowed from his spectral hands, intertwining with the guardian's golden light, reinforcing the barrier just as the cracks threatened to shatter it completely.

"You too, ponytail," Legba barked at Talien. "Four against one—let's show this trespasser what happens when you violate the sacred laws of death."

Talien added his power to the defense, his energy a midnight blue that filled in the remaining cracks. Nissa hesitated only a moment before joining them, her contribution a softer lavender light that seemed to seek out specific weaknesses in Kestrel's attack, neutralizing them with surgical precision.

"Betrayin' your own blood, girl?" Kestrel snarled at her daughter, the green lightning faltering slightly as her focus shifted. "After everything I taught you?"

"You taught me pain and fear," Nissa replied, her voice steady despite the tremor in her spectral form. "These people showed me I had a choice."

Kestrel's attack suddenly ceased, the green lightning disappearing as if switched off. The abrupt silence was almost as shocking as the attack had been, leaving them momentarily disoriented. Legba maintained the barrier, but exchanged a concerned glance with Sam.

"She's up to somethin'," the guardian muttered. "That was too easy."

Kestrel's form had retreated several steps, shrinking in on itself until she appeared almost diminutive, harmless. But her eyes still burned with that unnatural light, and her smile had grown, if anything, more terrible.

"You're right to be worried, Papa," she said, her voice dropping to a silky whisper. "Because I brought a friend with me. Someone who's been waitin' a long, long time to settle some old scores."

She raised her hands, but instead of attacking again, she began to weave them in complex patterns, her fingers trailing that same green light through the air. The words she chanted were in no language any of them recognized—not Creole, not English, not even the ancient necromantic tongue of Eldoria. This was something older, something that made the air itself seem to recoil from the sound.

"What's she doing?" Bree asked, her spectral form tensing beside Sam.

"Something terrible," he replied, his face grim with recognition. "She's using a summoning spell—drawing another spirit to her location."

"But who—" Bree began, then fell silent as understanding dawned. "Malakai."

The air behind them—between their group and the Tower—began to distort, a mirror image of the corruption Kestrel had emerged from. But where her entrance had been a violent tear in reality, this distortion formed more slowly, more deliberately, as if whatever was coming through had considerably more power and control.

Papa Legba spun around, his ancient eyes widening in alarm. "No!" he bellowed, swinging his walking stick toward the new threat. "Not in my realm!"

But before he could complete whatever defensive measure he intended, the distortion solidified into a tall, imposing figure. Where Kestrel's spirit form was wild and chaotic, this presence was coldly controlled, radiating power that seemed to bend the very rules of the Realm of the Dead around it.

Malakai Drach stood before them; his spirit form more substantial than should have been possible for a soul in this realm. He appeared as a handsome, aristocratic man in his prime, dressed in what might have been military regalia from another world. His eyes glowed with the same green light as his daughter's, but where hers burned with chaotic malevolence, his shone with calculated cruelty.

"Sameril!" he called out, his voice carrying easily across the distance. "Well, well, well. After all these centuries." His gaze fixed on Sam with hungry recognition. "The destroyer of Eldoria, still running from his failures."

Sam's spectral form went rigid, his face a mask of shock and old pain. "Malakai," he whispered, the name itself seeming to carry the weight of countless deaths, of a world lost to madness and power brought about by the General's military forces.

"The proper address," Malakai corrected smoothly, "is General Drach. Even in death, certain formalities should be observed." His gaze swept over the group, dismissing Legba with barely a glance before settling on Talien. "And Talien Nevos as well. Two of Xaloth's favored students. How convenient."

He turned slightly, acknowledging his daughter with a nod that carried more pride than warmth. "Well done, Kestrel. You've brought me exactly what I asked for."

"Always happy to please you, Daddy," she replied, her wild grin widening further. "Just like you taught me."

"You have no authority here, spirit," Legba declared, stepping forward to confront the new arrival. "This is my domain, my crossroads, my rules."

Malakai turned to the guardian with an expression of polite disinterest. "Rules," he repeated, as if tasting the word and finding it distasteful. "Always so many rules. But rules can be... rewritten." He gestured casually, and a pulse of green energy knocked Legba's walking stick from his hand, sending it clattering across the path. "Especially by those with the power to do so."

Sam took a step forward, placing himself between Malakai and the others. "This ends now, General. You destroyed one world. We won't let you corrupt another."

Malakai's laugh was nothing like his daughter's—where hers was wild and jarring, his was cultured, controlled, and infinitely more chilling for its normalcy. "Corrupt? I prefer to think of it as... evolution. The strong consuming the weak. The natural order of things."

His gaze shifted to Bree, studying her with newfound interest. "And what have we here? A witch, by the feel of her spirit. But not just any witch..." His eyes narrowed with sudden recognition. "Ah, I see it now. The resemblance is quite remarkable. Briella's bloodline, isn't it? How poetic."

Before anyone could react, Bree thrust her hands forward, channeling her power into a defensive spell. "Stay away from my friends," she warned, golden light gathering around her spectral fingers.

"Spirited, just like her ancestor," Malakai observed with cold amusement. Then, faster than seemed possible, he counterattacked. A blast of green energy erupted from his outstretched hand, cutting through Bree's incomplete spell with terrifying ease.

The impact caught her squarely in the chest, lifting her spectral form off the ground and sending her flying backward. She tumbled through the air like a discarded doll, her cry of pain cut short as she disappeared over the ridge they had climbed earlier, rolling down toward the Valley of Reflection.

"Bree!" Sam shouted, taking an instinctive step in her direction.

At that same moment, Kestrel launched her own attack from behind. A crackling bolt of green lightning arced toward the remaining defenders, aimed directly at Papa Legba's unprotected back.

"No!" Nissa cried, lunging forward with her hands raised. Violet energy burst from her palms, intercepting her mother's attack and deflecting it upward, where it dissipated harmlessly into the twilight sky.

Kestrel's eyes widened in shocked fury. "You dare?" she snarled at her daughter. "You dare use my own teachin' against me?"

"I learned from the best," Nissa replied, her voice steadier than her trembling spectral form suggested. "And then I learned better."

Sam stood frozen in indecision, torn between rushing to Bree's aid and facing the more immediate threat of Malakai and Kestrel. His gaze met Talien's, a moment of silent communication passing between the two necromancers.

"Go!" Talien urged. "We'll hold them here."

But before Sam could move, Malakai stepped forward, placing himself directly in Sam's path. "Always running to the rescue, Sameril?" he taunted. "Just as you did on Eldoria. Remind me again how well that worked out for everyone?"

"This isn't about the past," Sam growled, his spectral form pulsing with barely contained power. "This is about stopping you from destroying another world."

"Then stop me," Malakai invited, spreading his arms wide in apparent vulnerability. "If you can."

Papa Legba had retrieved his walking stick, his ancient eyes burning with a fury that made even Kestrel hesitate. "You violate my realm," he thundered, his Louisiana drawl thick with power. "You threaten the Tower of Souls. You attack those under my protection. Three strikes, spirit. And in this game, three strikes means you're out."

He slammed his walking stick against the ground, and the path buckled beneath Malakai's feet. The general stumbled momentarily, his perfect composure slipping for just an instant.

"Now!" Legba shouted to the others. "Hit 'em with everything you got!"

Sam and Talien responded instantly, channeling their necromantic power in a coordinated attack they had perfected centuries ago on Eldoria. Purple and blue energy merged into a pulsing wave that crashed toward Malakai, while Nissa and Legba focused their efforts on Kestrel.

The battle for the Tower of Souls had begun in earnest—four defenders against two corrupted spirits whose power threatened the very fabric of the afterlife itself. And somewhere down the ridge, Bree's spectral form lay motionless, separated from her allies when they needed her most.

In the library, the physical bodies of the travelers remained in their trance state, surrounded by the protective circle of witches. The air hummed with the energy of their chanting, a sacred barrier between worlds maintained by sheer will and collective power.

Suddenly, Bree's body jerked violently, as if struck by an invisible force. Her knees buckled, and though she remained upright, her physical form now knelt within the circle, head bowed as if in submission or pain. Her hands, previously hanging limp at her sides, began to twitch and reach outward—fingers stretching toward the table where the Tanner Hat sat glowing with inner light.

A collective gasp rippled through the witches, though none dared break the protection chant. Mary Ann covered her mouth with one hand, her eyes wide with shock and fear for her daughter, but she too maintained her place in the circle, her voice never faltering in the ritual words.

Sarah Fond, stood beside her mother Susan, their hands linked in the protective formation. With the heightened perception that sometimes came to those with natural talent, she saw what others missed—the intent behind Bree's movements, the desperate reaching of her hands.

"Mom," she whispered urgently between chanted phrases, "Bree's trying to reach the Hat."

Susan's eyes widened in understanding. She squeezed her daughter's hand, then leaned toward Mary Ann. "The Hat," she murmured, nodding toward Bree's grasping fingers. "She needs the Hat."

Mary Ann's gaze darted between her daughter's kneeling form and the glowing Hat just feet away. Understanding blazed in her eyes, but frustration quickly followed—she couldn't break the circle, couldn't interrupt her chanting without potentially endangering everyone's spiritual connection.

"We can't—" she began, the words barely audible between ritual phrases.

A movement from the outer ring caught their attention. Arthur Denim, who had been standing in silent wonder throughout the ritual, suddenly stepped forward. Having no magical ability himself, he wasn't part of the chanting circle, merely an observer to events beyond his understanding.

"Arthur, what are you—" Carol began, but couldn't risk breaking the chant to finish her question.

Without hesitation, Arthur slipped between two witches, careful not to break their joined hands, and stepped into the inner circle. His wire-rimmed glasses reflected the golden glow of the Hat as he approached it, uncertainty written across his face but with determination in his stride.

He reached the table and paused, staring at the Hat with trepidation. This object had been at the center of everything strange in his neighborhood for years—the focus of gatherings he'd observed from a distance, the catalyst for events that defied his carefully cataloged municipal regulations.

Taking a deep breath, Arthur picked up the Hat, feeling a strange vibration pass through his hands as he did so. It was lighter than he expected, almost as if it wanted to be carried.

With careful steps, he moved behind Bree's kneeling form. Her hands were still reaching blindly forward, her eyes closed in that same deep trance. For a moment, Arthur hesitated, unsure if what he was doing was right, if he was helping or interfering.

Then he thought of Carol, of the witches who had welcomed him despite his years of suspicious observation, of the palpable sense of crisis that filled the library. Without further hesitation, he placed the Tanner Hat gently on Bree's head.

The effect was immediate and dramatic. A pulse of golden light radiated outward from the Hat, washing over Bree's kneeling form in waves that seemed to pass through her physical body and beyond—reaching toward some distant point that only she could perceive.

There was no ceremony, no ritual words of transition, no formal passing of power from one generation to the next. But in that moment, as the Hat settled onto Bree's head, something profound shifted in the fabric of reality. The Hat had found its new bearer. What mattered was that Bree Tanner was now the true owner of all the Hat contained—all its power, all its knowledge, and all the spirits of those who had worn it before her.

Including Molly.

The battle raged across the path to the Tower of Souls, the very fabric of the Realm of the Dead shuddering under the onslaught of opposing powers. Green lightning crackled against golden barriers, necromantic energy twisted and writhed in the twilight air, and spirits scattered in all directions, fleeing the confrontation that threatened the natural order of their afterlife.

Papa Legba had faced many challengers in his eternal guardianship of the crossroads—spirits who thought themselves above the rules, mortals who believed they could cheat death, entities from other worlds who sought to impose their will on his domain. But never had he encountered anything like the combined might of Kestrel and Malakai Drach.

"How?" he gasped, his walking stick quivering under the strain of maintaining his defenses. Sweat beaded on his ancient brow, his Louisiana drawl thickened by exertion. "How they got this much power? No spirit should be able to—"

"They've been preparing for this for generations," Sam replied through gritted teeth, his own spectral form flickering as he channeled more energy into their shared barrier. "Malakai was corrupting necromancy before Eldoria fell. And Kestrel has spent her entire life building on his work."

The barrier between them and the Drach's cracked further, a web of fractures spreading outward from the center. Malakai stepped forward, his composed features betraying only the slightest hint of satisfaction as he observed their struggle.

"You always were a quick study, Sameril," he remarked, as casually as if they were discussing academic theories rather than battling for the fate of two realms. "But you never quite grasped the full potential of our art. Always so... constrained by ethics."

Kestrel cackled; her wild eyes gleaming with triumph. "Ethics don't mean nothin' when you're standin' in the land of the dead, sugar. Power's all that matters here. And we got more than enough to take what we want."

With a synchronized gesture, father and daughter intensified their attack. The green lightning from Kestrel's fingers doubled in intensity, while Malakai's more controlled blasts of energy struck the barrier in precisely the places it was weakest. The combination was devastating—methodical destruction guided by chaotic force.

"We can't hold them much longer," Talien warned, his spectral form straining with effort. "If that barrier falls—"

"When that barrier falls," Malakai corrected smoothly, "we will proceed to the Tower, and you will be nothing but scattered fragments of spirit, lost forever in the void between worlds."

Nissa, who had been channeling her power into reinforcing specific parts of the barrier, suddenly faltered. "I can't—" she gasped, her lavender energy flickering. "Mother's too strong."

As if on cue, the barrier shattered with a deafening crack, fragments of golden light dissipating into the twilight air. The defenders staggered backward from the force of the implosion, momentarily stunned.

Kestrel's triumphant laugh echoed across the path. "That's it! The Tower's ours now, Daddy. Just like you always wanted."

Malakai didn't join in her celebration, his calculating gaze already fixed on the path ahead, planning his next move with the precision of a military strategist. "Subdue them properly, Kestrel. No loose ends."

"With pleasure," she drawled, raising her hands for a finishing strike.

Down the ridge, where Malakai's attack had sent her tumbling, Bree's spectral form lay sprawled on the edge of the Valley of Reflection.

She was conscious but dazed, the impact having scattered her thoughts like leaves in a windstorm. Through blurred vision, she could see the battle unfolding above, could sense the moment the defenders' barrier shattered.

And then, something changed.

In the library of the living world, Arthur Denim had just placed the Tanner Hat upon her physical head. The connection between body and spirit, already tenuous in this between-place, suddenly blazed with newfound strength. Power coursed through Bree's spectral form—not just her own magic, but the accumulated knowledge and strength of generations of witches.

Her eyes flew open, blazing with golden light. Her body convulsed once, twice, as if adjusting to an electrical current too powerful for its circuits. Then, with fluid grace that belied her recent injuries, she rose to her feet.

The world around her seemed different now—clearer, more defined, as if she were seeing it through multiple sets of eyes simultaneously. The pools of reflection that had threatened them earlier no longer appeared as mere water but as windows into countless lives and memories. The path beneath her feet hummed with connections to other places, other realms. The Tower in the distance sang with the chorus of a million souls, each one distinct yet part of a greater harmony.

Bree raised her hands, palms upward in a gesture as ancient as witchcraft itself. "I call upon the Tanner line," she intoned, her voice resonating with power beyond her years. "Witches of my blood, guardians of two worlds. Stand with me now."

The air around her shimmered, coalescing into translucent forms that gradually solidified into distinct figures. Women of varying ages materialized in a semicircle behind her—some in colonial dress, others in more modern attire, each bearing the unmistakable stamp of family resemblance. At the center stood Nancy Tanner, her weathered face set with determination, and beside her, Molly, her spirit now fully defined and present in a way it hadn't been within the Hat.

"We stand with you, Bree," Nancy said, her voice carrying the weight of authority passed down through centuries. "As we have always stood with each Keeper of the Tanner Hat."

Molly stepped forward, taking her sister's hand. "Together," she said simply.

Power surged between them; a golden light that spread outward to encompass all the Tanner witches. As one, they began to ascend the ridge, moving with the synchronicity of those who share not just blood but purpose.

Above, on the path to the Tower, Kestrel prepared to unleash her finishing blow. Green energy swirled around her hands, building to a crescendo of destructive force. "Say goodbye, Papa," she taunted Legba. "Your time as guardian is—"

Her words cut off abruptly as she noticed something approaching from the ridge. The green energy faltered as her concentration broke. "What in the..."

Malakai turned, his composed features showing the first genuine surprise since his arrival. "Impossible," he whispered, the word falling from his lips like a stone.

An army of witches crested the ridge, golden light flowing around and between them like a living thing. At their head walked Bree, flanked by Nancy and Molly, her eyes blazing with the combined power of every Tanner witch who had ever lived.

"Stand aside, General Drach," Bree commanded, her voice carrying the authority of generations. "Your war is long over."

Malakai's surprise gave way to cold fury. "You dare address me in that tone, child? Do you have any idea who I am? What I've accomplished?"

"I know exactly who you are," Bree replied, as the Tanner witches began fanning out behind her in a formation that somehow resembled both a battle line and a ritual circle. "You're a relic of a dead world, clinging on to dreams of power that were never yours to claim."

With a snarl, Malakai thrust out both hands, sending a concentrated blast of green energy directly at Bree. But this time, she was ready. With a gesture that seemed both ancient and instinctive, she divided the attack, redirecting its energy harmlessly to either side.

"Now!" she called to the witches behind her.

As one, all of the spirits of the Tanner line began a chant in a language older than any still spoken on Earth. Their voices blended in perfect harmony, rising and falling in a pattern that seemed to resonate with the very fabric of the Realm of the Dead. Golden light flowed from their outstretched hands, weaving together into a complex pattern of energy that surrounded Malakai within its web.

"What is this?" he demanded, his composure finally cracking as the golden web tightened around him. "Release me at once!"

"You don't belong here, General," Bree said steadily, directing the combined power of her ancestors. "You've violated the natural order long enough."

Malakai struggled against the binding, green energy flaring as he fought to break free. But the combined power of dozens of witches, channeled through Bree and the Hat, proved stronger than even his corrupted necromancy.

"This isn't over, Sameril!" he snarled at Sam as the binding pulled him inexorably backward, toward the Tower. "I will find a way back! I always do!"

"No," Sam replied quietly. "You won't."

With a final surge of power, the Tanner witches completed their binding. Malakai's form compressed, constricted, and then shot backward like a stone from a sling, disappearing into the distant Tower—not as a conqueror, but as a prisoner, bound by magic older than his ambitions.

Papa Legba stared in open amazement; his ancient eyes wide with wonder. He turned to Sam, his walking stick briefly forgotten in his shock. "Well, now..." he murmured. "I wasn' expectin' this!"

Sam could only nod in agreement, his own spectral form momentarily paralyzed by the display of power. Talien let out a low whistle of appreciation, while Nissa watched in awe, knowing that her mother would not submit so easily.

Indeed, Kestrel's reaction to her father's binding was immediate and terrible. A howl of rage tore from her throat, the sound distorting the air around her as her form shifted back to that writhing mass of shadow and green light.

"You'll pay for that!" she shrieked, all pretense of control abandoned as raw, destructive power built around her. "I'll tear your spirits apart so thoroughly even the Tower won't recognize what's left!"

She unleashed her attack—not the controlled lightning of before, but a maelstrom of chaotic energy that lashed out in all directions. The very ground beneath them cracked and buckled as her corrupted magic sought to destroy everything in its path.

Bree stepped forward, the Tanner witches moving with her in perfect coordination. They raised their hands in unison, creating a shield of golden light that absorbed the worst of Kestrel's attack. Behind them, Sam, Talien, and Papa Legba added their own power to the defense, while Nissa focused on specifically counteracting her mother's voodoo techniques.

"You can't win, Mother," Nissa called out, her voice steadier than it had ever been when addressing Kestrel. "Not against all of us together."

"Ungrateful child!" Kestrel spat back, her form becoming more unstable as her rage increased. "I gave you everything! Taught you every secret! And this is how you repay me?"

"You taught me pain," Nissa replied calmly. "They taught me purpose."

With methodical precision, the combined forces began to press forward. The shield of their golden light advanced step by step, compressing Kestrel's chaotic energy back toward its source. The voodoo witch fought with increasing desperation, her attacks growing wilder and less focused as the noose of combined magic tightened around her.

"No!" she screamed as they closed in. "I won't go back! I won't be trapped again!"

"You ain't goin' back," Papa Legba said grimly. "You goin' somewhere you can't hurt nobody ever again."

With a precise, measured gesture from his intricately carved ancient walking stick, he opened a small, shimmering rift in reality beside the unsuspecting Kestrel—a revealing glimpse into her physical body, lying pale and vulnerably inert in her secluded Louisiana shack surrounded by protective voodoo talismans. The mystical connection between body and spirit vibrated visibly like a taut, glowing cord, a magical tether that had dangerously stretched but not completely broken during her ambitious journey to the forbidden Realm of the Dead.

"Now!" he commanded.

Sam and Talien moved with practiced coordination, channeling their necromantic power directly at that tether. Their combined energy, honed through centuries of working together, sliced through the connection with surgical precision. Kestrel's scream took on a new dimension of anguish as she felt the severing of her last link to the living world.

"What have you done?" she wailed, her form fluctuating wildly as she lost the anchor that had allowed her to maintain her identity in the Realm of the Dead. "What have you DONE?"

"Set you free," Nissa said quietly. "From everything that bound you—including yourself."

Bree stepped forward alone, the other Tanner witches forming a circle around the increasingly unstable form of Kestrel Drach. "Your journey ends here," she said, her voice carrying the authority of the Hat and all it contained. With a complex gesture that seemed to draw power from the very air around them, she wove a binding spell unlike any Sam had seen before—a combination of Earth witchcraft and techniques that must have originated on Eldoria.

The binding took hold, constricting Kestrel's wildly fluctuating form into a more defined shape. She fought against it, green energy flaring in desperate bursts, but the combined power channeled through Bree proved stronger than even her corrupted magic.

"Where?" Papa Legba asked, nodding toward the Valley of Reflection behind them. "Which pool will hold her?"

Bree turned, her gaze sweeping across the countless reflective surfaces that dotted the valley floor. "That one," she said, pointing to a pool slightly apart from the others, its surface darker and more still than those surrounding it. "It will show her nothing but the truth of what she's done, for as long as the Realm exists."

With a final gesture that seemed to carry the weight of judgment itself, Bree sent Kestrel's bound form flying backward, just as her father had been. But where Malakai had been banished to the Tower, Kestrel plummeted down into the valley, her scream of rage cut short as she plunged into the designated pool.

The surface rippled once, twice... and then went perfectly still, as if nothing had disturbed it. But those with eyes to see could make out a faint green glow deep within its depths—Kestrel Drach, trapped for eternity in a prison of her own reflection.

A profound silence fell over the path. The defenders stood motionless, processing the enormity of what had just occurred. Then, slowly, the spectral forms of the Tanner witches began to approach Bree, each one pausing briefly to acknowledge her before fading back toward the Tower.

Nancy was among the last to approach, her weathered face splitting into a proud smile as she stood before her granddaughter. "You did well, Bree," she said, reaching out to touch her cheek with a translucent hand. "Better than I could have hoped. Wear the Hat wisely."

"I couldn't have done it without all of you," Bree replied, her voice thick with emotion. "Without everything you left behind in the Hat."

"That's how it works, dear," Nancy said with a wink. "Each generation builds on what came before. And now it's your turn to add your own chapter to our story." She glanced over at Molly, who stood slightly apart, watching the exchange with a soft smile. "Both of you, in your own ways."

With a final nod of approval, Nancy's form began to fade. "We'll be waiting in the Tower, when your time eventually comes. But not too soon, I hope." And with that, she was gone, along with the remaining ancestral witches.

Only Molly remained, standing alone before her sister. For a moment, neither spoke, the weight of everything that had passed between them—life, death, and now this strange in-between—hanging in the air like an unasked question.

Then Molly broke into a grin, the same irreverent smile that had lit up her face in life. "So," she said, gesturing around at the ethereal landscape, "this is the afterlife. Gotta say, the decorating could use some work."

Bree laughed, the sound surprising her with its normalcy in this most abnormal of settings. She stepped forward and wrapped her arms around her sister, somewhat startled to find that Molly's spectral form felt solid to her touch.

"I miss you so much," she whispered into Molly's shoulder. "Every day. Every hour."

"I know," Molly replied, returning the embrace with equal fervor. "I can feel it, through the Hat. But I'm okay, Bree. Really. It's... different here. But not bad different." She pulled back slightly, meeting her sister's gaze. "And now I know you're okay too. That's what matters most."

Their reunion was interrupted by a sound like thunder—deep, resonant, and undeniably irritated. The ground beneath them trembled slightly as heavy footsteps approached from the direction of the Tower.

"WHAT DA HELL BE GOIN' ON DOWN HERE?"

The voice boomed across the path with enough force to make even Papa Legba wince. The guardian of the crossroads turned toward the approaching figure, his expression a mixture of respect and wariness.

"Baron," he acknowledged with a slight nod. "Wasn't expectin' you to take notice of our little... situation."

"Little situation?" The newcomer emerged fully into view, his very presence seeming to intensify the twilight around them. "You call dis a LITTLE SITUATION?"

Baron Samedi cut an imposing figure even by the standards of the Realm of the Dead. Dressed in formal black attire complete with a top hat, his face was a death's head—part skull, part flesh, with dark sunglasses perched incongruously on his skeletal nose. He carried a cane that he used to punctuate his words with sharp jabs at the air, and the smell of rum and tobacco followed him like a cloud.

"Papa," he continued, gesturing expansively with his free hand, "why you not at da roads crossing? Who mindin' da store while you out here playin' with these..." he paused, examining the assembled group with open curiosity, "...whatever dey are?"

"These 'whatever they are' just saved your realm, Baron," Legba replied evenly. "Woman named Kestrel Drach was tryin' to reach the Tower, consume the souls there. Would've upset the balance somethin' fierce."

Baron Samedi paused, his skeletal grin somehow managing to convey surprise. "Dat so?" He leaned in closer, examining Sam, Talien, Bree, Molly, and Nissa with newfound interest. "Living folk willingly come to da realm of death to protect it?" He threw his head back and laughed, the sound echoing like bones rattling in a box. "Now dat's somethin' you don't see every day!"

He sauntered closer, moving with the casual confidence of one who feared nothing in any realm. "So," he drawled, drawing out the word, "you fine folks decided to risk your own souls to protect my Tower?" He raised his sunglasses briefly, revealing eyes that burned with a light both terrifying and mesmerizing. "Well, anyone willin' te come here and risk their own souls to protect my realm be alright by me."

Sam stepped forward, offering a respectful nod to the powerful loa. "We did what was necessary, Baron. The threat posed by Kestrel and Malakai Drach endangered both our worlds."

"Hmm." Baron Samedi tapped his cane thoughtfully against the ground. "And where dey at now? These troublemakers?"

"Malakai's bound in the Tower," Talien explained. "And Kestrel is..." he gestured toward the Valley of Reflection, "contained."

"Good, good," Baron Samedi nodded approvingly. "Saves me the trouble of dealin' with them myself." His gaze swept over the group again, lingering on Bree and Molly. His skeletal head tilted to one side. "Now what's dis? Sisters, eh? One living, one dead?"

Bree nodded solemnly, her eyes reflecting unresolved grief and determination, stepping protectively closer to Molly's fragile spiritual form. "Yes. My sister died recently, sacrificing herself heroically while protecting our family's ancient and powerful magical artifact."

"Hmm." Baron Samedi circled the pair, examining them from all angles with unnerving intensity. "Died protectin' something important, did you?" he asked Molly directly. "Honorable way to go. More honorable than most."

His erratic pacing stopped abruptly as a brilliant, unexpected thought seemed to strike him with supernatural force. He looked thoughtfully between the Tanner sisters with his hollow, calculating eye sockets, then at Papa Legba's imposing figure, then back at the sisters with renewed interest and ancient cunning. A skeletal grin spread across his bone-white face, somehow wider and more mischievous than before, revealing teeth that gleamed with otherworldly knowledge.

"Well now," he said, drawing himself up to his full, imposing height. "I suppose I should repay you somehow for all of da trouble you went through." He fixed his gaze on Bree while pointing a bony finger at Molly. "Go on, then. Take her back wit' you."

The silence that followed was absolute. Even Papa Legba seemed stunned, his ancient eyes widening in disbelief.

"Baron," he began cautiously, "you know the rules about—"

"Rules?" Baron Samedi cut him off with a dismissive wave. "Who makes da rules here? Me! And if I say dis girl goes back, den she goes back!" He leaned in, his skeletal face inches from Legba's. "You got a problem with dat, Papa?"

Legba raised his hands in surrender, though the corner of his mouth twitched in what might have been the beginning of a smile. "No problem at all, Baron. Your domain, your decision."

"Damn right it is!" Baron Samedi turned back to the sisters, who stood frozen in shock. "Well? What you waitin' for? A formal invitation? Go on!"

"You mean..." Bree began, hardly daring to believe what she was hearing. "Molly can come back with me? Back to life?"

"Dat's what I said, isn't it?" Baron Samedi huffed impatiently. "Girl dies protectin' something important, then her sister comes all the way to the land of the dead to fix the problem. Seems to me both of you earned something special." He gestured expansively. "Besides, I'm in a good mood today. Don't happen often, so you better take advantage!"

Molly looked as stunned as Bree felt. "But... how?" she asked. "My body is..."

"Details, details," Baron Samedi waved away her concern. "You think the Baron of Death don't know how to fix a little thing like dat? Please." He tapped his cane imperiously on the ground. "Now hurry up before I change my mind!"

The sisters exchanged a look of wonder, hope blooming where moments before there had been only acceptance of their separation. Sam and Talien watched in amazement, while Nissa smiled softly at the unexpected turn of events.

Baron Samedi surveyed the group with impatience. "Well? What you all standin' around for? Show's over! You can't be stayin' here disrupting the way things should be!" He made a shooing motion with his cane. "Legba, get them outta here!"

With that, he turned and strode back toward the Tower, his formal black attire and top hat making an incongruous silhouette against the ethereal landscape. Just before he disappeared from view, he called back over his shoulder, "And don't be comin' back too soon, you hear? I got better things to do than hand out resurrections all day!"

Papa Legba chuckled softly as the Baron vanished into the distance. "Well," he said, turning back to the group, "you heard the man." He raised his walking stick high, then brought it down with a solid thump that seemed to resonate through the very fabric of the Realm of the Dead. "Let's go."

A golden light began to swirl around them, similar to the one that had brought them to this place but somehow warmer, more vibrant. Bree felt Molly's hand slip into hers, solid and real in a way that seemed impossible given all they'd been through.

"Ready?" she asked her sister.

Molly's grin was answer enough. "Let's go home."

The golden light intensified, enveloping them completely. The last thing Bree saw before her vision was overwhelmed was Papa Legba's ancient face, creased in a smile that held both wisdom and wonder at the ways of death and life, endings and new beginnings.

Chapter 38
Second Homecoming

The library hummed with tension as the witches of the Andromeda coven maintained their protective circle, bodies swaying slightly with the rhythm of their chanting. At the center, the four motionless figures—Sam, Talien, Bree, and Nissa—had remained in their deep trance for what felt like hours, though no one dared check the time. The Tanner Hat still sat upon Bree's head, emitting a soft golden glow that occasionally pulsed stronger, as if responding to events unseen by those keeping vigil.

Mary Ann Tanner hadn't taken her eyes off her daughter since the ritual began. Her hands remained clasped with Susan Fond's, their voices blending in the protective chant, but her attention never wavered from Bree's still form. The loss of one daughter was still a raw wound; the thought of losing another was unbearable.

"Something's happening," Sarah Fond whispered, her young voice barely audible over the collective chant.

A change had come over the figures in the circle. A subtle shift in the air, a deepening of the golden light around them. The chanting faltered momentarily as the witches sensed the impending return, then strengthened as they focused on providing a stable bridge back to the physical world.

The air within the circle shimmered like heat rising from summer pavement. The four figures seemed to become more solid, more present, as if returning from a great distance. Sam was the first to draw a deep breath, his eyes opening with a sudden awareness of his surroundings. Talien followed seconds later, then Nissa and Bree, each returning to their bodies with varying degrees of disorientation.

But it was the space between Bree and Nissa that drew every eye in the library. The air there rippled and distorted, a nimbus of white light coalescing into a vaguely human shape. The light intensified until it was almost painful to look at directly, then began to solidify, features emerging from the radiance like a sculptor's work taking form.

First came the outline of a young woman, then details—dark hair, a familiar profile, hands that had once mixed potions and cast spells with confident dexterity. The light seemed to melt into solid flesh, color blooming across pale skin until, with a final flash of golden radiance, Molly Tanner stood in the circle, whole and alive and unmistakably present.

For a heartbeat, the library was utterly silent. Even the protective chant died away as every witch present stared in disbelief at what should have been impossible.

Then Mary Ann Tanner broke the silence with a sob that contained all the grief and joy a mother's heart could hold. She released Susan's hands and rushed forward, breaking the circle without a thought for magical protocol or proper procedure. All that mattered was reaching her daughters—both of them, impossibly, miraculously together again.

"Molly!" she cried, sweeping both her daughters into an embrace so fierce it nearly knocked them over. "Molly, Bree—my girls, my girls!"

Molly's laugh was exactly as it had been in life—bright, slightly mischievous, and utterly genuine. "Hey, Mom," she said, her voice thick with emotion despite her light tone. "Sorry for the dramatic exit. And, uh, entrance."

Mary Ann could only sob harder, one hand cradling the back of Molly's head as if to convince herself this was real, that her daughter was truly solid and present and alive again. Bree joined the embrace, the Tanner Hat still perched somewhat incongruously on her head, tears streaming down her face.

Around them, the library erupted in amazed exclamations as the protective circle dissolved into a crowd of astonished witches. Some wept openly, others laughed in disbelief, and still others simply stared, trying to process the miracle they were witnessing.

Talien turned to Sam, slapping him on the back with enough force to make him stagger slightly. "Well, that brought back some memories!" he exclaimed, his usual exuberance returning full force. "Not bad for a day's work, eh? Save the Tower of Souls, defeat a couple of power-mad necromancers, witness a resurrection—just like old times!"

Sam was too overwhelmed to reply immediately, his gaze fixed on the reunited Tanner family. There was something in his expression beyond mere satisfaction at a crisis averted—a wonder, a vulnerability that few had ever seen in the centuries-old necromancer.

The goblins emerged from their respectful distance, Morden straightening his impeccable suit as he approached. Tord and Glenken followed, their usually dour expressions replaced by cautious smiles.

Even Margaret and Ezekiel had materialized more fully than was their habit, their spectral forms almost solid as they hovered near the celebrating witches.

"We won," Bree announced, finally extricating herself from her mother's embrace to address the coven. Her voice carried easily through the library, commanding attention without effort—a new authority evident in her bearing. "Kestrel Drach has been defeated. The Tower of Souls is safe. And—" her voice caught slightly, "—we got Molly back."

A cheer went up from the assembled witches. Questions erupted from all sides—how had they defeated Kestrel? What was the Tower of Souls like? And most pressingly, how was Molly standing among them again, alive and whole when they had all seen her lifeless body?

"Baron Samedi," Molly explained, grinning at the confused faces around her. "Head honcho of the death loas. Apparently, he was impressed with our family's heroics and decided I deserved a second chance." She shrugged, as if returning from the dead was a minor inconvenience rather than a fundamental violation of natural law. "Who was I to argue?"

The celebrations continued to spread throughout the library. Witches who had known each other for decades embraced as if meeting for the first time, the shared danger and miraculous outcome creating new bonds between them. The goblins moved among the guests, looking somewhat bemused by the emotional display but clearly pleased with the outcome.

Eventually, Bree managed to disentangle herself from the crowd of well-wishers and found her way to where Sam stood slightly apart, watching the proceedings with a thoughtful expression.

"Hey," she said, suddenly feeling oddly shy despite everything they had just experienced together. "I wanted to thank you. For everything. For helping us, for believing in me, for..."

"You don't need to thank me," Sam interrupted gently. "You're the one who saved us all. I was just along for the ride."

Bree shook her head firmly, the ancient Tanner Hat—now settled more comfortably on her head after the powerful binding ritual—catching the library's warm golden light with subtle magical glimmers. "That's not true at all. Without you and Talien working tirelessly behind the scenes, we would never have known what was really happening in the spiritual realm, never have been able to reach Papa Legba despite Kestrel's interference, never have had even the slightest chance against Kestrel and Malakai's combined dark powers." She reached out impulsively, taking his weathered hand in her smaller one, feeling the familiar connection between them. "I'm just glad you were alright after that confrontation. When Malakai suddenly appeared in his full terrifying glory, I was so afraid for you..."

"Afraid for me?" Sam looked genuinely surprised, his ancient eyes softening with emotion. "You were the one who got magically blasted off a cliff into another dimension."

Before Bree could respond with the words forming on her lips, Talien appeared silently beside them, his timing as impeccable as ever when it came to interrupting moments of emotional vulnerability between the pair.

"You know what was particularly odd about that entire cosmic confrontation?" he said without preamble or greeting, his expression thoughtful despite his deliberately casual tone.

Sam sighed deeply, long accustomed to his centuries-old friend's tangential thinking and poor social timing. "What was odd, Talien? Please enlighten us immediately."

"All of the Tanner line appeared in spiritual form except Briella herself." He glanced meaningfully between Sam and Bree with uncharacteristic seriousness in his usually mischievous eyes. "You know exactly what that means, don't you, Sam?"

Sam frowned slightly, tension returning to his shoulders. "What are you talking about now?"

"Briella couldn't appear because she was already here," Talien said, his voice dropping as if sharing a profound secret. "In Bree." He tapped his temple meaningfully. "She really was reincarnated!"

Sam stared at his friend, then at Bree, his expression shifting from confusion to dawning realization. "I... I suppose you're right," he said slowly. The resemblance had always been striking, but he had attributed it to family genetics rather than something more mystical. Now, though, with everything they had witnessed in the Realm of the Dead...

Bree smiled, a slow, knowing smile that transformed her face. There was something in her eyes—a wisdom beyond her years, a recognition that seemed to confirm Talien's theory. "Well," she said, her voice carrying a hint of mischief that reminded Sam painfully of Briella, "I guess I found my soulmate!"

For a moment, Sam hesitated, acutely aware of the crowded library, of the dozens of witches who might be watching, of centuries of carefully maintained distance from the human world around him. But something had changed during their journey to the Realm of the Dead—some wall had crumbled, some self-imposed restriction had lifted.

Before he could overthink it further, Bree stepped forward, eliminating the distance between them. Their lips met in a kiss that felt simultaneously like an ending and a beginning—the conclusion of a separation that had lasted centuries, and the first page of a story yet to be written.

From somewhere nearby came the sound of Molly's delighted laughter. "About time!" she called out, causing several nearby witches to turn and stare. "Do you know how long she's been talking about the 'mysterious neighbor'?"

Bree broke the kiss, her cheeks flushed, but she didn't look remotely embarrassed. Instead, she smiled up at Sam with a confidence that was entirely her own, regardless of any past-life connections. "We have a lot to talk about," she said quietly.

"We do," Sam agreed, his expression more open than anyone in Ballad had ever seen it. "And we have time."

At the edge of the gathering, Carol Andors found herself standing beside Arthur Denim, whose wire-rimmed glasses had slipped down his nose as he watched the unfolding scene with undisguised fascination.

"What were you thinking?" she asked, nodding toward the center of the library where Bree still wore the Hat that Arthur had placed on her head. "Walking into the middle of a magical ritual like that? You could have been hurt, or worse!"

Arthur adjusted his glasses with one finger, a gesture that had once seemed fussy to Carol but now struck her as endearingly precise. "Carol," he said with unexpected dignity, "I'm a man of action."

She stared at him for a moment, then burst into laughter. "Yes, you are!" she agreed, taking his hand and leading him away from the crowd. "Yes, you definitely are."

As they moved toward a quieter corner of the library, Arthur glanced back at the impossible space around them, his bureaucratic mind still struggling to reconcile what he had witnessed with the orderly world of municipal regulations he had inhabited for so long.

"Do you think there's a building code for interdimensional libraries?" he asked, only half-joking. "Or a zoning ordinance for resurrection rituals?"

Carol's laugh was warm and genuine as she squeezed his hand. "I'm sure if there isn't, you'll write one."

Morden had been circulating among the guests with the impeccable manners of a butler at a society function, despite the extraordinary circumstances. After ensuring that the goblins' unexpected houseguests were settled, he approached the outer circle of celebrating witches.

"Would anyone like something to eat or perhaps a refreshment?" he inquired politely, his tiny spectacles gleaming in the library's golden light. "We have an excellent selection of teas, and I believe there are some biscuits that might be suitable for human consumption."

But no one seemed to notice his offer. The witches were deep in animated discussions about what had happened, about the implications for the coven, about the miracle of Molly's return. Theoretical debates about the intersection of necromancy and traditional witchcraft had broken out in several corners, while others were already planning how to document these events in the coven's records.

Morden sighed, a small, dignified sound of resignation. With a shrug that somehow remained elegant despite his diminutive stature, he made his way to a small table where he had indeed set out refreshments earlier. Settling himself in a chair that might have been sized specifically for goblin proportions, he selected a biscuit and began to eat, watching the celebration with the air of one who has seen many extraordinary events and expects to see many more.

"Humans," he murmured to himself, though there was more fondness than criticism in his tone. "Always so excitable."

As the initial shock and celebration began to settle into a more measured joy, Bree found herself standing by one of the library's vast windows, gazing out at a view that couldn't possibly exist inside Sam's modest suburban home. The Tanner Hat sat more comfortably on her head now, as if it had always belonged there. In a way, she supposed, it had.

Molly joined her, nudging her sister with familiar playfulness. "So," she said, nodding toward where Sam was deep in conversation with Talien and several of the older witches, "you and the necromancer next door, huh? Mom's going to have questions."

Bree laughed. "Mom's going to have a lot of questions. Starting with 'how are you alive again?' and probably ending with 'when did you start dating our neighbor who turns out to be hundreds of years old?'"

"Hey, at least family dinners won't be boring," Molly replied with her characteristic irreverence. She sobered slightly, looking out at the impossible view. "It's strange, you know. Being back. Part of me remembers everything about the Realm of the Dead—the Tower, the spirits, Papa Legba and Baron Samedi—but it's already starting to feel distant, like a dream."

"Is that hard?" Bree asked, studying her sister's profile. "Coming back?"

Molly considered the question seriously. "No," she said finally. "Just different. Like there's a part of me that knows things I didn't before, that understands things differently." She grinned suddenly. "Plus, now I have the best comeback ever when someone tells me to go to hell. Been there, done that, got resurrected by a voodoo death loa."

Bree snorted with laughter, the sound so normal, so wonderfully ordinary after everything they had experienced. "Only you would see it that way."

"That's why I'm the fun sister," Molly replied, bumping Bree's shoulder with her own. She nodded toward the Hat. "So, Keeper of the Hat now, huh? How does it feel?"

Bree reached up to touch the brim thoughtfully. "Like responsibility. Like connection." She paused. "Like home, in a way I didn't expect. All those generations of witches, all their knowledge and experiences... they're all there, all accessible." She smiled ruefully. "Turns out Great-Aunt Prudence really was as judgmental as everyone said, by the way. She has opinions about my casting technique."

Molly laughed, the sound carrying across the library and drawing smiles from those who heard it—a living reminder of what they had all fought to protect.

"You know what this means, right?" she said, her expression turning mischievous. "You're going to have to teach me everything. All the stuff Nancy was going to show us, all the secrets of the Hat. I've got catching up to do."

"We've all got catching up to do," Bree replied, her gaze finding Sam again across the library. He looked up as if sensing her attention, offering a smile that contained centuries of waiting and newfound hope. "But we have time now. Thanks to you, thanks to all of us—we have time."

The celebration continued around them, witches and goblins and spirits mingling in the impossible library hidden within an ordinary suburban home. Outside, beyond the magical boundaries that separated this sanctuary from the world, Ballad remained unchanged—a quiet town unaware of how close it had come to catastrophe, how deeply its fate was intertwined with realms and powers beyond ordinary understanding.

But within the walls of Sam's home, within the expanded reality of the library, something profound had shifted. Ancient boundaries had been crossed, seemingly immutable laws had bent, and in the process, connections had formed that would reshape the futures of everyone present.

Bree adjusted the Tanner Hat on her head, feeling its comforting weight, its accumulated wisdom, and its promise of challenges yet to come. Whatever the future held—for the Andromeda coven, for her family, for her unexpected relationship with Sam—she would face it with the strength of generations behind her and the courage that had always been her own.

The Keeper of the Hat and new High Priestess of the Andromeda Coven had come into her own. And somewhere, in the distant Tower of Souls, Nancy Tanner and all the witches who had come before watched with pride as a new chapter in their family's long story began.

I would like to share a special thank you to Chris, for reading and making edits to my books. You make my books better.

Born in 1963 in the city of Berea, Ohio, Ron Blacksmith grew up in the 60's when science-fiction was truly taking off. Throughout his childhood he read books from his favorite author, Robert A. Heinlein such as 'Space Cadet' 'Time for the Stars' and 'Stranger in a Strange Land' while watching the original 'Lost in Space' and 'Star Trek'.

Out of High School, Ron went straight into Manufacturing working for a company that produced Steam Generator cooling tubes for the Navy's Nuclear Powered Air Craft Carriers and Seawolf-class Submarines.

He continued in the steel industry in supply chain, fabrication and shipping.

While working, Ron spent most of his days thinking of his stories and other worlds. He only decided to write about them after leaving his last job and with the encouragement of his family.

Ron Blacksmith lives in Cleveland, Ohio.

All books by: Ron Blacksmith

Science-Fiction Series: Rangers of the Realm

The Eye of Farem	(Book 1, 2024)
The Drax	(Book 2, 2024)
Child of the Stars	(Book 3, 2025)
Blackreef	(Book 4, 2025)

Stand-alone Books:

Thieves of Alcyone Alpha (Published 2024) Sci-Fi

Coven of Andromeda (Published 2025) Fantasy

All reviews on Amazon are greatly appreciated. Please feel free to check-out ronblacksmith.com for future book updates and to contact Ron Blacksmith.

FIRST-WORLD BOOKS

Made in the USA
Monee, IL
11 June 2025

c8829ae9-9fb0-422c-af0c-b7554bb52931R01